And gladly wolde he lerne and gladly teche

ESSAYS ON MEDIEVAL ENGLISH

PRESENTED TO PROFESSOR MATSUJI TAJIMA

ON HIS SIXTIETH BIRTHDAY

Matsuji Tajima

And gladly wolde he lerne and gladly teche

ESSAYS ON MEDIEVAL ENGLISH PRESENTED TO PROFESSOR MATSUJI TAJIMA ON HIS SIXTIETH BIRTHDAY

Edited by

Yoko Iyeiri and Margaret Connolly

Kaibunsha

Tokyo 2002

Published by Kaibunsha Publishing Co.
26 Sakamachi, Shijuku-ku,Tokyo 160-0002, Japan

ISBN 4-87571-577-3

Printed in JAPAN

CONTENTS

Preface

The present volume is published to celebrate Professor Matsuji Tajima's sixtieth birthday. First of all, we would like to express our gratitude to the contributors to this volume for their cooperation. Due to the global nature of Professor Tajima's academic background, our contributors are based in Japan, Canada, the U.S.A., the U.K., Ireland, Germany, and Denmark. Different countries have different conventions in terms of style in writing academic essays even in this global world. We would like to thank our contributors for their readiness to compromise for the sake of consistency throughout this volume.

We would also like to convey our appreciation to Professor David Staines (University of Ottawa), Professor Risto Hiltunen (University of Turku), Professor Graham Caie (University of Glasgow), and the late Professor David Burnley (University of Sheffield). They all expressed their interest in contributing to the present volume, although eventually they had to withdraw for various reasons. We would especially like to mention Professor Burnley, whose untimely death hindered him from contributing an essay to this volume. He was a close friend to Professor Tajima for a long time, and in 1994 he collaborated with Professor Tajima in the compilation of *The Language of Middle English Literature* (Annotated Bibliographies of Old and Middle English Literature, 1). When we wrote to Professor Burnley about the present volume, he was already in hospital. Although he expressed his eagerness to write at least a short essay for Professor Tajima, he was unable to do so in the end.

Finally, we would also like to acknowledge the patience of, and assistance of, Mr Yoichi Yasui at Kaibunsha Publishing Co., Tokyo. We embarked upon this project in May 2001. On the one hand, one and half years may sound short, but on the other hand it is quite an extensive space of time. During this period Yoko Iyeiri moved from Kobe City University of Foreign Studies to Kyoto University, and Margaret Connolly gave birth to a baby named Robert. Due to the change of our circumstances, the speed of our editing of this volume was often delayed, but Mr Yasui was always patient. Without his continuing help, the present volume could hardly have been completed in this form.

Yoko Iyeiri
Margaret Connolly

Ceres, Fife
July 2002

Contributors

Thomas Cable, *University of Texas at Austin, USA*
Margaret Connolly, *University College Cork, Republic of Ireland*
Laurence M. Eldredge, *University of Ottawa, Canada*
Yoko Iyeiri, *Kyoto University, Japan*
Edward Donald Kennedy, *University of North Carolina at Chapel Hill, USA*
E. F. K. Koerner, *University of Cologne, Germany*
Sadahiro Kumamoto, *Kumamoto University, Japan*
Robert E. Lewis, *University of Michigan, USA*
Yoshiyuki Nakao, *Hiroshima University, Japan*
Hans Frede Nielsen, *SDU Odense University, Denmark*
Jeremy J. Smith, *University of Glasgow, UK*
Eric G. Stanley, *University of Oxford, UK*
Jun Terasawa, *University of Tokyo, Japan*
Hideki Watanabe, *Osaka University, Japan*
Joseph Wittig, *University of North Carolina at Chapel Hill, USA*

Abbreviations

ASPR	The Anglo-Saxon Poetic Records, ed. G. P. Krapp & E. V. K. Dobbie. 6 vols (New York: Columbia University Press, 1931-53).
EETS e.s.	Early English Text Society, Extra Series
EETS o.s.	Early English Text Society, Original Series
EETS s.s.	Early English Text Society, Supplementary Series
LALME	*A Linguistic Atlas of Late Mediaeval English*, ed. A. McIntosh, M. L. Samuels, & M. Benskin, et al. 4 vols (Aberdeen: Aberdeen University Press, 1986).
Manual	*A Manual of the Writings in Middle English 1050-1500*, gen. ed. J. B. Severs & A. E. Hartung. 10 vols published to date (New Haven, CT: Connecticut Academy of Arts and sciences, 1967-98).
ME	Middle English
MED	*Middle English Dictionary*, ed. H. Kurath, S. M. Kuhn, R. E. Lewis, et al. 13 vols (Ann Arbor: University of Michigan Press, 1952-2001).
MnE	Modern English
OE	Old English
OED	*The Oxford English Dictionary*, ed. J. A. H. Murray, et al. 2nd ed., prepared by J. A. Simpson & E. S. C. Weiner, and combined with *A Supplement to the Oxford English Dictionary*, ed. R. W. Burchfield (Oxford: Clarendon Press, 1989).
OF	Old French

OFris	Old Frisian
OHG	Old High German
OS	Old Saxon
PDE	Present-day English
TOE	*A Thesaurus of Old English*, ed. J. Roberts & C. Kay with L. Grundy. 2 vols (London: Centre for Late Antique and Medieval Studies, King's College, 1995).
WGmc	West Germanic

Professor Matsuji Tajima and his Scholarship

Professor Matsuji Tajima, born in Kanoya City, Kagoshima in 1942, was educated at Kyushu University from 1961 to 1967, where he was awarded the degrees of BLitt and MLitt, both in English. Shortly after he started to teach at Fukuoka Women's University, he decided to be educated further at Simon Fraser University (British Columbia, Canada), where he obtained the degree of MA in English. Also, he returned to Canada in 1977, when simultaneously he was an associate professor at Kyushu University. After being a registered student at the University of Ottawa for two years, he was successful in completing his dissertation and was awarded the degree of PhD in English Literature. As mentioned above, his teaching career starts at Fukuoka Women's University in Japan (1967-72). Subsequently, he also taught at Hokkaido University (Sapporo, Japan) between 1972 and 1975, before he moved to Kyushu University, where he is currently a professor. He celebrated his sixtieth birthday on 10 October 2002.

Professor Tajima's research interests are wide-ranging, although his main interest lies in the development of verbals from later ME to early MnE as the list of his publications attached at the end of this volume clearly shows. The very first publication of his, i.e. Tajima (1965), discusses participial constructions in Shakespeare. It was followed by the three articles entitled 'Verbals in Langland (I)' and 'Verbals in *Piers the Plowman* (II) (III)' (Tajima 1966, 1968a, & 1968b), where he investigates the participles, gerunds, and infinitives in Langland. Apparently, his interests extend further to the group of alliterative poems in general in late ME. Hence the publication of Tajima (1970, 1971, & 1972), where he discusses the *Gawain*-poet's use of the participles, gerunds, and infinitives.

In the 1970s, Professor Tajima's research career saw the growth of two major fields of interest. The first was the authorship issue of the *Gawain*-poems, about which he published several articles including 'The *Gawain*-Poet's Use of *Con* as a Periphrastic Auxiliary' (Tajima 1975b) and 'Additional Syntactical Evidence against the Common Authorship of MS. Cotton Nero A.x.' (Tajima 1978). The second major field he pursued was the syntactic development of the gerund in ME, which culminated in the publication of the monograph entitled *The Syntactic Development of the Gerund in Middle English* (Tajima 1985). Evidently, the gerund was selected from among the English verbals which always interested him. This does not mean, however, that he lost interest in infinitives and participles. He discusses, for instance, the development of the auxiliary *ought* in late ME in Tajima (1990 & 2000), both of which are clearly linked to the issue of infinitives.

It may at first be surprising for those who know Professor Tajima as a medievalist that he has published a number of works in the field of PDE usage. Indeed in the 1990s, he published more than ten articles in this field, either alone or with other scholars. One could surmise that this arises from his firm position as a historian of the English language. Needless to say, the history of the English language covers the present day. In fact, this principle of his philosophy is observable already in Tajima (1975a) (i.e. 'Some Notes on the Correlative Conjunction "NOT ONLY...BUT (ALSO)" and its Similar Expressions'), although his major publications in PDE are found in the 1990s. Eventually, the publications of this series were consolidated and presented in the form of a book entitled *Present-day British and American English Usage: A Corpus-Based Study* (Tajima, et al. 1995).

As the title of Tajima, et al. (1995) indicates, one of the characteristic features of his research into PDE is the use of electronic corpora. This is not in contradiction with his attitude as a philologist, since for him close reading is always the most important. The use of electronic corpora simply signifies the change of devices and does not invalidate the importance of the close reading of texts. As a matter of fact, he was always interested in the concept of using electronic corpora for research purposes from the very beginning of his career, although circumstances allowed him to utilize them effectively only in the 1990s. Incidentally, this was when the Japan Association for English Corpus Studies was established, which today holds as many as 300 members. Whether consciously or not, he knows how to react rightly to academic trends.

While the above account clarifies the linguistic aspects of his research, it is equally significant to stress how Professor Tajima's interest lies in literature. He uses a large number of literary works in his research. This is of course partly based upon the traditional methodology in philology, but also reveals how much he enjoys reading literature. Works by Chaucer, Langland, the *Gawain*-poet(s), and Shakespeare especially are constantly analyzed in his works. His recent publication entitled 'The Earliest Instance of the Expression "American dream"' (Tajima 1998) is not unrelated when viewed from this perspective. Once he even translated a Canadian novel into Japanese, although unfortunately the manuscript of this translation disappeared by some technical errors of the computer. Furthermore, he has edited and annotated several college textbooks of modern British and American stories.

Finally but not least, one has to describe Professor Tajima as an efficient editor and an organizer of various kinds. He has compiled four bibliographies, either alone or with other scholars: (1) *Noam Chomsky: A Personal Bibliography 1951-1986* (Koerner & Tajima 1986); (2) *Old and Middle English Language Studies: A Classified Bibliography 1923-1985* (Tajima 1988); (3) *The Language of Middle English Literature* (Burnley & Tajima 1994); and (4) *A Bibliography of English Language Studies in Japan 1900-1996* (Tajima, et al. 1998). It is highly important for researchers to be devoted to their own works, but it is equally important for them to make positive and tangible contributions to the establishment of scholarly tradition. He feels responsible for publicizing the bibliographical data he holds for this purpose, hence the publication of the four bibliographies mentioned above. Moreover, he is currently an advisory editorial board member for *Amsterdam Studies in the Theory and History of Linguistic Sciences, Series V: Library and Information Sources in Linguistics* (Amsterdam & Philadelphia, 1985-), for *NOWELE: North-Western European Language Evolution* (Odense, Denmark, 1989-), and for *English Language and Linguistics* (Cambridge, 1996-). Also, he has founded an academic journal entitled *The Kyushu Review*, for which he is at present the chief editor. Furthermore, he was the principal founding member of The Japanese Association for Studies in the History of the English Language (1999-). The publication of its newsletter entitled *The Bulletin of the Japanese Association for Studies in the History of the English Language* owes much to the effort of Professor Tajima, who is currently the principal editor. Furthermore, he has recently launched a new project: 'Eighteenth-Century English: An Historical and Sociolinguistic Study'. It is a large collaborative project involving several of his former students. As a matter of fact, he has supervised a large number of postgraduate students in his career, who could also have contributed their works to the present volume but who are working in different fields from medieval studies.

References

Burnley, D. & M. Tajima, eds. 1994. *The Language of Middle English Literature*. Annotated Bibliographies of Old and Middle English Literature, 1. Cambridge: D. S. Brewer.

Koerner, E. F. K. & M. Tajima, eds. 1986. *Noam Chomsky: A Personal Bibliography 1951–1986*. Library and Information Sources in Linguistics, 11. Amsterdam & Philadelphia: John Benjamins.

Tajima, M. 1965. 'Participial Constructions in Shakespeare'. *Cairn* (Kyushu University) 6:72–90. [in Japanese]

———. 1966. 'Verbals in Langland (I): Participle'. *Cairn* 8:76–90. [in Japanese]

———. 1968a. 'Verbals in *Piers the Plowman* (II): Gerund'. *Essays in Literature and Thought* (Fukuoka Women's University) 31:29–53.

———. 1968b.'Verbals in *Piers the Plowman* (III): Infinitive'. *Essays in Literature and Thought* 32:1–55.

———. 1970. 'On the Use of the Participle in the Works of the *Gawain*-poet'. *Essays in Literature and Thought* 34:49–70.

———. 1971. 'On the Use of the Gerund in the Works of the *Gawain*-poet'. *Essays in Literature and Thought* 35:1–24.

———. 1972. 'On the Use of the Infinitive in the Works of the *Gawain*-poet'. *Essays in Literature and Thought* 36:1–56.

———. 1975a. 'Some Notes on the Correlative Conjunction "NOT ONLY ...BUT (ALSO)" and its Similar Expressions'. *Hokkaido University Essays in Foreign Languages and Literatures* 21:341–57. [in Japanese]

———. 1975b. 'The *Gawain*-poet's Use of *Con* as a Periphrastic Auxiliary'. *Neuphilologische Mitteilungen* 76:429–38.

———. 1978. 'Additional Syntactical Evidence against the Common Authorship of MS. Cotton Nero A.x.'. *English Studies* 59:193–8.

———. 1985. *The Syntactic Development of the Gerund in Middle English*. Tokyo: Nan'un-do.

———, ed. 1988. *Old and Middle English Language Studies: A Classified Bibliography 1923–1985*. Library and Information Sources in Linguistics, 13. Amsterdam & Philadelphia: John Benjamins.

———. 1990. 'The Development of the Modal Auxiliary *Ought* in Late Middle English'. *Studies in English Philology in Honour of Shigeru Ono*. Tokyo: Nan'un-do. 227–48. [in Japanese]

———. 1998. 'The Earliest Instance of the Expression "American Dream"'. *The Kyushu Review* 3:33–9. [in Japanese]

———. 2000. 'Chaucer and the Development of the Modal Auxiliary *Ought* in Late Middle English'. *Manuscript, Narrative, Lexicon: Essays on Literary and Cultural Transmission In Honor of W. F. Bolton*, ed. R. Boenig & K. Davis. Lewisburg, PA: Bucknell University Press; London: Associated University Presses. 195–217.

———, et al. 1995. *Present-day British and American English Usage: A Corpus-Based Study*. Tokyo: Kaibunsha. [in Japanese]

———, et al., eds. 1998. *A Bibliography of English Language Studies in Japan 1900–1996*. Tokyo: Nan'un-do. [in Japanese]

More than Thirty Years of Friendship with Professor Matsuji Tajima*

E. F. K. Koerner

In the summer of 1988, having become conscious of approaching the fiftieth anniversary of my birth in February 1989, I persuaded two colleagues and friends to serve formally as the editors of a little volume which I had conceived as an opportunity for a variety of long-time friends to talk about their experiences with yours truly and the kind of relationships they had established with me over the years. I had previously organized with them the Edward Sapir Centenary Conference held in Ottawa in September 1984 and subsequently edited the proceedings (see Cowan, Foster & Koerner 1986). To this collection of a dozen testimonials (Cowan & Foster 1989) I had added an autobiographical sketch and, as I had recently managed to get my list of publications on disk (remember: it was the time when a 'Mac Plus' was the non-plus-ultra of word processing). I also added a detailed accounting of all my scholarly or not so scholarly sins. (I guess we all have written reviews of the works of others which we later feel a bit ashamed of and maybe a few rather inept papers too, when we were young and foolish—not that I mean to claim that old age alone prevents us from making fools of ourselves!) One of these twelve testimonials—which included pieces by

---

* A first draft of this piece was written in Austin, Texas, March 2001, during my sojourn as a visiting scholar at the University of Texas. The final version was completed in October 2001, when I was a fellow-in-residence at the Netherlands Institute for Advanced Study in the Humanities and Social Sciences (NIAS) in Wassenaar/Holland. I would like to thank the host institutions for providing the congenial conditions for writing this ditty, and the editors of this volume for helping me to make it more readable.

scholars whom I first met in the early 1970s (Raimo Anttila, Rudolf Engler, J. Peter Maher, Hans-Josef Niederehe, and others) as well as by my Amsterdam publisher, John Benjamins—was by our honoree Matsuji Tajima. The time has now come for me to reciprocate and say something about our first meeting and our enduring friendship which preceded those I formed with others several years later. I would like to put on record that Matsuji Tajima was my first scholarly friend, if we talk in terms of post-graduate relationships.

The French writer Nicolas Boileau (1636-1711) is credited with the observation that 'Le style c'est l'homme', meaning, I suppose, that we betray what kind of person we are through the manner in which we express ourselves. I'm sure that there is much truth to this; at least, I'm ready to accept this for myself. So let's make no bones about the fact that I'm an extrovert and that, for reasons that could only be fully explained by early life experiences as a German born in Poland shortly before World War II, and the resulting loss of homeland, family property and various kinds of discrimination in post-war Germany, I am a democrat with a strong sense of justice, fairness and equality. If I see things right, Matsuji Tajima is quite a different sort of person: he, by family tradition and culture, is reserved, with a ready sibylline smile, and a strong sense of duty—and he earns respect and affection through his readiness to help others and through his old-fashioned sense of loyalty and human kindness. It should not be forgotten, however, that Dr Tajima and his family, too, were affected by the Second World War, the loss of his father in the war, and the drastic social changes that occurred thereafter, and so I'm inclined to believe that we have more in common than meets the eye. Keeping Boileau's dictum in mind, let's now hear how our distinguished friend and colleague described, back in 1988, his first meeting with me twenty years earlier:

> December 26, 1968, Shell House (the men's residence), Simon Fraser University, Burnaby, British Columbia, Canada—this date and place remains fixed in my memory. On that day, toward the evening, I arrived there, direct from Japan. Since it was during the Christmas holidays, there were only a handful of students around, most of them from Asian countries. In the cafeteria where all those students had gathered for dinner, a 'Westerner' approached me speaking to me in a courteous manner. It was EFKK (as he referred to himself humorously and as I ever since refer to him when I talk about him among family members and friends) who subsequently turned out

> to be my very neighbour in the residence, with only a wall separating us. Whenever I come to think of this 'historic' meeting and of the friendship that soon developed thereafter, my heart is filled with memories of all the events and places which I shared with him during my 16-month stay at Simon Fraser.
>
> I had come to SFU to study Medieval English philology as an M.A. student; it was my first exposure to the English-speaking world and, for that matter, my first direct contact with the world outside my own country. The shift in environment, tone, and atmosphere was a tremendous experience to me. I felt isolated, completely out of place. It would have been extremely difficult for me to adjust to these totally new and strange circumstances had it not been for EFKK. He turned out to be a true 'friend in need' to me. From the very beginning he made himself freely available to me, although he appeared to be very busy. We soon became close friends; we were about the same age, our research interests overlapped a little, and both of us were thousands of miles away from our respective home countries. Almost daily we had a chat about all sorts of things either in his room or mine, during walks around the treed and hilly areas around the campus, or on trips in his recently-acquired Simca 'Aronde'. (Tajima 1989:80)

I had better stop the quotation here before our friend says too many things in my favour. As is obvious from these passages, the narrator gives all the credit to his friend, almost to the extent of disappearing himself. For instance, what he did not mention was that he arrived from his long and tiring travel from Japan to Canada's West Coast suffering from an infection which for the first couple of weeks prevented him from tasting the varied food that the Christmas and New Year holidays especially have to offer; instead, self-prepared soup, rice, and green tea, all of which (plus medication) he had brought with him, was his regular fare. It's hardly surprising that he was so appreciative of anyone (who himself had come from a country of an almost equal distance from Vancouver) who was ready to engage with him. There was, however, another reason that brought us together: we were several years older than most other students in the residence and on campus; also, we both were determined to use our time to further our studies (and skip most parties which, during the late 1960s, were the preoccupation of many). And so when Dr Tajima reports in the same appraisal 'I soon became immensely struck with admiration for that graduate student in linguistics who was beginning to establish himself as a scholar, writing papers and reviews for professional journals in Europe and North America and compiling a full-scale Saussure bibliography' (1989:80), he, typically, forgot to mention the fact that he himself was cramming in as many courses at the English Department as he could, including one given by a distinguished visiting professor from the University of Reading, U.K. I also noticed that the piles of 3 x 5 inch white cards on the shelves in his room on which he had entered primary data from Middle English literary texts (using, I believe, one card for each sample of one sentence) were steadily increasing. Only many years later, well after 1977, when he first came to Ottawa to take the required courses for his doctorate, did I begin to realize that he had already mapped out the subject for his thesis then and there. His PhD dissertation on the development of the gerund in Middle English, submitted to the University of Ottawa on a later visit to Canada's capital in the late summer of 1983 (published as Tajima 1985), was based on the careful excerption, one sentence at a time, from about 95% of the entire primary literature available. Such a feat was matched only by a handful of 19th-century European scholars.

So when our distinguished colleague credits me by saying 'I think that to no small degree because of his encouragement, support, and academic stimulation I managed to complete my MA by the end of the Spring term 1970' (1989:81), we need not accept his claim to modesty. I believe instead that he had the drive in himself well before we met. Being ready to leave home for a far-away, foreign country in order to compete with the 'natives' on their terms is, I submit, a kind of auto-selection and usually not a choice made by the feeble-minded. Indeed, we probably had more in common than either of us recognized at the time. Like Matsuji Tajima, I had been a philologist (Anglicist and Germanist in my case) before switching to linguistics about a year before my enrolment at Simon Fraser University. Academically, we were about the same age, although I am his senior by three and a half years: I had spent several years in the military before enrolling at the University of Göttingen in 1962, and I had served for one year as a foreign language teacher in France (1965-6). However, our honoree, unlike myself, had already held a regular academic appointment for some time before coming to Vancouver. Besides, finishing a Master's degree at a foreign university under rather different conditions within less than sixteen months is no small feat. If anything, the many rainy days of British Columbia probably helped him (and me) to spend more days in the library than we might have done had it been Southern California.

Still, friendships do not last if there is no follow-up. The exchange of letters bridges years, it's true, but subsequent meetings in person usually deepen such relationships. And it so happens that life has given us several such opportunities. The first such opportunity came when I accepted a position in Ottawa in 1976, something which revived Matsuji Tajima's idea of pursuing a PhD (an plan which he had buried as the English Department at Simon Fraser had not yet established a doctoral program at the time he arrived there). Once the necessary paperwork had been done, our professor from Kyushu University spent two full years under, if truth be told, rather modest conditions with his young family in Ottawa (1977-9). Having to live on personal savings and borrowed money and like a graduate student again, is not for everybody. But, as we know, perseverance has been one of our friend's main character traits. Add to this a self-effacing demeanour even if you are a proud man in your heart, and you cannot but have warm admiration for Dr Tajima, the human being.

But our story does not end here. During his sojourn in Ottawa, Matsuji Tajima worked with me on a variety of projects which I had initiated either as the director of the Linguistics Documentation Centre, or as the editor of a journal and several monograph series which I had launched with a young and enterprising Amsterdam publisher in 1973. One was a plan to continue work on a sequel to my 1972 *Bibliographia Saussureana*; while this plan never materialized, at least we published a survey of Saussurean studies in Japan (Tajima & Koerner 1978; cf. also Koerner 2000, for some background information). I recall also that we invested lots of time on other projects too. One of them, compiling a list of all linguistic and philological journals of the world, remained incomplete; another, bringing the book of a senior Japanese scholar into publishable form (Hayashi 1978), was happily completed: It was ready on time for the first International Conference on the History of the Language Sciences (ICHoLS), which I organized at the University of Ottawa on 28-31 August 1978, with the unstinting support of our great friend (cf. the Acknowledgements in Koerner 1980:v). Last, but not least, we amassed a considerable amount of data for a bibliography of Noam Chomsky's writings in linguistics and politics, which I had initiated in March 1978 on a visit to this famous professor's office at the Massachusetts Institute of Technology in Cambridge, Massachusetts (see Koerner 1999a:208-14, for an account of this meeting). I don't recall whether we worked again on the Chomsky bibliography in 1983, when

Matsuji Tajima returned to Ottawa in preparation of his thesis defence. At any rate, I think we both were relieved (and the publisher, too) when the work finally appeared three years later (Koerner & Tajima 1986). In the meantime, we had both met again; this time at Princeton, New Jersey, in August 1984, on the occasion of the Third International Conference on the History of the Language Sciences (ICHoLS III).

For more than fifteen years thereafter we did not see one another, each of us continuing research and related academic work such as lecturing, directing theses, and editing in our respective fields. As the record shows, Dr Tajima has not been idle. Au contraire, in a time where an IBM Selectric typewriter was the most advanced technical aid, our distinguished colleague produced the most comprehensive bibliography of Old and Middle English philological research of the preceding sixty-five years of international scholarship (Tajima 1988), and as if to prove that he was by no means finished with *fare la bibliografia*, he first co-authored a lengthy reference work (Burnley & Tajima 1994), and then brought together a 1,000-page bibliography covering almost one hundred years of English language studies in Japan (Tajima 1998). For this work he received the Conrad Gesner Prize of the Japanese Library Association in 1999, surely the most competent organization in the country when it comes to judging and appreciating the tremendous effort involved in such a feat. (Only those familiar with the inner workings of university library facilities in Japan may be able to appreciate fully this achievement.) But regular scholarship was not left behind, and so we see Dr Tajima writing, presenting and publishing a series of papers (for details, see the honoree's full list of writings in this volume). A further service to his profession must be mentioned to round out at least a small picture of Professor Tajima's scholarly activities. In 1996, Professor Tajima launched, in truly admirable fashion (and at his own cost), *The Kyushu Review*, an annual periodical catering to his colleagues in the English language and literature field.[1] If the rise in paid subscriptions to the

[1] I can say little about Dr Tajima's scholarship; I am sure that other contributors to this Festschrift will do this, and much more competently. That his work has found international recognition may be gathered from the fact that the editors of the journal *NOWELE: North-Western European Language Evolution* (Odense, Denmark) invited him in 1989 to join their editorial board, and when Cambridge University Press launched *English Language and Linguistics* in 1996, Professor Tajima was one of those

journal is any guide, *The Kyushu Review* has in a short time become a fixture on the scholarly horizon in his country. I cannot claim to have contributed to English philology in any serious way; and so while volumes IV and V of *The Kyushu Review* carried two little pieces from my pen (Koerner 1999b, 2000), I regard this as mainly a token of our long friendship.

As we had not seen each other for some fifteen years, Matsuji Tajima took the decision to join me in March 2000 in Tucson, Arizona, where I was spending most of the winter as a visiting scholar at the University of Arizona. This time, however, our project was to travel to the Grand Canyon, and not to hit the library or undertake anything scholarly: I think it was a well-deserved change for both of us. On the occasion of his 60th birthday on 10 October 2002, I am sure we all wish Professor Tajima, BA MLitt MA PhD, many more years of good health and enjoyment in his work.

References

Burnley, David & Matsuji Tajima. 1994. *The Language of Middle English Literature* (= *Annotated Bibliographies of Old and Middle English Literature*, 1.) Cambridge: D. S. Brewer.

Cowan, William & Michael K. Foster, eds. 1989. *E. F. Konrad Koerner Bibliography*. Bloomington, IN: Eurolingua.

Cowan, William, Michael K. Foster & [E. F.] Konrad Koerner, eds. 1986. *New Perspectives in Language, Culture, and Personality: Proceedings of the Edward Sapir Centenary Conference (Ottawa, 1-3 October 1984).* Amsterdam & Philadelphia: John Benjamins.

Hayashi, Tetsuro. 1978. *The Theory of English Lexicography 1530-1791.* Amsterdam: John Benjamins.

Koerner, E. F. K[onrad]. 1971. *Ferdinand de Saussure: Origin and Development of His Linguistic Thought in Western Studies of Language. A Contribution to the History and Theory of Linguistics.* PhD dissertation, Simon Fraser University, Vancouver, B.C. (Published, Braunschweig: Friedrich Vieweg & Sohn, 1973; 2nd printing, 1974.)

Koerner, E. F. K. 1972. *Bibliographia Saussureana 1870-1970: An Annotated, Classified Bibliography on the Background, Development, and Actual*

who were asked to join its board, too.

Relevance of Ferdinand de Saussure's General Theory of Language. Metuchen, NJ: Scarecrow.

Koerner, E. F. K., ed. 1980. *Progress in Linguistic Historiography: Papers from the International Conference on the History of the Language Sciences, Ottawa, 28-31 August 1978.* Amsterdam: John Benjamins.

Koerner, E. F. K. 1982[1973]. *Saussure no Gengoron* [Saussure's linguistic thought]. Authorized translation by Kei-ichi Yamanaka. Tokyo: Taishukan.

Koerner, E. F. K. 1999a. *Historiography of Linguistics: Projects & Prospects.* Amsterdam & Philadelphia: John Benjamins.

Koerner, E. F. K. 1999b 'My Edinburgh Connections, 1964-1999'. *The Kyushu Review* 4:89-102.

Koerner, E. F. K. 2000. 'Saussure's Importance in 20th-Century Linguistic Thought'. *The Kyushu Review* 5:5-16.

Koerner, E. F. K. & Matsuji Tajima. 1986. *Noam Chomsky: A Personal Bibliography, 1951-1986.* Amsterdam & Philadelphia: John Benjamins.

Tajima, Matsuji. 1985. *Syntactic Development of the Gerund in Middle English.* Tokyo: Nan'un-do.

Tajima, Matsuji. 1988. *Old and Middle English Language Studies: A Classified Bibliography 1923-1985.* Amsterdam & Philadelphia: John Benjamins.

Tajima, Matsuji. 1989. 'Twenty Years of Friendship with EFKK'. Cowan & Foster (1989), pp. 80-1.

Tajima, Matsuji. 1998. *A Bibliography of English Language Studies in Japan, 1900-1996.* Tokyo: Nan'un-do.

Tajima, Matsuji. 1999. 'The Compound Gerund on Early Modern English'. *The Emergence of the Modern Language Sciences: Studies on the Transition from Historical-Comparative to Structural Linguistics in Honour of E. F. K. Koerner, vol. II: Methodological Perspectives and Applications*, ed. Sheila Embleton, John E. Joseph & Hans-Josef Niederehe. Amsterdam & Philadelphia: John Benjamins. 265-77.

Tajima, Matsuji. 2001. *English Language Studies in Japan, 1900–2000: Retrospect and Prospect.* Tokyo: Nan'un-do.

Tajima, Matsuji & E. F. K. Koerner. 1978. 'Saussure in Japan: A Survey of Research, 1928-1978'. *Historiographia Linguistica* 5(1/2):121-48.

ESSAYS ON MEDIEVAL ENGLISH LANGUAGE

The Old English Sound System from a North-Sea Germanic Perspective

Hans Frede Nielsen

1. Introduction

Old English is usually classified as a West Germanic language, but there is some controversy as to how the WGmc branch of Germanic should be subdivided. Did OE derive from an Anglo-Frisian sub-branch (OE/OFris) contrasting with a German one (OHG/OS)? Or did Old Saxon join OE and Old Frisian in a North-Sea Germanic (or Ingveonic) sub-branch as opposed to a southern WGmc one with Old High German as its only member? The assumption underlying both models is that the Anglo-Saxon colonists brought linguistic features to England stemming from the northern part of the WGmc speech area. The chief aim of this paper will be to investigate the extent to which the features that the OE sound system shares with its continental closest of kin did in fact develop on the Continent. First we shall have a brief look at the labels Anglo-Frisian and North-Sea Germanic (Ingveonic).

2. Anglo-Frisian and North-Sea Germanic

Although long before the latter half of the nineteenth-century scholars considered English and Frisian to be particularly closely related (cf. Bremmer 1982:79-81; 1989), there is some justification in regarding Henry Sweet as the father of the *Anglo-Frisian* hypothesis (cf. Sjölin 1973:329), because Sweet (1877:162) was the first linguist to claim that Anglo-Frisian was the common ancestor of English and Frisian and of the idiom spoken both by the Anglo-Saxon invaders of Britain and by those who stayed behind. Sweet received support in the Low Countries from Sipma (1913:1-3) and in Germany from Bremer (1900:809-10), who had no hesitation in accepting the concept of Anglo-Frisian language unity in view of all the linguistic features shared by OE and OFris (1900:843). However, Siebs dissociated himself from Sweet's term, preferring instead the more modest label *englisch-friesisch* ('English-Frisian', cf. 1889:7; 1901:1154), a designation which referred only to the totality of phonological features common to the Anglo-Saxon and Frisian dialects prior to the colonization of Britain. The notion of an Anglo-Frisian sub-branch of WGmc is reflected in a number of our handbooks, e.g. in Streitberg (1896:4) and Steller (1928) and more recently in Robinson (1992:12-13, 248) and Kisbye (1992:19).

The first linguist to offer a plausible explanation for assigning OS to the northern group, was Morsbach (1897), who, in accordance with the principles of dialect geography, attributed innovations shared by OFris, OE and OS to geographical proximity on the Continent prior to the Anglo-Saxon emigration. Morsbach employed neither the tribal term *Ingveonic* nor the geographical designation *North-Sea Germanic* for referring to his dialect group, expressions which were later to be used by, respectively, Rooth and Dal. Both of these last-mentioned scholars believed that, in addition to OFris and OE, OS belonged to an Ingveonic / North-Sea Gmc *Sprachkreis* which had come into existence prior to the Anglo-Saxon exodus (cf. Dal 1983:88, 78), and that the features which OS shared solely with OHG, were secondary. But while Rooth (1932:40, 54) thought that the German element in the OS manuscripts was a reflection of Franconian scribal influence, Dal interpreted it as a genuine influx of High German linguistic forms. Together Rooth and Dal represent the mainstream view of the dialectal position of OS within WGmc. A scholar to have come out recently in favour of the same hypothesis is Århammar (1990), who presupposes the existence of an Ingveonic continuum comprising Proto-OFris, Proto-OE, Proto-OS and Proto-Old Dutch (1990:10). Frisian became an independent language through innovations of its own (1990:21-2), but even more so through the deingveonicization of Low German, which started no later than the time of the subjugation of the Saxons by Charlemagne. Århammar (1990:13) also points to the deingveonicization of Old and early Middle Dutch, and is thus in line with the view held by specialists on Dutch historical dialectology such as Frings, Kloeke and Schönfeld, who believed that the autochthonous Gmc language in the Low Countries was Ingveonic and that the mixed character of Dutch was due to Franconian linguistic influence, especially after 700. In the north, Ingveonic was retained and developed into Frisian (cf. Schönfeld/van Loey 1970:xxiv-v; xxxiii; Frings 1944; 1957; Vleeskruyer 1948).

The considerable degree of resemblance between OE and OFris is also explained in terms of 'their status as Ingvæonic relict areas' by Stiles (1995:212); but as descendants from a dialect continuum their shared development did not reach beyond the fronting of WGmc long *a* (1995:198-200). Stiles thus endeavours 'to nail down the coffin lid' (1995:184) on the Anglo-Frisian thesis. In a very recent paper, Fulk has tried to pull out some of the coffin nails by claiming that the fronting of WGmc short *a* and palatalization were also shared innovations implemented before OE and OFris began to diverge (cf. 1998:153). Since a definition of the northern sub-branch of WGmc has come to depend heavily on phonological issues, we shall proceed to discuss the historical development of the OE sound system. In so doing, we shall pay attention to the chronological aspects involved.

3. Accented Vowels

3.1. Old English

In standard OE (West Saxon), there were seven long monophthongal phonemes:

ī	ȳ	ū
ē		ō
ǣ		ā

Examples (long monophthongs):

/i:/ *wrītan* 'to write' (< WGmc *ī*)
/e:/ *mēd* 'meed', cf. OS *mēda*, OHG *miata* (< WGmc *ē*)
/æ:/ *dǣd* 'deed', cf. OS *dād* (< WGmc *ā*)
/a:/ *stān* 'stone', cf. OHG *stein*, Goth. *stains* (< WGmc *ai*)
/o:/ *gōd* 'good', cf. OHG *guot*, Goth. *gōþs* (< WGmc *ō*)
mōna 'moon', cf. OHG *māno* (< WGmc *ā* + N)
/u:/ *mūs* 'mouse', *fūs* 'eager for, willing' (< WGmc *ū*)
/y:/ *fȳsan* 'to send forth, stimulate', cf. OS *fūsian*

Compared to Proto-Germanic and WGmc, the most spectacular change is the split of *ā* into OE *ǣ* (fronting) and *ō* (merger with the reflex of WGmc *ō*), cf. *dǣd*, *mōna*. A new *ā* phoneme has come into being through the monophthongization of WGmc *ai*, cf. *stān*. *ȳ* as in *fȳsan* is the result of *i*-umlaut. The *ē* of *mēd* is clearly a reflex of WGmc *ē*.

Two WGmc diphthongs were retained by standard OE: *ēo* (< WGmc *eu*) and *ēa* (< WGmc *au*). In early OE, WGmc *eu* was reflected as *īu* and *ēu*, but the *-u* segment was soon to be succeeded by *-o*, and eventually the two early diphthongal forms were replaced by *ēo*. An early orthographic rendering of the reflex of WGmc *au* is <æa>, cf. early OE *þǣah* 'through' (standard OE *þēah*). Krupatkin (1970:61) explains the early spellings as indications of the incorporation of *iu*, *eu*, *au* into the long OE vowel system in agreement with the front-back parameters of the system: *īu*, *ēo*, *ǣa*. The *i*-mutated reflex of all three diphthongs was *īe* in West Saxon.

Examples (long diphthongs):
/i:u/ dat.pl. *flīusum* (Leiden Riddle) 'fleece' (< WGmc *eu*)
/e:o/ *bēodan* 'to command' (< WGmc *eu*)
/ɛ:a/ *bēad* '(he) commanded', cf. Goth. *bauþ* (< WGmc *au*)
/i:e/ WS *flīes* 'fleece' (*i*-umlaut of WGmc *eu*))

The short vowel system came to acquire front-back correlations on the pattern of the long system (Krupatkin 1970:63; Hogg 1992:102), including a contrast between *æ* and *a* (both stemming from WGmc *a* through, respectively, fronting and fronting plus retraction before a following back vowel). The front-back parameters are likely to have facilitated the introduction of breaking (fracture), which entailed diphthongization of *i*, *e*, *æ*, *ǣ* before 'velar(ized)' consonants (*h*, *r* + cons., *l* + cons.) to respectively, *io*, *eo*, *ea*, *ēa* (Campbell 1959:§139-54). The short vowel system with the short, fractured diphthongs inserted:

i	iu	u
e	eo	o
æ	æa	a

completely parallels the early long system. I can only agree with Hogg (1992:105) that a significant effect of breaking was 'the introduction of a phonological contrast of length in diphthongs'. The functional yield of the short diphthongs was later increased when through back mutation *i, e, æ* were diphthongized to *io, eo, ea* before a following unaccented vowel at the time of the earliest OE manuscripts (ca. 700).

Two additional vowel phonemes were represented in the standard OE short vowel system, viz. *y* and *ie*, which had both arisen through *i*-mutation and which fully parallelled their long counterparts.

Examples (short vowels):

/i/ *writen* 'written' (< WGmc *i*)
/e/ *beran* 'to bear' (< WGmc *e*)
/æ/ pt.sg. *bær* 'bore', cf. OHG *bar* (< WGmc *a*)
/a/ *sadol* 'saddle', cf. OHG *satal* (< WGmc *a*)
/o/ *holt* 'forest, wood' (< WGmc *o*)
/u/ *full* 'full', cf. Goth. *fulls* (< WGmc *u*)
/y/ *fyllan* 'to fill', cf. Goth. *fulljan* (*i*-umlaut of WGmc *u*)
/io/ *tiohhian* 'to consider' (breaking of *i*)
/eo/ *weorpan* 'to throw' (breaking of *e*)
/ea/ *healf* 'half' (breaking of *æ* < WGmc *a*)
/ie/ *ieldra* 'older' (< **ealdira* < **ældira* < WGmc **aldiza*-)
(*i*-umlaut (breaking, fronting))

3.2. Old Frisian

The OFris manuscripts exhibit an accented vowel system with five short monophthongs and five long ones (cf. Sjölin 1969:19-22; Boutkan 1996:18-22; and Hofmann 1964:162):

i		u	ī		ū
e		o	ē		ō
	a			ā	

Examples:

/i/ *fisk* 'fish' (< WGmc *i*)
/e/ *bera* 'to bear', cf. OE/OS/OHG *beran* (< WGmc *e*)
stef 'staff', cf. OHG *stab* (< WGmc *a*)
fella 'to fill', cf. OE *fyllan*, Goth. *fulljan* (< *u* + *i, j*)
/a/ *was* 'was', *falla* 'to fall' (< WGmc *a*)
/o/ *folk* 'people', *holt* 'wood' (< WGmc *o*)
/u/ *full* 'full', *tunge* 'tongue' (< WGmc *u*)

/i:/ *wrīta* 'to write'; *mīde* 'rent' (< WGmc *ī*; *ē*)
/e:/ *dēd*(*e*) 'deed', cf. OE *dǣd*, OS *dād* (< WGmc *ā*)
mēde 'rent', cf. OE *mēd* 'meed', OS *mēda*, OHG *miata* (< WGmc *ē*)
stēn 'stone', cf. OE *stān*, OS *stēn*, Goth. *stains* (< WGmc *ai*)

	hēra 'to hear', cf. OE *hīeran*, OS *hōrian*, Goth. *hausjan* (< WGmc *au* + *i, j*)
	hēd 'skin', cf. OE *hȳd*, ModDu. *huid* (< WGmc **hūdi-*)
/a:/	*māra* 'more', cf. OE *māra*, OS *mēro*, Goth. *maiza* (< WGmc *ai*)
	hāch 'high', cf. OE *hēah*, OS *hōh*, Goth. *hauhs* (< WGmc *au*)
/o:/	*fōt* 'foot', cf. OE/OS *fōt* (< WGmc *ō*)
	mōna 'moon', cf. OHG *māno* (< WGmc *ā* + N)
/u:/	*hūs* 'house', cf. OE *hūs* (< WGmc *ū*)

In comparison with OE, the OFris short monophthongal system has no *æ* and *y*. Fronting as well as *i*-umlaut have taken place in OFris, but the fronted reflex of *a* (cf. *stef*) and the *i*-mutated product of *u* (cf. *fella*) have both merged with the reflex of Gmc *e* (cf. *bera*).

Similarly, there is no long *ǣ* or *ȳ* in the OFris long system of monophthongs. No fewer than five WGmc vowels are reflected in the examples provided for OFris *ē*, viz. WGmc *ā* (cf. *dēd*(*e*)), *ē* (cf. *mēde*), *ai* (cf. *stēn*), *au* + *i, j* (cf. *hēra*) and *ū* + *i, j* (cf. *hēd*), corresponding to five different vowel phonemes in OE (West Saxon), respectively *ǣ*, *ē*, *ā*, *īe* and *ȳ*. It should be noted that a split plus merger has taken place in OFris in the development of WGmc *ā* just as in OE, cf. *dēd*(*e*) and *mōna* and the exemplification given above. Further, a split of WGmc *ai* into *ē* and *ā* has occurred in OFris as shown by *stēn* and *māra*, where, e.g., OE only has one reflex, cf. *stān* and *māra*. Note that WGmc *ē* is reflected as both *ī* and *ē* in OFris, cf. *mīde*, *mēde*; *hīr*, *hēr* 'here', etc. As for the WGmc diphthongs, *ai* and *au* were monophthongized in OFris.

Not all scholars have taken at face value the evidence of the manuscripts on the basis of which the OFris system of vowel phonemes has been posited. Hofmann (1964:162), e.g., suggests that the OFris orthographic rendering of *ē* perhaps conceals a phonemic distinction between /e:/ and /æ:/.

Taking both northern and southern Frisian dialectal evidence into account, Jørgensen (1946:109-10) reconstructs the following system of long monophthongs for Proto-Frisian prior to the introduction of *i*-mutated long vowels, i.e. a system which had no currency beyond the eighth century:

ī	ū
ē	ō
ǣ (< ai)	ā (< au)

West Gmc *ē* has here merged with the reflexes of WGmc *ī* and *ā* (/i:/ and /e:/), and /æ:/ and /a:/ have been added to the system through the monophthongization of WGmc *ai* and *au*.

3.3. Old Saxon

The following short and long monophthongs can be posited for the OS vowel system:

i		i		ī		ū
e		o		ẹ̄		ọ̄
	a			ę̄		ǭ
					ā	

Examples:

e	/e/	*beran* 'to bear' (< WGmc *e*)
a	/a/	*staf* 'staff', cf. OE *stæf*, OFris *stef*, OHG *stab* (< WGmc *a*)
i	/i/	*fisk* 'fish' (< WGmc *i*)
o	/o/	*holt* 'wood', *holm* 'island', cf. OE *holt*, *holm* (< WGmc *o*)
u	/u/	*gumo* 'man', cf. Goth./OE *guma* (< WGmc *u*)
ī	/i:/	*wrītan* 'to write' (< WGmc *ī*)
ẹ̄	/e:/	*lēt* 'allowed', cf. OE *lēt*, OHG *liaʒ* (< WGmc *ē*)
ę̄	/ɛ:/	*lēđ* 'hateful', cf. OE *lāð*, OFris *lēth*, OHG *leid* (< WGmc *ai*)
		lēstian 'to perform', cf. OE *lǣstan*, OHG *leisten*, Goth. *laistjan* (< WGmc *ai* + *i*, *j*)
ā	/a:/	*jār* 'year', cf. OHG *jār*, OFris *jēr* (< WGmc *ā*)
		māno 'moon', cf. OHG *māno*, OE/OFris *mōna* (< WGmc *ā* + N)
ǭ	/ɔ:/	*ōra* 'ear', cf. OE *ēare*, OFris *āre*, Goth. *auso* (< WGmc *au*)
		gihōrian 'to hear', cf. OE *hīeran*, OFris *hēra*, Goth. *hausjan* (< WGmc *au* + *i*, *j*)
ọ̄	/o:/	*bōk* 'book', cf. OHG *buoh*, OE *bōc* (< WGmc *ō*)
ū	/u:/	*ūt* 'out' (< WGmc *ū*)

It will be seen from the examples that the WGmc diphthongs *ai* and *au* have been monophthongized to half-open long vowels.

In contradistinction to what happened in OE, *i*-umlaut has apparently not affected the (monophthongized) reflexes of WGmc *ai* (cf. *lēđ*; *lēstian*) and *au* (cf. *ōra*; *gihōrian*). Also, OS shows no split plus merger of WGmc *ā*, which is neither fronted nor rounded to *ō* before nasals (cf. *jār*, *māno*). Nor is short *a* regularly fronted (cf. *staf*).

But some OS texts show vocalic features that are much more North-Sea Germanic or Ingveonic than those shown here. In the most North-Sea Germanic of all versions of the OS Heliand epic, viz. the recently discovered Straubing fragments, there are several instances of long, fronted reflexes of *ā*, e.g. in *forlētan* 'to give up, to abandon' (Cotton MS *forlātan*) and *uuērun* 'were' (Cotton and Monacensis MSS *uuārun*), and one example of *ō* (< WGmc *ā*) before a nasal, cf. *sōn* 'at once' (C/M *sān*; cf. OFris *sōn*, OE *sōna*). There are even a few fronted reflexes of short WGmc *a*, e.g. *creht* 'power, might' (C/M *craft*; cf. OE *cræft*).

In the majority of attested cases the reflex of WGmc *au* in the Straubing fragments is *ā* as in certain other OS manuscripts as well as in OFris: *āk* 'also', *thāh* 'though', *āstan* 'from the east', *bākna* (gp.) 'sign' (C/M *ōc*, *thōh*, *ōstan*, C *bōcno*/M *bōgno*; cf. OFris *āk*, *thāch*, *āsta*, *bāken*).

A derivation of the OS accented vowels from WGmc presents few problems. It is less clear how the OS accented vowel system relates to the OE and OFris systems, and how the North-Sea Germanic vocalic features outlined above should be accounted for. We shall now proceed to a discussion of these difficult problems.

3.4. The Old English, Old Frisian and Old Saxon vowel systems compared

Traditionally, the fronting of WGmc *ā* in OE is thought to have preceded the monophthongization of WGmc *ai* to *ā* since otherwise the reflex of *ai* would also have become *ǣ*. However, the monophthongization must have occurred prior to the fronting of short *a*, because otherwise the first element of *ai* would have become *æ* (**æi*), which could not have developed into *ā*. Because of its front first element, the OE diphthong *ēa* (< WGmc *au*) is supposed to have evolved contemporaneously with the fronting of short WGmc *a*. This is the relative chronology offered by Campbell (1959:§132) as well as some more recent scholars, e.g., Hogg (1992:100-1) and Stiles (1995:198-9).

From a modern phonological viewpoint, a more obvious analysis of the changes would be to see a chain shift (co-occurrence) in the fronting of WGmc *ā* and the monophthongization of WGmc *ai* to *ā* (Lass 1994:39-41). In the light of the fronted (cf. *dǣd*) and back rounded (cf. *mōna*) reflexes of WGmc *ā* in OE (West Saxon), a so-called push-chain development would seem to be a plausible scenario.

In addition to restricting the extensive phonological space occupied by the reflex of WGmc *ā* in the open and half-open area, the introduction of *ā* (< WGmc *ai*) led to a phonemic split (plus merger) in which (1) an open front-back correlation arose (*ǣ* (< *ā*) - *ā* (< *ai*)) and (2) the nasalized *ā̃*-allophones of *ā*, joined by the reflexes of WGmc *a* plus nasal plus voiceless fricative (e.g. OE *ōðer* 'other', cf. OHG *ander*, Goth. *anþar*), eventually merged with *ō* (Krupatkin 1970). As mentioned earlier, the reflex of WGmc *au* (*ēa*) was incorporated into the front-back pattern of the long vowel phonemes; and the split of short WGmc *a* into *æ* and *a* was modelled on, and therefore secondary in relation to, the front-back contrast established in the open area of the long system.

In Proto-Frisian, a push-chain process triggered by the monophthongization of WGmc *ai* and *au* is likely to have restricted the phonological space in the open front and back areas considerably: except in the position before a nasal (where a nasalized back allophone had arisen that eventually merged with *ō* as in OE, cf. OFris/OE *mōna*), the reflex of WGmc *ā* was confined to the mid front area, WGmc *ē* merging partly with WGmc *ī*, partly with WGmc *ā*. Before *i*-mutated *ā* (< WGmc *au*) joined the *ǣ* phoneme, *ǣ* was exposed to a phonemic split in that its allophones in 'grave' environments coalesced with *ā*, cf. OFris *rāp* 'rope', *māra* 'more' vs. *stēn* 'stone', *brēd* 'broad' (OE *rāp*, *māra*, *stān*, *brād*). Had *i*-umlaut antedated 'gravity' assimilation, *i*-mutated *ā* (< WGmc *au*) would not have come out consistently as *ǣ* (spelt <e> in OFris, e.g. *hēra* 'to hear'), cf. Nielsen (1983). Vowel monophthongizations in pre-OE and Proto-Frisian may thus have sparked off split-plus-merger developments as regards the fate of WGmc *ā* in the two languages, but as mutually independent processes.

Jørgensen's hypothesis (1946:109-10) that the monophthongization of *au* and *ai* preceded *i*-umlaut in Frisian, was anticipated by Campbell (1939: 104-5) in the relative chronology he posited for the same events. The Jørgensen/Campbell model receives empirical support from several inscriptions belonging to the so-called Frisian runic corpus which evidence the shift of Gmc *au* to *ā*. The earliest item is the sixth-century London gold solidus, which bears the runic legend **skanomodu** *skānomōdu* < **skaunamōd-* 'Schönmut'. The name of the rune (ᚪ) denoting **a** *ā* was *āc* 'oak' in OE, a name deriving from WGmc **aik-*. In runic Frisian, there is no evidence of the use of ᚪ for *ā* < WGmc *ai*, and according to the acrophonic principle (by which the runes had the sound value of the first letter of their names) the rune is therefore likely to have been invented in England and been exported from there to Frisia, where WGmc *ai* became *ǣ* (cf. OFris *ēk* 'oak'), and where for phonetic reasons, but contrary to the acrophonic principle, the runic letter was used with the sound value *ā*, e.g. to denote *ā* < WGmc *au*. The circumstance that ᚫ is attested in runic English only from the seventh century may be fortuitous in view of the paucity of early extant inscriptions. The effect of the emergence of new open monophthongized vowels in the early English and Frisian long vowel systems was to restrict the phonological space of the respective reflexes of WGmc *ā* (cf. Hofmann 1979:15), making the fronting of WGmc *ā* secondary in relation to monophthongization.

In the OS long vowel system, there was no fronting of WGmc *ā*. In the light of the events determining the development of the systems of the OE and OFris long vowels, it is easy to see that the monophthongization of WGmc *ai* and *au* to *ę̄* and *ǭ* in OS reduced the phonological space in the half-open area, preventing *ā* from undergoing a split-plus-merger process which an open monophthongized vowel might have triggered, cf. OE and OFris.

But there are clear traces of a vowel system in OS characterized by North-Sea Germanic evolutionary features. A case in point is the Straubing version of the Heliand epic, where fronted reflexes of WGmc long and short *a* are found (cf. *uuērun* 'were'; *creht* 'power'); where *ā* before a nasal may come out as *ō* (cf. *sōn* 'at once'), coalescing with the reflex of *a* + nasal + voiceless fricative (cf. *ōđer* 'other'); and where WGmc *au* is reflected as *ā* (cf. *thāh* 'though')

Perhaps the eventual split of OS *ę̄* (cf. above)—and merger with the reflexes of (1) WGmc *ē* and (2) the *i*-mutated allophone of WGmc *ā* (which was kept apart from the non-mutated reflex of WGmc *ā*)—is easier to comprehend if an OS vowel system is posited in which WGmc *ā* is seen within a North-Sea Gmc framework (Klein 1977:516). This would make the split of OS *ę̄* comparable to that of *ǣ* (< WGmc *ai*) in Frisian, but it must be stressed that such a parallel between Saxon and Frisian is structurally conditioned, requiring no explanation in terms of shared origin and diffusion by contact, cf. Hofmann (1995).

However that may be, Klein thinks that, apart from southern Westphalian, NSG vocalism (split-plus-merger of WGmc long and short *a*) may have occurred anywhere in the OS speech area, 'wenn wir auch über ihre dialektale Verbreitung und ihre genauen phonetischen Bedingungen kaum Sicheres wissen' (1977:523).

3.5. Concluding remarks

The evolution of the accented vowel systems of OE, OFris and OS showed a number of similarities, but as we have seen, the monophthongization of WGmc *ai* and *au* and the fronting and rounding of the reflexes of WGmc long (and short) *a* took place independently in each of the three languages. We may repeat here that WGmc *au* was not even monophthongized in OE and add that the OE runic letter (ᛠ) denoting *ēa* did not emerge in the runic inscriptions of England until after the earlier seventh century.

But did the North-Sea Germanic languages exhibit any specific shifts of accented vowels shared only by them and assignable to a period preceding (or co-occurring with) the Anglo-Saxon colonization of England? Presumably there is only one plausible candidate for such a shift, and that is nasalized long and short *ã*.

The earliest finds in England and Frisia to show any of the new runic letters included in the extended 'Anglo-Frisian' futhorc are the Undley bracteate (East Anglia) from the late fifth century and the Chessell Down scabbard plate (Isle of Wight) from the sixth (or perhaps even from the late fifth century), which both have ᚩ. Apparently, the letter denotes an accented vowel only in the Undley legend, where it is transliterated as **o**, by Odenstedt as a rendering of long *ō* and by Eichner as a representation of the corresponding short vowel.

In my view, it is worth considering whether ᚩ could not at first have been designed to represent the nasalized reflexes of, respectively, long and short *a*. According to Krupatkin (1970:54-6), the events leading up to this were that in the North-Sea Gmc dialects the reflex of WGmc long *ā* split into nazalized $\bar{a}^n$ and non-nazalized $\bar{a}^v$, $\bar{a}^n$ occurring before nasals and merging with the reflexes of Gmc *a* + nasal before voiceless fricatives (**anh*, **ans*, **anf*, **anþ*), and that WGmc short *a*, to restore systemic equilibrium, split into a^v and a^n. The advantage to the vowel system was that long and short vowels remained qualitatively equivalent. The eventual shift to *ō* was triggered (in pre-OE) by the intrusion of the new monophthongized vowel *ā* (< WGmc *ai*), which obviated the non-nasality - nasality opposition, a front-back contrast developing with the fronting of WGmc *ā* to *ǣ*. The by now isolated nazalized vowel $\bar{a}^n$ merged with *ō*, and in the short system the opposition a^v-a^n was replaced by a front-back contrast modelled on the long system. After a^n was denazalized, it was represented by both *a* and *o* spellings (Krupatkin 1970:59-69). Both the long and short vowels thus ended up with a three-tier system with a front-back contrast also in the open area. In any case, Krupatkin's scenario opens up for the possibility that a split into $\breve{\bar{a}}^v$-$\breve{\bar{a}}^n$ was an early shared North-Sea Germanic shift, the phonemic distinction being expressed graphemically by the contrast between ᚨ and the new ᚫ rune.

4. Unaccented Vowels

4.1. Old English

The earliest unaccented vowel system that can be established for OE on the basis of the earliest extant manuscripts is the following (Hogg 1992:119-22):

i	u
æ	a

In the eighth-century Northumbrian (Moore) version of Cædmon's Hymn the gsm/n. suffix is spelled *-aes, -œs*, cf. *-rīcaes* 'kingdom's', *metudœs* 'God's', *-cynnœs* 'kin's' (gs. *-œs* < **-as*) and not *-es* as is the standard OE spelling (*rīces, metodes, cynnes*). Similarly, the early version of Cædmon's Hymn exhibits unaccented *-i*(-), cf. *ēci dryctin* 'eternal Lord', corresponding to later OE *-e*(-) (*ēce dryhten*), cf. also n/asm. *i*-st. early OE *-wini*, standard OE *wine* 'friend'. This would seem to show that a phonemic distinction was maintained between the two unaccented front vowels *œ* and *i* in the earliest surviving type of OE; it should be noted, however, that in its rendering of 'heaven', Cædmon's Hymn vacillates between *hefaen-* and *heben*, the unaccented vowel going back to *œ* (< **a*, cf. OS *heƀan*), which might be taken as a sign that the front-vowel distinction had been blurred in this early text. It is interesting also that whereas the Moore version has the dsm. *a*-st. form *hrōfe* 'roof', the Leningrad version of Cædmon's hymn (early

Northumbrian as well) has *hrōfæ*; the *-æ* of this form is the 'regular' early OE reflex of Gmc **-ai*, being replaced in standard OE by *-e*. As for the back vowels, early OE distinguishes clearly between *a*, cf. gpn. *uundra* 'wondrous things' and *u*, cf. dpn. *barnum* 'children' with the same suffixes as OE (West Saxon) *wundra, bearnum*, cf. also standard OE nsm. *n*-st. *guma* 'man', n/asm. *u*-st. *sunu* 'son'.

The merger of unaccented /i/ and /æ/ brought about a triangular system with the back-vowel distinction retained:

	u
e	
	a

There are indications, however, that the back vowels were not kept apart beyond the tenth century and that all phonemic distinctions in the unaccented system were given up in the course of the eleventh century (Nielsen 1998:§4.3.1.2, §7.2.3.1).

4.2. Old Frisian

As Sjölin (1969:22) points out, nearly all OFris manuscripts render the vowels of the unaccented syllables graphically by means of *e* in free variation with *a, i, o* and *u*. Nevertheless, in the most archaic of the major OFris texts, the first riustring manuscript (R_1) from ca. 1300, there are signs of a triangular unaccented vowel system represented graphemically by <i, e>, <a> and <u, o>, in which *i* and *u* would seem to occur in complementary distribution with *e* and *o*, cf. dsm. *godi* 'God', npn. *skipu* 'ships' where *i* and *u* are used after short stem vowels. If the stem is long/polysyllabic or the stem vowel is *e* (or *o*), the spelling of the unaccented vowels is *e* and *o* instead, cf. e.g. dsm. *hōue* 'hoof', n/a/dsm. *kere* 'statute' (cf. Boutkan 1996:9, 27). Examples of words ending in *-a* are gpm. *kininga* 'kings' and nsm. *n*-stem *skeltata* 'legal magistrate'.

The first Riustring manuscript has, in other words, an unaccented vowel system closely resembling that of ninth-century OE with two back-vowel phonemes but without any front-vowel distinctions being retained, cf. also the R_1 forms *drochten* 'Lord', gsm. *godis* 'God's' vs. OE *dryhten, godes* (but early Northumbrian *dryctin*, gsm/n. *-æs*).

4.3. Old Saxon

The earliest OE system has quadrangular counterparts in OS, where all texts have unaccented *-i* (cf. *wini* 'friend', *drohtin* 'Lord') and *-u* (cf. *sunu* 'son'). But one group of texts, the most prominent members of which are the Lublin psalm-fragments and the Straubing Heliand-fragments, prefer *-e* and *-a* (cf. OFris and OE), where other texts, e.g. the Cotton Heliand-manuscript, exhibit *a* and *o* (cf. OHG). The Heliand S *n*-stem forms nom.sg.f. *thiorne* 'maiden, virgin' and nom.sg.m. *uuillia* 'will' as opposed to Heliand C *thiorna* and *uuilleo* illustrate this dichotomy.

Geographically, the OS texts with *-e, -a* spellings derive from Eastphalia and Engern, whereas the *-a, -o* group texts stem largely from Westphalia. According to Klein (1977:529), the phonological systems of the two groups are, respectively, /-i, -æ, -a, -u/ and /-i, -a, -o, -u/, which in Klein's view are both later reflections of an early OS system consisting of the four phonemes /-i, -æ, -ɔ, -u/. This system is attested basically only in the Monacensis-manuscript of the Heliand (Klein 1977:416), which combined *-o* /-ɔ/ with a great deal of orthographic variation between *-a* and *-e* to render /-æ/. The reason for this variation should be attributed to the fact that in the OHG mother tongue of the scribes there were five unaccented short vowels /-i, -e, -a, -o, -u/ as against four in the OS language which the scribes were supposed to put down in writing (Klein 1977:390-1).

Decisive for this difference in the number of unaccented (short) vowels between OHG and OS was the North-Sea Gmc fronting of *-a* to *-æ*, whereby the vowel merged with *-e* /-æ/ < Gmc **-ai*, cf. dat.sg.m. *a*-stem OHG *kuninge,* OE *cyninge,* OFris (R_1) *kininge* 'king', the *-e* suffixes of which derive from **-ai* (Gmc **kuningai*). The merger between the reflexes of Gmc **-ai* and WGmc **-a* took place in all of the OS speech area, the merged phoneme being rendered chiefly as *-e* in the *-e, -a* texts and as *-a* in the *-a, -o* group, cf. the variation between OS dat.sg.m. *cuninge* (Heliand S) and *cuninga* (Heliand C 696) 'king' corresponding roughly to that between *thiorne* and *thiorna* 'maiden, virgin'.

In the *-e, -a* group, however, the fronting of WGmc **-a* was followed by a shift of *-o* to *-a*, giving this brand of OS the same type of unaccented vocalism as that of early OE and pre-OFris. It is thus possible to posit a common North-Sea Gmc unaccented vowel system, but it is clear that such a system could not have come about until the fronted reflex of **-a* had coalesced with the monophthongized descendant of **-ai*. The fronting process must have followed in the wake of the fronting of long and short *a* in accented syllables, which, as I proposed earlier, is likely to have occurred independently in the various North-Sea Gmc dialects. As for the shift of *-o* to *-a*, this is best interpreted as a (late) drag-chain process. The coalescence of the reflexes of WGmc **-a* and **-ai* in the North-Sea Gmc languages must thus have been preceded by an unaccented system consisting of five vowels: /-i, -æ, -a, -o, -u/. It might be added that, like OHG, Old Dutch had been exposed to no merger between **-a* (cf. nom.sg.f. *n*-stem *tunga*) and **-ai* (cf. dat.sg.m. *a*-stem *dage*). Old (West) Flemish, on the other hand, seems to have joined the North-Sea Gmc group as suggested by, e.g., nom.sg.m. *n*-stem and gen.pl. *a*-stem forms in *-a*, cf. the Old West Flemish names *Sassa* (nom.sg.m.) and *Erniga*[*-ham*] (gen.pl.). In both instances the Old Dutch suffix would be *-o*, cf. *namo* 'name', *dago* 'days' (Schönfeld/van Loey 1970:§107, §100; Quak 1992:85, 83). A drag-chain shift of *-o* to *-a* would thus appear to have taken place in Old (West) Flemish.

5. Consonants

In OE, the number of consonant phonemes was increased through the palatalization and affrication of the WGmc velar stops /k/ and /g/: /k/ became /tʃ/ before original front vowels and /j/ and after /i/ in word-final position, cf. OE *cēosan* 'to choose', *lǣce* 'doctor' and *ic* 'I'; and /g/ changed to /dʒ/ between a nasal and /j/, cf. *sengan* 'to singe', and when geminated before *j*, cf. *lecgan* 'to lay'. The phonemic split of the old /k/ phoneme (as well as /g/) arose as a result of *i*-umlaut, cf. the contrast between initial /tʃ/ and /k/ in the minimal pairs OE *cēn* (< **kēna-*) 'torch' and *cēne* (< **kōni-*) 'keen'. Another important change pertains to the allophonic variation among fricatives in OE. Except in the case of /s/ ≠ /z/ voice was not a distinctive feature as regards the Proto-Gmc fricatives, *[ƀ, đ, ǥ] being allophones of */b, d, g/ (≠ */f, θ, χ/). In West Gmc, [đ] coalesced with /d/, and in OE, [ƀ] merged with the voiceless fricative /f/, which like the other voiceless fricatives became voiced in medial position ([v]). /f/, /θ/ and /s/ have the following allophonic distribution in OE: [f] *fisc* 'fish', *grōf* 'dug', [v] *grafan* 'to dig'; [θ] *þonkian* 'to thank', *bæþ* 'bath', [ð] *weorðan* 'to become'; and [s] *sunu* 'son', *hūs* 'house', [z] *wesan* 'to be'. It should be added that the velar voiceless fricative disappeared in medial position in OE, perhaps as a further stage in the voicing process, cf. OE *tēon* 'to pull', pret. *tēah* (Goth. *tiuhan*, *tauh*).

In OFris, palatalized and affricated stops developed in much the same way as in OE: /k/ became /tˢ/ before original front vowels and *j*, cf. *tsiāsa* 'choose', *lētza* 'doctor'; and /g/ changed to /dᶻ/ when geminated before *j*, cf. *ledza* 'to lay', or when occurring between *n* and *i*, cf. *keninze* (< **kuningi-*) 'king'. /k/ was not palatalized and affricated before *i*-mutated vowels, cf. *kenn* (< Gmc **kunja-*) 'kin', which shows that *i*-umlaut postdated the palatalization and affrication of /k/ (and /g/), cf. OE *cynn*. The OFris fricative system and the relationship between fricatives and stops are more or less identical to what we found in OE, e.g. [f] *fisk* 'fish', *gref* 'grave', [v] *greva* 'to dig'; [θ] *thonkia* 'to thank', *beth* 'bath', [ð] *wertha* 'to become'; and [s] *sunu* 'son', *hūs* 'house', [z] *wesa* 'to be'. Similarly, the velar voiceless fricative disappeared in medial position, cf. OFris *tiā* 'to pull', pret. *tāch*.

A significant difference between the OS and the OE/OFris consonant systems is the absence of affricated stop phonemes in OS, cf. OS *kiosan* 'to choose', *lāki* 'doctor' and *leggian* 'to lay'. Another difference is the retention of the fricative /h/ in medial position where it disappeared in OE and OFris, cf. OS *tiohan* 'to pull'. The remaining OS fricatives (/f/, /θ/, /s/) are treated in the same way as the OE and OFris ones, e.g. [f] *fisk* 'fish' *graf* 'grave', [v] *bigraƀan* 'to bury'.

The reorganization of the obstruent structure in the North-Sea Gmc languages, whereby a complementary (non-phonemic) distribution of voiceless and voiced fricatives arose, occurred before the emergence of the earliest manuscripts. In runic Frisian, the contrast between Gmc */b/ [ƀ] and */f/ [f] has been retained graphemically in, respectively (Oostum comb, ca. 800) **habuku** 'hawk' (< Gmc **habukaz*) and the personal name (Folkstone tremissis, ca. 600) **æniwulufu** (< Gmc nsm. **wulfaz* 'wolf'). It should be noted that in early OE there are examples comparable to those attested in runic Frisian, cf. Cædmon's Hymn which in the early Northumbrian Moore MS version has *heben* 'heaven' and not *heofon* as in the later West Saxon text. In the early OE glosses and glossaries, e.g. in the Epinal Glossary, we meet forms such as *gibaen* 'given', *-hebuc* 'hawk', *halb-* 'half', *salb-*

'ointment' vs. *uulfes* gsm. 'wolf' and *scofl* 'shovel', but without full etymological consistency, cf. *sifun-* 'seven' (Gmc **sebun*). Note also that the Leningrad MS of the early Nhm. version of Cædmon's Hymn has *hefen* for 'heaven'. In terms of relative chronology, the voicing of *-s-* and *-þ-* in medial position postdated, respectively, the change of medial Gmc **z* to *r* and that of **đ* to *d* in WGmc.

As for the palatalization and affrication of Gmc **k* and **g*, these changes affected the phonemic systems only of OE and OFris, where the initial plosives retained in, e.g., OE *cynn* and OFris *kenn* 'kin' (< Gmc **kunja-*) show that the new phonemes must have come about in the two languages before the operation of *i*-umlaut. But since, e.g., **k-* is affected also before the fronted reflexes of West Gmc short and long *a* in OE and OFris, cf. OE (WS) *ceaf* 'chaff', *ceald* 'cold'; *cēace* 'cheek' and OFris *tsetel* 'kettle' (< Lat. **catīnus, catīllus*); *tzīse* 'cheese' (< Lat. **cāseus*), it can safely be assumed that the new affricated phonemes arose independently in the two languages. Nevertheless, Fulk has now come out in favour of the view (1998:153; cf. 1998:145-8) that palatalization, but not the phonemicization of 'palatals', antedated the split between English and Frisian, conceding at the same time that 'there is no compelling reason to date palatalization [...] so early, aside from the desire to make it an Anglo-Frisian development' (1998:154)!

There is textual evidence in OS to suggest that palatalization occurred also there, at least with regard to *k*, cf. the following forms of *antk(i)ennian* 'to understand', a weak Class I verb (< Gmc **-kanjan-*): Hel. M *antkiennien*, Hel. S *untkiende* (Nielsen 1991:259). But these examples should not be linked to the OE and OFris developments because the OS palatalised stop appears before a vowel fronted through *i*-umlaut. And significantly, *i*-mutation was implemented later in OS than in OE and OFris (cf. Krogh 1996:210-12; cf. also Gysseling 1962:17).

6. Further Chronological Deliberations

Unlike Dal, Rooth and others, Hans Kuhn believed, partly for ethnographical and archaeological reasons (1955:41-2, 26), that North-Sea Gmc came into being only at the same time as or after the fifth-century Anglo-Saxon emigration to Britain. The linguistic innovations that came to prevail, originated along the shores of the southern North-Sea region, from where they spread into the Low German and Low Franconian hinterland (1955:36-44, 46). Later investigators have tended to accept that a number of the North-Sea Gmc innovations postdate the emigration, but maintain that the earliest correspondences arose on the Continent. This holds true of, e.g., Markey (1976:36-71), whose inventory of 36 'typically Ingvæonic' (1976:44) parallels, contained three features thought to have developed before 450: (1) loss of nasals before fricatives, (2) uniform verbal pl. endings and (3) loss of *-r* in monosyllabic pronouns; and of Stiles, who in addition to the development of a back timbre and nasalization in long and short *a* (1995:198-9) and the fronting of WGmc long *ā* accepted Markey's items (1) and (2) as pre-invasion shifts.

Except for the fronting of *ā*, I have no problems in assigning the contrast between (what Krupatkin designated as) *ā̆*^{v} and *ā̆*^{n}, the loss of nasals before fricatives (whereby *a*^{n} occurring before nasals merged with the reflexes of Gmc *a* in the sequences **anh*, **ans*, **anf*, **anþ*) and the uniform 1/2/3 pres.pl. endings in, e.g., OE *drīfaþ* 'drive', OFris *nemat*(*h*) 'take', OS *drīƀath/drīƀad* (which had as their starting point the loss of *-n-* in 3 pres.pl. **-anþi*) to the period preceding the Anglo-Saxon exodus (cf. also Markey 1976:48-9, 70; Krogh 1996:331-6; and Nielsen 1985:118-19, 149-51; for a different view, see Kuhn 1955:35). I agree, too, that the loss of *-r* in monosyllabic pronouns such as OE *hē̆*, *wē̆*, *mē̆*, OFris/OS *hī̆* /*hē̆* 'he', *wī̆* 'we', *mī̆* 'me', ODu *hē̆*, *uī̆*, *mī̆*, is a pre-invasion change in view of the loss of Gmc **-z* in unaccented position in West Gmc, which led to variation between unaccented monosyllabic pronouns exhibiting consonantal loss and accented ones retaining *-r* (the accented reflex of **-z*). Subsequent levellings brought about a generalization of *-r* forms in OHG (cf. *er*, *wir*, *mir*) and forms without a final consonant in North-Sea Gmc. Further, I believe that the addition of *h-* to the nom.sg.m. forms of the 3 sg. pers.pron. 'he' in OE, OFris, OS and ODu was a pre-invasion innovation (cf. Krogh 1996:319-22, 401), which was also an indirect consequence of the West Gmc loss of unaccented **-z*. In OHG the accented reflex of Gmc **iz*, **ez* 'he' was selected (*er*), but in the North-Sea Gmc languages, where the unaccented form (**i*, **e*) was generalized, a phonologico-semantic remedy was required, and initial *h-* was available as raw material (cf. OS *hiudu* 'today', OHG *hiutu*; Goth. (dsm.) *himma* (*daga*)). However, the intraparadigmatic extension of *h-* to other case and gender forms in OE, OFris and MDu probably occurred independently in the languages concerned (Nielsen 1985: 98).

Among the phonological items discussed, the following OE changes were interpreted as independent innovations: the monophthongization of *ai* (in OFris *ai* and *au*), the fronting of long and short *a*; the palatalization and affrication of *k* and *g*; *i*-mutation; and breaking. The all-important difference between this model and that proposed by Stiles is the relative position of the fronting of long *ā*, an 'Ingvæonic' change preceding the monophthongization of *ai* (in OFris, *ai* and *au*) according to Stiles (1995:199-200), but seen by me as an independent innovation postdating (or co-occurring with) the monophthongization processes.

References

Århammar, N. 1990. 'Friesisch und Sächsisch'. *Aspects of Old Frisian Philology*, ed. R. H. Bremmer, G. van der Meer, & O. Vries. Amsterdamer Beiträge zur älteren Germanistik, 31/32. Amsterdam: Rodopi. 1-25.

Boutkan, D. 1996. *A Concise Grammar of the Old Frisian Dialect of the First Riustring Manuscript*. Odense: Odense University Press.

Bremer, O. 1900. 'Ethnographie der germanischen Stämme'. *Grundriß der germanischen Philologie, III*, ed. H. Paul. 2nd ed. Straßburg: Trübner. 735-950.

Bremmer, R. H. 1982. 'Old English—Old Frisian: The Relationship Reviewed'. *Philologia Frisica Anno 1981*. Ljouwert: Fryske Akademy. 79-90.

———. 1989. *Late Medieval and Early Modern Opinions on the Affinity between English and Frisian: The Growth of a Commonplace*. Dutch Working Papers in English Language and Linguistics, 9. Rijksuniversiteit Leiden.

Campbell, A. 1939. 'Some Old Frisian Sound-Changes'. *Transactions of the Philological Society* 1939:78-107.

———. 1959. *Old English Grammar*. Oxford: Clarendon.

Dal, I. 1983. '2.1. Altniederdeutsch und seine Vorstufen'. *Handbuch zur niederdeutschen Sprach- und Literaturwissenschaft*, ed. G. Cordes & D. Möhn. Berlin: Schmidt. 69-97.

Eichner, H. 1990. 'Die Ausprägung der linguistischen Physiognomie des Englischen anno 400 bis 600 n. Chr.'. *Britain 400-600: Language and History*, ed. A. Bammesberger & A. Wollmann. Heidelberg: Winter. 307-33.

Frings, T. 1944. *Die Stellung der Niederlande im Aufbau des Germanischen.* Halle: Niemeyer.

———. 1957. *Grundlegung einer Geschichte der deutschen Sprache.* 3rd ed. Halle: Niemeyer.

Fulk, R. D. 1998. 'The Chronology of Anglo-Frisian Sound Changes'. *Approaches to Old Frisian Philology*, ed. R. H. Bremmer, T. S. B. Johnston, & O. Vries. Amsterdamer Beiträge zur älteren Germanistik, 49. Amsterdam: Rodopi. 139-54.

Gysseling, M. 1962. 'Het oudste Fries'. *It Beaken* 24:1-26.

Hofmann, D. 1964. '"Germanisch $\bar{e}^2$" im Friesischen'. *Festschrift für Jost Trier zum 70. Geburtstag*, ed. W. Foerste & K. H. Borck. Köln: Böhlau. 160-85.

———. 1979. 'Die Entwicklung des Nordfriesischen'. *Friesisch heute*, ed. A. Walker & O. Wilts. Schriftenreihe der Akademie, Neue Folge, 45-6. Sankelmark: Akademie Sankelmark. 11-28.

Hogg, R. H. 1992. 'Phonology and Morphology'. *The Cambridge History of the English Language, I: The Beginnings to 1066*, ed. R. H. Hogg. Cambridge: Cambridge University Press. 67-167.

Jørgensen, P. 1946. *Über die Herkunft der Nordfriesen.* København: Munksgaard.

Kisbye, T. 1992. *A Short History of the English Language.* Aarhus: Aarhus Universitetsforlag.

Klein, T. 1977. *Studien zur Wechselbeziehung zwischen altsächsischem und althochdeutschem Schreibwesen und ihrer Sprach- und kulturgeschichtlichen Bedeutung.* Göppingen: Kümmerle.

Krogh, S. 1996. *Die Stellung des Altsächsischen im Rahmen der germanischen Sprachen.* Göttingen: Vandenhoeck & Ruprecht.

Krupatkin, Y. B. 1970. 'From Germanic to English and Frisian'. *Us Wurk* 19:49-71.

Kuhn, H. 1955. 'Zur Gliederung der germanischen Sprachen'. *Zeitschrift für deutsches Altertum und deutsche Literatur* 86:1-47.

Lass, R. 1994. *Old English. A Historical Linguistic Companion.* Cambridge: Cambridge University Press.

Markey, T. L. 1976. *Germanic Dialect Grouping and the Position of Ingvæonic.* Innsbruck: Inst. für Sprachwiss. d. Univ.

Morsbach, L. 1897. Review of O.F. Emerson, *The History of the English Language* (1894). *Beiblatt zur Anglia* 7:321-38.

Nielsen, H. F. 1983. 'Germanic ai in Old Frisian, Old English and Old Norse'. *Indogermanische Forschungen* 88:156-64.

———. 1985. *Old English and the Continental Germanic Languages*. 2nd ed. Innsbruck: Inst. für Sprachwiss. d. Univ.

———. 1991. 'The Straubing Heliand-Fragment and the Old English Dialects'. *Language Contact in the British Isles*, ed. P. S. Ureland & G. Broderick. Tübingen: Niemeyer. 243-73.

———. 1998. *The Continental Backgrounds of English and its Insular Development until 1154*. Odense: Odense University Press.

———. 2000. *The Early Runic Language of Scandinavia. Studies in Germanic Dialect Geography*. Heidelberg: Winter.

Odenstedt, B. 1983. *The Inscription on the Undley Bracteate and the Beginnings of English Runic Writing*. Umeå Papers in English, 5. Umeå: Department of English, Umeå University.

Quak, A. 1992. 'Versuch einer Formenlehre des Altniederländischen auf der Basis der Wachtendonckschen Psalmen'. *Zur Phonologie und Morphologie des Altniederländischen*, ed. R. H. Bremmer & A. Quak. Odense: Odense University Press. 81-123.

Robinson, O. W. 1992. *Old English and Its Closest Relatives*. London: Routledge.

Rooth, E. 1932. 'Die Sprachform der Merseburger Quellen'. *Niederdeutsche Studien*, pp. 24-54.

Schönfeld's Historische Grammatica van het Nederlands. 1970. 8th ed., prepared by A. van Loey. Zutphen: Thieme.

Siebs, T. 1889. *Zur Geschichte der englisch-friesischen Sprache*. Halle: Niemeyer.

———. 1901. 'Geschichte der friesischen Sprache'. *Grundriß der germanischen Philologie, I*, ed. H. Paul. 2nd ed. Straßburg: Trübner. 1152-1464.

Sipma, P. 1913. *Phonology and Grammar of Modern West Frisian with Phonetic Texts and Glossary*. Oxford: Oxford University Press.

Sjölin, B. 1969. *Einführung in das Friesische*. Stuttgart: Metzler.

———. 1973. 'Anglofriesisch'. *Reallexikon der Germanischen Altertumskunde, I*, ed. H. Beck, et al. 2nd ed. Berlin: Gruyter. 329-31.

Steller, W. 1928. *Abriß der altfriesischen Grammatik*. Halle: Niemeyer.

Stiles, P. V. 1995. 'Remarks on the "Anglo-Frisian" Thesis'. *Friesische Studien II*, ed. V. F. Faltings, A. G. H. Walker, & O. Wilts. Odense: Odense University Press. 177-220.

Streitberg, W. 1974 [1896]. *Urgermanische Grammatik*. 4th ed. Heidelberg: Winter.

Sweet, H. 1877. 'Dialects and Prehistoric Forms of Old English'. *Transactions of the Philological Society* 1875-6:543-69.

Vleeskruyer, R. 1948. 'A. Campbell's Views on Inguaeonic'. *Neophilologus*, pp. 173-83.

The Origins of Old English Breaking *

Jeremy J. Smith

1. Introduction

The hypothesis presented in this paper is that the prehistoric OE diphthongizations known collectively as 'Breaking' are to be explained plausibly as contact phenomena, brought about through the interaction of the Saxon and Anglian sound-systems. This hypothesis is based upon the analysis of both extralinguistic and intralinguistic correspondences. On the way to this conclusion, the status of Breaking as a unitary phenomenon is brought under review. The characteristic Old Anglian developments known as 'Retraction' and 'Smoothing' are also discussed, as are the changes known as 'First Fronting' (witnessed in both OE and OFris), 'Back Umlaut' and 'Late West Saxon Smoothing'.

2. A description of OE Breaking

'Breaking' (or 'Fracture') is the term generally used by Anglicists to describe the process of diphthongization during the prehistoric OE period whereby, between a front vowel and certain single consonants or consonant clusters, a back glide vowel developed, at first as [u], but subsequently lowered and centred to [ə]. This back vowel combined with the original front vowel to form a diphthong. The process seems to have taken place most fully in the West Saxon variety, but it is manifested to a lesser extent in

* I am grateful to Mike MacMahon and Robert McColl Millar, and especially to the late Les Collier, for insights leading to this paper. I am of course responsible for all errors and omissions.

other varieties as well. Breaking is fully described and illustrated in standard grammars and narratives, e.g. Campbell (1959:54-60), Hogg (1992:84-5), Lass (1994:48-51).

The term 'Breaking' is of course used by students of other Germanic languages to describe similar diphthongizations, although these seem to be quite distinct processes. Thus OFris Breaking is exemplified in *riucht* 'law, right' (cf. OE *riht*), *siunga* 'to sing' (cf. OE *singan*) and *thiukke* 'thick' (OE *þicce*); there are a few similarities (e.g. OFris *fiuchta* 'to fight', cf. OE *feohtan*), but Breaking in the two languages is generally distributed quite differently within the lexicon. The term 'Breaking' is applied in Old Norse studies to two changes which are treated distinctly by Anglicists (Breaking and Back Umlaut). It may be exemplified by such forms as Old Icelandic *björn* 'bear' (cf. OE *beorn* 'warrior', with Breaking), but also *jötunn* 'giant' (cf. OE **eoton*, *eoten* with Back Umlaut).

OE Breaking is usually dated to the prehistoric period immediately after the *Adventus Saxonum*. It does not appear in cognate languages, cf. OE *weorþan* 'become', *weaxan* 'grow' beside Old Icelandic *verða*, *vaxa*, OHG *werdan*, *wahsan*, OFris *wertha*, *waxa*. The fact that the phenomenon works quite differently in OFris indicates that OE Breaking arose after the divergence of the two Ingvaeonic languages.

The process of diphthongization seems to be triggered in the environment of following 'back' (i.e. velarised, uvularised) consonants and consonant-clusters, i.e.

(1) the fricative /x/ <h>, both on its own and in the sequence [xC] (where C = any consonant) (/x/-Breaking);

(2) /r, l/ + following consonant (including geminate /rr, ll/), <rC>, <lC> (but not when /ll/ was originally followed by /j/) (= /r/-, /l/-breaking).

(For a third environment (3), see p. 41 below.)

Bearing these two environments in mind, the following developments may be presumed from the West Saxon written record:

[i] > [iu], <io> (later <eo>): (1) only, traditionally exemplified by *meox* 'manure', *tiohhian* 'consider', *Peohtas* 'Picts'.

[i:] > [i:u], <īo> (later <ēo>): (1) only, e.g. *lēoht* 'light' (in weight).

[e] > [eu], <eo>: (1), and sometimes (2), e.g. *feoh* 'money', *feohtan* 'fight', *feorh* 'life', *eolh* 'elk', but *helpan* 'help' (infinitive); breaking of <e> before /l/-groups generally only takes place when [x] follows. Before <lc>, breaking of <e> is regularly indicated in the written record only when <s> precedes, e.g. *aseolcan* 'become languid' beside *melcan* 'milk' (verb). Because /l/-breaking only takes place in the environment of a following /lC/-cluster (where C = velar consonant), it could be argued that (2) in this case is perhaps not to be strictly separated from the developments with a following velar grouped together as (1). Breaking before /r/-groups is, however, common, thus *eorþe* 'earth', *weorþan* 'become', *weorpan* 'throw', *eorl* 'warrior', *sweord* 'sword' etc.

[æ:] > [æ:u], <ēa>: (1) only, e.g. *nēah* 'near'

[æ] > [æu], <ea>: (1), (2), e.g. *seah* 'saw', *bearn* 'child', *eald* 'old', and *healp* 'helped'.

It is generally held that the phonemic status of Breaking was established when apparent minimal pairs arose through the development of metathesised or syncopated forms, e.g. *ærn* 'house' (< **rænn*) beside *earn* 'eagle', *bern* 'barn' (< **berern*) beside *beorn* 'warrior'. However, see further section 5 below.

Breaking was more restricted in its outputs in the other OE dialects. Breaking in environment (1) seems to have affected both Saxon and Anglian varieties of OE, though subsequent sound-changes (see especially section 6 below) frequently obscured this development. However, breaking in environment (2) was rarer in varieties of Anglian than in Saxon. Thus Anglian has *ald* 'old' and *halp* 'helped'; for West Saxon and Mercian *bearn* 'child', Old Northumbrian texts have *barnum* (dative plural), *barna* (genitive plural). Old Northumbrian also has <o> for <eo> in <r>-groups when the vowel is preceded by <w>, e.g. *worða* 'become', *worpa* 'throw', *sword* 'sword'. These places where varieties of Old Anglian have a presumed back vowel in place of a West Saxon presumed diphthong are traditionally referred to as 'Retraction'.

It is traditional to allow for Breaking in a third environment, i.e. (3) with following /w/. However, the evidence for /w/-Breaking is problematic. That there is uncertainty about the precise process involved in diphthongization before /w/ is indicated by Lass (1994:49), who exemplifies /w/-breaking with the form *eowu*, 'ewe'; this form is, however, cited by Campbell (1959:90, §211), and by Hogg (1992:157-60, §5.105(1)) as an example of the later diphthongization known as 'Back Umlaut'.

The view taken here is that the diphthongization ascribed to /w/-influence is better considered as distinct from the other components of Breaking and really part of the later change known as Back Umlaut. It is noticeable that many examples used by the standard handbooks to illustrate /w/-breaking are either explicable by Back Umlaut or otherwise problematic; moreover, it is surely significant that /w/-breaking fails in the environment of an [i] in the following syllable, cf. *niowul* 'prostrate' beside the by-form *niwel* (see Campbell 1959:57, §148 and 1959:59, §154(2), Hogg 1992:90, §5.24; also Luick 1914-40:139, §134). The <eo> in the form *hweowul* could also have been brought about through Back Umlaut, cf. Germanic */xwexula/.

Other forms traditionally used as examples of /w/-breaking may also be excluded from consideration. *āsēowen* 'sifted' (past participle) could be accounted for by analogy with the infinitive *āsēon*, where the *ēo* is the result of /x/-breaking (see Campbell 1959:58, §153); it is noticeable that a past participle *āsiwen* is also recorded. Hogg (1992:89, §5.22, n.7) dismisses OE *cnēo* < */kneu/, cf. Gothic *kniu*, from consideration; the forms *cneowe* (dat.sg) etc. may be simple analogical extensions; and *þēow* would seem, from its etymology, to follow the same pattern as *cnēo* (cf. Gothic *þius*). As for Retraction before /w/ being exemplified by *clawu* 'claw', Hogg (1992: 80-1, esp. §5.13) has argued that /w/ was a post-vocalic environment where Ingvaeonic First Fronting failed, and thus forms like *clawu* 'claw', far from deriving from [æ] through Retraction, derive from forms which retained a back vowel and never developed a stressed front vowel [æ] in the first place.

3. Why did Breaking occur?

If, then, /w/-breaking is left aside as part of a distinct process, the three principal environments for Breaking in West Saxon are /l/, /r/ and /x/. If all three environments are conceived of—quite plausibly—as in some sense 'back' environments, then a process of diphthongization seems phonetically reasonable (Lass 1994:49). But one important question, never really addressed in the handbooks, remains: why did this set of sound-changes happen when and where it did, and not before or after (see further Smith 1996:89)?

As is well-established in the theoretical literature (e.g. Samuels 1972;

Milroy 1992), language-change, including sound-change, depends crucially on contact. The raw material for sound-change always exists, in the continually-created variation of natural speech, but sound-change only happens when a particular variable is selected in place of another as part of systemic regulation. Such processes of selection take place when distinct systems interact with each other through linguistic contact, typically through social upheavals such as invasion, revolution or immigration. And interestingly the set of changes known as Breaking corresponds very closely, as was flagged in section 2 above, to a key moment of contact: the coming together of Anglian and Saxon varieties to produce Anglo-Saxon. This would suggest that the explanation for Breaking lies in the interaction of these two varieties. It therefore behoves us, at least as an opening strategy, to look at the nature of Anglian in relation to Saxon at the time of the *Adventus Saxonum* in the fifth century A.D.

The distribution of the various Germanic peoples on the eve of the *Adventus Saxonum* is both uncertain and controversial. However, most modern scholars agree that the Angles occupied the area in modern Denmark known as Angeln, to the north of modern Schleswig-Holstein, whereas the Saxons seem to have lived rather more to the south, in the area bordering Jade Bay, centred on the river Elbe and between the rivers Weser and Ems. This distribution is confirmed *inter alia* by the distribution of brooch-types in grave-goods; saucer-brooches characteristic of the Saxons appear in Southern England and in the Elbe-Jade region, whereas cruciform brooches characteristic of the Angles appear in burials in Angeln and in the English Midlands and North.

Given the principles of dialect geography, it is not therefore surprising that Anglian, though a West Germanic variety, differed from Saxon by being more like North Germanic. While still in use in the Germanic *Heimat*, Anglian is the variety nearest the North Germanic dialects, and it evidently shared a common cultural and even linguistic heritage distinct from that of Saxon. It is no coincidence that Anglian cultural sites such as the Sutton Hoo ship-burial look to Scandinavian artistic models, and that the epic-poem *Beowulf*, which seems to have originated in the Anglian culture of the East Midlands, tells a trans-Baltic story linking Denmark with the land of the Geats, usually interpreted as Southern Sweden (see Hines 1984: *passim*).

And there is some slight intralinguistic evidence in the Old Anglian texts for an Anglian-North Germanic linguistic connexion which predates the Viking invasions of the ninth century, e.g. the preposition *til* for West Saxon *tō* in the Moore version of Cædmon's *Hymn*, dating from ca. 737. The verb *aron* 'are' in the tenth-century Lindisfarne Gospels Gloss is also perhaps of relevance; it is distinct from the Norse form, cf. Old Icelandic *eru*, but clearly closer to the North Germanic pattern than the West Saxon *sind(on)*, cf. Present-Day German *sind*.

Since historical explanation in linguistic study depends—like (arguably) all historiography—on the observation of correspondences, it would seem that Anglian/Saxon linguistic divergence relates at least in part to the closer placing of Anglian, during the period of the Germanic *Heimat*, to North Germanic. It would seem therefore logical to investigate whether the distinct developments with regard to Breaking in Anglian and Saxon derive from their distinct Germanic ancestries and their different original geographical locations.

4. The origins of /l/-Breaking

We might begin with the most obvious distinction between Anglian and Saxon: the difference between the two varieties in /l/-Breaking environments.

To illustrate the process we might trace the development of one form: West Saxon *eald* 'old', Anglian *ald*. Traditionally it has been held that both forms derive from WGmc */ɑld/, the vowel of which has been retained in Present-Day German *alt*. It was therefore held that the common ancestor of Anglian and Saxon—along with the ancestor of OFris, the other Ingvaeonic variety—underwent the sound-change known variously as 'First Fronting' or 'Anglo-Frisian Brightening': thus West Germanic */ɑld/ became Ingvaeonic */æld/.

The usual assumption seems to be that OE was originally a single variety which subsequently diverged into various accents and dialects: Anglian and Saxon. According to this view, Ingvaeonic */æld/ underwent Breaking in West Saxon to produce the historical *eald*, whereas in Anglian the form underwent a distinct sound-change known as 'Retraction' to produce *ald*. Thus the vowel in the Anglian form underwent a pendulum shift from /ɑ/ to /æ/ and then back to /ɑ/.

Recently, however, scholars have looked again at the plausibility of this pendulum shift. Hogg (1992:80-1, esp. §5.13), following a suggestion originally made by Bülbring (1902), has argued that, in the ancestor of recorded Old Anglian, Proto-Germanic /ɑ/ failed to undergo First Fronting in the environment of a 'covered *l*' (i.e. /l/ + consonant).

If Hogg's view is accepted—and it is certainly plausible, not least in terms of economy—then this would suggest that the realization of /l/ in the ancestor of Anglian was markedly 'back' in quality even before the advent of First Fronting. The question then arises: is there any independent evidence for a distinct back realization of /l/ in Anglian?

As is the case when dealing with phonetic details of a language-variety of such antiquity, we have to build on a mixture of small indications, including the analysis of correspondences. With regard to a velar /l/, the best and most relevant evidence comes from the Present-Day Danish of East Jutland, where a velarised /l/ is still in use (see Haugen 1976:275 and reference there cited). In more northerly Scandinavian dialects this sound eventually merged with the acoustically somewhat similar so-called 'cacuminal' or 'thick' /l/ (see Haugen 1976:274-8); thick /l/ is usually considered to be an '/r/-like /l/' ([r, l] are of course in many languages not distinct phonemes, e.g. in Japanese). Haugen (1976:273) argues that a velarised /l/ was the usual realization in Pre- (i.e. pre-550 A.D.) and Common (550-800) Scandinavian.

It therefore seems at least possible that Anglian, the variety of West Germanic closest to North Germanic, could have developed its early velarised /l/ through contact with Pre-Scandinavian while still in the Germanic *Heimat*. The velarised /l/ prevented the development of First Fronting in the ancestor of Anglian: thus the retention of *ald* /ɑld/. This velarised /l/ moved with the Anglians during the invasions of Britain during the fifth century. In England the velarised /l/—perceptually quite a significant feature—was adopted by the West Saxons, possibly for sociolinguistic reasons given that political hegemony was in England early situated within the Anglian kingdoms: England, after all derives its name from the Angles and not the Saxons, and this choice seems to have been made early on (see Myres 1986:109, also section 7 below). But since the ancestor of West Saxon had had First Fronting, the outcome of the velarization in that variety was somewhat distinct from Anglian in terms of vocalic development.

There remains the question of Anglian forms such as *ældra* 'older' (derived from *[ɑldira]) with the *i*-umlaut of 'retracted' *a*. That /l/ has not restrained fronting due to *i*-umlaut suggests either that the /l/ has changed in its realization or—more probably—that the 'front' vowel-harmony effects of *i*-umlaut outweigh or compensate for the 'back' quality of /l/. Such effects are still recorded in PDE (see Wells 1982:533-4).

5. The origins of /r/-Breaking

The question of /r/ is a little more problematic. The distinct Northumbrian development of /r/-breaking, combined with the evidence of Present-Day Northumbrian dialects, would suggest that a 'back' /r/ first developed in Northumbrian varieties of Anglian, subsequently spreading—again in England—to Mercian and Kentish.

'Uvular *r*' [ʀ] develops earliest in North Germanic in Danish (see Haugen 1976:72-3), and has spread from there into Southern Sweden. The evidence would seem to indicate that the variety of Anglian which ultimately became Northumbrian derived its uvular realization of /r/ from the period of contact between West and North Germanic varieties. A weakened, velar form of the uvular /r/, rather akin to that found in some varieties of American English (see Lass 1983), could have been subsequently adopted by other varieties of Anglo-Saxon. Such a development would account for the early, Ingvaeonic-period failure of First Fronting in the ancestor of Old Northumbrian (producing *barnum* etc.) beside the later, post-Ingvaeonic and post-First Fronting developments in more southerly varieties of OE. If this hypothesis is accepted it would of course also suggest that the precursor of Old Northumbrian was developing as a variety distinct from the rest of Anglian even before the Angles left their Germanic homeland.

However, it is interesting that metathesised or syncopated forms, e.g. *ærn* 'house' (< **rænn*), *bern* 'barn' (< **berern*) (see section 2 above) were not subjected to breaking-type diphthongizations. This fact would suggest either that these metatheses took place after Breaking had been completed or that the conditions which triggered Breaking had ceased to be operative. One possibility, which would depend on there being a chronological gap between Breaking and metathesis, is that the realization of /r/ had lost its back quality by the time the metathesised forms developed.

Another, perhaps more likely, possibility is that the /r/ involved in metathesis was realised in a distinct way from that involved in Breaking, perhaps syllabically (as in some varieties of present-day Scandinavian, e.g. Dano-Norwegian; cf. Haugen 1976:74-5), or with a glide-vowel between /r/ and /n/. Such developments as the latter are frequently found as intermediate stages in some kinds of metathesis (see Samuels 1972:16-17), and would seem a logical development of the syncopated forms as well; cf. Common Slavic **zolto* 'gold' > Russian *zoloto* (East Slavic) beside Czech *zlato* (West Slavic) (I owe this last example to Robert McColl Millar). As has been pointed out, the precise mechanisms involved in metathesis have received surprisingly little attention (see Jones 1989:191).

6. The origins of /x/-Breaking

The third, and most productive, Breaking environment is the fricative /x/. All varieties of OE demonstrate breaking before /x/, and this would suggest that it was invariably realised in all environments, at an early date, as a 'back' velar fricative consonant, as in present-day Yiddish or Afrikaans and in some varieties of Dutch (see Lass 1994:75). It would thus have differed from the modern front/back distribution seen in (e.g.) Present-Day German *hoch*, *höchst*, with [x, ç] respectively. Such a distinction seems to have emerged towards the end of the OE period, and it is sustained by those varieties which have kept /x/ as part of their phonemic inventory, e.g. the Scots distinction between [nɔxt, nɪçt] 'not', 'night'. However, the contrast between OE *feoh* 'property' (with Breaking) and its cognate OHG *feho*, or between OE (West Saxon) *seah* 'saw' and its cognate OHG *sah*, would seem to indicate that the general realization of /x/ <h> as a back consonant whatever the environment was an innovation in prehistoric OE.

Given the argument put forward so far, is it possible to argue that Anglian /x/ came to be realised solely as a velar (as opposed to a palatal) fricative, after the operation of First Fronting, and that it in turn affected the realization of West Saxon /x/? The evidence for such an argument is problematic, but there does seem to be a correspondence in dating between the presumed establishment of velar realizations of /x/ in the ancestors of Anglian and Saxon and a redistribution of fricatives in what became Common Scandinavian (see Haugen 1976:155). Could the Anglian change have been triggered by this change—and subsequently spread to West Saxon when the two varieties came into contact? Certainly there would seem to be room for further investigation in this area.

However it arose, the diphthongizations were not sustained later in the OE period. Just before the time of historical records, Anglian dialects underwent the development known as 'Smoothing', whereby the diphthongs produced by /x/-breaking were monophthongised; thus Anglian had undergone the change **nēh* 'near' > **nēoh* > *nēh*. Now such pendulum shifts have already been considered unlikely (see section 4 above), but Hogg has offered a fairly convincing explanation on prosodic grounds (see Hogg 1992:143-4). The result would be the rightward transfer of '[j]-prosody' from the first (front) element of the diphthong to the following consonant, as a result of the obscuration of the second element of the diphthong, probably in [ə]. The fact that Smoothing fails in /x/-Breaking environments when a back vowel remains in the following syllable indicates that something along these lines had taken place, cf. the alternation *ðuerh* 'crooked' (with /rx/-Breaking) beside *ðweoran* acc. sg. (Hogg 1992:144).

The preconditions for Smoothing would seem to be two: obscuration of the second element of the diphthong, and subsequent fronting of the phoneme /x/. Something similar occurs in Late West Saxon ('Late West Saxon Smoothing', Campbell 1959:131); this development has generally been seen as distinct from Anglian Smoothing, but it may simply be a later development of the same kind. There is some evidence that more southerly dialects of OE and ME were more conservative with regard to diphthongal developments, and it may be that the obscuration of the second element of the diphthong, one of the two preconditions, took longer to develop here, and that smoothing was therefore also somewhat delayed in consequence. (See also Hogg 1992:101-6, esp. 1992:103, §5.44, for the lowering of the second element of the diphthong produced by Breaking, which seems to be detectable earliest in Anglian.)

The outcome of the developments just discussed was that the ME distinction emerged between 'front vowel + front /x/' and 'back vowel + back /x/' in (e.g.) *knight*, *nought*, a distinction which would only be (partially) obscured by later developments.

7. An hypothesis as to the origins of Breaking

It will be fairly obvious from the preceding discussion that much remains obscure about the origin of the OE sound-changes, including Breaking. However, it is argued here that a reasonable hypothesis as to the origins of this sound-change may be put forward, while noting (of course) that final proof for such a course of events will almost certainly always be lacking.

The hypothesis depends on two insights:

(1) that linguistic historiography (like other historical disciplines) depends upon the careful analysis of extra- and intralinguistic correspondences; and

(2) that the interaction of varieties in present-day situations has a relevance for the understanding of past states of the language.

The first of these points has been covered explicitly in the preceding argument. The second point has been made somewhat implicitly hitherto, and thus needs a little expansion. The history of OE is often taken as the history of the emergence of 'standard' OE, West Saxon. Yet West Saxon as we have it, it has been argued here, is really the product of an earlier interaction with Anglian where Anglian was the sociolinguistically dominant variety—something which we would expect from what is known of the earliest history of the Anglo-Saxons. As Myres (1986:107-8) puts it:

> It has recently been suggested ... that when the main tide of migration to Britain took place in the fifth century, the Angles on the Continent were already becoming the dominant element in the *Mischgruppe* of peoples pressing south-westward into Frisian from all the lands around the lower valleys of the Elbe and the Weser. There is no doubt that this southward pressure of Angles, Jutes, and related tribes was a major force behind the migration to Britain at this time. If in fact the Angles played a leading part in the movement, that might well account for the substitution of their name for that of the Saxons over so much of eastern Britain. It would mean that in the fifth century, as distinct from what had happened in the fourth or third, the main impetus was now coming from what German scholars have termed a *Großstamm der Angeln.* It would have incorporated all the restless peoples on the north German and Frisian coasts under the leadership of Angle or Jutish chieftains pressing down from Jutland, Schleswig, and the Baltic lands beyond the lower Elbe.

In short, the evolution of the classic OE sound-changes, often treated as a rather esoteric set of formalisms, becomes most explicable when seen in the context of the historically attested movement of peoples—and thus may be explained by reference to present-day sociolinguistic theory.

References

Bülbring, K. 1902. *Altenglisches Elementarbuch, I: Lautlehre*. Heidelberg: Winter.

Campbell, A. 1959. *Old English Grammar*. Oxford: Clarendon Press.

Haugen, E. 1976. *The Scandinavian Languages*. London: Faber.

Hines, J. 1984. *The Scandinavian Character of Anglian England in the Pre-Viking Period.* British Archaeology Reports, British Series, 124. Oxford: British Archaeology Reports.

Hogg, R. 1992. *A Grammar of Old English I: Phonology*. Oxford: Blackwell.

Jones, C. 1989. *A History of English Phonology*. London & New York: Longman.

Lass, R. 1983. 'Velar /r/ and the history of English'. *Current Topics in English Historical Linguistics*, ed. M. Davenport, H. Hansen & H. F. Nielsen. Odense: Odense University Press. 67-94.

——. 1994. *Old English: A Historical Linguistic Companion.* Cambridge: Cambridge University Press.

Luick, K. 1914-40. *Historische Grammatik der englischen Sprache*. Leipzig: Tauchnitz. Reprint, Oxford: Blackwell, 1965.

Milroy, J. 1992. *Linguistic Variation and Change*. Oxford: Blackwell.

Myres, J. N. L. 1986. *The English Settlements* (The Oxford History of England, vol. 1B). Oxford: Clarendon Press.

Samuels, M. L. 1972. *Linguistic Evolution.* Cambridge: Cambridge University Press.

Smith, J. J. 1996. *An Historical Study of English.* London: Routledge.

Wells, J. C. 1982. *Accents of English.* Cambridge: Cambridge University Press.

Old English *þæt deofol*; se *deofol* or Just *deofol*

Eric G. Stanley

1. Recognizing the definite article in early English

Whether the Anglo-Saxons had fully developed the definite article from the demonstrative pronoun is unlikely, or at least debatable: it is not clear when and where and to what extent the definite article emerged, and whether *pari passu* in verse as in prose. Not surprisingly in view of the number of occurrences that would have to be parsed and taken into account, quantified statistics are not presented, though some exemplification is given, when such statements are made as by Traugott (1992:172):

> Modifying *se* (i.e. *se* functioning as a determiner) does not contrast in OE with a definite article. In many ways it covers the domains of both the demonstrative *that* and the definite article *the* in PDE. However, there are some differences. For example, *se* can be used with proper nouns where either no demonstrative or *this* would be preferred in PDE... On the other hand, *se* is often not present where an article or demonstrative might be expected in PDE. This is especially true of the early poetry.

Dating of OE poetry as 'early' is fraught with insecurity. Little is known for certain about changes in style, metre, and syntax through the long period of Anglo-Saxon verse, from *Cædmon's Hymn* to the poems in MSS Corpus Christi College Cambridge 201 and Bodleian Library (Oxford) 121, all of them edited by Dobbie (1942). It is not surprising that in the same book (Hogg 1992) in which Traugott's chapter appeared, another chapter (Godden 1992) gives similarly, and similarly highly probable, generalizations on syntactic matters; the presumption about emphasis, here asserted as the history of the article in literary OE is considered, is undemonstrable (Godden 1992:504):

> One important aspect of Old English poetic diction is its specialised grammar and syntax, extending all the way from matters of inflexion and the use of demonstratives to the structure of the sentence. Historically, the Old English demonstrative (*se*, *seo*, *þæt*, *etc.*) developed gradually into something approaching a definite article in function..., but even in late Old English prose it is used less frequently, and presumably therefore with more emphasis, than the PDE article. In poetry the demonstrative / definite article is generally used less frequently than in prose. This is easily exemplified even in a passage from a very late poem like *The Battle of Maldon.*

The Battle of Maldon lines 166-70 are quoted, and they contain only one definite article; but lines 136-9 could have been quoted, by way of contrast, with five definite articles.[1] If comparison with MnE usage is considered relevant, it may be useful to adduce the 'close translation' of the poem by Scragg (1991:23-5): lines 166-70 have four articles against the single OE article, but the translation of lines 136-9 with five definite articles and one indefinite article is not so very different in this respect from the OE original.

2. Neuter gender of *deofol* in OE verse

From the concordance to OE verse (Bessinger 1978:201-2) it appears that in poetry the use of *deofol* without definite article is common, and when, not very often, a definite article is used and the gender is clear, it is never masculine, always neuter, but 'always' amounts to only four occurrences, three times in *Juliana* and once in *Solomon and Saturn*.[2] *Juliana*, line 288b,

---

[1] That we cannot distinguish in OE, and therefore should perhaps not attempt to distinguish, the definite article from the demonstrative adjective is no fundamental complication for this paper. Whenever in this paper the term 'definite article' is used it should be understood as 'the demonstrative adjective or, if weakened, the demonstrative adjective used as definite article' (cf. Wülfing 1894-1901, I:277, §133; Einenkel 1916: 157, §55α; Mitchell 1985:§237). I am reluctant to use the term 'definite determiner', because that is too comprehensive for the purposes of this paper, though it avoids the problem of distinguishing the demonstrative from the article.

[2] The etymon, (Greek *διάβολος* >) Latin *diabolus* is masculine, as are the loanwords in Germanic as far as can be determined, except for OE where masculine is common in prose, neuter (as far as gender is clear) is the rule in verse and occurs in prose too, though less often than masculine. According to the Toronto *Dictionary of Old English* (Cameron, et al. 1986-:D frames 265-71) the word occurs some 2500 times in OE verse

Heo ðæt deofol genom ('She seized the devil'): the metrical pattern of this half-line is common, with 256 b-lines of this pattern (Hutcheson 1995:212), and if the article were omitted the pattern would be somewhat rarer, with 55 b-lines of this pattern (1995:211). *Juliana*, line 460b, *Hyre þæt deofol oncwæð* ('The devil answered her'): its metrical pattern is somewhat rarer, with 123 b-lines of this pattern (1995:213), and if the article were omitted the pattern would be that of line 288b, that is, quite common. *Juliana*, line 534, *Heo þæt deofol teah* ('She dragged the devil along'): its metrical pattern is very common, with 1201 b-lines of this pattern (1995:205); and if the article were omitted the pattern would be rare, with only 27 b-lines of its pattern (1995:205). It is noteworthy, how significant it is I do not know, that all three half-lines in this poem with neuter definite article qualifying *deofol* have a finite verb as the second stress. It is striking, but may be chance, that all three of these b-lines open a sentence, with (in modern editions and translations) a full stop (once a semi-colon) preceding as in Thorpe's translation (1842:259/27, 270/5, 274/17), in Grein (1857-8:59, 64, 65), a semi-colon in Gollancz's translation (1895:259), in Wül(c)ker and Assmann (1881-98:III/1 (Wülker 1897), 125, 131, 133), in Strunk (1904:13, 20, 23), in Krapp (Krapp and Dobbie 1936:121, 126, 128), and in Woolf (1955:33, 41, 46). None of the three half-lines has a mark of punctuation preceding it in the manuscript (Chambers, Förster, & Flower 1933:f.69v, last line; f. 72v, line 2; f. 73v, line 6). *Solomon and Saturn*, line 122b is a half-line sentence (preceded by a semi-colon in the editions, or by a colon in the German editions), its second stress is an adjective, not a finite verb: *him bið ðæt deofol lað*, 'loathly to them is the Devil' in the translation in Kemble's edition (1845-58:142, Kemble's line 246). The manuscript, Corpus Christi College Cambridge 422 p. 5 (Robinson & Stanley 1991: facsimile reference 12.4 [for 12.2.4], line 1), has no mark of punctuation.

---

and prose; *DOE* does not comment on the distribution of the gender or on the use of the word in the singular with or without definite article. Jones (1988) specializes on gender and 'neutralization' in late OE, Transitional English, and early ME; but 'devil' is not discussed by him, presumably because none of the small number of texts, on which he bases his study, has the word as a neuter. In the discussion of the metre the date 1995 refers to Hutcheson's book of that date whose statistics I have accepted.

3. No definite article before *deofol* in verse

In verse *deofol* is commonly used without definite article; and that not only in such genitival phrases as *helle deofol* 'devil of hell' at *Juliana* line 629b and *Elene* line 900b, *helle dioful* at *Andreas* line 1298b.[3] It may be coincidental that the only uses in verse of *deofol* with definite article in the genitive are to be found in *Solomon and Saturn*, three times, *ðæs deofles*, at lines 44a, 401a, and 458a, and that this poem has one of the four occurrences of neuter *deofol*. Of course, *ðæs* can be either genitive singular masculine or neuter and there is no way of proving that *deofol* is neuter in these three lines as it must be at line 122b. It may not be significant that the four certain occurrences of the neuter in *Juliana* and in *Solomon and Saturn* come in the second half-line, whereas the three genitival uses come in the first half-line. At *Solomon and Saturn* line 145b *deofle* is used without definite article, as is usual in verse.

4. Grammatical gender of *deofol* is quite often neuter, not masculine, in both verse and prose

In the voluminous linguistic and literary studies of OE there is much on the devil in illustration of the Christian influence on OE writings; much on the date of borrowing the loanword *deofol* into the language. Whether it was borrowed direct from Greek or via Latin features in many historical treatments, well summarized by Chapters 1 and 2 of Wollmann (1990). Work has been done on the devil as a manifestation of the demonic and the sinful, (Bloomfield 1952:28 & 328, n. 243; 110; 113-14); and those who etymologize and literalize any possible association of *deofol* with northern gods and elvish beings take the devilish wording far towards Valhalla (Jente 1921:29-31; North 1997:54-6, 77, 325). There are good accounts of how the complexity of forms of the word in some OE dialects might have arisen via Celtic (Thomson 1961:24-8). Good work has been done on change of gender (Mitchell 1985:§§62-5), and it may well be that I have missed an account of how the inherited masculinity of the devil was turned to neuterness as early as Cynewulf to whom a ninth-century date is usually assigned (cf. Fulk

---

[3] The treatment of genitival phrases and compounds in the editions and in translations is exemplified in the Appendix.

1992:368, §393), and *Solomon and Saturn* perhaps a little later (cf. Fulk 1992:3-4, fn. 5; 195 fn. 46). Neuter *deofol* is unrelated to neutralization in very late OE and in Transitional English.

Neuter *þæt deofol* occurs not uncommonly in prose too, quite often in the Blickling Homilies; often it is sentence-initial. Reasons of dialect or sentence accentuation come to mind as possible, but they remain doubtful reasons. The following are some examples: *Þæt deofol hine þa genam þriddan siþe* (Morris 1874-80:27/13-14) 'The devil then took him a third time'; ... *swa Crist oferswiþde þæt deofol mid þisse cyþnesse* (Morris 1874-80:31/19) '... as Christ overcame the devil with this testimony'; *Se mæssepreost se þe bið to læt þæt he þæt deofol of men adrife ... þonne bið he geteald to þære fyrenan ea* (Morris 1874-80:43/22-5) 'The mass-priest who is too slack in driving out the devil from a person ... shall then be assigned to the fiery river'; *And æfter þam breades sticce eode him on þæt wiðerwearde deofol*[4] (Assmann 1889:163/256-7) 'And after that piece of bread the inimical devil entered into him [Judas]'; *Þæt deofol þa cwæþ to þam folce* (Cassidy and Ringler 1971:214/193) 'The devil then said to the people';[5] *þa raþe eode Satanas þæt deofol* (Morris 1874-80:149/32) 'then immediately the devil Satan went'; *Þis is se halga heahengel Sancte Michael ⁊ se æþela scyldend wið deofles swipornesse, swa se witega sægde, þæt þæt deofol þohte þæt he scolde gelæran þæt folc* (Tristram 1970:156/64-7) 'This is the archangel St Michael and the glorious protector against the devil's cunning, as the prophet said, that the devil intended that he should teach that people'; *gif ge nellað gelefan ... þæs ærendgewrites, þonne geþencað ge na hu þæt* [above *þæt* in another hand *se*] *deofol þam ancre sæde hwylc hit in helle wære to wunianne* (Napier 1883:214/19-22) 'if you will not believe the written message, then you do not at all consider how the devil said to the anchorite what it might be like to dwell in hell'; *Ða þæt deofol hyre to cwæð* (Thorpe 1840:f. 467, line 7 from bottom; octavo II,

---

4 Two of the manuscripts quoted in Assmann's apparatus have the masculine *se wiðerwearde deofol*. The source is St John's Gospel 13:27, and *breades sticca* 'stick of bread' renders *buccella* 'morsel'.

5 In the version from Corpus Christi College Cambridge MS 198 (article 64) of this anonymous life of St Andrew neuter *Þæt deofol* comes no fewer than six times, always sentence- (or clause-)initially; and similarly, in the version in the Blickling Homilies (Morris 1874-80:241/5, 241/10, 243/4, 243/14).

398/1-2) 'Then the devil said to it [the soul]'; *Þæt deofol ongan þa cleopian* (Thorpe 1840:f. 468/19-20; octavo II, 398/18-19) 'The devil did then call out'; *Ðæt deofol bið ærest on geogoðhade on cildes onlicnisse, ðonne bið deofol on dracan onlicnisse* (Menner 1941:168/4-5)—neuter *deofol* occurs frequently in the first two paragraphs of this text (as edited).

In very late OE, in Transitional English, in ME, and in MnE the natural gender of the devil is masculine, immutably so: in the England after the tenth century, as Shakespeare puts it, 'The Prince of Darkenesse is a Gentleman' (Hinman 1968:806 = *King Lear*, III.iv.[143]). *Juliana* and *Solomon and Saturn* are early enough for *þæt* immediately preceding *deofol* (or with only an adjective intervening) to be grammatical neuter, not the epicene demonstrative.[6]

No satisfactory explanation for the neuter gender of *deofol* has been advanced, as far as I know. One might think of the many senses in MnE of 'devil-' in abstract formations: *devildom*, *devilhood*, *devilishness*, *devilism*, *devilment*, *devilry*, *devilship*, and *deviltry* are to be found in *OED*, and several more, now obsolete. There is a scale of seriousness from heavy to light in these senses. He is laden with sin and induces sin, did so when he brought about the Fall of Man; he is mischievous and induces mischief, he is a lighthearted rogue and induces laughter. What did Mephistopheles say about the devil in Goethe's *Faust*?:[7] 'Consider it well: the devil, he's old;

---

[6] The demonstrative pronoun *þæt* does of course not specify gender when used in explanation or in deixis, as in the opening of Ælfric's Catholic Homily 'De Initio Creaturae', *An angin is ealra þinga: þ[æt] is God ælmihtig* (Clemoes 1997:178), 'There is a beginning of all things: that is God almighty'; or *Beowulf* 11b *þæt wæs god cyning!* (Klaeber 1950:1), 'that was an excellent king' (cf. Mitchell 1985:§§323-7; Brunner 1962, II:133). From the latest OE (or earliest ME) onwards, when gender was beginning to break down, neuter *þæt* is used occasionally with feminine or masculine nouns, even as far south as Peterborough, as in the Chronicle annal for 1070 (copied in 1121), with feminine OE *dæd* in the accusative *þ[et] yfel dæd hæfden don* (Clark 1970:3/62) 'had done that evil deed', annal for 1154, with OE *dæg* masculine, *þat ilce dæi þat* ... (Clark 1970:60/8), 'the very day that ...'. Perhaps 'that' in the 1070 annal is a stressed use of the demonstrative, but levels of stress are not demonstrable in English so far removed from us in time. It may be that in verse, where the demonstrative adjective is thought to have weakened into the definite article later than in prose, a higher degree of emphasis on it is possible; if so, it was insufficient for demonstrative adjectives to take metrical stress and exceptions are very rare (cf. Stanley 1994:127-8 and n. 26).

[7] 'Bedenkt: der Teufel der ist alt, | So werdet alt, ihn zu verstehen!' (Goethe 1832:103; 1888:100/6817-18).

grow old to understand him!' Yet the scale suggested by these modern abstract nouns is unlikely to be applicable to the devil as presented in the writings of the Anglo-Saxons who, weighed down by the burden of Original Sin, knew only the heavy end of the scale. Moreover, the neuter devil whom St Juliana drags along, *Juliana*, line 534, *Heo þæt deofol teah*, is very far from any abstraction. Why then is he neuter? The only answer I can think of is that in the virtual absence of an indefinite article in OE verse (cf. Mitchell 1985:§§232-5) the neuter grammatical gender is used to indicate that it is not '*the* devil' but 'a devil'—yet that cannot apply to *Satanas þæt deofol* of the Blickling Homilies (Morris 1874-80:149/32); and that he is of the male sex in *Juliana* appears to be indicated by the rest of the sentence in which two adjectives, *fæstne* and *hæþenne*, have the accusative, masculine singular ending *-ne* (*Juliana* 534b-6a):[8]

Heo þæt deofol teah
breostum inbryrded bendum fæstne,
halig hæþenne.

[She, inspired in her innermost being, dragged along the devil held securely in bonds, the holy one (dragged along) the heathen one.]

5. The use of *deofol* without definite article in prose

The devil appears more often without an article in verse, and that may well have, in part, the metrical explanation that unstressed syllables are to some extent avoided in verse, or, rather, are subject to some constraints.[9] For prose, it has long been a well-known item of OE syntax that, on the whole, Ælfric, and many other writers of OE, use the definite article with *deofol*, whereas

[8] Rosemary Woolf (1955:46), in her note on these lines, draws attention to a similar lack of concord involving *þæt deofol* in the OE Martyrology for 25 August, St Bartholomew (Kotzor 1981, II:187/9-11): *Þæt wæs þæt deofol þæt seo þeod hyre ær for god beeodon, ond hi nemdon þone Astaroþ* 'That was the devil whom that people had venerated as god for them, and they named that one Astaroth'. In this sentence, after the neuter *þæt deofol þæt*, the demonstrative pronoun *þone* is accusative masculine singular. Mitchell (1985:§§69-71) gives examples of several kinds to illustrate such 'Triumphs of sex over gender', among them neuter *cild* 'child', *wif* 'woman', and masculine *wifman* 'woman' followed by pronouns referring to them, masculine for a boy, feminine for a woman.

[9] The best account of what these constraints might be is given in Russom 1987, *passim*. Such genitival phrases as *helle deofol* are of course normal without article in verse as in prose (cf. MnE 'the/a devil of hell, hell's devil').

Wulfstan, on the whole, omits the definite article.[10] The matter is complicated, of course, by the fact that not all the 'genuine' writings of either Ælfric or Wulfstan are transmitted in manuscripts that preserve such details with meticulous care.

In this study I concern myself only with *deofol* in the singular used without definite article (other than in genitival phrases) or used with the neuter definite article. First of all, there are some Ælfrician uses without definite article. These are easily isolated by reference to the *OE Concordance* (Venezky & Healey 1980:s.v.); the following are some illustrative examples.

First, Ælfric uses *deofol* without definite article not infrequently in his non-rhythmical prose: *Nu cwædon gedwolmen þæt deofol gesceope sume gesceafta* (Clemoes 1997:182-3/117-18) 'Now heretics said that the devil created some creatures'; *He wearð þa deofle gehyrsum ⁊ Gode ungehyrsum* (Clemoes 1997:184/157-8) 'He was then obedient to the devil and disobedient to God'; *On ðreo wisan bið deofles costnung, þæt is, on tyhtinge, on lustfullunge, on geðafunge: deofol tyht us to yfele* (Clemoes 1997:271/138-9) 'The devil's temptation is in three ways, namely, in incitement, in amusement, and in consent: the devil incites us to evil'; *Is nu ... micel neod gehwam þæt he leornige ... hu he mage deofol forbugan* (Godden 1979:27/287-9) 'It is now ... very needful for everyone that he may learn ... how he can shun the devil'; *'ðu hæfst deofol on ðe'. Se Hælend andwyrde, 'Næbbe ic deofol on me'* (Godden 1979:127-8/19-22) 'thou hast the devil in thee". The Saviour answered, "I have not the devil in me"'.

Secondly, from Ælfric's rhythmical prose where *deofol* without definite article is uncommon:[11] *þas halgan mægnu oferswyðaþ ða leahtras þe deofol*

---

[10] As far as I know, the first to draw attention to the absence of the definite article in the writings of Wulfstan was Mohrbutter (1885:3; cf. Jost 1950:157): 'deofles (*sic* for *deofol*, or for *deofle* and *deofles* of his examples) steht immer ohne Artikel' (*deofol* occurs always without article). Mohrbutter's dissertation covers only 'the four genuine homilies'; these are the four homilies recognized as genuine by Napier (1882:7-8).

[11] Ælfric, both in his non-rhythmical and his rhythmical prose, like other writers of OE often has no definite article in prepositional phrases; *fram deofle*, *mid deofle*, *of deofle*, *ongean deofol*, *þurh deofol*, *to deofle*, *wið deofol*. For example: *Se Hælend wæs gelæd fram ðam Halgan Gaste to anum westenne, to ðy þæt he wære gecostnod fram deofle* (Clemoes 1997:266/8-9) 'The Saviour was led by the Holy Ghost to a desert, in order that he might be tempted by the devil'; *Þonne farað ða uncystigan and ða unrihtwisan*

besæwð on us (Skeat 1881-1900, I:62/375-6) 'these holy virtues overpower the sins which the devil sows in us'; *On þam flotan wæron þa fyrmestan heafodmen Hinguar and Hubba, geanlæhte þurh deofol* (Skeat 1881-1900:II, 316/29-30) 'In that fleet the most important leaders were Ingwar and Ubba, united by the devil'; *Deofol is se stranga þe ure Drihten embe spæc* (Pope 1967-8:I, 274/188) 'The devil is the strong one our Lord spoke about'; *Nu sceolon we biddan ... þæt he ure synna fram us adyle(gie) þurh ðone Halgan Gast, and us gehealde wið deofol* (Pope 1967-8, I:325/278-82) 'Now we must pray that he purge away from us our sins through the Holy Ghost, and that he sustain us against the devil'; *Full dysig byð se mann and ðurh deofol beswicen se ðe nele gelyfan ðæt se lifigenda God æfre wære wunigende ær ðam ðe he worhte gesceafta* (Crawford 1921:36/39-41) 'That man is very foolish and deceived by the devil who will not believe that the living God always existed before he made creatures'; *dæghwamlice drecð deofol mancyn mid mislicum costnungum* (MacLean 1884:24/227-8) 'every day the devil afflicts mankind with divers temptations'.

Wulfstan commonly, but not invariably, uses *deofol* without definite article; thus, *Antecrist bið soðlice deofol 7 mann* (Bethurum 1957:128/8) 'Antichrist is truly devil and man'; *Ac sona swa deofol ongeat þæt mann to ðam gescapen wæs þæt he scolde 7 his cynn gefyllan on heofenum þæt se deofol*[12] *forworhte ðurh his ofermodignesse...* (Bethurum 1957:145/39-42)

---

into ecere cwicsusle mid deofle (Godden 1979:66/174-5) 'Then the niggardly and the unrighteous go into everlasting living torment with the devil'; *Ælc bletsung is of Gode, 7 wyriung of deofle* (Clemoes 1997:230/174-5) 'Every blessing is from God, and (every) cursing is from the devil'; *Oþer cyn is ancrena ... þe ... on lancsumere mynsteres drohtnunge geleorniað þæt hie ... þurh broðra getrymnesse ongean deofol ... winnan magan* (Schröer 1885-8:9/5-9) 'The second kind is of anchorites ... who ... in the long monastic way of life learn that they ... can fight against the devil through the support of the brethren'; *se ðe fram Gode bihð to deofle he forlyst Godes gife* (Clemoes 1997:235/110-11) 'he who turns from God to the devil forfeits God's grace'; *He wyrcð eac þurh deofol fela tacna* (Napier 1883:195/22-3) 'He performs also many miracles through the devil'; *wundorlic wæs þæt martyrcynn, and wið deofol strang gewinn* (Skeat 1881-1900, I:402/84-5) 'wondrous was that company of martyrs, and mighty the strife against the devil'.

12 Bethurum (1957:295) has a note: '**se deofol.** Wulfstan is probably influenced by Ælfric's text to use the article with *deofol* which he usually does not do'. The reference is to the parallel account in Ælfric's Creation homily (Clemoes 1997:183/125-9), but, in fact, *se deofol*, though common in this homily, does not come at this point in the extant

'But as soon as the devil perceived that man had been created to this end that he and his progeny were to take their place in heaven, which the devil had forfeited through his pride...'. Wulfstan also has *þurh deofol*, but that may be considered as merely part of his normal usage without article, thus ... *⁊ ðonne to hrædlice ðurh deofol beswicene* (Bethurum 1957:117/27-8) '... and then [they are] too quickly deceived by the devil'. There are exceptions: ... *fore ealne þone egsan þe ðurh þæne deofol on worulde geworðan sceal* (Bethurum 1957:132/66-7) '... on account of all that terror which is to come about in the world through the devil'.

The use of *deofol* without definite article is not uncommon in other prose (and that not only in prepositional phrases, for which see n. 11); for example: *God us læreð eadmodnessa and deofol us lærð ofermodnesse* (Assmann 1889:168/110-11) 'God teaches us humility and the devil teaches us pride'; *Utan þeah us georne wið deofol scyldan eallum tidum* (Scragg 1992:318/68) 'Let us, however, earnestly shield ourselves at all times against the devil'; *ne helpeð þam men ænig wiht, þeah þe he ealne þysne middaneard on his agene æht gestryne, gif deofol nimð þa sawle* (Napier 1883:264/22-265/1) 'it is of no help whatever to that person, though he accumulates all this world to his own possessions, if the devil takes his soul'; *and nu þu oferswiðdest deofol* (Skeat 1881-1900:II, 196/111-12) 'and now thou hast overpowered the devil'; *Deofol þonne ... beswac þone ærestan wifmon* (Morris 1874-80:3/17-5/2) 'The devil then ... deceived the first woman'; *Crist wunað on eaðmodnysse ⁊ deofol on modignysse* (Napier 1916:8/25) 'Christ abides in humility and the devil in pride'.

The following are slightly different uses without definite article, different in that aspects of signification are involved; thus in naming: *oþer us lærð to hellewites brogan þæs nama is deofol* (Napier 1883:233/5-6) 'the second teaches us of the horror of the torment of hell the name of which is "devil"'; ... *on muðe and on fæðme þæs deaðberendan dracan þe is deofol genemned* (Napier 1883:188/9-10) '... in the mouth and in the embrace of that mortiferous dragon that is named "devil"'. Sometimes the absence of an article might perhaps be explained by the fact that *deofol* means 'a devil' rather than 'the devil', and the indefinite article was not firmly established in

---

text, and in any case Wulfstan is not consistent in his usage. On the relationship between Wulfstan's and Ælfric's homily see Jost (1950:57) and Godden (2000:4).

OE (cf. Mitchell 1985:§§220-5), thus: *ne sæde ic hit ær þæt he wære deofol nalles munuc?* (Hecht 1900-7, I:29/16-18) 'did I not say before that he is a devil and not at all a monk?' When *sylf* follows *deofol* the latter does not have the definite article;[13] thus, reinforcing Wulfstan's common practice with *deofol* of having no definite article, *Nys nan swa yfel sceaða swa is deofol sylf* (Jost 1959:89, §107; cf. Liebermann 1898-1916, I:306, I Cnut 26.2) 'There is no ravager so evil as is the devil himself'; and (probably by Wulfstan) *his wiðerwinnan, þæt is deofol sylfne, he besencte* (Ure 1957:82/9-10) 'his adversary, that is the devil himself, he caused to go under'. Other than in Wulfstan we find: in Corpus Christi College Cambridge MS 322 *he is deofol sylf* (Hecht 1900-7, I:28/5) 'he is the devil himself', but Bodleian MS Hatton 76 reads *he is swutol deofol*; in the same text MS Corpus reads *þæt wæs deofol sylf* (Hecht 1900-7, I:156/29) 'that was the devil himself', where MS Hatton has the order *sylf deofol*.

6. In conclusion, only a partial explanation

With so many occurrences of the word *deofol* it is unlikely that every complication has been caught by me. Some complexities have been illustrated above; but to the basic question, how did the neuter gender get attached to *deofol*, which I failed to answer, I now add another unanswered, perhaps equally unanswerable, question: how did it come about that the style shown by the writers of OE differed so greatly as regards the use of the definite article with *deofol*? One might hazard a guess, why some writers, Wulfstan fairly systematically so, have no definite article with this noun, whereas others, Ælfric fairly systematically so, use the definite article. The words for God, *Drihten*, *Crist*, and *Hælend* are often treated as if they were

[13] In a sense, the use of the demonstrative adjective, *se deofol* 'that devil', obviates the use of *sylf*, and it is rare in Ælfric: *Se deað and seo hell is se deofol sylf* (Pope 1967-8:441/463-5) 'That death and that hell is the devil himself'. It is of interest that, whereas Corpus Christi College Cambridge MS 178 reads *and se deofol sylf andwyrde* (Pope 1967-8:708/587) 'and the devil himself replied', MS Corpus Christi College Cambridge 303 omits *sylf*; similarly the following five words in the reading of Corpus Christi College Cambridge MS 178 *ne furþan se deofol sylf* (Pope 1967-8:793/61) 'nor indeed the devil himself', are omitted in Bodleian MS Hatton 116. Note also: *Þæt wæs se sylfa deofol þe on ðam synfullum rixað* (Pope 1967-8:404/190) 'That was the selfsame devil who reigns over sinners'.

names.[14] *Drihten* is often qualified by a possessive adjective preceding it, *ure, min, his, hire, heora, þin,* etc.; *Drihten sylf* is not uncommon. The definite article, however, is not idiomatic with *Drihten*, though there are exceptions: (perhaps *se* is to be regarded as demonstrative rather than as the article—if that distinction is valid for OE): *Þa us gegearwige se Drihten, þe mid Fæder ⁊ mid Sunu ⁊ mid þam Halgum Gaste leofað and rixað on ecnysse a buton ende* (Assmann 1889:150/157-9) 'May that Lord then make us ready, who with the Father and with the Son and with the Holy Ghost lives and reigns in eternity world without end'; with *drihten* intercalated in MS Corpus Christi College Cambridge 162 but *se drihten* in MS Corpus Christi College Cambridge 303, *Hwæt is us rihtwislicre þonne we God lufion ⁊ his bebodu gehealdon, þurh þone ... we wæron gesceapene, ⁊ syððan we wæron alysede fram deoflicum þeowdome, se `Drihten´ us forgeaf ealle þa þing þe we habbað?* (Szarmach 1981:80/G28-31; cf. Scragg 1992:341-2/173-6 and apparatus) 'What is more righteous in us than that we love God and hold his commandments, by whom ... we were created, and thereafter we were redeemed from diabolic enslavement, that Lord who granted us everything we have?'[15] Before a qualifying adjective the definite

[14] With definite article, *se Hælend* 'the Saviour' is quite common. *Hælend* is also used for the name Jesus, crucially so in the Gospels, Matthew 1:25 *peperit filium suum primogenitum et uocauit nomen eius Iesum* 'she brought forth her first borne sonne: and called his name IESUS' (*New Testament* 1582:4), *Heo cende hyre frum-cennedan sunu; ⁊ nemde hys naman hælend* (Corpus Christi College Cambridge MS 140, and similarly (with dialectal differences) in all versions, early and late West Saxon, Northumbrian, and Mercian; Skeat 1887:28-9), and cf. Luke 2:21 *Et postquam consummati sunt dies octo ut circumcideretur uocatum est nomen eius Iesus quod uocatum est ab angelo priusquam in utero conciperetur* 'And after eight daies were expired, that the childe should be circumcised: his name was called IESUS, which was called by the Angel, before that he was conceiued in the wombe' (*New Testament* 1582:140), *Æfter þam þe ehta dagas gefyllede wæron þæt ðæt cild emsnyden wære: his nama wæs hælend; Se wæs fram engle genemned ær he on innoðe geeacnod wære* (Corpus Christi College Cambridge MS 140, and similarly in all versions, early and late West Saxon and Northumbrian, except that Lindisfarne has *se hælend*; Skeat 1874:30-1). The combination *Drihten Hælend*, literally 'the Lord Saviour', is probably better regarded as 'the Lord Jesus'.

[15] The editors punctuate these clauses differently, and the alternative reading, without *Drihten* gives a further possibility. For this paper the important point is that the word, present in the later manuscript, was intercalated in the earlier. Without the word the end of the quotation may be translated, '... God ... by whom ... we were created and ... were redeemed ..., that one who granted us everything we have?'

article is not unusual, thus: *se ælmihtiga Drihten* (Förster 1913:136[= 120]/8-9) 'the almighty Lord', and so also Tristram (1970:174/34; = Bazire & Cross 1982:70/22); *se ilca Drihten þe ...* (Morris 1874-80:123/28) 'that same Lord who ...'; *se mildheorta Drihten 7 se Alysend þysses menniscan cynnes* (Morris 1874-80:65, line 3 from bottom) 'the merciful Lord and the Redeemer of human kind'. We may compare MnE usage: *OED*, s.v. *God*, 5., characterizes this as 'the specific Christian and monotheistic sense', used without definite article 'As a proper name', but when an adjective precedes the word *the* may be used, as in a quotation in *OED* dated 1741: 'God, the all-gracious, the all-good, the all-bountiful, the all-mighty, the all-merciful God'.

We may seek to explain the fact that the definite article is unidiomatic with *Drihten* by taking the use of the word in English to be poetic in origin, and in verse such absence of the article is usual. There is little point in going back to Germanic militarism for the meaning and usage of the divine epithet *Drihten* (well discussed by Green 1965:275-9)—no more than users of *garlic* think of the Germanic military origins of its first syllable: in religious contexts *Drihten* is wholly christianized, and the word has become a proper name for the Deity.[16] The name *deofol* of the Antichrist is, as proper names are, idiomatically used without definite article.

Appendix

A masculine (or neuter) definite article agreeing with *deofol* could only precede feminine *helle* if the two words were a 'genitival compound' (with *helle* its first element), but there is no definite article before this locution at any of its three occurrences, as there is for other locutions with *hel-*, for example, *Genesis B*, line 447a *hwearf him þurh þa helldora* 'hastened through the gates of hell', and, significantly, *Genesis B*, line 694b *Hwæt se hellsceaða* 'Behold, the hellish ravager', but *Elene*, line 956b *þone hellesceaþan* 'the hellish ravager' (accusative).

---

[16] The early ME ending of *Drihhtin* in Orm, like the *-in* in Orrmin itself, is probably modelled on Latin endings in *-inus*, as, for example, Awwstin (*pace* d'Ardenne 1936:148-9).

In his edition, Grein (1857-8, II:126 *Elene* his line 901b *helle deófol*, 128 *Elene* his line 957 *þone helle sceađan*) is inconsistent with the principles of recognizing compounds in traditional OE grammars; he ignores the definite article *þone* which leads others to regard *hellesceaþan* as a compound, but he changes his mind because of that (Grein 1865:424). The problem was posed more generally by Grein a little earlier, in 1864, when he gives *helle* + noun as a genitival phrase, at other times as a compound (Grein 1861-4, II:29-31), and so also inconsistently in his edition (Grein 1857-8); Grein (1861-4, II:29) s.v. *hel*, genitive *helle*, says 's[iehe] auch *helle-* in den Compositis, die vielleicht z[um] T[heil] getrennt zu schreiben sind' [see also *helle-* in the compounds which are perhaps to be written as two separate words], and these are listed in the two pages that follow (here listed in the forms as in Grein's texts, slightly altered to bring occasionally into line with modern editorial orthography for OE, the line-numbers adjusted to the titles and numeration in ASPR): (1) *Christ III* 1426 *helle-bealu*, (2) *Judith* 116 *helle-bryne*, (3) *Genesis B* 373 *helle-clommas*, (4) *Christ III* 1619 *helle-cinn* (also with alternative explanation), (5) *Juliana* 629 and *Elene* 900 *helle-deófol*, *Andreas* 1298 *helle-dióful*, (6) *The Descent into Hell* 87 *helle-dorum*, (7) *Elene* 1229 *helle-duru*, (8) *Christ and Satan* 70 *helle-flôras*, (9) *Christ III* 1269 and *Meters* 8.51 *helle-fŷr*, (10) *Beowulf* 1274 *helle-gâst*, *Juliana* 457 and 615 *helle-gǣst*, (11) six times in five different poems *helle-grund*, (12) *Christ and Satan* 431 *hylle-gryre*, (13) *Christ and Satan* 629 *helle-hæftas*, (14) *Beowulf* 788 *helle-hæfton*, (15) *Andreas* 1342 and *Juliana* 246 *helle-hæftling*, *Solomon and Saturn* 126 *helle-hæftlig*, (16) *Genesis A* 38 *helle-heáfas*, (17) *Andreas* 1171 *helle-hinca*, (18) *Guthlac A* 677 (Grein 649) *helle-hûs*, (19) *Genesis B* 775 *helle-nîð*, (20) *Elene* 956 *helle-sceaþan*, (21) *Christ and Satan* 132 *helle-scealcas*, (22) *Juliana* 422 *helle-seað*, (23) *Guthlac B* 1069 (Grein 1042) *helle-þegna*, (24) *Genesis B* 303 and *The Lord's Prayer III* 36 *helle-wītes*, *Andreas* 1052 *helle-wītu*, *Soul and Body I* 32 and 47 *helle-wītum*. Grein's understanding of these supposed OE compounds is best represented by his translation into German alliterative verse (Grein 1857-9), either as compounds or, more often, as genitival phrases (which is determined by alliteration, so that he never compounds when both nouns begin with *h*), thus: (1) Höllenübel, (2) der Hölle Brandglut, (3) Höllenklammern, (4) der Hölle Volk, (5) Höllen-teufel, der Hölle Teufel, (6) der Hölle Thoren (Grein 1857-9, I:197), (7) der Hölle

Thor, (8) der Hölle Flure, (9) Höllenfeuer, der Hölle Feuer (10) Höllengeist, (11) Höllengrund, der Hölle Grund, (12) Höllengraus, (13) der Hölle Häftlinge, (14) der Häftling der Hölle, (15) der Hölle Häftling, der Häftling der Hölle, (16) der Hölle Heulen, (17) der Hölle Hinker, (18) das Haus der Hölle, (19) der Hölle Qualen, (20) der Höllenschädiger, (21) der Hölle Knechte, (22) der Hölle Pfuhl (23) Höllenknechte, (24) Höllenstrafe, der Hölle Strafen, der Hölle Qualen, Höllenqualen. In his important edition, Grimm (1840:77 *Elene* line 900, 79 *Elene* 956) treats both *helledeófol* and *hellesceaðan* (*sic*) as compounds. Thorpe (1836 or 1837:127 his line 1805, 129 his line 1917) prints *helle deofol* and *þone helle sceaþan*. In his edition, Kemble (1844-6, II:53 *Elene* his line 799, 57 *Elene* his line 1911) is content to follow Grimm (including eth for manuscript thorn).

Later editors often follow Grein in his inconsistent handling of genitive phrases as compounds. As regards *helle-deofol*, Gradon (1958:59/900, 61/956) commendably treats Grein's *helle-deofol*, as a genitival phrase, and she does so also for his *þone helle-sceaþan*, unlike Krapp (1932:91 *Elene* line 900, 92 *Elene* line 956), who was content to follow the revised edition of Grein [Wül(c)ker and Assmann 1881-98:II/1 (Wülker 1888), 177/900, 181/956]. If it is granted that 'genitival compounds' existed in OE—*se domes-dæg* 'Doomsday', for example— (and 'genitival compound' is a morphological concept in which I have no faith for OE), then it is when the article preceding the genitival first element of the nominal collocation is not in the genitive, that is, when it agrees with the second element of the genitival compound in gender and case; and so Gradon might have treated *helle-sceaþa* as a compound. In the phrase *þæt deofles temp(e)l* the case of the article goes with (neuter) *temp(e)l*; thus in Ælfric, *þæt deofles tempel grundlunga tofeoll* (Skeat 1881-1900:48/387) 'the devil's temple fell to the ground utterly'; *He het þa gedæftan þæt deofles templ* (Skeat 1881-1900, I:112/368) 'He then ordered that the devil's temple be prepared'. Similarly, and likewise only rarely, other genitives may qualify 'temple', *Godes tempel*, etc., thus: *he sume dæg eode to þam Godes temple* (Skeat 1881-1900, I:220/23-4) 'on a certain day he went to God's temple'; *heo ... brohte Crist ... to þam Godes tempel* (Scragg 1992:282/43-4) 'she ... brought Christ ... to that temple of God'; *hi tobræcon þa burh grundlinga and þæt mære Solomones templ forbærndon* (Godden 1979:36/215-16) 'they razed to the ground the city and destroyed the glorious temple of Solomon by fire'.

References

Assmann, B., ed. 1889. *Angelsächsische Homilien und Heiligenleben*. C. W. M. Grein's Bibliothek der angelsächsischen Prosa III. Reprinted, Darmstadt: Wissenschaftliche Buchgesellschaft, 1964, with a supplementary introduction by Peter Clemoes.

Bazire, J., & J. E. Cross, eds. 1982. *Eleven Old English Rogationtide Homilies*. Toronto Old English Series 7. Toronto, Buffalo, London: University of Toronto Press.

Bessinger, J. B., Jr, ed. with P. H. Smith, Jr. 1978. *A Concordance to the Anglo-Saxon Poetic Records*. Ithaca & London: Cornell University Press.

Bethurum, D., ed. 1957. *The Homilies of Wulfstan*. Oxford: Clarendon Press.

Bloomfield, M. W. 1952. *The Seven Deadly Sins: An Introduction to the History of a Religious Concept, with Special Reference to Medieval English Literature*. East Lansing: Michigan State University Press. Reprinted, 1967.

Brunner, K. 1962. *Die englische Sprache—ihre geschichtliche Entwicklung*. 2 vols. Tübingen: Max Niemeyer.

Cameron, A., A. C. Amos, A. diP. Healey, et al., eds. 1986-. *Dictionary of Old English*. Toronto: Pontifical Institute of Medieval Studies.

Cassidy, F. G., & R. N. Ringler, eds. 1971. 'The acts of Matthew and Andrew in the city of the canibals', *Bright's Old English Grammar and Reader*, pp. 203-19. 3rd ed. New York & London: Holt, Rinehart and Winston. Reprinted, 1974.

Chambers, R. W., M. Förster, & R. Flower, eds. 1933. *The Exeter Book of Old English Poetry*. London: Percy Lund, Humphries & Co. for the Dean and Chapter of Exeter Cathedral.

Clark, C., ed. 1970. *The Peterborough Chronicle 1070-1154*. Oxford: Clarendon Press.

Clemoes, P. A. M., ed. 1997. *Ælfric's Catholic Homilies. The First Series. Text*. EETS s.s. 17.

Crawford, S. J., ed. 1921. *Exameron Anglice or The Old English Hexameron*. C. W. M. Grein's Bibliothek der angelsächsischen Prosa X. Reprinted, Darmstadt: Wissenschaftliche Buchgesellschaft, 1968.

d'Ardenne, S. R. T. O., ed. 1936. *An Edition of þe Liflade ant te Passiun of Seinte Iuliene*. Bibliothèque de la Faculté de Philosophie et Lettres de l'Université de Liége LXIV. Reprinted, EETS o.s. 248, 1961.

Dobbie, E. V. K., ed. 1942. *The Anglo-Saxon Minor Poems*. ASPR VI. New York: Columbia University Press.

Einenkel, E. 1916. *Geschichte der englischen Sprache II: Historische Syntax*. 3rd ed. H. Paul, gen. ed., Grundriss der germanischen Philologie (3rd ed.). Strasburg: Karl J. Trübner.

Förster, M., ed. 1913. 'Der Vercelli-Codex CXVII nebst Abdruck einiger altenglischer Homilien der Handschrift'. *Festschrift für Lorenz Morsbach*, Studien zur englischen Philologie L, 20-179. Also issued separately (as pp. 1-164).

Fulk, R. D. 1992. *A History of Old English Meter*. Philadelphia: University of Pennsylvania Press.

Godden, M. R., ed. 1979. *Ælfric's Catholic Homilies. The Second Series. Text*. EETS s.s. 5.

——. 1992. 'Literary Language'. In Hogg (1992), pp. 490-535.

——, ed. 2000. *Ælfric's Catholic Homilies: Introduction, Commentary and Glossary*. EETS s.s. 18.

Goethe, J. W. v. 1832. *Faust. Der Tragödie zweyter Theil in fünf Acten.—(Vollendet im Sommer 1831)*. Goethe's Werke, Vollständige Ausgabe letzter Hand XLI, Goethe's nachgelassene Werke I. Stuttgart & Tübingen: J. G. Cotta'sche Buchhandlung. Reprinted, Goethes Werke Herausgegeben im Auftrage der Großherzogin Sophie von Sachsen XV/1. Weimar: Hermann Böhlau, 1888.

Gollancz, I., ed. 1895. *The Exeter Book*, I. EETS o.s. 104.

Gradon, P. O. E., ed. 1958. *Cynewulf's* Elene. London: Methuen & Co.

Green, D. H. 1965. *The Carolingian Lord—Semantic Studies on Four Old High German Words: Balder. Frô, Truhtin, Hêrro*. Cambridge: University Press.

Grein, C. W. M., ed. 1857-8. *Bibliothek der angelsächsischen Poesie*. I. Text. 2 vols. Göttingen: Georg H. Wigand.

——, trans. 1857-9. *Dichtungen der Angelsachsen stabreimend übersetzt*. 2 vols. Göttingen: Georg H. Wigand.

——, ed. 1861-4. *Sprachschatz der angelsächsischen Dichter*. 2 vols = Bibliothek der angelsächsischen Poesie, II. (1861) Cassel & Göttingen: Georg H. Wigand, (1864) Göttingen: Georg H. Wigand.

——. 1865. 'Zur Textkritik der angelsächsischen Dichter'. *Germania* 10:416-29.

Grimm, J., ed. 1840. *Andreas und Elene*. Cassel: Theodor Fischer.

Hecht, H., ed. 1900-7. *Bischof Wærferths von Worcester Übersetzung der Dialoge Gregors des Grossen*. 2 vols. C. W. M. Grein's Bibliothek der angelsächsischen Prosa V. Reprinted, Darmstadt: Wissenschaftliche Buchgesellschaft, 1965.

Hinman, C., ed. 1968. *The Norton Facsimile The First Folio of Shakespeare*. New York: W. W. Norton & Company.

Hogg, R. M., ed. 1992. *The Cambridge History of the English Language, I: The Beginnings to 1066*. Cambridge: University Press.

Hutcheson, B. R. 1995. *Old English Poetic Metre*. Cambridge: D. S. Brewer.

Jente, R. 1921. *Die mythologischen Ausdrücke im altenglischen Wortschatz*. Anglistische Forschungen 56. Heidelberg: Carl Winter.

Jones, C. 1988. *Grammatical Gender in English: 950 to 1250*. London, New York, Sydney: Croom Helm.

Jost, K. 1950. *Wulfstanstudien*. Schweizer anglistische Arbeiten (Swiss Studies in English) 23.

———, ed. 1959. *Die «Institutes of Polity, Civil and Ecclesiastical»*. Schweizer anglistische Arbeiten (Swiss Studies in English) 47.

Kemble, J. M., ed. 1844, 1856. *The Poetry of the Codex Vercellensis*. Ælfric Society, No. 5, part I The Legend of St. Andrew, No. 6, part II *Elene* and Minor Poems.

———. 1845-8. *The Dialogue of Salomon and Saturnus*. Ælfric Society, No. 8, part I (1845), No. 13, part II (1847), No. 14, part III (1848).

Klaeber, F., ed. 1950. *Beowulf and the Fight at Finnsburg*. 3rd ed. (last revision). Boston Massachusetts (later issues, Lexington, Massachusetts): D. C. Heath and Company.

Kotzor, G., ed. 1981. *Das altenglische Martyrologium*. 2 vols. Bayerische Akademie der Wissenschaften; Philosophisch-historische Klasse, Abhandlungen, neue Folge 88. Munich: Bayerische Akademie der Wissenschaften.

Krapp, G. P., ed. 1932. *The Vercelli Book*. ASPR II. New York: Columbia University Press.

——— & E. V. K. Dobbie, eds. 1936. *The Exeter Book*. ASPR III. Morningside Heights, New York: Columbia University Press.

Liebermann, F., ed. 1898-1916. *Die Gesetze der Angelsachsen*. 3 vols. Halle: Max Niemeyer; rptd Aalen: Scientia, 1960.

MacLean, G. E., ed. 1884. 'Ælfric's Version of *Alcuini Interrogationes Sigeuulfi in Genesin—Fortsetzung*'. *Anglia* 7:1-59.

Menner, R. J., ed. 1941. *The Poetical Dialogues of Solomon and Saturn*, The Modern Language Association of America Monograph Series, XIII. New York: The Modern Language Association of America; London: Oxford University Press.

Mitchell, B. 1985. *Old English Syntax*. 2 vols. Oxford: Clarendon Press. Quoted by section numbers, which are continuous in the two volumes.

Mohrbutter, A. 1885. *Darstellung der Syntax in den vier echten Predigten des angelsächsischen Erzbischofs Wulfstan.* Doctoral dissertation of the Königliche Akademie, Münster. Lübeck: printed by H. G. Rahtgens.

Morris, R., ed. 1874-80. *The Blickling Homilies of the Tenth Century.* EETS o.s. 58, 63, 73.

Murray, J. A. H., H. Bradley, W. A. Craigie, & C. T. Onions, eds. 1884-1928. *A New English Dictionary on Historical Principles.* 10 vols in 12 vols. Craigie & Onions, eds. (1933), *Introduction, Supplement, and Bibliography.* Reissued in 1933 as *The Oxford English Dictionary on Historical Principles.* 13 vols. R. W. Burchfield, ed. (1972-86), *A Supplement to the Oxford English Dictionary.* 4 vols. These 17 vols integrated by J. A. Simpson & E. S. C. Weiner (1989) as *The Oxford English Dictionary Second Edition.* 20 vols. Oxford: Clarendon Press.

Napier, A. S. 1882. *Über die Werke des altenglischen Erzbischofs Wulfstan.* Doctoral dissertation, Göttingen University. Weimar: printed by the Hof-Buchdruckerei.

———, ed. 1883. *Wulfstan—Sammlung der ihm zugeschriebenen Homilien...* Sammlung englischer Denkmäler in kritischen Ausgaben IV. Berlin: Weidmannsche Buchhandlung. Reprinted with a bibliographical appendix by K. Ostheeren. Berlin, Zürich, Dublin: Weidmann, 1966.

———. 1916. *The Old English version of the enlarged rule of Chrodegang... An Old English version of the Capitula of Theodulf... An interlinear Old English rendering of the Epitome of Benedict of Aniane.* EETS o.s. 150.

New Testament, The. 1582. *The New Testament of Iesus Christ Translated Faithfully into English, out of the authentical Latin.* Rhemes: printed by Iohn Fogny.

North, R. 1997. *Heathen Gods in Old English Literature.* Cambridge Studies in Anglo-Saxon England 22. Cambridge: Cambridge University Press.

Pope, J. C., ed. 1967-8. *Homilies of Ælfric: A Supplementary Collection.* 2 vols. EETS o.s. 259, 260.

Robinson, F. C., & E. G. Stanley, eds. 1991. *Old English Verse Texts from Many Sources.* Early English Manuscripts in Facsimile XXIII. Copenhagen: Rosenkilde and Bagger.

Russom, G. R. 1987. *Old English Meter and Linguistic Theory.* Cambridge: Cambridge University Press.

Schröer, A., ed. 1885-8. *Die angelsächischen Prosabearbeitungen der Benediktinerregel.* C. W. M. Grein's Bibliothek der angelsächsischen Prosa II. Reprinted, Darmstadt: Wissenschaftliche Buchgesellschaft, 1964, with an appendix by H. Gneuss.

Scragg, D. G., ed. 1991. *The Battle of Maldon AD 991*. Oxford: Basil Blackwell.

———. 1992. *The Vercelli Homilies and Related Texts*. EETS o.s. 300.

Skeat, W. W., ed. 1874. *The Gospel According to Saint Luke in Anglo-Saxon and Northumbrian Versions Synoptically Arranged...* Cambridge: University Press.

———. 1881-1900. *Aelfric's Lives of Saints*. 2 vols. EETS o.s. 76, 82, 94, 114.

———. 1887. *The Gospel According to Saint Matthew in Anglo-Saxon, Northumbrian, and Old Mercian Versions, Synoptically Arranged...* Cambridge: University Press.

Stanley, E. G. 1994. *In the Foreground:* Beowulf. Cambridge: D. S. Brewer.

Strunk, W., Jr, ed. 1904. *The Juliana of Cynewulf*. Boston & London: D. C. Heath and Co.

Szarmach, P. E., ed. 1981. *Vercelli Homilies IX-XXIII*. Toronto Old English Series 5. Toronto, Buffalo, London: Toronto University Press.

Thomson, R. L. 1961. 'Aldrediana V: Celtica'. *English and Germanic Studies* 7:20-36.

[Thorpe, B., ed. 1836?] (calligraphic, handwritten title-page) *Report on the New Edition of Rymer's Fœdera by C. P. Cooper. —Appendix B.* [London: distributed on His Majesty's Service to Members of the Record Commission.]

Thorpe, B., ed. 1840. *Ancient Laws and Institutes of England...; also, Monumenta Ecclesiastica Anglicana*. [London:] published in one volume folio, and in two volumes octavo, under the direction of The Commissioners on the Public Records of the Kingdom.

———, ed. 1842. *Codex Exoniensis. A Collection of Anglo-Saxon Poetry, from a Manuscript in the Library of the Dean and Chapter of Exeter, with an English Translation...* London: William Pickering for the Society of Antiquaries of London.

Traugott, E. C. 1992. 'Syntax'. In Hogg (1992), pp. 168-289.

Tristram, H. L. C., ed. 1970. *Vier altenglische Predigten aus der heterodoxen Tradition...* Doctoral dissertation of the University of Freiburg im Breisgau.

Ure, J. M., ed. 1957. *The Benedictine Office . An Old English Text*. Edinburgh University Publications, Language and Literature 12. Edinburgh: University Press.

Venezky, R. L., & A. diP. Healey, compilers. 1980. *A Microfiche Concordance to Old English*. Toronto: Centre for Medieval Studies, University of Toronto.

Wollmann, A. 1990. *Untersuchungen zu den frühen lateinischen Lehnwörtern im Altenglischen—Phonologie und Datierung*. Münchener Universitäts-

Schriften, Philosophische Fakultät, Texte und Untersuchungen zur Englischen Philologie 15. Munich: Wilhelm Fink.

Woolf, R., ed. 1955. *Juliana.* London: Methuen & Co.

Wül(c)ker, R. P., & B. Assmann, eds. 1881-98. *Bibliothek der angelsächsischen Poesie begründet von Christian W. M. Grein.* 3 vols. I/1. R. P. Wülcker, ed., Das Beowulfslied (1881). I/2. R. P. Wülcker, ed., Das Beowulfslied nebst den kleineren epischen, lyrischen, didaktischen und geschichtlichen Stücken (1883). Kassel: Georg H. Wigand. II/1. R. P. Wülker, ed., Die Verceller Handschrift (1888); II/2. R. P. Wülker, ed., Die Handschrift des Cambridger Corpus Christi Collegs CCI, die Gedichte der sogen. Cædmonhandschrift, Judith, der Hymnus Cædmons, Heiligenkalender (1894). III/1. R. P. Wülker, ed., Die Handschrift von Exeter (1897). III/2. R. P. Wülker & B. Assmann, eds., Metra des Boetius, Salomo und Saturn, die Psalmen (1898). Leipzig: Georg H. Wigand's Verlag.

Wülfing, J. E. 1894-1901. *Die Syntax in den Werken Alfreds des Grossen.* 2 vols. Bonn: P. Hanstein.

Modality and Ambiguity in Chaucer's *trewely*: With a Focus on *Troilus and Criseyde*

Yoshiyuki Nakao

1. The aim of this paper

History is etymologically related to *story* in meaning the 'narrative of past events, account, tale, story' (*OED* s.v. *history* ad L *historia*). The synonymous *tale* can also mean 'falsehood' (*OED* s.v. *tale* 5. c1250～). Crosslinguistically the Japanese equivalent of *tale*, *katari* can also mean 'falsehood'. It is, therefore, inferred that events and states are, when described, easily susceptible to the speaker's perspectives and intended controls. Chaucer seems to be sensitive to this speaker involvement and brings it into full play at important phases in his narrative. This is achieved through a variety of expressions of speaker-hearer semantic negotiations, such as swearing, proverbs, intensifiers, modal expressions (modal auxiliaries, modal adverbs, modal lexical verbs), set-phrases such as *soth to say*, *without lesing/wene/drede*, etc., verb inflections (indicative/subjunctive forms), and intonation. *Trewely* (variant forms *trewelich/e, trewly, truely, truly*), which may be classified as a modal adverb, is a case in point. My particular attention will be paid to *Troilus and Criseyde* in which this *trewely* is repeated with reference to significant events, most typically Criseyde's *untrouthe* in the story, encouraging the audience to participate in interpretation of them. I will make clear the processes in which this word is concerned with degrees of truth, and as a result with Chaucer's ambiguity.

2. Modal expressions in *Troilus and Criseyde*

Dealing with Criseyde's *untrouthe* in *Troilus and Criseyde*, Chaucer focuses on its inner and psychological meaning, not on the external meaning. It is projected to the audience not as having an absolute and objective value but as open to a dualistic interpretation. In *The House of Fame* its thematic importance is repeatedly stressed in that one and the same event or a *loves tydynge* comprises truth and falsehood at the same time. Regarding this combination, see: 'Bothe sawes and lesinges' (*HF* 676); 'And of fals and soth compouned' (*HF* 1029); 'A lesyng and a sad soth sawe' (*HF* 2089); 'Thus saugh I fals and soth compouned / Togeder fle for oo tydynge' (*HF* 2108-9).[1] It is no wonder that the audience should more often than not be placed in a psychological tension between 'truth' and 'falsehood'.

Troilus and Criseyde uses a variety of modal expressions perhaps because it deals with the continually altering natures of events such as the mutability of Fortune, metaphysical discussions, and characters' promises and predictions. Of the modal meanings, my central concern is with 'epistemic' meaning (not 'deontic'/ 'dynamic'), with regard to which see Palmer (1979: 50-1). Modal auxiliaries in Chaucer's time had developed to what Traugott (1989) describes as 'weak epistemic', typical instances of which are *shal*, *wil*, *may*, and *must*. Some adverbs of Germanic origin, going beyond propositional domains, had developed additional meaning in late ME showing the speaker's propositional attitude, e.g. *iwis*, *sothe*, *nedes, maybe*, *sikerly*, etc. To these adverbs there were added in ME *certes*, *certain*, *douteles*, *peraventure*, *peraunter*, etc. of Romance origin. The same is true of modal lexical verbs. *I trow, I wene* and *I gesse* are of Germanic origin, and *I suppose* is of romance origin. Moreover, through intonation contours (falling/rising tones), the speaker could describe degrees of certainty of events.

Trewely, of Germanic origin, can be classified as one of the epistemic adverbs mentioned above. Comparatively, *trewely* is used with reference to the two extremes of the value of the event, one factual, the other counterfactual, whereas others like *certes*, *douteles*, *peraunter* indicate degrees of certainties between the two extremes. It should also be noted that this *trewely* still retains its etymological sense along with its developed

[1] Quotations from Chaucer and abbreviations of his works are taken from Benson (1987).

epistemic sense, as shown in 3 below, while others like *certes* or *iwis* are epistemically restricted.

3. Previous studies of *trewely* and remaining issues

From a lexical point of view, the *OED* defines *trewely*, as shown below:

OED s.v. *Truly* OE *treowliche*
1. Faithfully, loyally, constantly, with steadfast allegiance. *arch.* 1000-1852
*2. Honestly, honourably, uprightly. Obs. 1362-1558
3. In accordance with the fact; truthfully; correctly (in reference to a statement). 1303-1875
4. In accordance with a rule or standard; exactly, accurately, precisely, correctly. 1375-1875
5. Genuinely, really, actually, in fact, in reality; sincerely, unfeignedly. c1380-1874
b. Used to emphasize a statement (sometimes as a mere expletive): Indeed, forsooth, verily. c1205-1869

While the *OED* definitions 1, 2, 3, 4 and 5 are used as adverbs of manner, 5b is used epistemically to show the speaker's attitude towards the propositional content. 3 includes examples of *trewely* co-occurring with verbs of utterance (*bid*, *speak*, *tell*, *swear*), and 5 includes an example of *trewely* co-occurring with a verb of thinking (*believe*). Here we find borderline cases similar to epistemic expressions like 'trewely to tell' (*Ywaine & Gawaine*, 329). As regards 5b, the *OED* only describes the function 'to emphasize the statement (sometimes as a mere expletive)' of *trewely.* It does not refer to the modal aspect of this word nor distinguish between the modal sense and the speech act sense.

As far as epistemic meaning is concerned, there is substantially no difference between the *OED* and the *MED*, as shown in:

MED s.v. *treuli*: 8.
actually, in fact; really, indeed; genuinely, sincerely; also as intensifier or in parenthetical expressions with reduced semantic content; also in stock simile.

Kerkhof (1982:404-5) lists 'Adverbs of Modality' grammatically, but does not describe them in semantic and pragmatic terms. He does not include *trewely* there.

A modern descriptive grammar, for instance, Quirk, et al. (1985:615) examines the semantics and syntax of these adverbials from a synchronic point of view, and deals with them as style disjuncts expressing the speaker's modality and manner to what he/she says and as content disjuncts expressing the degrees or conditions of the truth of the content. The idea of disjuncts in contradistinction to adverbs of manner can be applied to Chaucer'*s trewely.*

From the semantic and pragmatic point of view, Brinton's (1996:230-1) description is valuable. She examines the historical development of 'first person epistemic parentheticals' from the point of view of grammaticalization and subjectification. Her comments on the relation between these parentheticals and the contents to which these are attached are very useful: 'they are most often appended to utterances expressing personal opinion, evaluation, or interpretation' (218).[2] But with regard to modal adverbs, she sketches them very briefly and stresses the same function with the first person epistemic parentheticals. And her sketch does not include *trewely.* Traugott's (1989:46-7) discussion of adverbs like *apparently/evidently* as regards the rise of epistemic meaning is also of interest. But like Brinton she does not deal with *trewely.* Their discussion is primarily about grammaticalization, and therefore ambiguity is not really their concern.

From a stylistic or literary critical point of view, many scholars have focused on these expressions, but mainly in relation to narrative devices typical of orally transmitted literature. Bennett (1947:85) describes the following effects.

> This is not to deny, however, as has been admitted above, that Chaucer made use of rhyme-tags and padding material. All medieval writers drew upon a large rag-bag full of tags, alliterative and stock phrases to save themselves trouble, to give their listeners time to absorb some fact or interesting detail, or to drive home the importance of a statement.

Malone (1951) focuses on the effects of those tags in GP as ascribable to a secret conversation between the narrator and the audience. In relation to the interaction between the narrator and the audience, Mehl (1974) points out that those expressions are functional in encouraging the audience to

---

[2] For the eight types of 'utterances expressing personal opinion…', see Brinton (1996:218-23).

participate in the interpretation of the narrative text. From a metrical point of view, Masui (1964:237-45) deals with those phrases in relation to Chaucer's rhyming techniques. He says: 'This word (i.e. *trewely*) is sometimes used to emphasize a statement, sometimes as a mere expletive, the latter being often the case with Chaucer' (239). These studies have contributed to the study of narrative devices in ME oral transmission, but are little concerned with a modal point of view by which to question the quality of a statement, and therefore with the question of ambiguity.

Donaldson (1970:74) and Elliott (1974:115) have directed their attention to *trewely*. Donaldson emphasizes the anti-climactic effect of *trewely* comparing it with a MnE *surely*, and Elliott attended to the effect of 'ironical twist'. Elliott does not distinguish between *trewely* as an adverb of manner and as an epistemic one. In rhetorical terms, they both seem to confine the effect of *trewely* to the counterfactual, although *trewely* can be functional as objective epistemic.[3]

To get the full potential of Chaucer's *trewely*, we need to investigate it from the point of view of modality and ambiguity.

4. The semantics of *trewely* and the theoretical background to its ambiguity

To borrow the terminology of Sweetser (1990), the senses of *trewely* range over the three different domains listed below:

[a] proposition
[b] propositional attitude
[c] speech act

Trewely [a] works as an adverb of manner within the scope of the predication, whether the modified word is a verb, adjective or adverb. [B] works as a disjunct or modally functioning adverb, indicating that the truth of the proposition is not self-evident, but open to the speaker's/listener's judgement. [C] is more subjectively oriented with the implications of the speaker's politeness/familiarity/attention-calling to the listeners and, when the most formalized, comes to be restricted to a local context, working as a mere tag or filler with some tautology in the narrative communication. In

---

[3] Traugott (1989:46): … weaker epistemic precedes stronger epistemicity.

historical terms, the sense of *trewely* is developed from [a] to [c], and the three senses are found in Chaucer's English. The functional senses in [a] correspond to the *OED* 1, 2, 3, 4, 5, those functional in [b] to the *OED* 5.b, and those functional in [c] again to the *OED* 5.b, the latter two senses being undifferentiated in the *OED*. *Trewely* in combination with the verbs of utterance/thinking like 'truly to tell', 'truly I believe', etc. comes close to [b]/[c], some examples of which are included in the *OED*'s 3 and 5.

Chaucerian scholarship treated above in 3 has, bypassing [b], placed too much emphasis upon the speaker's intention [c] like pause-making, attention-calling, etc. projected to the audience, or on a rhetorical implication like irony, again [c]. [B] has thus been taken for granted and therefore been given very little attention. This sense is our central concern here. Mere intensification, tagging or irony does not exhaust the use of this word.

Theoretically, the ambiguity due to *trewely* can occur horizontally on the assumption that it varies between the three senses [a], [b], [c] and vertically according to the polysemy of each level. In the former, [a] and [b]/[c] are syntactically easily distinguished, since while the former is immediately before or after the word it modifies, most examples of the latter are sentence-initial with a pause before the proposition that follows, as shown in Table 1 below. Of course, there are some fuzzy cases like 'For *treweliche* he swor hire as a knyght' (*Tr* 5.113), where on our assumption of a pause before 'he swor ...', the function of *treweliche* varies from [a] to [b]/[c] (see 5.2 below). On the other hand, [b] and [c] overlap, since [b] is basically retained in [c]. If there is any difference perceived between them, it is a matter of degree. We might say that on occasion they work together. Our primary concern here is vertical, especially with [b] in that *trewely* is used to modalize the content of an utterance, and ambiguity is most likely to occur (such as a plus or minus truth value of the content, ambiguity due to the duality of the proposition that *trewely* may be applied to, or the fuzziness in the scope of *trewely*'s modality). Ambiguity in [c] is also expected, but separate treatment is difficult because of the overlapping semantic status.

Trewely [b] is functional in that the speaker negotiates with the audience about the truth of the statement. This phenomenon can be classified into two types, according to Oh (2000:252-3): one functions in a local scope and the other in a global scope. The former 'locally intensifies the meaning of the clause in which it occurs', which might correspond to the *OED* 5.b, and the latter is more pragmatic, 'the function of contradicting prior expectations'. Chaucer's modalizing use of *trewely* and its subsequent ambiguity is central to this global function. The speaker's bare statements devoid of epistemic phrases, by contrast, tell the listeners that what is treated is self-evident.

Evidence of modalization of a statement through *trewely* is obvious in Chaucer. It is applied to utterances expressing evaluation (e.g. 'And *trewely*, as to my juggement, / Me thynketh it a thyng impertinent', ClP IV (E) 53-4); the word order of his *trewely* is most frequently sentence-initial,[4] which indicates that it functions semantically as a disjunct to the content that follows (e.g. 'For *trewely*, ye have as myrie a stevene / As any aungel hath that is in hevene' NPT VII (B2) 3291-2). Some examples (e.g. 4.1415, 5.1051, 5.1072) in *Troilus and Criseyde* even begin a new stanza, which may function as a discourse marker to direct the reader's attention to the development of the story; the initial position of *trewely* tends to be introduced by the coordinate conjunctions *and/but/for* suggesting *the existence of* speakers' inference. See Table 1 below.

I have checked the semantic frequency of Chaucer's *trewely*. Most examples are used epistemically in the sense of [b], and a pure example of [c] is hard to discover, because when we find one, as mentioned earlier, it tends to retain its modal colourings. For instance, *trewely* is not grammaticalized to the extent of *iwis* or *certes*. Quantitatively I dealt with [b]/[c] at the same time. Distinguishing between [b] and [c] is only possible by a qualitative analysis. See Table 2 below. The use of *trewely* only for the poet's metrical demands is not prominent. The frequency of this word in a rhyming position is about one third, and it is easy to shift on a verse line. It is highly probable that functions other than metrical ones are more important.

[4] Brinton (1996:259-60): ...when modal forms in sentence-initial, modality is 'thematized', while in sentence-medial position, it is 'interpolated' and in sentence-final position it is 'adjoined'.

Table 1: Frequency of epistemic *trewely* in relation to preceding conjunctions and its positions in a sentence in Chaucer

Conjunction and Position	CT	BD	HF	Anel	PF	Bo	Tr	LGW	SH	Astr	Rom	Total
And-I	7/0	1/0	0	0	0	0	8/2	0	0	0	0	16/2
And-M	0	0	0	0	0	0	0	1/1	0	0	0	1/1
And-F	1/1	0	1/1	0	0	0	2/2	0	0	0	0	4/4
For-I	6/0	2/1	0	0	0	0	7/0	0	0	0	0	15/1
For-M	0	0	0	0	0	0	0	1/0	0	0	0	1/0
But-I	5/0	0	0	0	0	0	6/1	2/0	1/0	0	0	14/1
But-M	0	1/0	0	0	0	0	1/1	0	0	0	0	2/1
But-F	0	1/1	0	0	0	0	0	0	0	0	0	1/1
Others-I	3/1	0	0	0	0	0	1/0	0	0	0	0	4/1
Others-M	0	0	0	0	0	0	1/1	0	0	0	0	1/1
Others-F	0	1/1	0	0	0	0	0	0	0	0	0	1/1
Zero-I	0	1/0	0	0	0	0	1/0	0	0	0	0	2/0
Zero-M	1/1	2/0	0	0	0	0	3/3	2/0	0	0	2/2	10/6
Zero-F	5/5	3/2	1/1	0	0	0	0	0	1/0	0	0	10/8
That-I	3/0	4/1	0	0	0	0	2/1	0	0	0	0	9/2
That-M	1/1	2/1	0	0	0	0	0	0	0	0	0	3/2
That-F	1/1	0	0	0	0	0	1/1	0	0	0	0	2/2
Total	33/10	18/7	2/2	0	0	0	33/12	6/1	2/0	0	2/2	96/34

(I = sentence-initial, M = sentence-medial, F = sentence-final; zero = devoid of conjunctions; Others = other elements starting the sentence; That = within the subordinating conjunction; SH = Short Poems; The number to the left of the slash indicates the total items, and to the right the frequency of the item in a rhyming position.)

Table 2: Semantic frequency of *trewely* in Chaucer

Function of *Trewely*	CT	BD	HF	Anel	PF	Bo	Tr	LGW	SH	Astr	Rom	Total
adverb of manner	6/0	0	2/2	0	0	0	5/1	2/1	1/0	1/0	0	17/4
with verb of utter.	4/2	0	1/1	0	0	0	0	0	1/0	0	0	6/3
with verb of thinking	3/0	4/2	0	0	0	0	2/1	0	0	0	0	9/3
episte-mic adv.	33/10	18/7	2/2	0	0	0	33/12	6/2	2/0	0	2/2	96/35
Total	46/12	22/9	5/5	0	0	0	40/14	8/3	4/0	1/0	2/2	128/45

('with verb of utter.' = *trewely* co-occurring with verb of utterance)

Cf. Semantic frequency of *trewely* in Langland, Gower, and four contemporary romances

Function of *Trewely*	Langland	Gower	Amis	Launfal	Squire	Wedding	Total
adverb of manner	7/7	6/0	1/0	1/0	0	0	15/7
with verb of utter.	3/3	1/1	1/0	0	0	0	5/4
with verb of thinking	1/1	4/3	0	0	0	0	5/4
epistemic adv.	4/4	3/2	0	0	0	2/2	9/8
Total	15/15 [alliteration]	14/6	2/0	1/0	0	2/2	34/23

(Langland = *Piers Plowman*, Gower = *Confessio Amantis*, Amis = *Amis and Amiloun*; Launfal = *Sir Launfal*, Squire = *The Squire of Low Degree*, Wedding = *The Wedding of Sir Gawain and Dame Ragnell*)

5. Modality and ambiguity of Chaucer's *trewely* in *Troilus and Criseyde*

Trewely appears in *Troilus and Criseyde* almost as frequently as in *The*

Canterbury Tales which is about twice the size. In the four contemporary romances I investigated (see Table 2 Cf.), only five instances were found. Although *Troilus and Criseyde* has much language affinity with romance genre works, the frequent use of *trewely* therein seems to display a deviation from them.[5] This story focuses on the processes of Criseyde's betrayal. The degree of truthfulness involved in it is made problematic in the story, and as a result its explanation or justification comes close to an expository genre such as a sermon, with regard to which see *CT* Mel VII 1363 and ParsT X (I) 628. Who uses *trewely* to whom and when (what Book) is shown in Table 3. It should be noted that *trewely* is found where Chaucer departs from his original, Boccaccio's *Il Filostrato*, with the exception of 4.687 and 5.483. Most instances cluster together in Books 4 and 5, where we see the progress from the Trojan Parliament's decision to exchange her for Greek prisoners, to her yielding to Diomede in the Greek camp. *Trewely* is increasingly used as the relationship between Troilus and Criseyde is increasingly disrupted. The kinds of statements descriptive of her *trouthe/untrouthe* are significantly introduced by *trewely*. Pragmatically, who uses *trewely* to whom is also important in affecting the degrees of modalization. Comparatively, its near equivalents like *by my trouthe/have my trouthe* or *soth to seyne* seem not to be conditioned greatly by the development of the story nor the contents of the statements, although *by my trouthe/have my trouthe* is restricted to the dialogues of characters. These asseverations are more accidental and light in tone than *trewely*. For the detailed information, see Nakao (1997:148-57). I will first deal with the narrator and then these characters.

[5] I have investigated a variety of epistemic expressions (modal adverbs, modal lexical verbs, prepositional phrases, etc.) in Chaucer and some contemporary romances in Nakao (1997). My investigation shows that *Troilus and Criseyde* is conspicuous in the variety of epistemic expressions and also their frequency, and in them *trewely* captures the reader's attention because of its unusual frequency there.

Table 3: Frequency of *trewely* according to Book and who uses it to whom in *Troilus and Criseyde*

who uses *trewely* to whom	Book 1	Book 2	Book 3	Book 4	Book 5	Total
T → C			1489	1450		2
T → P					483	1
T : M				1055 1063	1704 1720	4
C → T				1288	1623	2
C → P		164, 241 1161	835	939		5
C → D					987	1
C : M					1075 1082	2
P → T	985				380, 410 494	3
P → C		541				1
Calkas → Greek				116		1
Women → C				687		1
D → C					146	1
N	246	628		1415	19, 816 826, 1051 1086	8
Total	2	5	2	8	16	33

(T = Troilus, C = Criseyde, P = Pandarus, D = Diomede, N = narrator, M = monologue, → = speaks to)

5.1. Narrator

The love between Troilus and Criseyde develops in the unstable situation of the Trojan war. Their love reaches a climax in Book 3. Soon after, in Book 4, the exchange of Criseyde for Greek prisoners is settled by the Parliament, and she is forced to go to the Greek camp, where her father, a betrayer of Troy, waits to be reunited with her. Troilus and Criseyde argue about how to cope with the exchange. She asserts that once she will go to the Greek camp, deceive her father, and come back to Troy within ten days in obedience to her promise. She says that if she cannot persuade his father into believing her within one day or two, she will be obliged to kill herself. Soon after comes the narrator's introduction of *treweliche*, as shown below. He modalizes with *treweliche* on how 'trewe' she was at that time, perhaps expecting him/her to expect the opposite—a typical example of 'global scope' mentioned in 4.

And but I make hym soone to converte
And don my red withinne a day or tweye,
I wol to yow oblige me to deye".

And *treweliche*, as writen wel I fynde
That al this thyng was seyd of good entente,
And that hire herte trewe was and kynde
Towardes hym, and spak right as she mente,
And that she starf for wo neigh whan she wente,
And was in purpos evere to be trewe:
Thus writen they that of hire werkes knewe. (4.1412-21)

Treweliche is introduced not by the adversative *but* nor by the causal *for*, but the coordinate and unobtrusive *and*. We are encouraged to understand the following speech as a matter of course. *Treweliche* is placed at the beginning of the stanza (or an important turning point in the story) as well as in the initial position of the sentence with a topicalized implication under which the statement is to be understood. The statement, consisting of evaluative adjectives, describes Criseyde's moral status and involves the speaker's judgement. This is typical of *trewely* in [b]. Incidentally, no scribal variants are found for *trewely* according to Windeatt (1984). To make clear the full potential of *treweliche,* we need to ask the following five questions.

(1) What is the statement to which *treweliche* is attached?

(2) Assuming that the statement is determined, what about the audience's response to the speaker's evaluation?

(3) What is the scope of the modal force of *treweliche* in relation to the repetition of the statements through the coordinate conjunction *and*?

(4) Why is the reconfirmation of the evidential 'Thus written they that of hire werkes knewe' necessary?

(5) Is there any effect of *paronomasia* perceivable in the co-occurrence of *treweliche* and *trewe*?

Regarding (1), *treweliche* is semantically applied to the statement in the 'That'-clause, since the contents are evaluative. After *treweliche*, it should be noted that an evidential or source of information, 'as written wel I fynde', is inserted to substantiate his opinion.[6]

However, in relation to the complement marker *that*, *treweliche* is taken grammatically as attached to 'I fynde ...'. If this is correct, the modality is overtly attached to the quotation of the narrator, and only indirectly to the validity of her *trouthe* since it is located in the embedded clause. The narrator's references to the authorities are in ME poetry conventionally used to strengthen the validity of the statements he conveys to the audience, but psychologically they imply that the statements in question are not necessarily self-evident, and therefore need some evidential support for their justification, with regard to which see Fukaya & Tanaka (1996:265-70). This is the case with Chaucer. When he makes a metacomment on the sources of the proposition concerned, this tends to be paradoxically his original, but when he is reticent about authorities, the proposition in question is likely to be based on authorities. In Chaucer, therefore, his references to authorities and subsequently their validities are occasionally open to the listener's judgement. As seen about Fame in *HF*, the sources themselves can be biased. We are reminded of the message 'of fals and soth compouned'.

Thus when the proposition is framed both by an epistemic *treweliche* and an evidential, the relation between *treweliche* and its modified proposition gets loosened, involving two propositions. The interpretative oscillation is reflected in the modernizations of this part as in the following:

Windeatt (1998): And truly, I find it written that all of this was said with good intentions, that...

Coghill (1971): And truly, it is written, as I find, / That all she said was said with good intent, / And that ...

Stanley-Wrench (1965): And truly, as I find it written, too, / All this was said to him with good intent, / And I believe her heart was kind and true

Tatlock and MacKaye (1912): And truly, as I find it written, all this was said

---

[6] The detailed information of 'evidential' is found in Traugott (1989:47-8) and Brinton (1996:231-5).

> with sincerity and good intent, and her heart was true and loving towards him...

In Windeatt and Coghill quotative forms are construed grammatically as superordinate clauses, but in Stanley-Wrench and Tatlock-MacKaye those forms are treated parenthetically, where *treweliche* is more directly related to the statements.

With regard to (2), the validity of the adjectives (*good, trewe, kynde*) are generally dependent on the criteria that readers set up in their minds. One of the criteria here is the question of time involved in Criseyde's shifting heart. Readers who pay only limited attention to this particular occasion in which she copes with the issue of her exchange, may take her intentions as sincere and devoid of deception. On the other hand, readers who take a longer view of her promises (and assume that these will be broken) are likely to be sceptical of her sincerity. Further, Troilus argues against her, saying that 'Men may the wise atrenne, and naught atrede' (4.1456), and points to her optimism. She does not accept this. Paradoxically, her excessive sensitivity and sincere obedience to the varying situations she faces can be said to imply a future shift of mind. Dependent on the assumptions of the audience, the degrees of the subjectivity of the statement vary.

With regard to (3), the scope of modality is made problematic. In accordance with the repetition of the statements depictive of her truth through *and*, the force of modality is acoustically weakened, and as a result the truth of those statements is gradually strengthened. This is, as Pearsall (1986) says, reflective of Criseyde's processes of reasoning—she accumulatively lists reasons for her justification, gradually comes to recognize them as objective, and then concludes. Of course, if we are aware of and stress the repeated use of the complement marker *that*, the weakening of modality is likely to be abandoned. Here we have an ambiguity due to the scope of modality.

With regard to (4), the reconfirmation of the evidential (4.1421) is probable because of the gradual weakening of *treweliche* and the evidential (4.1415). However, as mentioned before, this quotative is open to interpretation.

With regard to (5), it should be noted that *treweliche*, at the important turning point in the story, focuses on Criseyde's truth (*trewe* 4.1417, 1420).

There is likely to be an effect of chiming in that *treweliche* (4.1415) and *trewe* are semantically linked together by their similar sounds. This is what medieval rhetorics call *paronomasia*. Here with an earlier meaning of [a] ('faithfully') superimposed on a later epistemic meaning [b] ('surely'), *treweliche* enriches its implications. This is an example classified as a horizontal ambiguity. This cannot be replaced by *certes* or *iwis*.

We have similar instances of *trewely* by the narrator, which are shown below:

Ful redy was at prime Diomede
Criseyde unto the Grekis oost to lede,
For sorwe of which she felt hire herte blede,
As she that nyste what was best to rede.
And *trewely*, as men in bokes rede,
Men wiste nevere womman han the care,
Ne was so loth out of a town to fare. (5.15-21)

Men seyn—I not—that she yaf hym hire herte.
But *trewely*, the storie telleth us,
Ther made nevere womman moore wo
Than she, whan that she falsed Troilus.
She seyde, "Allas, for now is clene ago
My name of trouthe in love, for everemo!
For I have falsed oon the gentileste
That evere was, and oon the worthieste! (5.1050-7)

But *trewely*, how longe it was bytwene
That she forsok hym for this Diomede,
Ther is non auctour telleth it, I wene.
Take every man now to his bokes heede,
He shal no terme fynden, out of drede.
For though that he bigan to wowe hire soone,
Er he hire wan, yet was ther more to doone. (5.1086-92)

In the first example Criseyde is escorted by Diomede to the Greek camp. The narrator sheds light on Criseyde's sorrow, which is in *Il Filostrato* Troilo's (see Windeatt 1984:447). It should be noted that the line immediately preceding *trewely* 'As she that nyste what was best to rede' is open to a dual interpretation ('<u>since</u> she nyste what was best to rede'; '<u>like one who</u> nyste what was best to rede'). Its direct/indirect-vacillating ambiguity seems to be contagious to *trewely*.[7]

The second example is given just after Criseyde's yielding to Diomede's wooing. Because of the climactic hint of her betrayal (5.1050), the narrator needs to use the adversative conjunction *But* to introduce his sympathetic comment upon her great sorrow owing to her betraying Troilus. But here again *trewely* is added with the evidential 'the storie telleth us' before going to the content of her sorrow. It should be noted that her devotion to Diomede and her great sorrow due to her betraying Troilus are both epistemically directed. The evidential is again added by Chaucer. 'The storie telleth us' can be within the scope of *trewely*, not necessarily 'Ther made …'.

The context of the third example is this. In her monologue, Criseyde regrets her betrayal of Troilus, tries to cope with the predicament she is confronted with, gradually recovers herself, and concludes her speech: 'And gilteles, I woot wel, I yow leve. / But al shal passe; and thus take I my leve.' (5.1084-5). The narrator's sympathetic comment is introduced again by the adversative *But* at the beginning of the stanza, since in the immediately preceding stanza Criseyde betrays her parting from Troilus and justifies it with the proverbial 'But al shal passe'. The content to which *trewely* is attached refers to the time to be taken for her forsaking Troilus for Diomede although in an interrogative way 'How long it was …'. This is presented to the audience as if to get rid of their skepticism of her sudden change. This temporal implication becomes obvious in the line 'Er he hire wan, yet was ther more to doone' (5.1092). And as is seen before ('I not' 5.1050), the content is again put in the framework of the negative quotation 'Ther is non auctour telleth it'.[8] So much unfavorable evidence for her honour is accumulated that he is less and less assured of it.

The narrator views Criseyde's *untrouthe* with a shifting perspective, as a sympathetic and detached observer. It is significant that his use of epistemic *trewely* is closely related to the estimation of the moral status of Criseyde.

---

[7] For the meaning and use of *as he/she that*, see Nakao (1993) and Nakao (1995).

[8] E'n breve spazio ne cacciò di fuore
Troilo e Troie, ed ogni altro pensiero
Che 'n lei fosse di lui o falso o vero. (*Il Filostrato* 6.8.6-8)

[In brief space he (i.e. Diomede) drave forth from it Troilus and Troy and every other thought which she had of him, or false or true.]

5.2. Characters

The characters' use of *trewely* is affected by their intentions on particular occasions or more likely by their characterized features. Troilus's use of epistemic *trewely* is in a local scope and honest in that few or no inconsistencies are admitted between what he says and what actually happens. His absolute commitment to Criseyde as her servant/knight (3.1489) is, for instance, confirmed superlatively, and this is actually well attested by his later services. For similar examples, see 4.1450, 5.1704, 5.1720. Two (4.1055, 4.1063) are used in his debates between free will and predestination based on Boethius. Significantly enough, no epistemic *trewely*s are found in *Boece* although a variety of epistemic expressions such as *certain*, *certes*, *forsothe*, *without doute*, *nedes*, *I trow,* etc. are used.[9]

Criseyde's use of *trewely* is more complex than that of Troilus in that her words and her actions do not necessarily correspond, which might be considered as belonging to 'a global scope'. Her promises and vows are likely to shift not in spite of but because of her sensitivity or obedience to the situations she faces. For instance, her proposal to go first to the Greek camp and then come back to Troy is taken as optimistic by Troilus:

> And, for the love of God, foryeve it me,
> If I speke aught ayeyns youre hertes reste;
> For *trewely*, I speke it for the beste. (4.1286-8)

Her decisions are relative, since her superlative 'for the beste' is applied only to this occasion. This decision is soon altered by her father and her surrounding situation in the Greek camp. She prays to God that Troilus would have good days as the noblest knight to serve her faithfully and keep her honour best although she recognizes herself as his betrayer. See the following example:

> "But, Troilus, syn I no bettre may,
> And syn that thus departen ye and I,
> Yet prey I God, so yeve yow right good day,
> As for the gentileste, *trewely*,
> That evere I say, to serven feythfully,
> And best kan ay his lady honour kepe". (5.1072-7)

---

[9] According to Nakao (1997), it is interesting to note that Chaucer makes use of *certes* as often as 190 times, *forsothe*, 27 times, in *Boece*.

Whether *trewely* is used to strengthen her recognition of Troilus as such or added in relation to the illocutionary force (e.g. request) extended to him or works as a mere rhyme filler is hard to determine. If these interpretations are possible, *trewely* is ambiguous as between [a] and [b] and [c]. For similar examples, see 2.241, 2.1161, 4.939, 5.987, 5.1082, 5.1623.[10]

Pandarus's use of *trewely* is more or less the same as Criseyde's. His use is strategically directed for the purposes he has on particular occasions. Pandarus, for instance, resorts to the belief/feelings attributed to other people for persuasion, as shown below.

> For *trewelich*, of o thing trust to me,
> If thow thus ligge a day, or two, or thre,
> The folk wol seyn that thow, for cowardice
> The feynest sik and that thow darst nat rise!" (5.410-13)

He thus induces Troilus to go out although the above belief is not certified or might be cancelled later. For similar examples, see 1.985, 5.380, 5.494.

Since we are given information about Diomede's hypocritical attitude towards Criseyde (5.92-105, 771-98), his use of *trewely* is open to question. His commitment to Criseyde is linguistically more or less the same as Troilus's, but in function similar to the fox in the NPT (VII (B2) 3289-92) or the canon in the CYT (VIII (G) 1063-5): 'For *trewely*, ther kan no wyght yow serve, That half so loth youre wratthe wold disserve' (5.146-7). Incidentally, the narrator's use of *treweliche* about Diomede's verbal behaviour ('For *treweliche* he swor hire, as a knyght, / That ther nas thyng with which he myghte hire plese' (5.113-14)) is worthy of note. I take it to be collocated with the verb of utterance *swor*, but introduced by the coordinating conjunction *For* and placed sentence-initially, it is conditionally motivated to be taken as an epistemic adverb with implied irony.

5.3. A comparative note on trewely

Langland and Gower do not use *trewely* as frequently as Chaucer, as shown

---

[10] Cf. In her vow to Troilus 'And I shal *trewely*, with al my myght, / Youre bittre tornen al into swetenesse' (3.178-9), *trewely* is functional as an adverb of manner. However, if we are allowed to put a pause before it and convert it to a parenthetical phrase, it is likely to be modally coloured.

in Table 3. Their use of it is mainly to strengthen their statements, as the *OED* says in 5.b, and straightforward like those examples by Troilus, which might be classified as 'a local scope'. Typical examples of each poet are *The Vision of Piers Plowman* 7.180 and *Confessio Amantis* 5.2536.

One of the Early MnE equivalents of *trewely* is *sure*. Shakespeare's use of this in *Julius Caesar* merits attention. At Caesar's funeral Antony is making a speech with repeated reference to Brutus's evaluation of Caesar, not forgetting to comment on Brutus's character, 'Brutus is an honourable man'. See the following:

> ... The noble Brutus
> Hath told you Cæsar was ambitious....
> (For Brutus is an honourable man, ...)
> But Brutus says he was ambitious,
> And Brutus is an honourable man....
> Yet Brutus says he was ambitious,
> And Brutus is an honourable man....
> Yet Brutus says he was ambitious,
> And *sure* he is an honourable man. (*Julius Caesar*, Act III, Sc. II 79-101)

Antony's fourth comment on his character is given an epistemic parenthetical, *sure*, which may suggest to the audience that whether he is honourable or not is open to question. This *sure* occurs only once, but is contiguous to the preceding judgements by Brutus, whose character and evaluation are put in question. Antony brings the potential of *sure* into full play to ensure the audience's assessment of Brutus's character.

6. Conclusion

From the above discussion, we can recapitulate:

(1) Previous scholarship of Chaucer's *trewely* has stressed its intensifying function. Little attention has been given to its modal function and therefore to the question of ambiguity.
(2) Most of Chaucer's *trewely*s are epistemic: 75% (epistemic adverbs only).
(3) *Trewely* tends to be introduced by the coordinating conjunctions *and/but/for*. These conjunctions suggest speaker inference.
(4) Most *trewely*s are located sentence-initially functioning as theme (73%).

(5) The frequency of *trewely* in *Trolilus and Criseyde* is conspicuous among Chaucer's works, particularly in Books 4 and 5 where Criseyde's betrayal of Troilus becomes obvious. The narrator treats Criseyde's sincere attitude involved in coping with the variable situations sympathetically, while at the same time he suggests to the audience an opposing or shifting image of her.

(6) The narrator uses *trewely* to highlight the moral status of Criseyde. The relation between *trewely* and its attached proposition allows for multiple interpretations (the truth of the proposition, the kinds of the proposition (events, quotative forms) the modality is applied to, the scope of the modality).

(7) How are the functions of evidentials combined with *trewely*? Chaucer's resort to the authorities is fictional and their validity is also open to question as shown in *HF*.

(8) Troilus's use of *trewely* is on a local scope with little discrepancy between his statements and their realization in deed. Criseyde's use, on the other hand, is apt to shift because her decisions or vows are temporarily limited, over time easily abandoned owing to her obedience to the varying situations with which she is confronted. Pandarus's use is made strategically for persuasion of Troilus into actions. Diomede's use is apparently similar to Troilus's, but their validity is questionable, because his way of wooing Criseyde is tactically based unlike a romantic lover's.

(9) In terms of ambiguity, we can generalize in this way: provided that the relatedness of two textual elements are weakened and the reader's participation in relating them is strengthened, the ways in which they are related are expanded and therefore ambiguity is motivated to arise. Here we have concentrated on the interaction between the two elements: the modality and the proposition through *trewely*.[11]

---

[11] For a general framework for describing the rise of Chaucer's ambiguity, see Nakao (2001).

References

Bennet. H. S. 1947. *Chaucer and the Fifteenth Century.* Oxford: Clarendon Press.

Benson, L. D., gen. ed. 1987. *The Riverside Chaucer*. 3rd ed. Boston: Houghton Mifflin.

Brinton. L. J. 1996. *Pragmatic Markers in English: Grammaticalization and Discourse Markers.* Berlin & New York: Mouton de Gruyter.

Coghill, N., tr. 1971. *Geoffrey Chaucer: Troilus and Criseyde*. London: Penguin Books.

Donaldson, E. T. 1970. *Speaking of Chaucer*. London: Athlone Press.

Dorsch, T. S., ed. 1979. *Julius Caesar*. Arden Edition. London: Methuen & Co Ltd.

Elliott, R. W. V. 1974. *Chaucer's English*. London: André Deutsch.

Fukaya, M. & S. Tanaka. 1996. *Kotobano Imizukeron* (*The Mechanics of Signification in Daily Language*). Tokyo: Kinokuniyashoten.

Griffin, N. E. & A. B. Myrick, eds. & trs. 1978. *The Filostrato of Giovanni Boccaccio.* New York: Octagon Press.

Kerkhof, J. 1982. *Studies in the Language of Geoffrey Chaucer.* Second, Revised and Enlarged Edition. Leiden: E. J. Brill/Leiden University Press.

Kurath, H., S. M. Kuhn, & R. E. Lewis, et al., eds. 1952-2001. *Middle English Dictionary*. Ann Arbor: University of Michigan Press.

Leach, M., ed. 1960. *Amis and Amiloun*. EETS o.s. 203. London, New York, & Toronto: Oxford University Press.

Macaulay, G. C., ed. 1900 & 1901. *The English Works of John Gower*, 2 vols. EETS e.s. 81 & 82. London, New York, & Toronto: Oxford University Press.

Malone, K. 1951. *Chapters on Chaucer*. Westport: Greenwood Press, Publishers.

Masui, M. 1964. *The Structure of Chaucer's Rime Words—An Exploration into the Poetic Language of Chaucer*. Tokyo: Kenkyusha.

Mehl, D. 1974. 'The Audience of Chaucer's *Troilus and Criseyde*'. *Chaucer and Middle English Studies: In Honour of Rossell Hope Robbins,* ed. B. Rowland. London: George Allen & Unwin. 173-89.

Nakao, Y. 1993. 'The Ambiguity of the Phrase *As She That* in Chaucer's *Troilus and Criseyde*'. *Studies in Medieval English Language and Literature* 8:69-86.

———. 1995. 'A Semantic Note on the Middle English Phrase *As He/She That*'. *NOWELE: North-Western European Language Evolution* 25:25-48.

———. 1997. 'The Semantics of the Epistemic Expressions—"ye sey me soth,"

"soth to sey," "soth is," "soothe," and "forsoth" in Chaucer's *Troilus and Criseyde*'. *English and English-American Literature* 32:115-60. [Originally in Japanese.]

———. 2001. 'Chaucer's Ambiguity in *Troilus and Criseyde*—A Consideration of the Degrees of Relatedness between Textual Elements from a Reader's Point of View'. *A Festschrift in Honour of Professor Masahiko Kanno: Originality and Adventure—Essays on English Language and Literature,* ed. Y. Nakao & A. Jimura. Tokyo: Eihosha. 225-59. [Originally in Japanese.]

Oh, S. 2000. '*Actually* and *in fact* in American English: a data-based analysis'. *English Language and Linguistics* 4 (2):243-68.

Palmer, F. R. 1979. *Modality and the English Modals*. London: Longman.

Pearsall, D. 1986. 'Criseyde's Choices'. *Studies in the Age of Chaucer Proceedings* 2:17-29.

Quirk, R., et al. 1985. *A Comprehensive Grammar of the English Language*. London: Longman.

Sands, D. B., ed. 1986. *Middle English Verse Romances*. Exeter: University of Exeter Press.

Schmidt, A. V. C., ed. 1995. *William Langland The Vision of Piers Plowman—A Critical Edition of the B-Text Based on Trinity College Cambridge MS B. 15.17*. 2nd ed. London: J. M. Dent.

Simpson, J. A. & E. S. C. Weiner, eds. 1989. *The Oxford English Dictionary*. 2nd ed. Oxford: Clarendon Press.

Stanley-Wrench, S., tr. 1965. *Troilus and Criseyde by Geoffrey Chaucer*. London: Centaur Press Ltd.

Sweetser, E. E. 1990. *From Etymology to Pragmatics: Metaphorical and Cultural Aspects of Semantic Structure*. Cambridge: Cambridge University Press.

Tatlock, S. P. & P. MacKaye, trs. 1912. *The Complete Poetical Works of Geoffrey Chaucer: Now First Put into Modern English.* London: Macmillan.

Traugott, E. C. 1989. 'On the Rise of Epistemic Meanings in English: An Example in Subjectification in Semantic Change'. *Language* 65 (1): 31-51.

Windeatt, B. A., ed. 1984. *Geoffrey Chaucer Troilus and Criseyde—A New Edition of 'The Book of Troilus'*. London: Longman.

———, tr. 1998. *Geoffrey Chaucer Troilus and Criseyde: A New Translation*. Oxford & New York: Oxford University Press.

The Function of Word Classes and the Import of French in Middle English Poetry: A Comparative Study of *The Romaunt of the Rose*-A and *Le Roman de la Rose*

Sadahiro Kumamoto

1. Introduction

The main aim of this paper is to describe the function of word classes as rhyme words in the ME translation text *The Romaunt of the Rose* (the A-fragment in particular), in comparison with its OF original text, *Le Roman de la Rose*. Because the rhyme position is a significant location where various distinctive features of the vocabulary in either text are seen, our investigation of rhyme words will provide a clue for looking into some questions about the vocabulary of ME. In this regard, we may discover how and to what extent the native and Romance vocabularies were interrelated at that time, how the two kinds of vocabulary functioned in literary works (especially poetical works), how French words had actually been imported into English, and so on. Another aim of this paper is therefore to present an actual historic case revealing one specific process by which French words have been imported into ME. First, a general survey of the ingredients of rhyme words will be made according to word classes, and, next, each word class will be examined in detail.[1]

The French text (*Rn*) and the English text (*Rt*) display fairly different proportions of word classes with respect to their rhyme words: [*Rn*] n. 664

---

[1] The French text used in the present paper is Langlois's (1914-24) edition, and the English text is A. David's edition included in Benson (1989:686-767).

(39.8%), adj. 241 (14.4%), v. 664 (39.8%), adv. 79 (4.7%), pron. 11 (0.7%), prep. 0, broken rhymes 11 (0.7%); [*Rt*] n. 675 (39.6%), adj. 186 (10.9%), v. 445 (26.1%), adv. 274 (16.1%), pron. 108 (6.3%), prep. 9 (0.5%), broken rhymes 6 (0.4%) (note: 'broken rhyme' is the rhyme comprising two words as a rhyme factor like *countenaunces : daunce is*). These figures show that nouns appear at almost the same rate in the two texts, showing a high frequency; the prominence of verbs is characteristic of the French text; adverbs and pronouns appear in quite different proportions in the two texts, both word classes occurring far more frequently in the English text. We shall take a closer look at each word class in the following.

2. Nouns

The nouns used as rhyme words in the two texts are diverse in their forms. Still, there are certain endings of nouns available for rhyming in both texts, though the lexical forms of nouns are so various that the use of such endings does not typically come to the reader's attention. The endings noticeable in the French text are: *-ance*, *-ure*, *-ie*, *-iaus*, *-té* (*acointance*, *acordance*, *bienvoillance*; *ardure*, *aventure*, *ceinture*; *baillie*, *compaignie*, *cortoisie*; *chevriaus*, *combiaus*, *damoisiaus*; *biauté*, *clarté*, *delitableté*).

The variety of specific ending-types is not as great in the English text as in the French text, because many native nouns take part in the rhyme stock. Be that as it may, Romance nouns account for more than half of the nouns in the rhyme position in the English text (R = Romance nouns, E = native nouns): R 401 (59.4%), E 262 (38.8%), Others 12 (1.8%). Approximately half of the translator's Romance nouns are borrowed from the original text (208/51.9%), while the other half are used as substitutes, in paraphrases and as additions (respectively, 79/19.7%, 50/12.5% and 64/16.0%). One of the reasons for the high frequency of borrowed nouns is that they are often imported as rhyme pairs: *age/corage*, *envie/Pavie*, *flowtours/jogelours*, *semblaunce/remembraunce*, *moysoun/sesoun*, etc. Of the 208 borrowings, 78 are borrowed in this way.[2]

[2] Geissman (1952:161) says that the translator's tendency is 'wherever possible, to preserve the original rime in his translation'. This remark seems true of the translator's manner of borrowing such paired nouns, but his attitude shows different inclinations on several occasions.

The nouns borrowed from the French text, whether as pairs or not, give the English text a rhyming tone common to the two texts: [-*ure*] *creature*, *coverture*, *peyntures*, etc.; [-*ye*] *envye*, *curtesye*, *felonye*, etc.; [-*oun*] *gounfanoun*, *moysoun*, *foisoun*, etc.; [-*aunce*] *semblaunce*, *signyfiaunce*, *countenaunce*, etc.; [-*te*] *beaute*, *bounte*, *crueltee*, etc. Some of these borrowed nouns are cited as the earliest instances in the *OED* and the *MED* (the figure in parentheses denotes the line number): *jagounces* (< *jagonces* 1117), *chevesaille* (< *cheveçaille* 1081), *moysoun* (< *moison* 1677).[3] The Romance nouns in the original text are sometimes imported into the English text with the native suffix -*ing* added: *disseyvyng* (< inf. n. *decevoir* 1590), *praiyng* (< inf. n. *preier* 1484), *karolyng* (< *querole* 804), *refreynynge* (< *refraiz* 749). The *refreynynge* of line 749 is the only citation in the *OED* and the *MED*. By examining those words imported into the English text which are the first instances in the two dictionaries, with or without modification in form, we may be able to catch a glimpse of the circumstances under which French words actually participated in the English vocabulary at the time.

The Romance nouns used as substitutes, in paraphrases, or as additions also indicate, to a certain extent, a tendency similar to the borrowed nouns with respect to their endings. That is, the nouns with the ending -*oun*, -*our* and -*age* are particularly often encountered in the three cases: (as substitutes) *portreiture*, *chyvalrie*, *countenaunces*, *jolite*, *quystroun*, *langour*, *outrage*, etc.; (in paraphrases) *mysaventure*, *curtesie*, *myschaunce*, *relygioun*, *colour*, *passage*, etc.; (as additions) *norture*, *masonrye*, *proporcioun*, *valour*, *rage*, etc. We also find here the Romance nouns in -*ing* that are cited as the first instances in the *OED* and the *MED*: *jargonyng* (< *serventois* 716) (as a substitute), *myscounting* (< v. *mesconter* 196) (in a paraphrase), *ribanynges* (1077) (as an addition), etc.

The native nouns used in the rhyme position do not present the same degree of conspicuous identifying features in their forms as the Romance nouns. A variety in forms of word-stems is one of the characteristics of the

---

[3] If we accept the year 1366 as that of the production of the *Romaunt*-A, as is generally recognized in Chaucer scholarship, the noun *moysoun* (< *moison*) is also taken as the earliest instance even in the *MED* (s.v. *moisoun* n.). As Rothwell says repeatedly in his article (1998) on French loans in ME, the first citation of a word in the *OED* and the *MED* does not necessarily signify the first appearance of the word in English. It must be admitted, however, that the date of the first citation may be close to that of the word's entry into English. Cf. also J. de Caluwé-Dor (1983).

native nouns even in the rhyme position. As for the endings, the nouns in *-ing*, *-nesse*, *-ight*, etc., especially those in *-ing*, display a tendency to be used to fulfill the requirement of rhyme: *syngyng*, *lykyng*, *shadowing*, *gladnesse*, *worthynesse*, *wight*, *myght*, etc.

3. Adjectives

The lexical relationship of adjectives between the two texts is similar to that of nouns. Some lexical forms show a comparatively strong tendency to recur in the rhyme position in both texts; for instance, the adjectives in *-eus* and *-able* in the original text, and those in *-ous* and *-able* in the translation. What seems interesting here is that there is a difference in the proportions of the two forms between the two texts. The adjectives in *-ous* are more often used in the translation than the adjectives in *-eus* in the original text, while the adjectives in *-able* show the opposite tendency.

Some examples from the original text are: *amoreus*, *angoisseus*, *bocereus*, *amiable*, *covenable*, *delitable*, etc. In the translation text, the proportion of Romance and native adjectives is different from that of Romance and native nouns: R 70 (37.6%), E 113 (60.8%), Others 3 (1.6%). More than half of the seventy Romance adjectives are borrowings from the original text (40/57.1%), and the rest are shared by substitutes (16/22.9%), paraphrases (5/7.1%) and additions (9/12.9%). The percentage of the adjectives which are imported into the English text by borrowing the original rhyme pairs is slightly higher than that of the nouns (16/40 = 40.0%). Examples are: *egre/megre*, *jolyf/ententyf*, *pers/dyvers*, *resonable/stable*, etc.

The adjectives borrowed from the original text feature the endings *-ous* and *-able*: *envyous*, *curyous*, *outrageous*, *resemblable*, *resonable*, *dilectable*, etc. The adjective *curyous* (< *curieus* 1052) is cited as the first instance in the sense of 'anxious, concerned, solicitous' in the *OED* (s.v. *curious* a. 1. b), and also in the *MED* in the sense of 'solicitous, concerned' (s.v. *curious* adj. 1. (c)) if we accept the generally recognized year of the work's production, 1366. On the other hand, in the case of substitutes, paraphrases and additions, the translator often resorts to the Romance adjectives in *-ous*, but, strangely enough, those ending in *-able* are not found at all: *dispitous*, *daungerous*, *outrageous*, *delytous*, etc. Among these Romance adjectives used as substitutes and others, *roynous* (988) and *volage* (1284) are the first instances in the *OED* (s.v. *roinous* a., and *volage* a.), and also in the *MED* according to the accepted year of the poem's production, 1366 (s.v. *roinous(e* adj. (b), and *volage* adj. (a)).[4]

In the English text, adjectives are syntactically available to be used in the rhyme position in two ways; as a post-modifier, and as a supplementary epithet connected by the conjunction *and* (as a kind of hendiadys). The translator has often used such adjectival styles, with native adjectives in particular, to create additional rhyming elements which are not found in the original text. Among various native adjectives thus employed, those ending in *-ight(e)* are of frequent occurrence: (as a post-modifier) *the stoon so bright* (1088), *his bemys brighte* (1574), *with wawis brighte* (1561), *with braunches grene* (1511), *ful of stones shene* (127), etc.; (as a supplementary epithet with *and*) *so amiable and free* (1226), *so queynt his robe and faire* (65), *so clere was and so bright* (1121), *hertes grey and lyght* (32), etc. Such an adjectival usage is especially often met with in the English text, particularly with native adjectives. This usage demonstrates one of the functions of the native adjectives in English rhymed verse.

The translator's manner of using his native adjectives as equivalents to the original adjectives shows another important function of that word class in the rhymed lines. Adjectives are generally broader in their semantic range than other word classes, and the translator enjoys this advantage in employing his native adjectives which should correspond to the original adjectives: *free* (corr. to F. *genz*, *douz*, *franches*, *delivres*), *bright* (corr. to F. *serin*, *blonz*, *cler e luisant*), *swete* (corr. to F. *savoree*, *saine*, *douce*). Such a semantic advantage of adjectives as observed here would be possibly used

---

[4] The contemporary currency of French words may influence the translator's decision as to whether he should import the words in the original text directly into his translation or replace them with other words. Romance words in *-able* and *-age* offer one example. They respectively appear eleven and twenty-two times in the original text, and eight and twenty-four times in the translation. The original words *fable*, *table*, *delitable*, *estable*, *raisnable* and *resemblables* are directly imported into the translation, but *amiable*, *covenables*, *piteable* and *esperitables* are not, though *amiable* and *covenables* had already entered the English language in 1350 and 1340 according to the *OED*. The adjective *piteable* appeared later, in 1456, and English never adopted *esperitables*. Likewise, the words in *-age*, such as *aage*, *corage*, *image*, *lignage*, *outrage*, *rage*, *usage* and *visage*, are imported into the translation, but *paage*, *enrage*, *ombrage*, *sage* (adj.) and *cuvertage* are not. According to the *OED*, the adjective *sage* entered English in 1297, and nouns *paage*, *enrage* and *ombrage* in 1456, 1502 and 1647 respectively.

not only in translations but generally in rhyming poetry.

4. Verbs

The verbs used as rhyme words in the two texts reveal quite different aspects of usage. The difference is mainly due to the dissimilarity of the inflectional forms of French and English verbs. Many inflectional endings of French verbs can work as rhyme elements in the original text, but in the translation the inflectional ending *-ing* is the only one that can serve for rhyming—the inflections *-ed* and *-eth*/*-ith* being unable to serve for that purpose on account of their weak accentuation. In the English text, consequently, word stems must be exploited as rhyme elements, whether they are inflected or not. Such a distinctive feature decisively affects not only the overall frequency of verbs in rhyme (*Rn* 674; *Rt* 450), but also the structure of rhymes made by verbs in the two texts.

Most of the verbs used as rhyme words in the French text make use of their inflectional endings as rhyme elements, rhyming with each other or with other word classes: [*-er*] *aesmer*, *afubler*, *aporter*, etc.; [*-ier*] *acrochier*, *afaitier*, *apetisier*, etc.; [*-ir*] *deservir*, *enhastir*, *jaunir*, etc.; [*-ai*] *abaissai*, *arestai*, *escoutai*, etc.; [*-oit*] *anuitoit*, *bevroit*, *chantoit*, etc.; [*-oient*] *abatoient*, *chantoient*, *entrejetoient*, etc.; [*-ist*] *crainsist*, *morist*, *traisist*, etc.; [*-ant*] *agaitant*, *arestant*, *escoutant*, etc.; [*-(i)ee*] *apelee*, *coloree*, *desciriee*, etc.

In the translation text on the other hand, the verbs standing at the end of the line, both of Romance and native origins, make rhymes with their own stems, except for some instances in which the pr. ppl. ending *-ing* is made use of. With native verbs in particular, as a necessary result, their inflected stems are exploited to the fullest extent as rhyme elements by the translator. In consequence, there is a much higher frequency of native verbs than Romance ones for rhyming: R 72 (16.2%), E 345 (77.5%), Others 28 (6.3%). Approximately half of the 72 Romance verbs are borrowed from the original text—almost the same ratio as in the case of Romance nouns and adjectives. When the original verbs are borrowed, their inflectional endings are changed into English endings which are unavailable for rhyming. What interests us is that some of the Romance verbs thus imported into the translation are cited as the earliest instances in the *OED* and the *MED*: *anoynten* (1057), *enbatailled* (139), *bytrasshed* (1520), *costeying* (134), etc.[5]

Even among the Romance verbs which are not borrowings, we find some cited as the earliest instances in the *OED* and the *MED*: *poynten* (1058), *fyned* (1696), *ameled* (1080), *tasseled* (1079), etc.[6] The verbs *tasseled* and *ameled* in the following lines, the former used as an addition and the latter in a paraphrase, may have first appeared in English as a rhyme pair (the original lines are given on the right):

And with a bend of gold *tasseled*,	D'une bande d'or neelee
And knoppis fyne of gold *ameled*.	A esmaus fu au col orlee (1061-2)
(1079-80)	

One of the most salient features of the verbs used as rhyme words in the translation is, as mentioned above, the use of the inflected stem forms of native verbs. A great variety of them are made use of as rhyme elements and consequently promote the frequency of native verbs in the rhyme position: *wrought*, *wente*, *took*, *herde*, *tolde*, *left*, *mette*, *hyghte*, *torn*, *fond*, etc. The verb 'to be' also has several inflected forms of its own, which are prominent in frequency: *be* (33), *ben* (5), *bene* (1), *is* (13), *was* (2), *were* (15), *wane* (1). Another native verb which the translator resorts to is *se(e)*, which appears 22 times. The reason for the prominent frequency of the verb forms *be* and *se(e)* lies in that they can rhyme with each other, and moreover with the pronouns *he*, *she* and *me*. The verb form *be* is also used in correspondence with various forms of the French verb *estre*, such as *estre*, *est*, *fu*, *fusse*, *soit*, *seroie*, *soie*, *esté*. The verb form *se(e)* similarly substitutes for various forms of original verbs of perception, such as *trueve*, *regarder*, *regardoit*, *veoir*, *veianz*, *voie*, *voient*, *veïsse*, *veïssiez*.

Another reason for the high frequency of the form *se(e)* lies in its occurrence, in an infinitival form with *(for) to*, as a supplement to an adjective at the end of the line: *smal to se* (1017), *bright to see* (1084), *fair to see* (644), *semely for to see* (586), *the alther-fairest folk to see* (625), etc.

---

[5] Cf. the *OED*: *embattled* ppl.a. 1., *betraise, -traish* v. 4. ('To reveal, disclose incidentally') and *coast* v. 3. ('To proceed or travel by the coast of (sea, lake, river)'), and cf. also the *MED*: *enointen* v. 2. (c), *embatailled* adj., *bitraishen* v. 2. (a), and *costeien* v. 1. (a).

[6] Cf. the *OED*: *point* v.[1] I. 1, *fine* v.[3] 3. ('To make beautiful, handsome, or elegant'), *ameled* ppl. a. and *tassel* v. 1; and cf. also the *MED*: *pointen* v. (1) 1a. (a), *finen* v. (3) 3. (a) ('To make (something) beautiful, embellish'), *ameled* ppl. and *tasselen* v.

Such a supplementary use of the verb of visual perception after an adjective is often met with in the translation, but never in the original text. This manner of rhyming may originate in English poetry as a result of the availability of the verb form's /e:/ sound for rhyming (cf. the section of 'Pronouns' below). Another verb of perception, *here*, is employed only once in the same manner in the translation: *a wondir thing to here* (1114). The original text gives just one example of the verb *oïr* employed likewise: *Mout estoit bele l'acordance De lor piteus chant a oïr* (485) (the *a oïr* is connected to the adjective *bele*).

5. Adverbs

The first thing to be noted regarding the use of adverbs as rhyme words in the two texts is the difference in frequency (*Rn* 79; *Rt* 274). Two reasons may be offered for this difference; the difference in the number of word-types of adverbs in the two texts, and the tendency to use certain adverbs in a repetitive way in the translation. 64 types of adverbs are used as rhyme words in the original text, compared to 115 types in the translation. The proportion of adverbs in *-ment* in the original text is higher than that of adverbs in *-ly* in the translation; *-ment* 25/79 (31.6%), *-ly* 51/274 (18.6%). On the other hand, in the translation text, adverbs of intensity, affirmation, place and time, mostly of the native origin and without the *-ly* suffix, particularly contribute to the lexical variety of adverbs. Some of them are repeated frequently: *so* (9), *also* (9), *iwys* (21), *well* (18), *everydell* (6), *ay* (6), *tho* (7), *aboute* (7), *by* (5), *there/ther* (14), *withalle* (7), *eke/eek* (5), etc.[7] The result is the translator's heavy reliance on native words when he resorts to adverbs for rhyme: R 32 (11.7%), E 230 (83.9%), Others 12 (4.4%).

25 of the 32 examples of Romance adverbs are hybrid adverbs composed by a Romance stem and the native suffix *-ly*. By contrast, only four of the 32 Romance adverbs are borrowed from the original text, all of which bear the

[7] Pointing out the tendency to repeat certain words for rhyming in ME poetry, Borroff says: 'In Middle English verse, the traditional words, when used again and again in the same way and for the same purpose, seem dragged in "for the sake of the rhyme"; repetition becomes tiresome, and simplicity seems merely flatfooted. There is an additional danger for the Middle English poet in the form of an inherited body of expressions, suitable for use in rhyme, which are general and adaptable in meaning and thus can suggest themselves all too readily for use in filling out the lines when

suffix *-ly*, corresponding to the *-ment* of the original adverbs: *covertly* (< *covertement*), *queyntely* (< *cointement*), *comunly* (< *comunement*), *sotylly* (< *soutilment*). In both texts the suffixes serve as rhyme elements. The other 28 Romance adverbs are the translator's own used as substitutes (12), in paraphrases (6) and as additions (10), most of which also bear the suffix *-ly*. As for the translator's native adverbs, on the other hand, those with the suffix *-ly* are very few in number; 20 out of 230 examples (8.7%).

Geissman comments on the translator's manner of rendition of the original adverbs *mout* and *bien* that 'Chaucer, if he translates the words at all, almost always uses the adverb *ful*'.[8] However, they are often rendered into *well*, too, or into *right* or *parfitly* on some occasions, to stand in the rhyme position. While the French adverbs *mout* and *bien* appear unobtrusively in the interior of the original lines, the translator's adverbs *well*, *right* and *parfitly*, substituting for them, chime as rhyme words at the end of the lines:

There were, and that wot I full *well*, Of pome-garnettys a ful gret dell; (1355-6)	Pomiers i ot, *bien* m'en sovient, Qui charjoient pomes grenades: (1330-1)

The tendency to use such emphatic adverbs, including intensive and affirmative ones as already mentioned, is one of the characteristics of the English lines. It produces a kind of enhanced tone that is peculiar to the English.

6. Pronouns

As for pronouns, the difference in frequency particularly catches our attention: *Rn* 11; *Rt* 108. This is caused by the repetitive use of certain pronouns in the English text, rather than by any difference in lexical variety of this word class in French and English.

The distinctive structural feature of the rhyming pronouns in the French text is the use of the ending *-ui* or *-oi*: *lui*, *celui*, *soi*, etc. The word *neant*/*neient* also contributes to the frequency of pronouns in the rhyme position. The unstressed pronouns *il*, *ele*, *nos*, *vos*, etc. are never used as rhyme words.

---

inspiration flags' (Borroff 1998:232).

[8] Geissman (1952:182).

The 108 examples of pronouns in the translation text, all of which are of the native origin, are distributed as follows: 43 times (39.8%) as substitutes, 25 times (23.1%) in paraphrases, 40 times (37.0%) as additions. The 43 examples of substitutes are chiefly used to correspond to the pronouns *ele*, *il*, *me*, etc. which appear in the interior of the line in the original text. The employment of *ele* and its equivalent *she* in the next lines typically show the difference of the function of the word class in the two texts:

So for envie brenned *she* Whan she myght any man se (297-8)	Qu'*ele* fondoit d'ire ardoit Quant aucuns qu'ele regardoit (287-8)

Most of the 40 examples of additions in the translation are used to restore the pronouns which the original text has abbreviated out of existence:

A sorowful thyng wel semed *she*, Nor she hadde nothyng slowe be (321-2)	Mout sembloit bien estre dolente, Car el n'avoit pas esté lente (313-4)

The main reason for the convenience of using a pronoun in the rhyme position in the English text is the phonic value of the /e:/ carried by *she*, *he* and *me*. The long vowel of these personal pronouns makes it possible for them to rhyme with each other, with the verbs *be* and *see*, with the Romance nouns in *-te*, and so on: *she* (26), *he* (9), *me* (23).[9] Additionally, the ability of the personal pronoun *I* to rhyme with adverbs in *-ly*, and that of the demonstrative pronoun *this* to rhyme with the adverb *ywis* increase the number of instances of rhyming pronouns. For instance, we find *I* occurring nine times, and *this* ten times throughout the text.

7. Prepositions

Prepositions do not function as rhyme words in the French text, but serve that purpose nine times in the translation. Needless to say, the instances are all of native words: *to* (3), *by* (3), *among* (2), *aboute* (1). They appear once

---

[9] On the pronouns in rhyme in Chaucer's poems, Masui says: 'The personal pronouns like "me, he, she" are extremely frequently used at the end of the line. The reason is not far to seek. It is that Chaucer or any medieval poet could make an ending of a word rime with, against the modern tendency of versification, any word or any ending of a word which has the same quality of pronunciation as the former' (Masui 1964:46-7).

as a substitute, five times in a paraphrase, and three times as an addition. The following lines, as in the case of pronouns, demonstrate the difference of the function of prepositions in the two texts. The preposition *by* in rhyme in the translation corresponds to the preposition *delez* appearing at the beginning of the original line:

A mantyl heng hir faste *by*, (: beggarly)
Upon a perche, weik and small;
(224-5)

Delez li pendoit uns mantiaus
A une perchete graillete,
(212-3)

The prepositional phrase *hem among* in rhyme in the following lines does not have its equivalent in the original lines:

That songen for to wynne hem prys,
And eke to sormounte in her song
That other briddes *hem among*. (666-8)

Qui beoient a sormonter
Ces autres oisiaus par chanter;
(655-6)

These above lines, together with the previously cited lines, well indicate the rhyming function of prepositions in English.

8. Rhyme Pairs

Finally the general picture of the rhyme pairs which the six word classes make in the two texts is given (the figures in parentheses indicate the percentage):

	n:n	n:adj	n:v	n:adv	adj:adj	adj:v	adj:adv
Rn	202 (24.2)	101 (12.1)	128 (15.3)	36 (4.3)	41 (4.9)	45 (5.4)	5 (0.6)
Rt	189 (22.2)	73 (8.6)	128 (15.1)	69 (8.1)	25 (2.9)	31 (3.6)	22 (2.6)

	v:v	v:adv	adv: adv	n:pron	adj: pron	v:pron	adv: pron	n:prep
Rn	243 (29.1)	12 (1.4)	13 (1.6)	3 (0.4)	0	6 (0.7)	0	0
Rt	91 (10.7)	57 (6.7)	46 (5.4)	39 (4.6)	4 (0.5)	36 (4.2)	26 (3.1)	2 (0.2)

	v:prep	adv:prep	pron:pron	pron:prep	Total
Rn	0	0	1 (0.1)	0	835 (100)
Rt	3 (0.4)	1 (0.1)	6 (0.7)	2 (0.2)	850 (100)

As we can see from these figures, the types of rhyme pairs are not as varied in the original text as in the translation. In the original text, four types of combinations—n:n (202), n:adj (101), n:v (128), v:v (243)—account for 80.7% of the whole. The figure is much higher than that of 56.6% which is accounted for by the same four types in the translation. The rhyme pairs comprising verbs, adverbs and pronouns display especially distinct differences in both frequency and variety of combinations.

9. Conclusion

Some conclusions will be proposed by the statistics and examples presented in the foregoing pages. In the case of nouns and adjectives, the translator often uses French words in *-oun*, *-ye*, *-aunce*, *-ous*, *-able*, etc. to create the rhymes yielding a rather 'French' tone. Therefore such nominal and adjectival rhymes are often commonly held in both texts. The two texts, however, differ widely when it comes to the rhymes involving verbs, adverbs and pronouns, which serve to make distinctly English rhymes in the translation text. The differences in rhymes involving verbs are due to the distinctly different inflectional forms of French and English verbs; the former change their endings, and the latter their stems. The abundance and the syntactic flexibility of English adverbs serve to make them characteristic as rhyme words in the translation. Meanwhile, the vigorous use of pronouns in the rhyme position is entirely confined to the English text. This is most often due to the coincidence of the sound of the final vowel in some English personal pronouns (*he*, *she* and *me*), two English verb forms (*be* and *see*) and several Romance nouns ending in *-(t)e*. Certain adverbial rhymes, especially those involving intensive adverbs, conjure a heightened emotional mood and aesthetic tone which is almost unique to the English text.

The comparison made in the present paper between the French and the English texts goes some way, I hope, towards revealing some significant aspects of the function of word classes in ME poetry, and suggesting the manner by which a number of French words may have made their way into the English language. The extension of this comparative perspective to other OF and ME poems would contribute further to the elucidation of the formation and development of ME rhymed verse, and more generally of an aspect of the actual circumstances of the vocabulary of ME as well.

References

Benson, L. D., gen. ed. 1989. *The Riverside Chaucer*. Oxford: Oxford University Press.

Borroff, M. 1998. 'Chaucer's English Rhymes: The *Roman*, the *Romaunt*, and *The Book of the Duchess*'. *Words and Works: Studies in Medieval English Language and Literature in Honour of Fred C. Robinson*, ed. P. S. Baker & N. Howe. Toronto, Buffalo, London: University of Toronto Press. 223-42.

de Caluwé-Dor, J. 1983. 'Chaucer's Contribution to the English Vocabulary: A Chronological Survey of French Loan-Words'. *North-Western European Language Evolution* 2:73-91.

Geissman, E. W. 1952. 'The Style and Technique of Chaucer's Translations from French'. PhD dissertation, Yale University.

Langlois, E., ed. 1914-24. *Le Roman de la Rose par Guillaume de Lorris et Jean de Meun, publié d'après les manuscrits*. Paris: Librairie Ancienne Edouard Champion.

Masui, M. 1964. *The Structure of Chaucer's Rime Words: An Exploration into the Poetic Language of Chaucer*. Tokyo: Kenkyusha.

Rothwell, W. 1998. 'Arrivals and Departures: The Adoption of French Terminology into English'. *English Studies* 79:144-65.

Fifteenth-Century Rhythmical Changes

Thomas Cable

1. Introduction

Histories of the English language recognize the fifteenth century as a period of phenomenal change, perhaps most obviously in the beginnings and development of the Great Vowel Shift but in other aspects as well. The loss of final *-e* during this period is almost equally familiar—in some ways too familiar, because as a fact of the changing language it is often assumed by modern scholars as something we all know and take for granted, something to get beyond to other more interesting topics. The argument of the present essay is that scholarship of the past half century has not paid sufficient attention to what we collectively know about the loss of *-e* in the fifteenth century; furthermore, this inattention has caused a general misreading of the century's most prominent poet, John Lydgate.

The misreading of Lydgate in turn has caused a misunderstanding of the prosody of the poets who followed Lydgate later in the fifteenth century and in the early sixteenth century, including Thomas Hoccleve, Alexander Barclay, and Stephen Hawes. A new appreciation of these poets is not an especially urgent aim in itself, because their work is indisputably mediocre. However, they are the crucial links in the story of English prosody between Geoffrey Chaucer and the brilliant flowering of the Elizabethans.

Actually, the misunderstanding, or the current amnesia, begins with reading Chaucer, because the general grasp of his metre too has deteriorated during the past fifty years. A useful contrast might be drawn with the scholarly situation in another aspect of the changing language during the ME period, the syntax. Tajima (1985) was able to draw on published sources of materials by O. Jespersen, T. Mustanoja, T. Visser, and others. Yet he found that none of these monumental works nor smaller specialized studies presented an adequate analysis of the verbal aspects of the gerund. Tajima had to cover the ground himself for nearly 200 texts composed between 1100 and 1500, and from this survey he arrived at the original conclusions of his important work.

2. Geoffrey Chaucer (ca. 1343-1400)

The situation is strikingly different in the phonology of final *-e* and the metrical analyses that depend on it. Nearly everything we need to know about the phonology and the metrical practices of Chaucer, Lydgate, Hoccleve, Barclay, and Hawes, had been said by 1940. The problem was not in the analysis of the prosodical practice of individual poets but in the lack of a coherent narrative that tied the technical analyses together and gave them some kind of broader interest. Thus, ten Brink (1901) was really quite correct in all his comments on Chaucer except his quirky disallowance of headless lines. Standing alone in its rather stuffy way, however, his work has been an easy target for later metrists like Gaylord (1976), who wittily describes ten Brink's system as quaint and old-fashioned without naming specific errors in it: 'The effect is like examining some bulky engine in a museum, once designed, we are told, to perform some useful task, but whose precise function and workings are now obscure' (p. 32).

Halle & Keyser (1966) produced a much sleeker piece of technology driven by the Stress Maximum Principle. Numerous studies over the years have pointed out empirical and theoretical problems in this original model of generative metrics as well as problems in the inferences about Chaucer's phonology drawn from it, Chaucer being the first poet to whom the theory was applied. The main empirical problem is that all versions of generative metrics using the Halle-Keyser Stress Maximum Principle are too lax: most of Chaucer's metrical patterns can be described by the theory, but so can much ordinary prose.

Paul Kiparsky's Monosyllabic Word Constraint tightened the filter and allowed fewer unmetrical lines (Kiparsky 1975 & 1977); however, in importing syntactic description into the metre, it inappropriately mixed levels of ordinary linguistic description without avoiding the two theoretical problems that have always undermined generative metrics: (1) valuing the Strong position over the Weak position as the locus of metricality and (2) confusing the representation of the line with the line itself. Because the line itself must occur in time, this ontological matter is often vexed by a misapplication of the apparently straightforward distinction between the enduring line and the various performances of the line.

The summary in the last two paragraphs of nearly forty years of debate about generative metrics can only sound dogmatic as stated. Cable (2002) and Youmans & Li (2002) are the most recent exchanges in the debate, and they may be consulted for fuller explanations and arguments on both sides. For present purposes, it suffices to say that few new insights about Chaucer's metre or phonology have come from all this. The main claim in Halle & Keyser (1966) was that ten Brink's idea of two stress rules in Chaucer's language, Germanic and Romance, could be replaced by a single, more adequate Romance rule. Halle & Keyser (1971:102-5) gave up this idea in the face of evidence to the contrary and reverted to an account essentially the same as ten Brink (1901) and Luick (1896). Nearly everything we need to know about Chaucer's phonology had been said by 1940.

The same is true of Chaucer's metre. Several studies between the 1950s and the 1970s, including Southworth (1957) and Robinson (1971), argued against the regularly alternating pattern of stress that most metrists and editors assumed and in favor of a more modern, more natural reading. These extreme interpretations (extreme because of flying in the face of philology and historical linguistics) caused a brief stir and had the effect of prompting some metrists to look for a compromise between artificial stress and natural stress (see Woods 1984). It can now plausibly be argued that Chaucer's stress patterns were at least as artificial as ten Brink described—another return to the *status quo ante* (see Cable 1971 & 2002). However, the repetition of that argument is also not the present topic. We shall assume at the outset a very strict alternation of stress in Chaucer, brought about by a metre with the power to 'tilt' ordinary stress, promoting lightly stressed syllables in ictus positions, demoting heavily stressed syllables in non-ictus positions:

```
/    x / x   / x    / x / x
Whan that Aprill with his shoures soote
```

x / x / x / x / x / x
The droghte of March hath perced to the roote,

x / x / x / x / x /
And bathed every veyne in swich licour

x / x /x / x / x /
Of which vertu engendred is the flour;

x / x/ x / x /x /
Whan Zephirus eek with his sweete breeth . . . (*General Prologue*, 1-5)

It is with this pattern in mind that we now look ahead to interpretations and emulation of Chaucer in the fifteenth century.

3. John Lydgate (ca. 1370-1449)

Older histories such as Saintsbury (1906-10) and (1910) found little good to be said for English prosody of the fifteenth century except for that of the Scottish Chaucerians. For Saintsbury the two southern English poets John Lydgate, who is remembered for his 'broken-backed' lines, and Thomas Hoccleve were both 'struck with metrical palsy or metrical blindness' and 'sheer muddlement', producing 'a cacophony which is not even prosaic' (Saintsbury 1910:162). These assessments are unfair to Lydgate because of problems that scholars had already sorted through more completely for Chaucer but that still vexed Lydgate studies. Spurious works were attributed to Lydgate, and there was a dependence on corrupt texts, including sixteenth-century printed versions. In any light, Lydgate must still be seen as producing much uninspired poetry even at the technical level but some of it, at least, for reasons opposite to the chaos that Saintsbury saw. Lydgate is not so much metrically confused as ploddingly systematic.

In addition to spurious works and corrupt texts, there has been less willingness among prosodists to smooth rough lines with the sounding of historical *-e* in contexts where it is generally assumed for Chaucer and Chaucer's contemporary, John Gower. Saintsbury (1910:52-3), for example, illustrated the 'so-called "Lydgatian" missing syllable at cæsura' with a line from *The Siege of Thebes*:

The high | e hyl | les $_{\wedge}$ | gilt with | his stremes (1254)

However, if Lydgate is permitted a final *-e* on the past participial plural adjective *gilt*, such as Chaucer has in ‘With gilte cheynes on hire nekke hangynge’ (*Monk’s Tale* 2364), then Lydgate’s line is perfectly regular:

x / | x / | x / | x / | x / | x
The highe hylles gilt [-e] with his stremes

Similarly, Saintsbury (1910:52-3) scanned a ‘missing syllable at cæsura’ in a line from *The Temple of Glass* (stanza 16):

That ye | shall have | ^ ful | posses | sion

The occurrence of *-e* on *have* in the English language at the end of the fourteenth century depends on whether it is an infinitive, as here, on its position in the line, and on the usage of individual authors. Chaucer seems to allow disyllabic *have* only at the end of the line, where evidence for the sounding of *-e* is provided by the rhyme words. Gower clearly allows disyllabic *have* within the line when it is an infinitive construed with a modal auxiliary, the syntactic structure in Lydgate’s line:

x / x / x / x / x
What schal I have to my mede? (*Confessio Amantis*, 1554)

Following Gower’s usage, Lydgate’s line is regular:

x / x / x / x / x /
That ye shall have full possession

Even critics who find Lydgate’s metre less ‘disgusting’ than Saintsbury tend to let the broken-backed lines set the pattern and thus not give him the benefit of the doubt. Pearsall (1977:228), an authoritative study drawing on a deep knowledge of Lydgate’s poetry, marks six out of fifteen lines quoted from the *Troy-book* with a slash to show the caesura at the point where metrical stresses come together and the line is broken:

For she of cher / pale was and grene,
And he of colour liche to ashes dede;
And fro hir face was goon / al þe rede,
And in his chekis deuoided was þe blod,
So wofully atwene hem two it stood.
For she ne myȝt / nat a worde speke

And he was redy with deth / to be wreke
Up-on hym silfe, his nakid swerd be-side;
And she ful ofte gan to grounde glide
Out of his armys, as she fel a-swowne,
And he hym silf / gan in teris drowne;
She was as stille and dowmb as any ston,
He had a mouþe, but wordis had he non.
Þe weri spirit flikered in hir breste,
And of deth / stood vnder arreste.
(*Troy-book*, 3.4166-80)

It may be that some or all of these lines had clashing stress in Lydgate's mind. Because of somewhat different but equally vexing uncertainties in Chaucer's practice—especially his use of stress shift within and between words—it is hard to know whether Chaucer heard some of his own lines as broken-backed. However, Shakespeare clearly did, with a metrical pause separating the clashing stresses. Shakespeare used the pattern both in lines of nine syllables (conventionally 'broken-backed') and in lines of ten (conventionally 'trochaic substitution at the caesura'):

/x x / / x / x /
Horrible sight! ^ Now, I see, 'tis true (*Macbeth*, 4.1.122)

x / x / / x x/ x /
For brave Macbeth— ^ well he deserves that name (*Macbeth*, 1.2.16)

The pattern itself is not necessarily objectionable. For Lydgate the problem seems to be that it occurs too often, or inappropriately, or in a syntactically awkward way. Without trying to do away with all broken-backed lines in Lydgate, it should be noted that all six lines that Pearsall marks turn upon words that occur with the buffering syllable in Chaucer, or upon words that have been identified as peculiar—peculiar in a way that would smooth out the line. If Chaucer can use disyllabic *cheere* in:

x / x / x / x / x /x
Hem as he myghte, and cheere good he made
(*Troilus and Criseyde*, 2.1575)

then it is fair to scan Lydgate's first line as perfectly, almost boringly, regular:

```
x    /  x  / x  / x  /  x     / x
For she of chere pale was and grene        (4166)
```

Similarly, Chaucer's use of *face* followed by *was* gives a model for Lydgate's line:

```
  x   /  x   /x  /  x   / x / x
That, sith his face was so disfigured      (Knight's Tale, 1403)

x      / x   / x  /    x   /  x  /x
And fro hir face was goon all þe rede      (4168)
```

Furthermore, if the modal auxiliary *mighte* occurs with *-e* in *Troilus and Criseyde* 1.1082:

```
  x  /  x  / x  /   x  /  x  /
That in his tyme was, or mighte be
```

Then Chaucer's follower might well have sounded it in line 4171:

```
x   /  x  /   x  /  x  /     / x
For she ne myʒt-[e] nat a worde speke
```

Supplying the historical *-e* at the caesura doesn't help the end of the line, where the *-e* on *worde*, though appearing in the manuscript, is not justified historically for that neuter noun.

There is the possibility that Lydgate added an unhistorical *-e* to *worde,* but this complex topic is beyond the scope of the present study. It should be noted that Bergen (1924) discusses at length the possibility of Lydgate's adding 'an *e* to words to which it did not belong etymologically' (p. xxxii); and he considers specifically a disyllabic pronunciation of the key words that occur in the three remaining broken-backed lines above—*deth* (twice) and *silfe.* The topic is vexed. Babcock (1914) finds a diminution in the occurrence of final *-e* over Lydgate's career. Stanley (1989) is more sympathetic than most to Lydgate's broken-backed lines, though in his discussion of some thirty of them he does not pursue as fully as Bergen the possibility of disyllabic pronunciations of words such as *word.* The topic requires further investigation (the assertion above being that we know *nearly* everything we need to know).

4. Stephen Hawes (1475-1511)

To understand the metrical context out of which the glories of Elizabethan poetry grew, it is necessary to have a sense of the metrics of poets in the early sixteenth century, including Stephen Hawes and Alexander Barclay. However, dealing with the prosody of this period can be frustrating. Tillyard (1949) expressed a common opinion when he said of Hawes and Barclay, 'their sense of rhythm appears simply barbaric', and he described what many readers have felt:

> In Hawes and Barclay, too, there is no unifying pattern. If you read one line in a certain way, you will probably find that the next or the next but one cannot be read in that way; and in fact that the only way to read these people's verses is to gabble them breathlessly with the hopeful intention of lighting on four main accents a line (p. 18).

Saintsbury and C. S. Lewis have much the same opinion, and Pyle (1937), in trying to rationalize Barclay's metre seems to give up on Hawes, objecting to the modern linking of the two poets, as though they were pairs like Lydgate and Hoccleve or Wyatt and Surrey.

It will help to keep in mind several features of Hawes's literary heritage and his own language. The scholarly tradition that assigns metrical importance to the complete loss of final *-e* by the sixteenth century remains solid linguistic and literary history. We can assume that Hawes read or misread Chaucer in certain ways that we can make specific. He would probably have given similar readings to Gower, Lydgate, and Hoccleve, all of whom used final *-e*. Although in some superficial elements Hawes's rhythm recalls patterns of the fourteenth-century Alliterative Revival, that older metre was different in more basic ways, which again can be made precise. Finally, the 'caesura' figures prominently in Hawes's handling of unstressed syllables.

For a Chaucerian line such as the following, we can speculate that Hawes would have read eight syllables and four stresses:

x / x / x x / /
How koude I daunce to an harpe smale (*Wife of Bath's Prologue*, 457)

Both the infinitive *daunce* and the noun *harpe* (from OE *hearpe*) would have ended in an *-e* in at least some dialects and some registers of English in

Chaucer's time, including, we may infer, in Chaucer's own poetic voice. Because this syllable would not have occurred in any normal variety of English available to Hawes, the rhythm of a sixteenth-century performance of the line would be completely changed from its original rhythm. Not only is the line shorter but the trisyllabic pattern in the second half of the line (whether or not a trisyllabic foot) causes the line to break into two hemistichs. This hemistichic or half-line structure is indicated more or less regularly in the early editions by a mark of punctuation, a short oblique line.

Hawes's likely misreading of lines such as 'How could I daunce to an harpe smale' would lead him to compose many of his own lines in *The Pastime of Pleasure* with four stresses and a medial break:

```
 x  /  x  /        x   x     /  x /
So for to daunce / with my swete lady      (Pastime, 1589)
```

Throughout his poetry Hawes often shifts the stress, as in *lady*, for the sake of rhyme. By any scansion, only four stresses are plausible.

A similar effect is clear in a line such as this from the Knight's portrait as it might have been read by Hawes:

```
 x    /  x  /     x  x  /  x  /
That fro the tyme that he first bigan      (General Prologue, 44)
```

Notice that omitting *-e* on *tyme* does more than simply reduce the count of syllables. It makes stress on *that* much less likely than in the reading that was almost certainly Chaucer's own:

```
 x    /  x  /x  /  x  /   x  /
That fro the tyme that he first bigan
```

With the loss of stress on *that* the line divides naturally into two hemistichs:

```
 x    /  x  /      x  x  /  x  /
That fro the tyme / that he first bigan
```

It is this hemistichic reading that Lewis (1938) finds throughout Hawes, Barclay, and other writers of the 'fifteenth-century heroic line'. Lewis devises a clever rabbit-or-duck experiment to argue that all the lines in these poems should be read one way or the other: with five stresses and no structural caesura, or with four stresses and a caesura that amounts to a short-line break. The idea is that once a reader is in the mode of perceiving either a rabbit or a duck, all the lines will conform to the determinate mode. (Lewis opts for the four-stress reading, and he persuasively disavows the term 'caesura'.)

Each of Lewis's examples has its own clear rhythm. He quotes the following stanza from A. C. Swinburne's 'The Triumph of Time':

> I have given no man of my fruit to eat,
>   I trod the grapes, I have drunken the wine.
> Had you eaten and drunken and found it sweet,
>   This wild new growth of the corn and vine.

and he follows it with his own construction:

> I comfort few and many I torment,
> Where one is spared a thousand more are spent;
> I have trodden many down beneath my feet,
> I have given no man of my fruit to eat.

Lewis then says: 'I conjecture that you have read the last line of my second example differently from the opening line of my first' (p. 32).

Presumably, although Lewis does not scan the lines for us, the line in the first stanza would have the pattern:

```
x  x   /x  x    /  x  x  /  x  /
I have given no man of my fruit to eat
```

and in the second:

```
x  x   /x    /  x  /  x   /  x  /
I have given no man of my fruit to eat
```

While these examples are persuasive for showing how twentieth-century readers make lines conform to expectations, it is not at all clear that Hawes and his readers in the early sixteenth century would lock consistently into a four-stress reading—or into a five-stress reading. What is curious about the poetry of this transitional period is that the pattern often seems to change in the middle of a stanza. Consider a stanza, such as this one from *The Pastime of Pleasure,* that begins ambiguously with a line that could be either four-stress with a trisyllabic pattern or five-stress; followed by two lines that are almost certainly four-stress; then an ambiguous fourth line; a fifth line that could be scanned several ways though most likely with four stresses; a sixth line that could have either four or five stresses; and finally a concluding line that is almost certainly five-stress:

x / x x / or
x / x / / x / x /
Ha ha quod he / loue doth you so prycke

x / x / x / x x /x
That yet your herte / wyll nothynge be eased

x /x / x /xx /
But euermore / be feble and syke

x / x /x x x / x /x
Tyll that our lady / hath it well appesed

x x / / x / x x /x
Thoughe ye thynke longe / yet ye shall be pleased

x x / x x/ or
x / x / x / x / x/
I wolde quod I / that it were as ye saye

x / x / x / x / x /
Fye fye quod he / dryue suche dyspayre awaye

One can understand the frustrations of Saintsbury, Tillyard, Lewis, and other modern readers in sorting through the shifting metre and uncertainties of a stanza such as this.

However, if we take into account the difference between *sightreading* a stanza and reading a stanza that is familiar through practice, then the rhythmic shifts themselves are not unpleasing—only the irritation of being thwarted: being led down a 'garden path' that reveals itself halfway through the line as wrong, causing a false start and necessitating a second try. We can speculate that this trial-and-error way was how Hawes read Chaucer and Lydgate. Similarly, we can speculate that Hawes himself knew how he wanted his lines to go, and, were he reading them aloud, the shifting rhythms would not be aesthetically offensive.

Because the four-stress and five-stress readings are often referred to two grand traditions in English metre—strong-stress and syllable-stress respectively—it is important to say that such a bifurcation has certain problems. The four-stress hemistichic reading of Hawes's line does not belong with the eighth-century metre of *Beowulf* or with the fourteenth-century metre of *Piers Plowman* for reasons that bring into question some of the familiar generalizations of the handbooks and anthology introductions, to which we now turn in conclusion.

5. Implications

The uncertainties of metre and the lack of regular iambic pentameter in Hawes's poetry have exasperated many readers. It is interesting that some of these same metrical features of roughness have been valued in the poetry of Sir Thomas Wyatt two decades later and in John Donne's poetry three-quarters of a century after Wyatt—two poets, of course, of greater art than Hawes. If modern readers find much that is appealing in the speaking voice of Wyatt (leaving aside Donne, whose metre is clearly a form of iambic pentameter), it is worth asking whether poets of subsequent centuries have drawn upon similar metrical resources.

To get at an answer, it is necessary to state one of the overarching generalizations of English historical metrics and try to say what parts are right about it and what parts have been superseded by recent scholarship. The generalization was stated succinctly and persuasively in two classic essays, over a limited chronology by Lewis (1938) and more sweepingly by Wimsatt & Beardsley (1959). The main idea in both these studies was that the native accentual metre of English—most clearly seen in OE poems such as *Beowulf* and *The Battle of Brunanburh* and in poems of the ME Alliterative Revival such as *Sir Gawain and the Green Knight* and *Piers Plowman*—has sporadically reemerged as an alternative metre during the six centuries since Chaucer established the primacy of the iambic pentameter.

One of the most famous examples is Samuel Taylor Coleridge's *Christabel.* Also often cited are Edmund Spenser's *February Eclogue*, Gerard Manley Hopkins' 'The Windhover' and other poems in 'sprung rhythm', T. S. Eliot's *Four Quartets,* and various poems that would seem to be free verse were it not for the principle of counting a set number of stressed syllables regardless of how many metrically unstressed syllables occur before, between, and after the stressed ones. Almost any current book on reading or writing modern poetry will name accentual metre as one of the three or four main forms of English prosody.

The first problem with this story is that it doesn't get Old and Middle English metre right, and the consequences of beginning with the wrong set of historical assumptions amount to more than pedantic nitpicking. Much has been discovered about the internal dynamics of both OE and ME metre during the past thirty years, though none of this knowledge has made it into the college anthologies. The metrical notes in the *Norton Anthology of English Literature,* 7th ed. (2000) could have been written by Wimsatt and Beardsley in 1959.

One reason for the lag is that there is still debate among the specialists; nevertheless, what we know for certain is that the usual description of accentual metre does not hold. The key sentences in the present *Norton Anthology* (which does a better job of simplification than most) are these: 'The organizing device of the line is alliteration…. The Old English alliterative line contains, on the average, four principal stresses and is divided into two half-lines of two stresses each by a strong medial caesura, or pause'. And later: 'There is no rule determining the number of unstressed syllables' (I.19).

However, alliteration is not the 'organizing device'. It is the principal cue to the organizing device, which is word stress. The half-lines of *Beowulf* would have exactly the same metrical organization if all alliteration were ignored, an experiment easy to perform by looking only at the second half-lines, or b-verses. These have only one alliterating syllable and thus when read in isolation seem to have no alliteration at all. Yet there is no mistake about the metrical pattern. There is no mistake about where only one unstressed syllable is allowed, and where more than one is allowed, and where a syllable can be short or long.

Lest that last sentence seem coy, let's state the matter directly: the counting of unstressed syllables was a central element in the alliterative metres of both OE and ME, contrary to the usual statements, as in the *Norton*, 'There is no rule determining the number of unstressed syllables'.

Furthermore, recent studies of Kaluza's Law have shown that OE metre is much more quantitative than had been thought. The contexts for 'resolution' of short syllables and 'suspension of resolution' have been known at least since Sievers (1885) and Kaluza (1896), but they have generally been seen as technical details that can be omitted for simplicity, as in the *Norton* account. However, Fulk (1992) and Suzuki (1996) make clear how the quantitative structures have implications for the metre as a whole. I myself am persuaded that the melodic contours I had proposed in Cable (1974) would iron out the distinctions of quantity and the count of moras that have to be reckoned; therefore, the tunes as I proposed them cannot be sustained. ME metre does not have that quantitative element, but it does have a syllable count element, different from that in OE though overlapping in certain respects.

All this is to say that Old and Middle English metres were not the primitive metres that most prosodists think. First, it is not true that the Old and Middle English poets attended only to the count of stressed syllables and let the 'gabble of weaker syllables' fall where they might. Corn (1997:19) presents a typical description:

> Even though the number of syllables in a given line varies, and syllables in the line are of differing length, Germanic and Anglo-Saxon meters rely only on the *stress* given to certain of those syllables. A possible result is as follows, where syllable stress is indicated by upper-case letters:
> TA room room TA   room TA room room TA
> room TA room TA   TA room room TA room

The two hemistichs of Corn's second line are accurate abstractions of certain OE metrical types, but both hemistichs of his first line are problematic. 'TA room room TA', which would seem to be an expected rhythm in OE, given the handbook generalizations, occurs only twice in the 6,364 hemistichs of *Beowulf* (747b & 2150a). In fact, because it is so expected but so rare, most OE metrists rightly list the two occurring instances as suspect. The pattern 'room TA room room TA' may be considered a form of Sievers' type B, and there are some hemistichs in *Beowulf* that may be said to fit the pattern. However, most of these have such highly specific syntactic constraints that the pattern cannot be said to occur freely, and, by a plausible interpretation, it may be said to be unmetrical.

In general, Old and Middle English metres were so highly regulated, with such salient, multiple cues to their structure, that 'accentual metres' from the fifteenth century to the present, supposedly deriving from the older rhythms, are often pale, confusing reflections. Hawes used hemistichs, at least in many of his lines, often indicated by a diagonal mark. However, the regulation of unstressed syllables in Old and Middle English made the hemistich structure much more perspicuous in the older poetry, so that the half-lines could be considered independent short lines, as they appeared in early printed editions. If alliteration was icing on the cake in Old and Middle English, it has generally not occurred in Modern English poetry since the sixteenth century, where alliteration could be truly useful in the absence of the firm patterns of stressed and unstressed syllables that the older poetry had.

The idea persists to the present that accentual metre is a viable form for new poems in English—along with iambic, trochaic, anapestic, and dactylic metres. In a volume of poetry published in 2001 Dana Gioia intended the opening poem, 'Words', to be in accentual metre. A reviewer, puzzled by lines such as the first one, 'The world does not need words. It articulates itself', could only read it as a mix of iambic feet and free verse. The lesson to draw is that a line may seem accentual in the author's mind but be received as metrically indeterminate by a reader. Hawes surely knew the sound in his own mind even if we do not know it, or cannot be certain about it, and he frequently provided the cue of marked hemistichs, something that modern poems do not do. It may be that hemistichic structure—of clear syntactic phrases with two and occasionally three stresses—is essential for the perception of accentual metre in English. Without at least that much help, accentual poems of the twenty-first century may be as inscrutable to metrists of the year 2400 as many of Hawes's lines are to us.

References

Babcock, C. 1914. 'A Study of the Metrical Use of the Inflectional *e* in Middle English, with Particular Reference to Chaucer and Lydgate'. *Publications of the Modern Language Association* 29:59-92.

Bergen, H., ed. 1924. *Lydgate's Fall of Princes.* EETS e.s. 21. London: Oxford University Press.

Brink, B. ten. 1901. *The Language and Metre of Chaucer.* 2nd ed. Revised by F. Kluge. Trans. M. B. Smith. New York: Macmillan.

Cable, T. 1974. *The Meter and Melody of* Beowulf. Urbana: University of Illinois Press.

———. 1991. *The English Alliterative Tradition.* Philadelphia: University of Pennsylvania Press.

———. 2002. 'Issues for a New History of English Prosody' and 'A Rejoinder to Youmans and Li'. *Studies in the History of English: A Millenial Perspective,* ed. D. Minkova & R. Stockwell. Berlin: Walter de Gruyter. 125-51, 177-82.

Corn, A. 1997. *The Poem's Heartbeat: A Manual of Prosody.* Brownsville, OR: Story Line Press.

Fulk, R. D. 1992. *A History of Old English Meter.* Philadelphia: University of Pennsylvania Press.

Gaylord, A. T. 1976. 'Scanning the Prosodists: An Essay in Metacriticism'. *Chaucer Review* 11:22-82.

Gioia, D. 2001. *Interrogations at Noon.* Saint Paul, MN: Graywolf Press.

Halle, M., & S. J. Keyser. 1966. 'Chaucer and the Study of Prosody'. *College English* 28:187-219.

———. 1971. *English Stress: Its Form, Its Growth, and Its Role in Verse.* New York: Harper & Row.

Kaluza, M. 1896. 'Zur Betonungs- und Verslehre des Altenglischen'. *Festschrift zum siebzigsten Geburtstage Oskar Schade.* Königsberg: Hartung. 101-33.

Kiparsky, P. 1975. 'Stress, Syntax, and Meter'. *Language* 51:576-616.

———. 1977. 'The Rhythmic Structure of English Verse'. *Linguistic Inquiry* 8:189-247.

Lewis, C. S. 1938. 'The Fifteenth-century Heroic Line'. *Essays and Studies* 24:28-41.

Luick, K. 1896. *Untersuchungen zur englischen Lautgeschichte.* Strassburg: Trübner.

Mortensen, A. 2001. Review of '*Interrogations at Noon,* by Dana Gioia'. *Expansive Poetry & Music Online* (29 May). http://www.n2hos.com/acm/rev052001.html

Pearsall, D. 1977. *Old English and Middle English Poetry.* London: Routledge.

Pyle, F. 1937. 'The Barbarous Metre of Barclay'. *Modern Language Review* 32:353-73.

Robinson, I. 1971. *Chaucer's Prosody.* Cambridge: Cambridge University Press.

Saintsbury, G. 1906-10. *A History of English Prosody.* 3 vols. London: Macmillan.

———. 1910. *Historical Manual of English Prosody.* London: Macmillan.

Sievers, E. 1885. 'Zur Rhythmik des germanischen Alliterationsverses'.

Beiträge zur Geschichte der deutschen Sprache und Literatur 10:209-314, 451-545.

Southworth, J. G. 1954. *Verses of Cadence: An Introduction to the Prosody of Chaucer and his Followers.* Oxford: Blackwell.

Stanley, E. G. 1989. 'Chaucer's Metre after Chaucer'. *Notes and Queries* n.s. 36:11-23, 151-62.

Suzuki, S. 1995. 'Resolution and Mora Counting in Old English'. *American Journal of Germanic Linguistics and Literatures* 7:1-28.

———. 1996. *The Metrical Organization of Beowulf: Prototype and Isomorphism.* Trends in Linguistics, Studies and Monographs 95. Berlin & New York: Mouton de Gruyter.

Tajima, M. 1985. *The Syntactic Development of the Gerund in Middle English.* Tokyo: Nan'un-do.

Tillyard, E. M. W. 1949. *The Poetry of Sir Thomas Wyatt: A Selection and a Study.* London: Chatto & Windus.

Wimsatt, W. K., Jr, & M. C. Beardsley. 1959. 'The Concept of Meter: An Exercise in Abstraction'. *Publications of the Modern Language Association* 74:585-98.

Woods, S. 1984. *Natural Emphasis: English Versification from Chaucer to Dryden.* San Marino, CA: Huntington Library.

Youmans, G., & X. Li. 2002. 'Chaucer: Folk Poet or Littérateur?' *Studies in the History of English: A Millenial Perspective,* ed. D. Minkova & R. Stockwell. Berlin: Walter de Gruyter. 152-76.

The Development of Non-assertive *Any* in Later Middle English and the Decline of Multiple Negation

Yoko Iyeiri

1. Introduction

Non-assertive *any* most typically occurs in negative, interrogative, and conditional clauses in PDE. It also occurs in some constructions expressing comparison, temporal clauses introduced by *before*, after implicitly negative words, and after the preposition *without,* as claimed by Biber, et al. (1999: 176-7). Thus, negation is one of the most typical circumstances where non-assertive *any* is employed. The development of *any* in negation, however, goes back only to the end of the ME period, while the use of *any* in other non-assertive contexts was observed slightly earlier, according to previous studies. Burnley (1983:59-60) states that non-assertive forms are not found in negation in Chaucer's English. Likewise, Tieken (1995:126-7; 1997: 1548) argues that non-assertive *any* in Malory's *Morte Darthur* does not occur in negation, but in sentences with implicitly negative words (e.g. *without, loth*, and *unnethe*). Fischer (1992:282) also argues that non-assertive *any* is observed in ME, but fundamentally in contexts such as 'comparative clauses..., conditional clauses..., after verbs like *douten, denyen, forsaken*, etc. and after *lest'*. As I discuss in Iyeiri (2002:212-13), the development of *any* in negation must be slightly earlier than proposed by these studies. Still, it is only in the ME3 (1350-1420) of the Helsinki Corpus that some notable expansion of *any* in negation is attested for the first time. For details, see Iyeiri (2002:212-13).

There is a phenomenon which also occurred in the later part of ME and which is perhaps related to the development of *any* in negative sentences. It is the decline of multiple negation like the following:

Stomak *ne* conscience *ne* knowe I *noon* (*The Friar's Tale*, 1441).

Here, the negative sense is not cancelled out despite the repetition of negative words. Newly-developed *any* fills the place of redundant negative items, once the decline of multiple negation occurs in late ME (Jack 1978c: 70; Burnley 1983:60; Fischer 1992:283-4; Tieken 1995:125-7; Nevalainen 1998:268-70; Iyeiri 1998:136-7; 2001:153-5). The principal concern of the present study is to investigate how closely the development of non-assertive *any* and the decline of multiple negation are linked.

For this purpose, I have selected four late ME texts, whose details of negation I have already investigated for other purposes (see Iyeiri 2001). They are: (1) *The Canterbury Tales* by Chaucer; (2) *Confessio Amantis* by Gower (the first 300 pages of Macauley's edition only); (3) *Sir Gawain and the Green Knight*; and (4) *The York Plays*.[1] Chaucer's langauge is attributed to London (McIntosh, Samuels, & Benskin 1986, I:91), and the Ellesmere manuscript of *The Canterbury Tales* was produced at the beginning of the fifteenth-century (Samuels 1983:61; Owen 1991:8, n. 2). *Confessio Amantis* may be slightly earlier, while its language shows linguistic features of Suffolk and Kent (Fisher, Hamm, Beidler, & Yeager 1986:202-3; Samuels & Smith 1981:301). I have analyzed only the first 300 pages of Macauley's edition as mentioned above. This is in the interest of consistency, as I hold the data of negative constructions only for this part of the text (cf. Iyeiri 2001:13). To turn to *Sir Gawain and the Green Knight,* the manuscript date is around the same time, i.e. c.1400, while its language is localized in Cheshire (McIntosh, Samuels, & Benskin 1986, I:106). *The York Plays* is slightly later in date. The main scribe's work on MS Additional 35290 took place at some time between 1463 and 1477, and its principal language is localized in York in the North (McIntosh, Samuels, & Benskin, I:102).[2]

---

[1] The editions I have used are: (1) *The Riverside Chaucer*, 3rd ed., gen. ed. L. D. Benson, et al. (Boston, 1987); (2) *The English Works of John Gower*, 2 vols, ed. G. C. Macauley (London, 1900); (3) *Sir Gawain and the Green Knight*, 2nd ed., ed. J. R. R. Tolkien & E. V. Gordon and revised by N. Davis (Oxford, 1967); and (4) *The York Plays*, ed. R. Beadle (London, 1982).

[2] Although *The Canterbury Tales, Confessio Amantis,* and *The York Plays* are included in the Helsinki Corpus, which I have already studied in Iyeiri (2002), the parts selected for

2. The push-chain or the drag-chain

Tieken (1995:125-7) discusses the occurrence of *any* in negation as a functional extension from the use of *any* in interrogative, hypothetical and conditional clauses. She also employs the concept of the drag-chain shift to explain this, saying that the decline of multiple negation precedes or even triggers the extension of *any* to negative sentences. According to her, the spread of non-assertive *any* had not yet taken place in the language of Malory's *Morte Darthur* (p. 73), although the decline of multiple negation was already in progress. She exemplifies this by the following example where one feels a gap before *part* (p. 126):

none of you shall have part of her (Winchester MS, 72/28).

As she points out, Caxton's Malory runs as follows instead:

for none of yow shalle haue *no* parte of her ...
(Caxton's version, 114/31-2).

Tieken's contention is that Malory was unhappy about the gap and that he chose to repeat negative items in a single clause instead.

The concepts of the push-chain and the drag-chain shifts are generally applied to phonological changes, and most frequently to the Great Vowel Shift. It is, however, interesting to apply this framework to the relationship between the development of *any* and the decline of multiple negation. If the decline of multiple negation is a case of the push-chain shift, the relationship between the two is very strong, in that the recession of multiple negation occurs due to the extension of *any*. Provided that the extension of non-assertive *any* is a case of the drag-chain shift, the relationship is fairly strong, in that it is still a cause-and-effect relationship. There is also the third possibility that they do not illustrate either the push-chain shift or the drag-chain shift. In this case, the development of *any* and the decline of multiple negation may still be related, but the relationship between them is not as strong as in the case of the first two cases. The discussion below in fact supports the last inference.

the corpus are very short. To describe the details of the use of *any* in different syntactic conditions, it is essential to investigate a fairly lengthy portion of each text.

3. Non-assertive *any* in the four ME texts concerned

The four texts I have selected all display a reasonably extensive development of *any* itself. The frequency of *any* per 10,000 words in each text is given below:

Table 1. *Any* per 10,000 words

CT	CA	GGK	YP
11.77	13.04	11.87	9.29

CT = *The Canterbury Tales*
CA = *Confessio Amantis*
GGK = *Sir Gawain and the Green Knight*
YP = *The York Plays*

As Table 1 shows, nine to thirteen examples of *any* are witnessed in every 10,000 words. This is not below the average when compared with the data of the Helsinki Corpus, which I have investigated.[3] The mean frequency of *any* in ME3 (1350-1420) of the Helsinki Corpus is 20.30 per 10,000 words and that of ME4 (1420-1500) is 15.57 per 10,000 words. These large figures, however, include some texts with a distinctively frequent use of *any*. 'Proclamations, London (from *The Book of London English 1384-1425*)' in the category of 'Documents' in ME3, for example, present the rate of 144.74 per 10,000 words. Furthermore, *The Cloud of Unknowing* (ME3) shows the rate of 49.08 per 10,000 words. On the whole, however, offering around ten examples of *any* per 10,000 words is quite normal with ME3 texts. The same applies to ME4. In fact, even among prose texts of the ME3 and ME4 periods of the Helsinki Corpus, there are some without any examples of *any*. Thus, the state of the four texts selected for the present study is not particularly conservative, at least as far as the development of *any* in them is concerned.

The collocations of *any* in the four ME texts reveal the non-assertive nature of *any* fairly clearly. Table 2 shows the top ten to fifteen frequent

[3] Incidentally, the rates of *any* per 10,000 words in the relevant extracts included in the Helsinki Corpus are: *The Tale of Melibee* (11.10), *The Parson's Tale* (4.54), *The General Prologue of the Canterbury Tales* (19.28), *The Wife of Bath's Tale* (0), *The Summoner's Tale* (8.93), *The Merchant's Tale* (9.17), *Confessio Amantis* (9.56), and *The York Plays* (7.41). There are some discrepancies between the rates of the extracts (i.e. the Helsinki Corpus) and those of the entire texts.

words on the left of *any*:[4]

Table 2. Frequent words on the left of *any*

CT		CA		GGK		YP	
as	51	that	22	if	6	yf/if	20
that	37	in	16	then	6	withoute*	16
of	27	if	16	as	3	þat	7
for	22	of	9	and	3	in	7
if	22	and	9	other	2	be	6
and	21	as	7	in	2	as	5
to	20	withouten	6	er	2	or	5
or	15	bot	6	on	2	þer	5
withoute(n)	15	at	4	þat	2	þou	4
than	13	er	4	þay	2	of	3
ther	13	what	4	to	2	schall	3
in	11	which	4			with	3
whan(ne)	11	is	3				
		mihte	3				
		was	3				

* *Withoute* here stands for *withoute, withoutyn, withowten,* and *withowtyn.*

As the text length differs, the raw frequency of each word is not significant. The matter of interest is what kind of words are collocated with *any* in the four texts at issue. The words common to them are: *as, that, if, in*, and their orthographic variants. Clearly, *any* is often employed in conditional clauses with *if* in our texts. Some illustrative examples are:

And alle at ones doun thei falle,
If *eny* pite may be founde (*Confessio Amantis*, 95/2202-3)

Yf *any* man walke in þis way
Telle hym me bedene (*The York Plays*, 213/293-4).

Indeed, conditional clauses are one of the most typical non-assertive contexts. Of the total of 25 examples of *any* in *Sir Gawain and the Green Knight*, as many as ten (40%) belong to this category. Likewise, the proportions of *any* in conditional clauses to the totals of *any* in the other texts are: *The Canterbury Tales* (15.8%), *Confessio Amantis* (33.0%), and

[4] I have stopped the listing of words where appropriate.

The York Plays (31.4%).[5]

Secondly, the relatively frequent occurrence of *as* before *any* indicates that it is possibly used in comparative constructions of the following type:

For trewely, ye have as myrie a stevene
As *any* aungel hath that is in hevene (*The Nun's Priest's Tale*, 3291-2)

Indeed, examples of comparative constructions are particularly frequent in *The Canterbury Tales*, where 41 instances (19.1%) of the total of 215 illustrate comparative ones of various sorts. Here, I include examples of comparatives and superlatives:

for which it is moore digne than *any* oother preyere
(*The Parson's Tale*, 1040)

A theef of venysoun, that hath forlaft
His likerousnesse and al his olde craft,
Kan kepe a forest best of *any* man (*The Physician's Tale*, 83-5).

In fact, examples of these kinds would explain the fact that *of* and *than* are also listed in the frequent words collocated with *any* in Table 2 above. On the contrary, I have not counted examples of the following type as one of the 41 examples:

And tho were bent and blake as *any* sloo (*The Miller's Tale*, 3246).

This is a case of simile rather than equation, but it has certainly contributed to the appearance of *as* in the list in Table 2.

Finally, the appearance of *that* in Table 2 is also relevant to the non-assertive feature of *any*. As pointed out about PDE (cf. Quirk, Greenbaum, Leech, & Svartvik 1985:784), non-assertive *any* occurs in restrictive relative clauses qualifying generic noun phrases:

Witnesse on hym that *any* parfit clerk is (*The Nun's Priest's Tale*, 3236).

That-clauses can also be non-assertive when they are superordinated by a negative, interrogative, or conditional clause, as in:

---

[5] In these figures I have included conditional clauses with 'if', 'unless', and conditional clauses with inversion. I have also included examples of *any* in subordinated clauses

So wol I noght that *eny* time
Be lost of that thou hast do byme (*Confessio Amantis* 299/2701-2).

One thing that is not clear in Table 2 is how frequently *any* occurs in negative clauses, which is in fact the main concern of the present paper. Apparently, *any* was common in quasi-negative contexts at least, since *without* is listed under all of the four texts in Table 2. As I mention in the Introduction, previous studies maintain that the use of *any* is evidenced in quasi-negative contexts (e.g. *without, lest, unnethe, denyen,* and *douten*) before it spreads into negative sentences. The question is whether *any* in the four texts under consideration has expanded to negation. I have listed in Table 3 below the frequencies of *any* in negation (including *any* in clauses subordinate to a negative clause):

Table 3. Frequencies of non-assertive *any* in negative sentences
(per 10,000 words)

CT	CA	GGK	YP
1.48	2.22	1.42	0.43

Examples include:

seint Ambrose seith that Penitence is the pleynynge of man for the gilt that he hath doon, and namoore to do *any* thyng for which hym oghte to pleyne (*The Parson's Tale*, 84)

He was so full of veine gloire,
That he ne hadde no memoire
That ther was *eny* good bot he
For pride of his prosperite (*Confessio Amantis*, 112/2799-2802).

I have collected 51 examples of *any* in negative contexts, of which 25 are found in clauses dependent upon a negative clause. Furthermore, some of the collected examples are non-assertive in any case for other reasons. In this sense, the development of non-assertive *any* in negation in the four texts at issue is still at a preliminary stage. However, this state of affairs is not really conservative for their dates, since more than half of the texts of the ME3 and the ME4 periods in the Helsinki Corpus provide no examples of *any* in negation, although at the same time the corpus contains texts with a

---

dependent upon conditional clauses.

particularly frequent use of *any* in negative contexts, e.g. 'Proclamation, London' (32.89 per 10,000 words) and *The Cloud of Unknowing* (12.75 per 10,000 words). See Iyeiri (2002:217-18).[6] One notable point revealed in Table 3 is that the development of *any* in negation is not much in progress in *The York Plays*, at least in comparison with the situations of *The Canterbury Tales, Confessio Amantis,* and *Sir Gawain and the Green Knight.*

As I have the data of negative clauses in the four ME texts, I would like to use them to make sure that the frequent occurring of *any* in negation in Table 3 is not related to the frequent attestation of negative sentences themselves. Table 4 shows the number of *any* in negation per 100 negative clauses:

Table 4. Frequency of *any* in negation per 100 negative clauses

CT	CA	GGK	YP
1.06	1.39	1.57	0.30

It is clear from the above table that the sparseness of *any* in negation in *The York Plays* is not ascribable to the scarcity of negative clauses themselves. Even in proportion to 100 negative clauses, the use of *any* in negation is more limited in *The York Plays* than in the other three texts. This is interesting in relation to the issue of the push-chain and the drag-chain shifts, since *The York Plays* is a text which has undergone a fairly dramatic decline of multiple negation, at least in contrast to *The Canterbury Tales* and *Sir Gawain and the Green Knight.* If the demise of multiple negation and the development of *any* in negation are closely linked, one would expect a more expanded use of *any* in negation in texts like *The York Plays*. Table 5 below shows the proportions of multiple negation to the entire sample of negative clauses in the four texts under consideration:

Table 5. The proportions of multiple negation to the entire sample of negative clauses

CT	CA	GGK	YP
29.9%	8.6%	18.4%	10.2%

[6] The data of the Helsinki Corpus are based upon the same method of counting examples. In other words, the figures include examples of *any* in subordinate clauses dependent upon a negative clause, as well as those in negative clauses.

The York Plays is a progressive Northern text where the decline of multiple negation is much in progress, despite the restricted use of *any* in negation. It is also the latest text of the four. Another text which also displays a relatively progressed recession of multiple negation in Table 5 is *Confessio Amantis*, which however shows a comparatively extended use of *any* in negation. According to my study of non-assertive *any* in the Helsinki Corpus, there seems to be dialectal conditions related to the development of non-assertive *any* (Iyeiri 2002:219-20). *Any* develops in a most pronounced way in the East Midlands, which perhaps explains the difference between *The York Plays* and *Confessio Amantis*. In fact, *any* in negation seems to be rather indifferent to the degree of the decline of multiple negation as far as Tables 4 and 5 are concerned. I have plotted the relationship between the ratio of multiple negation and the frequency of *any* in negation per 100 negative clauses in Figure 1 below:

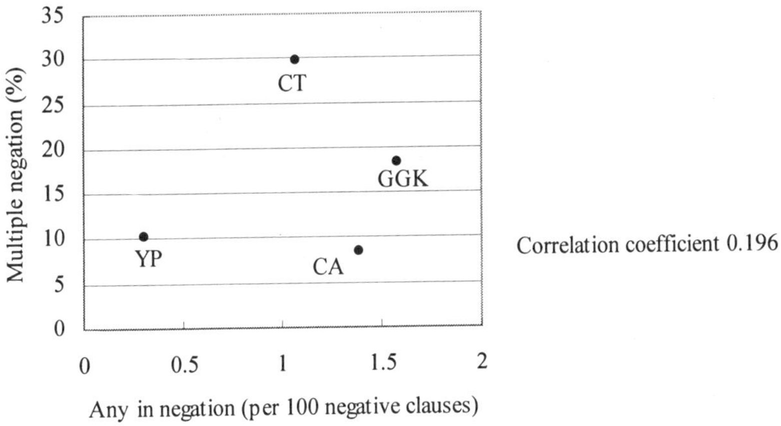

Figure 1. The ratio of multiple negation and *any* in negation per 100 negative clauses

If the depletion of multiple negation is automatically followed by the use of non-assertive forms in negation with or without time lag, there should be a fairly close negative correlation between the proportions of multiple negation and the rate of *any* in negation. Figure 1, however, yields the positive correlation coefficient of 0.196, although I do admit that the sample size is too small for accurate analyses. Since the relationship between the decline of multiple negation and the development of *any* in negation is much more reasonable among *The Canterbury Tales, Confessio Amantis,* and *Sir Gawain and the Green Knight*, I would surmise that the two issues are perhaps related once a certain extent of the development of *any* has been reached. There are texts which have attained this stage, while there are also others which have not. Apparently, the relationship between them is not necessarily of the cause-and-effect type.

4. Non-assertive *any* in *The York Plays*

As discussed in the previous section, *The York Plays* has not experienced the development of *any* in negation up to the stage where it fills the place of multiple negation, which is already close to depletion. This can also be proved by the fact that the proportion of *any* in negation to the entire sample of *any* in *The York Plays* is as small as 4.7%. The corresponding values in the remaining texts are: 12.6% in *The Canterbury Tales*, 17.0% in *Confessio Amantis*, and 12.0% in *Sir Gawain and the Green Knight*. As I argue in Iyeiri (2002:212-13), *any* in negation suddenly expands from a certain point of ME and its proportion to the entire sample of *any* also rises as time passes. I borrow the following figure to illustrate this point from my study of non-assertive *any* in the Helsinki Corpus (Iyeiri 2002:212):

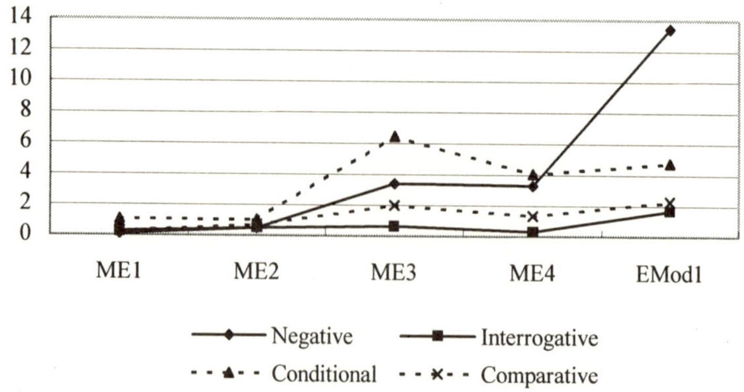

Figure 2. Non-assertive *any* in negative, interrogative, conditional, and comparative clauses in the Helsinki Corpus (per 10,000 words)

Figure 2 shows that the expansion of *any* in negation accelerates from a certain point of the ME period. *The York Plays* has not reached this state.

Another feature of non-assertive *any* in *The York Plays* is that it is more frequently followed by plural nouns than in the other texts:

And loke youre leggyng be lele,
Withowtyn any tryfils to telle (*The York Plays*, 223/107-8)

Yis lorde, we schall wayte if any wonderes walke,
And freyne howe youre folkis fare þat are furth ronne
(*The York Plays*, 243/27-8).

With the rate of one out of five, *any* is followed by a plural noun in *The York Plays*. In the remaining texts, by contrast, the employment of singular nouns after *any* is almost established, although there are a handful of exceptions. The following example where a singular noun follows *any* is cited from *The Canterbury Tales*:

Whan they were set, and hust was al the place,
And Theseus abiden hadde a space
Er *any word* cam fram his wise brest,
His eyen sette he ther as was his lest (*The Knight's Tale*, 2981-4).

Sahlin (1979:97) studies the use of *any* in PDE and reports that it is most frequently followed by singular nouns. Although the gap between the ME and the PDE periods has to be filled by further studies, it may be interesting to postulate that the non-assertive *any* used in PDE is the type which developed first in the East Midland areas in later ME, and not the type in *The York Plays*, where the plural usage is often found.

Finally, I would like to refer to non-assertive *ought* in *The York Plays*, the existence of which does not seem to hinder the development of *any*:

If ȝe amange you all in fere
Haue *ought* to ete (*The York Plays*, 368/65-6).

I have come across about 40 examples of *ought* of this kind, often in non-assertive contexts. *Ought* in various spelling forms, however, occurs in *The Canterbury Tales, Confessio Amantis,* and *Sir Gawain and the Green Knight*, as well. More importantly, there is a fairly clear division of domains between *any* and *ought*, so that *any* occurs fundamentally in the adjectival use followed by noun phrases. By constrast, *ought* is essentially nominal. This applies to all of the four texts under discussion.

5. Different tales of *The Canterbury Tales*

Before concluding this study, I would like to investigate the possible discrepancies of the use of *any* in different tales of *The Canterbury Tales*, with the hope that this would present some hints upon the origin of non-assertive *any*. Tottie (1994:425) takes the view that non-assertive *any* was colloquial in origin, whereas Tieken (1997:1551) argues that it originated in written language. According to my examination of the Helsinki Corpus, non-assertive *any* is most frequently attested at its early stage in genres like 'Documents', 'Law', and perhaps 'Letters' (Iyeiri 2002:218-19), showing the prosaic and non-fictional or non-literary nature of non-assertive *any*.

Although *The Canterbury Tales* includes tales of various types, the text length is often too short. I have, therefore, selected the following seven tales whose designated style is relatively clear and whose negative constructions I discussed in Iyeiri (1998:125-6): *The Knight's Tale, The Reeve's Tale, The Wife of Bath's Tale, The Clerk's Tale, The Tale of Melibee, The Canon's Yeoman's Tale,* and *The Parson's Tale*. Of the seven tales, *The Knight's Tale, The Clerk's Tale, The Tale of Melibee,* and *The Parson's Tale* are considered to be written in formal style, while the remaining texts are thought to be written in informal style. It is also relevant to point out that *The Tale of Melibee* and the most of *The Parson's Tale* are written in prose. The frequencies of *any* in them are given in Table 6 below:

Table 6. Frequencies of *any* of all types in different tales of *The Canterbury Tales*

Tales	Frequency	per 10,000 words
The Knight's Tale	28	16.28
The Clerk's Tale	2	2.11
The Tale of Melibee	14	8.26
The Parson's Tale	26	8.46
The Reeve's Tale	4	10.39
The Wife of Bath's Tale	9	8.93
The Canon's Yeoman's Tale	14	19.04

Clear tendencies are not available as far as the overall frequency of *any* is concerned. Although its use is limited in *The Clerk's Tale*, the other tales in the formal category offer a reasonably large figure. The frequency of *any* in *The Canon's Yeoman's Tale* is most pronounced, but *The Knight's Tale* written in formal style also presents a competingly large figure in Table 6.

Differences between formal and informal texts are available, however, in respect of *any* in negation, although relevant examples are not abundant. Table 7 shows the frequencies of *any* in negative contexts:[7]

Table 7. Frequencies of *any* in negation in different tales of *The Canterbury Tales*

Tales	Frequency	per 100 negative clauses
The Knight's Tale	5	2.46
The Clerk's Tale	0	0
The Tale of Melibee	4	1.44
The Parson's Tale	4	1.07
The Reeve's Tale	0	0
The Wife of Bath's Tale	0	0
The Canon's Yeoman's Tale	1	0.83

Although the use of *any* in negation is restricted in all of the seven tales, it is more frequently attested in formal style than in informal one. The relatively extensive use of *any* in negation in *The Tale of Melibee* and *The Parson's Tale* may be ascribable to the fact that they are mostly written in prose,[8] but *The Knight's Tale*, written in verse, also presents a comparatively frequent use of *any* in negation.

Incidentally, multiple negation is preserved well in tales of formal style in *The Canterbury Tales*, whereas it has declined to a much larger extent in informal style of writings. According to Iyeiri (1998:125-6), the proportions of multiple negation in the seven selected tales are: *The Knight's Tale* (30.0%), *The Clerk's Tale* (30.7%), *The Tale of Melibee* (39.6%), *The Parson's Tale* (43.3%); and *The Reeve's Tale* (10.7%), *The Wife of Bath's Tale* (21.6%), *The Canon's Yeoman's Tale* (22.6%). Thus, non-assertive *any* in negative contexts is more copious in formal style, where multiple negation is also better preserved. The decline of multiple negation, as found in informal texts, does not seem to trigger the use of *any* in negation. If there

[7] In the interest of consistency, I have counted examples in clauses superordinated by a negative clause.

[8] The prosaic nature of *any* is discussed in Iyeiri (2002:217-19).

is ever a visible relationship between the recession of multiple negation and the extension of *any* in negation, it is only among the three formal texts of *The Knight's Tale, The Tale of Melibee,* and *The Parson's Tale*, as Figure 3 indicates:

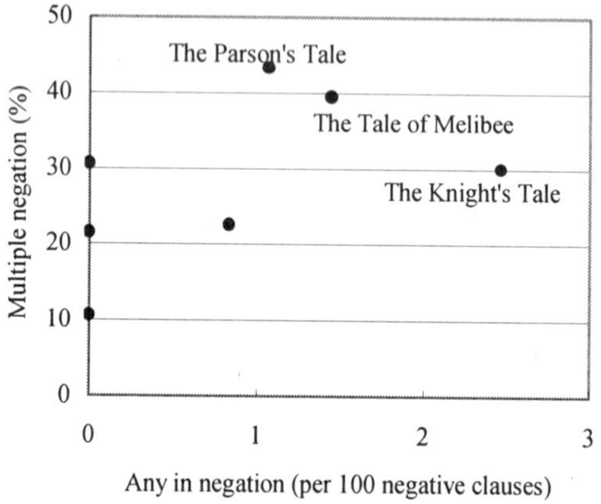

Figure 3. The relationship between the decline of multiple negation and the development of *any* in negation

Apparently, reduction of multiple negation itself does not directly lead to the extension of *any* into negative sentences. A reasonable correlation between the decline of multiple negation and the development of *any* in negation is visible only after the latter has reached a certain stage.

6. Conclusions

I have hitherto analyzed the development of non-assertive *any* in late ME. Although the expansion of non-assertive *any* in general has reached the standard level in terms of its frequency in *The Canterbury Tales, Confessio Amantis, Sir Gawain and the Green Knight*, and *The York Plays*, its use in negative contexts is restricted in *The York Plays*. Interestingly enough, it is a text from the North which has undergone a sharper decline of multiple negation than the other three texts. Thus, the recession of multiple negation itself does not seem to lead to the extension of non-assertive *any* into negative sentences. The correlation between them, however, improves when *The York Plays* is eliminated from analysis. Apparently, the relationship between them is a fairly loose one and is visible only after the development of *any* has reached a certain level.

That the use of *any* in negative sentences has not developed as much in *The York Plays* as in the other texts is also proved by the small proportion of *any* in negation to the entire sample of *any* in this text. Non-assertive *any* in negation goes through a dramatic increase from later ME onwards. Although *The York Plays* is the latest text of the four, it still displays a state before this jump. Another feature which distinguishes *The York Plays* from the other texts is that non-assertive *any* in it is more commonly followed by plural noun phrases, while noun phrases following *any* in the other texts are normally in the singular. Judging from the fact that present-day *any* is often followed by singular nouns, the type of *any* today may have developed from the type used in the texts other than *The York Plays*. In fact, the data of the Helsinki Corpus reveal that the use of non-assertive forms is most pronounced in the East Midlands in late ME. Apparently, the use of non-assertive *any* expanded from here, while the decline of multiple negation may have spread from the North.

Finally, the present study discussed the use of non-assertive *any* in different tales of *The Canterbury Tales*. I have especially concentrated upon four tales written in formal style, i.e. *The Knight's Tale, The Clerk's Tale, The Tale of Melibee, The Parson's Tale*, and three texts written in informal style, i.e. *The Reeve's Tale, The Wife of Bath's Tale,* and *The Canon's Yeoman's Tale*. The overall frequencies of *any* do not yield any differences between different styles, whereas *any* in negative contexts is more commonly found in formal texts. Interestingly enough, texts written in formal style of English tend to preserve multiple negation to a larger extent. On the other hand, *The Reeve's Tale, The Wife of Bath's Tale,* and *The Canon's Yeoman's Tale* display a recessed use of multiple negation, while they hardly offer *any* in negation. Here again, the relationship between the decline of multiple negation and the extension of *any* into negative contexts is fairly loose. The relationship improves when *The Knight's Tale, The Tale of Melibee,* and *The Parson's Tale* only are selected. It is perhaps safe to say, therefore, that the relationship is not necessarily of the cause-and-effect type. Indeed, the gap caused by the depletion of multiple negation was finally filled by non-assertive forms, but this was a result of things which had already been in progress.

References

Biber, D., S. Johansson, G. Leech, S. Conrad, & E. Finegan. 1999. *Longman Grammar of Spoken and Written English.* London: Longman.

Burnley, D. 1983. *A Guide to Chaucer's English.* London: Macmillan.

Fischer, O. 1992. 'Syntax'. *The Cambridge History of the English Language, II: 1066-1476*, ed. N. F. Blake. Cambridge: Cambridge University Press. 207-408.

Fisher, J. H., R. W. Hamm, P. G. Beidler, & R. F. Yeager. 1986. 'John Gower'. *A Manual of the Writings in Middle English 1050-1500, VII*, gen. ed. A. E. Hartung. New Haven, CT: Connecticut Academy of Arts and Sciences. 2195-210, 2399-418.

Iyeiri, Y. 1998a. 'MS Cotton Nero A.x. Poems Once Again: A Study of Contracted Negative Forms'. *English Historical Linguistics and Philology in Japan*, ed. J. Fisiak & A. Oizumi. Berlin: Mouton de Gruyter. 79-89.

———. 1998b. 'Multiple Negation in Middle English Verse'. *Negation in the History of English*, ed. I. Tieken-Boon van Ostade, G. Tottie, & W. van der Wurff. Berlin: Mouton de Gruyter. 121-46.

———. 2001. *Negative Constructions in Middle English.* Fukuoka: Kyushu University Press.

———. 2002. 'Development of *Any* from Middle English to Early Modern English: A Study Using the Helsinki Corpus of English Texts'. *English Corpus Linguistics in Japan*, ed. T. Saito, J. Nakamura, & S. Yamazaki. Amsterdam: Rodopi. 211-23.

Jack, G. B. 1978a. 'Negative Adverbs in Early Middle English'. *English Studies* 59:295-309.

———. 1978b. 'Negative Concord in Early Middle English'. *Studia Neophilologica* 50:29-39.

———. 1978c. 'Negation in Later Middle English Prose'. *Archivum Linguisticum* n.s. 9:58-72.

McIntosh, A., M. L. Samuels, & M. Benskin. 1986. *A Linguistic Atlas of Late Mediaeval English.* 4 vols. Aberdeen: Aberdeen University Press.

Nevalainen, T. 1998. 'Social Mobility and the Decline of Multiple Negation in Early Modern English'. *Advances in English Historical Linguistics*, ed. J. Fisiak & M. Krygier. Berlin: Mouton de Gruyter. 263-91.

Owen, C. A. 1991. *The Manuscripts of The Canterbury Tales.* Chaucer Studies, 17. Cambridge: D. S. Brewer.

Quirk, R., S. Greenbaum, G. Leech, & J. Svartvik. 1985. *A Comprehensive Grammar of the English Language.* London: Longman.

Sahlin, E. 1979. Some *and* any *in Spoken and Written English.* Studia Anglistica

Upsaliensis, 38. Stockholm: Almqvist & Wiksell International.

Samuels, M. L. 1983. 'The Scribe of the Hengwrt and Ellesmere Manuscripts of *The Canterbury Tales*'. *Studies in the Age of Chaucer* 5:49-65.

—— & J. J. Smith. 1981. 'The Language of Gower'. *Neuphilologische Mitteilungen* 82:295-304.

Tieken-Boon van Ostade, I. 1995. *The Two Versions of Malory's Morte Darthur: Multiple Negation and the Editing of the Text*. Cambridge: D. S. Brewer.

———. 1997. '*Any* or *No*: Functional Spread of Non-assertive *Any*'. *Language History and Linguistic Modelling: A Festschrift for Jacek Fisiak on his 60th Birthday, II: Linguistic Modelling*, ed. R. Hickey & S. Puppel. Berlin: Mouton de Gruyter. 1545-54.

Tottie, G. 1994. '*Any* as an Indefinite Determiner in Non-assertive Clauses: Evidence from Present-day and Early Modern English'. *Studies in Early Modern English*, ed. D. Kastovsky. Topics in English Linguistics, 13. Berlin: Mouton de Gruyter. 413-27.

ESSAYS ON MEDIEVAL LITERATURE

Beowulf 128: *æfter wiste*

Jun Terasawa

1. Previous notes on *æfter wiste*

Filled with bitter resentment against loud rejoicing at Heorot, Grendel departs for the royal hall under cover of the night. The following is the passage where the monster breaks into the hall and carries off thirty of the sleeping thanes:[1]

Gewat ða neosian, syþðan niht becom,
hean huses, hu hit Hring-Dene
æfter beorþege gebun hæfdon.
Fand þa ðær inne æþelinga gedriht
swefan *æfter symble*, sorge ne cuðon
wonsceaft wera. Wiht unhælo
grim ond grædig gearo sona wæs
reoc ond reþe ond on ræste genam
þritig þegna, þanon eft gewat
huðe hremig to ham faran
mid þære wælfylle wica neosan.
Đa wæs on uhtan mid ærdæge
Grendles guðcræft gumum undyrne,
þa wæs *æfter wiste* wop up ahafen
micel morgensweg. (ll. 115-29a, italics added)

(Then he [Grendel] went, after night was come, to seek out the lofty house, as to how the Ring-Danes had settled into it *after their beer-drinking*. Then he found therein a company of noblemen sleeping *after the banquet*; they did not know sorrow, men's misery. The creature of evil, fierce and greedy, savage and furious, was soon ready, and snatched thirty thanes from their rest. From

[1] The text used is Mitchell & Robinson (1998).

> there he departed, exulting in his booty, to go back home, to seek his dwelling with his feast of slaughter. Then at dawn before daybreak Grendel's war-strength was made plain to men. Then *after the feast* was raised up weeping, a great morning-cry.)

As one of the early Beowulfian scholars who discuss this passage, Ten Brink suggests that *æfter wiste* (128) should be associated with the preceding *wælfyllo* '(Grendel's) feast of slaughter' (125) to mean 'um die Beute, um den Frass'.[2] In their glossary, Heyne-Socin also define *wist* (128) as 'Speise, Frasz, Beute' and render line 128 as 'da war um die Beute (Grendels, die von ihm geraubten dreiszig Mannen) ein Wehgeschrei erhoben'.[3] This reading, however, met with severe criticism from scholars, notably from Cosijn, who states that '[t]o insist that OE *wist* has the sense of "prey" is equivalent to a public confession of utter incompetence'.[4] He relates *æfter wiste* to the preceding *æfter beorþege* (117) and *æfter symble* (119), and takes *wist* as 'the joyous feast of the heroes' in contrast with their lamentation (cf. *wop* 128). Cosijn's interpretation is followed by Trautmann[5] and Kock, the latter of whom voices another stern disapproval of Ten Brink's reading: 'The poet cannot have been unpoetical enough to express the grief of the Danes by saying that they were lamenting "on account of Grendel's food"!'.[6]

Most of the editors and translators seem to have since agreed that *æfter wiste*, appositive to the preceding *æfter beorþege* and *æfter symble*, refers to the Danish feasting held before Grendel's attack on Heorot.[7] Wyatt-Chambers interpret *æfter wiste* as 'after their [the Danes'] weal' or 'after their feasting', which 'seems a more likely interpretation than that there was lamentation concerning Grendel's feasting upon the thirty thanes'.[8] Klaeber translates the line in question as 'there was weeping where there was

---

[2] Ten Brink (1888:15).

[3] Heyne-Socin (1888:291). In his glossary, Holder (1884:181) takes *wist* as 'food, prey'.

[4] Cosijn (1991:4). The quotation is taken from Cosijn, *Notes on Beowulf* (1991), which translates the original Dutch *Aanteekeningen op den Béowulf* (1892) into English with annotations.

[5] Trautmann (1899:130).

[6] Kock (1904:223).

[7] Cf. also Holthausen (1929:II. Teil, 106), Hoops (1932:34), Sedgefield (1935:106), Dobbie (1953:122f.).

[8] Wyatt-Chambers (1914:9).

formerly feasting'.[9] In his award-winning verse translation of the epic, Heaney renders the phrase *æfter wiste* as 'their wassail was over'.[10] In this paper I shall reconsider *æfter wiste* in *Beowulf* (128) and shed fresh light on Ten Brink's (rather neglected) interpretation with reference to the use of words for 'drink' and 'food' in *Beowulf*.

2. Images of drink and food in *Beowulf*

As we have seen in the passage above, the *Beowulf* poet refers to the feasting of the night before as *beorþegu* (117). When Beowulf and his warriors are later welcomed in Heorot (cf. ll. 491-8, 611-30), the feast is again referred to as *beorþegu* (617) and takes place in *beorsele* 'beer-hall' (492) with frequent mention of drink (cf. *scir wered* 'bright sweet-drink' 496) and drinking vessels (cf. *hroden ealowæge* 'decorated ale-cup' 495, *ful* 'cup' 615, 628, *seleful* 'hall-cup' 619, *sincfato* 'precious cups' 622, *medoful* 'mead-cup' 624). As Magennis shows in his study of drink and food in OE literature, the poetic vocabulary of feasting is strongly associated with the image of drink and drinking.[11] To denote 'feasting hall', the *Beowulf* poet resorts to *medo-ærn* 'mead-hall' (69), *medo-heal* 'mead-hall' (484, 638), *medu-seld* 'mead-house' (3065), *win-ærn* 'wine-hall' (654), *win-reced* 'wine-hall' (714, 993), *win-sele* 'wine-hall' (695, 771, 2456) as well as *beor-sele* (482, 492, 1094, 2635). Notice that each of these compounds has a first element denoting 'liquor' and emphasises the idea of drinking.

By contrast, eating and food are, as Magennis notes, primarily associated with monsters and beasts.[12] In *Beowulf*, for instance, there occur two instances of *etan* 'eat' (444, 449), both of which refer to eating (of humans) by Grendel. *Beowulf* provides three instances of *fretan* 'eat up, devour': one is used of Grendel (1581) and the others metaphorically refer to 'consuming by fire' (3014, 3114). Besides *etan* and *fretan*, the poet uses the following

---

[9] Klaeber (1950:133).

[10] Heaney (2000:11).

[11] Magennis (1999:11, 28, *et passim*). Note that in *TOE*, **p** (= 'found only in Old English poetry') and **op** (= 'found once only in Old English poetry') flags cluster in category **04.01.03 Drink**.

[12] Magennis (1999:chapter 2). Eating and food are also related to humans who are represented as if they were beasts, such as the Mermedonians in *Andreas* and the Egyptians in *Exodus*.

verbs of eating, most of which refer to eating by non-human beings and objects, such as Grendel, sea-beasts, fire, swords:

bitan 'bite, cut': (Grendel ~) 742 , (sword ~) 1454, 1523, 2578
byrgean 'taste, eat': (Grendel ~) 448
gefeormian 'consume': (Grendel ~) 744
forswelgan 'swallow up': (fire ~) 1122, (Grendel ~) 2080
snædan 'eat, devour': (Grendel ~) 600
swelgan 'swallow': (Grendel ~) 743, (fire ~) 782, (sky ~) 3155
þicgan 'partake of': (sea-monsters ~) 563, (Grendel ~) 736 [Cf. (Hrothgar ~) 1010, (Wiglaf ~) 2633][13]

An examination of 'food' terms in *Beowulf* also reveals that they are mostly used in reference to Grendel, his mother, and beasts. The above-mentioned compound *wæl-fyllo* (125) denotes the food consumed by Grendel, i.e. people in Heorot. Both in simplex and compound, *fyllo* 'fulness (of food)' is with one exception (1014, associated with the Danes) used in reference to monsters: *fyllo* (562, sea-monsters; 1333, Grendel's mother), *wist-fyllo* 'fill of feasting' (734, Grendel).[14] Other terms for 'food' include *æs* 'food, carrion' (1332, Grendel's mother) and *æt* 'feasting' (3026, beasts of battle).[15]

3. A new interpretation

With these in mind, let us now go back to the passage of Grendel's attack on Heorot and consider the terms for feasting. While the compound *beor-þegu* (117) makes clear reference to drinking, no apparent association with drinking is found in the word *symbel* (119). It is to be noted, however, that *symbel* could be linked with the idea of drinking. Cleasby-Vigfusson (*Icelandic-English Dictionary*, s.v. *sumbl*) state that Old Norse *sumbl*, cognate with OE *symbel*, could be derived from the prefix *sam-* 'together'

---

[13] It is to be noted here that two instances of *þicgan* that take humans as subjects do not make a clear reference to 'eating': one (cf. 1010) takes *symbel* as object to mean 'take part in (the feast)' while the other (cf. 2633) denotes 'to drink' with *medu* as object.

[14] Cf. Magennis (1999:33).

[15] Klaeber (1950:144f.) takes (*lices*) *feorm* (451) as 'sustenance of my body' or 'disposal [of my body]'. Since *feorm* usually means 'food, feeding', however, I am inclined to accept Swanton's interpretation that 'possibly the phrase ironically alludes to the meal Grendel may make of the hero' (1997:191). Cf. also Jack (1994:54).

and *öl* 'ale'. According to Vries' *Altnordisches etymologisches Wörterbuch*, *sumbl* is a word indigenous to Germanic, the original sense being 'beitrag zu einem gemeinsamen gelage'.[16]

Unlike the preceding *beor-þegu* and *symbel*, the word *wist* does not relate to drink or drinking: since *wist* is often used for 'food', the image of eating and food could be present in the use of the word for 'feast' in line 128.[17] As we have seen above, the vocabulary of eating and food is primarily associated with monsters and beasts so that the use of *wist* for 'the Danish feasting at Heorot' would be a bit peculiar.[18] It might be worth recalling here that the compound in *wist-*, i.e. *wist-fyllo* (734), is used of Grendel. It is unlikely that the *Beowulf* poet would have used the word *wist* in this context just for the sake of the alliteration on *w-* with *wop*: the poet might have been able to choose *win-þegu* (cf. *Daniel* 17; *Gifts of Men* 74) for 'human feast' and satisfy the metrical requirement without resorting to the word *wist.*[19] These considerations would lead me to assume that, as Ten Brink suggests,[20] the word *wist* in line 128 would concern Grendel rather than the Danes. Unlike Ten Brink, who interprets *æfter wiste* as 'because of Grendel's prey or the thirty thanes', however, I would rather like to take the phrase as 'after Grendel's *banquet*, i.e. his feasting upon the thirty thanes' so that the successive use of the formula '*æfter* ~' can bring out the dramatic antithesis between the heroes' feasting of joy and Grendel's feasting of misery.

According to our interpretation, line 128 would be translated as follows: 'Then lamentation was raised up after Grendel's feasting (upon the thirty thanes)'.

---

16 Holthausen (*Altenglisches etymologisches Wörterbuch*, s.v. *symbel*), however, regards the etymology of *symbel* as unknown.

17 Cf. Magennis (1999:33).

18 The other instance of *wist* in *Beowulf* (1735), although applied to a human being, denotes abundance in general without specific reference to food.

19 The half-line *þa wæs æfter winþege* would have been a well-formed verse of Type C.

20 However, Ten Brink does not notice such a close association of 'eating and food' with monsters in the epic as Magennis has demonstrated. On the other hand, Magennis does not seem to relate *wist* (128) to Grendel.

References

Cleasby, R. & G. Vigfusson, eds. 1957. *An Icelandic-English Dictionary*. 2nd ed. with a supplement by W. A. Craigie. Oxford: Clarendon Press.

Cosijn, P. J. 1892. *Aanteekeningen op den Béowulf.* Leiden: Brill.

———. 1991. *Notes on Beowulf.* Introduced, translated and annotated by R. H. Bremmer Jr., J. van den Berg, & D. F. Johnson. Leeds Texts and Monographs, n.s., 12. Leeds: School of English, University of Leeds.

Dobbie, E. Van K., ed. 1953. *Beowulf and Judith.* ASPR, 4. New York: Columbia University Press.

Heaney, S. 2000. *Beowulf: A New Verse Translation.* New York: Farrar, Straus and Giroux.

Heyne, M., ed. 1888. *Beowulf.* 5th ed. Revised by A. Socin. Paderborn: Ferdinand Schöningh.

Holder , A., ed. 1884. *Beowulf. II.* Freiburg i.B.: J. C. B. Mohr.

Holthausen, F., ed. 1929. *Beowulf nebst den kleineren Denkmälern der Heldensage*. 5th ed. Part 2. Heidelberg: Carl Winter.

———, ed. 1974. *Altenglisches etymologisches Wörterbuch.* 3rd ed. Heidelberg: Carl Winter.

Hoops, J. 1932. *Kommentar zum 'Beowulf'*. Heidelberg: Carl Winter.

Jack, G. B., ed. 1994. *Beowulf: A Student Edition.* Oxford: Clarendon Press.

Klaeber, F., ed. 1950. *Beowulf and the Fight at Finnsburg*. 3rd ed. with 1st and 2nd Supplements. Lexington, MA: Heath.

Kock, E. A. 1904. 'Interpretations and Emendations of Early English Texts: III'. *Anglia* 27:218-37.

Magennis, H. 1999. *Anglo-Saxon Appetites: Food and Drink and their Consumption in Old English and Related Literature.* Dublin: Four Courts Press.

Mitchell, B. & F. C. Robinson, eds. 1998. *Beowulf: An Edition.* Oxford: Blackwell.

Roberts, J. & C. Kay, with L. Grundy. 1995. *A Thesaurus of Old English.* King's College London Medieval Studies, 11. 2 vols. London: King's College.

Sedgefield, W. J., ed. 1935. *Beowulf.* 3rd ed. Manchester: Manchester University Press.

Swanton, M., ed. 1997. *Beowulf.* Revised ed. Manchester: Manchester University Press.

Ten Brink, B. 1888. *'Beowulf.' Untersuchungen.* Quellen und Forschungen zur Sprach- und Culturgeschichte der germanischen Völker, 62. Strassburg: K. J. Trübner.

Trautmann, M. 1899. 'Berichtigungen, Vermutungen und Erklärungen zum *Beowulf*. Erste Hälfte'. *Bonner Beiträge zur Anglistik* 2:121-92.

Vries, J. de. 1962. *Altnordisches etymologisches Wörterbuch*. 2nd ed. Leiden: Brill.

Wyatt, A. J., ed. 1914. *Beowulf with the Finnsburg Fragment*. New ed. Revised, with introduction and notes by R. W. Chambers. Cambridge: Cambridge University Press.

Did Benvenutus Grassus Lecture at Montpellier?

Laurence M. Eldredge

1. Introduction

All the biographical details concerning Benvenutus Grassus, the thirteenth-century ophthalmologist, have been inferred from his only known treatise, the *De probatissima arte oculorum*. The fullest set of inferences are those drawn by Noè Scalinci (1935), and there is a summary updating of scholarship in Eldredge (1993). Benvenutus appears to have been an itinerant ophthalmologist who lived in the thirteenth century, probably educated before 1250 and in practice after 1250. Where and how he learned his craft we do not know. Some evidence suggests that he, like other medieval medical specialists, was trained by the apprentice method (Bullough 1959). But his facility with Latin, his ability to order his material coherently, perhaps even the range of his references to Salerno as well as to a number of medical authorities, all indicate some exposure to the lectures and discipline of a university setting (Siraisi 1990:48-77; Scalinci 1935:196-200).

2. The present theory

One fact about the reception of Benvenutus' treatise has teased his commentators into speculation: despite his evident Italian origins, his early reputation begins not in Italy but in northern Europe, where Jean de Yperman cites him for the first time in 1328 (Laborde 1901:8) and Guy de Chauliac mentions him often in his *Inventarium* (1997, I:323-46). This displacement from his supposed origins leads Scalinci to take up the theory first advanced by Pansier (1904) that Benvenutus lectured at Montpellier (Scalinci 1935:305-11). His presence there would nicely account for his reception in northern Europe and the evident neglect he experienced in Italy, but like so much concerning Benvenutus the theory rests on scant evidence.

The evidence that exists is, first, a note preceding the prologue in the manuscript of the French translation of Benvenutus' treatise (Paris, Bibliothèque Nationale MS Lat. 1327) to the effect that the tract was written at Montpellier: 'Cy apres sensuit le compendil qui a este ordonne par bien venu raffe maistre et docteur en medecine qui a este compose et compille et ordonne a montpellier pour la douleur et maladie des yeulx sur cette forme'. Second, another manuscript, Munich, Bayerische Staatsbibliothek MS CLM 331, records on the last leaf that the codex cost six crowns in Montpellier: 'Iste liber constat in monte pessulano VI coronas'. Third, Pansier (1904:443 & 537) observes that among the teachers of medicine at Montpellier there is a 'Guido Grassi nopolitanus', who lectured there in 1240.

These bits of evidence offer less than they seem to. Both the Paris and the Munich manuscripts are dated in the fifteenth century (Lindberg 1974:104; *Catalogus* 1868, I, 1:66), thus indicating that some two hundred or more years after Benvenutus' era his treatise was known at Montpellier, and he was himself thought to have written there. Finally, the Guido Grassi of Naples, who evidently did lecture in the medical faculty at Montpellier, appears there in an inconvenient year, 1240, putatively before Benvenutus began his actual career as an ophthalmologist. If a careless registrar entered the name Guido instead of Benvenutus, and if this Guido lectured there a generation earlier than the reception evidence suggests, then it may indeed be our man. But both the date and the irregularity of the name give pause.

Scalinci also provides a number of additional details in support of Benvenutus' academic credentials. He claims that medical degrees from Salerno came in more than a single variety, and that certain surgical specialities, such as ophthalmology, might have been granted a special recognition reserved for what he calls 'chirurghi idioti' (Scalinci 1935:204-5). 'Chirurghi idioti' are literally uneducated surgeons, those who might have learned their craft by the apprentice method, like tooth drawers or bone setters. But Frederick II's decree of 1231, which would certainly have applied to any Sicilian or Neapolitan medical candidate for at least the next few years, required of all such candidates the approval of the Salernitan masters of medicine (Mazza 1723:64; DeRenzi 1857, I:373-4). Moreover, Frederick's decree stipulated that only after such approval had been granted was the candidate entitled to fashion himself 'Magister' and to have the right to teach medicine. It is true that in some manuscripts Benvenutus refers to himself as *magister*;[1] in another he styles himself *physice professor*;[2] and in a third he refers to himself as *domino*.[3] But all of these titles occur in the prologue to his treatise, where the text is somewhat unstable (Eldredge 1993:127-8), and where the attribution may be a scribal addition. Even if Benvenutus is responsible for the title, calling oneself *magister* or *professor* confers no valid claim to a genuine title.

In further support of Benvenutus' academic qualifications Scalinci offers the didactic tone of the treatise (Scalinci 1935:305-6), noting the opening of the prologue with an address to all listeners: *Audientes audiant omnes circumstantes* (Naples MS: f.48 [51]r). And he goes on to quote a number of other passages where Benvenutus seems aware that he has an audience. For example 'and do this as I shall teach you' (*et operamini artem secundum ego docebo vos*); 'now I want to tell you' (*nunc volo vobis dicere*); 'here I want especially to explain further' (*hic vero in speciali volo vobis magis explanare*)—and many other similar expressions. There is no doubt that such expressions do figure in the text, partly indicating awareness of a group of listeners and partly marking off the end of one section and the beginning of another. But they do not occur with equal frequency in all the manuscripts. The Naples manuscript, from which Scalinci quotes most often, is especially generous with words of address to the listeners, and one of the five Vatican manuscripts runs it a close second.[4] But the majority of the manuscripts are more laconic, often moving from one section to another with only a slight indication of transition (Eldredge 1993:106-7). In other words it seems to

---

1 Naples, Biblioteca Nazionale MS VIII. G. 100, f.48 (51)r; Vatican, Biblioteca Apostolica MS Palat. Lat. 1320, f.97r; Oxford, Bodleian Library MS Bodley 484, f.56r; Munich, Bayerische Staatsbibliothek MS CLM 259, f.105r, and CLM 331, f.100r; Caen, Bibliothèque Municipale MS 93, f.40r; Wolfenbüttel, Herzog August Bibliothek MS Guelf. 51. 1 Aug. 2°, f.59 (60)r; Florence, Biblioteca Riccardiana MS 2150, f.286r; and Besançon, Bibliothèque Municipale MS 475, f.59r.

2 Boncompagni MS in Albertotti 1901.

3 Vatican, Biblioteca Apostolica MS Vat. Lat. 5373, f.166v.

4 Naples, Biblioteca Nazionale MS VIII. G. 100 and Vatican, Biblioteca Apostolica MS Vat. Lat. 5373.

me only sporadically possible to see Benvenutus' treatise as a lecture or series of lectures. Where the manuscripts are inconsistent, only uncertain conclusions can be drawn.

3. On the contrary

I contend that the only evidence available to us, namely the twenty-four Latin manuscripts and two early printed editions, do not testify unequivocally to a fully qualified academic lecturer, whether at Montpellier or elsewhere. I would like to argue that the *De probatissima arte oculorum* shows evidence of some acquaintance with university-style discourse but generally falls short of the treatises produced by university lecturers in the later thirteenth century. My reservations about the nature of the treatise are based wholly on style, and in what follows I shall argue by comparing Benvenutus' tract with other medical treatises by physicians whom we know to have lectured at universities. I want especially to single out the prologue and the anatomy section of Benvenutus' work, as I think here we can see most clearly what the author strives for and almost reaches. The physicians/surgeons whose work I shall consider are Lanfranc of Milan, whose *Cyrurgia magna* was completed in 1296; Theodorico Borgognoni, who published his *Cyrurgia* before 1266; William of Saliceto, whose *Cyrurgia* appeared in two versions, one in 1258 and the other in 1275. Because some of the directions indicated by these surgeons are more fully developed in the following century, I shall also refer to the work of Henri de Mondeville, whose *Cyrurgia* appeared in 1306, and Guy de Chauliac, who published his *Inventarium* in 1363. I would like to stress that my conclusions are all provisional, for this study represents a stage on the way to a fuller understanding of physicians, surgeons, and their education in the thirteenth and fourteenth centuries.

4. The argument

Most medical/surgical tracts are modestly addressed to a friend, a colleague, or someone who has asked the author to set down his knowledge and experience so that others may benefit from it. Theodorico Borgognoni explains in his prologue that a certain bishop, whom he had served as a chaplain, had asked him to write something about the unknown factors in the art of surgery, such things as he might have learned from his father, Ugo da Lucca.[5] Likewise, William of Saliceto accedes to the nagging of his friend Ruffinus, prior of St. Ambrose at Placentia, and his fellow monks, and to Leonardinus, (his son?) one of his prospective students, all of whom have moved him to write what he has been mulling over as a possibility for some time.[6] And this tradition continues throughout the thirteenth century and into the fourteenth: Lanfranc of Milan, moved to write in 1296 by the love of his dear friend Bernard, the prayers of his honoured professors, and his love for his fellow surgeons (Lanfranc of Milan 1500:f.176rb); Henri de Mondeville wrote at the request of his former teacher, William of Saliceto (Pagel 1892:10); Guy de Chauliac in 1363, names as his impulse to write his colleagues, past and present, at Montpellier, Bologna, Paris, and Avignon (McVaugh 1997, I:1-2).

This sort of modesty may be no more than a rhetorical convention, akin to Chaucer's farewell to his poem at the end of *Troilus and Criseyde*, but it does nonetheless convey a sense of becoming reticence and a lack of presumption. Benvenutus' rumbustious prologue stands in sharp contrast to this tradition of modesty, as he appears to write at his own instigation and to further his own ends. Instead of the few friends and colleagues addressed by the mainstream surgeons, Benvenutus addresses everyone: 'Listen up', he says, 'all you bystanders who want to hear about a new science and gain a marvellous reputation'.[7] It is true that Henri de Mondeville expounds at considerable length on the desirability of a good reputation for caution and medical conservatism, and on the relationship between reputation and income (Pagel 1892:67-76), but the information is offered judiciously and with many qualifications. Benvenutus in contrast gives the impression of a

---

[5] Domino A. dei gratia episcopo valentium … me uestrum tunc temporis capellanum … affectuose rogastis ut uobis quedam artis medicine cyrurgie, scilicet occulta et implicita et ab antiquis imperfecte dicta librum super hoc faciens secundum medicationem domini Hugonis de Luca … Borgognoni 1500:f.97ra.

[6] disposui in mente id quod reclusum erat in anima et aquisitum longo tempore per vsum rationalem in operatione medicinali in scriptis reducere. Et est tamen propter continuam instantiam domini Ruffini prioris sancti Ambrosii de Placentia et sociorum eius, et amore cuiusdam filij mei qui Leonardinus quem ad professionem artis medicinalis inducam pro posse. William of Saliceto 1502:f.2ra.

[7] Audientes audiant omnes circumstantes qui cupiunt audire nouam scienciam scientiam [sic] et habere famam et laudem … Naples MS, f.48 (51)r.

circus barker announcing a show or of a man mounting his soap-box at Hyde Park Corner to deliver a harangue to anyone listening.

One of the pieces invariably included in a compendious medical work is the writer's claim to authority, usually a statement that they rely on both ancient authority, especially Hippocrates and Galen, and on their own experience, with which they carefully supplement ancient learning. Theodorico Borgognoni notes that in the time he spent learning from his father he was not fully able to grasp all the older man's methods; to make up for this deficit he will rely both on his own experience and that of the ancients, chiefly Galen.[8] So too Lanfranc explains the source of his authority as the doctrine of old wise men and knowledgeable former professors together with his own experience extending over a long period.[9] Henri de Mondeville notes that his principal authority is Avicenna, or rather the better parts of Avicenna that have been noted both by himself and by better men, along with his own experience.[10] When it comes to the treatment of wounds, contusions, and ulcers, he depends upon Theodorico along with certain recent treatments of his contemporaries;[11] and Lanfranc is his authority for the treatment of fractures, dislocations, and sprains, ulcers, apostemes, and cancers, and for his antidotary or collection of medical recipes.[12] Guy de Chauliac is the most fulsome of all the early surgeons, presenting as an expression of gratitude to his predecessors what very nearly amounts to a history of physicians and surgeons up to his own own day (McVaugh 1997, I:5-8).

In contrast to these who acknowledge and depend upon their predecessors, Benvenutus gives only a passing nod to the sayings of the ancient phi-

---

[8] Quia uero modico ualde tempore fui cum domino Hugone praedicto, neque uidere neque comprehendere neque discere ad plenum potui expertissimas curas suas. Ideoque in parte ista imperfectum meum expropria experientia et antiquorum curabo perficem, Galieni maxime. Borgognoni 1500:f.97ra.

[9] … secundum doctrinam sapientum acceptam ueterumque ualentium magistrorum meorum et meis certis experimentis et rationabilibus ex longo tempore elaborata. Lanfranc of Milan 1500:f.176rb.

[10] sicut … proposuit Auicenna, prout per me et per quosdam meliores melius extrahi potuit ab eodem et sicut per experientiam eam uidi (Pagel 1892:10).

[11] … ex libro II Theodorici cum quadam cura nova et facili noviter acquisita et deducta in lucem per experientiam modernorum (Pagel 1892:10).

[12] … et istos tres ultimos tractatus eo modo quo nunc dictum est ordinauit Magister Lanfrancus de Mediolano in sua cyrurgia (Pagel 1892:11).

losophers.[13] The rest he claims for his own territory, opened up and explored by him alone. He has gained his experience, he says, through long exercise of his trade in diverse parts of the world, treating his patients in both cold and warm regions.[14] And this experience, described in general terms, he committed to writing, and by both note-taking and memorizing, he claims, he gained first-hand acquaintance with all the diseases of the eye and their cures. Not only did he make note of these illnesses and their causes and cures, but also he was the one who gave names to all of them.[15]

Having done all that, he then wrote it up in its present form, much in the manner of other physicians and surgeons. But where Theodorico Borgognoni says of his first version simply that he wrote it[16] and of his second that he is openly describing the secrets of surgery without any taint of envy,[17] Benvenutus notes that he put his material in order, wrote it all down, and gave it the title that it now bears.[18] In other words where most physicians/surgeons stated their case modestly, giving credit to the earlier authorities on whom they depended and claiming a small portion for their own experience, Benvenutus reverses the emphasis. He claims almost everything for himself and grants only a small bit to the 'sayings of the ancient philosophers'.

At this point in some surgical treatises the author plunges into the matter

---

[13] secundum dictum antiquorum philosophorum (Naples MS, f.48 (51)r).

[14] … et nostram experientiam per longum exercitium quod habui eundo per diuersas partes mundi, medicando tam in frigidis quam in calidis regionibus … (Naples MS, f.48 (51)r).

[15] … et semper augendo in noticiis oculorum et in conualescentiis eorum secundum accidentia cuiuslibet humoris iniuantiuis (?) et expertis medicinis et omnes certissimas et probatissimas medicinas reducebam in scriptis, semper notando et in memoria conseruando usquequo habui plenitudinem de omnibus egritudinibus oculorum et curis eorum tam de causis et accidentijs superuenientibus quam de curis necessarijs et pulueribus et colerijs et emplastris et vnctionibus et pillolis et purgationibus et electuarijs et cauterijs et abstinencijs a contrarijs et regimine bonorum ciborum. Et imposui nomen proprium cuilibet infirmitati per se (Naples MS, f.48 [51]r, with emendations from Vatican, Biblioteca Apostolica MS Vat. Lat. 5373, f.166v).

[16] … librum tunc edidi (Borgognoni 1500:f.97ra).

[17] … artis cyrurgie secreta deposito omnis liuoris aculeo apertissime manifesto (Borgognoni 1500:f.97ra).

[18] Hoc facto omnia hec congregaui simul ordinaui et reduxi in scriptis in libro meo et intitulaui ipsum artem probatissimam oculorum et digne sic nominatus est (Naples MS, f.48 (51)r, with corrections from Vat. Lat. 5373, f.166v).

at hand. Lanfranc's *Parua cyrurgia* and Rolandus' *Libellus de cyrurgia* both make very little introductory ado, Rolandus offering a definition of medicine and the three ways in which medicine treats a patient.[19] Lanfranc's *Parua cyrurgia* is a little more chatty and mentions again his good friend Bernard, but his prologue actually consists of little more than a summary of the work (Lanfranc *Parua* 1500:f.171ra). In other treatises the author offers further advice to his students, as William of Saliceto does in stressing to his young readers the importance of avoiding fools, of keeping a grave demeanour, of avoiding garrulity, of dressing soberly, of asking a proper wage (William of Saliceto 1502:f.2rb). Henri de Mondeville expatiates even more fully than William on a series of related topics: the need for a surgeon to be literate and educated, the need to observe carefully the work of experienced surgeons, the need to identify and avoid the false claimants to medical expertise—and here he names barbers, witches, livery stable managers (?pickpockets?), highwaymen, fakers, alchemists, prostitutes, givers of false measure (?), midwives, old women, converted Jews, and Saracens.[20]

But Benvenutus goes his own way at this point, saying that he has written his excellent book because he has noted a scarcity of books on ophthalmology, especially among Christians.[21] Such a statement very nearly denies the existence of all the authorities cited by the surgeons I have mentioned. Both the ancient authorities and the treatises contemporary with Benvenutus have something to say on diseases of the eye. Many of them describe, and prescribe treatments for, complaints that Benvenutus also deals with, though it is only fair to add that his treatise does mention more—and more varied—ailments than any of the other thirteenth-century treatises. It is true that Rolandus, writing around 1210 at Bologna, remarks on the scarcity of treatises on surgery, observing that only Roger Frugardi (fl. ca. 1170) had written one (Rolandus 1500:f.135ra). But Rolandus was right: at that time

---

[19] Medicina equivocatur duobus modis: uno enim … alio uero … Est autem triplex instrumentum medicine … scilicet dieta, potio, et cyrurgicum (Rolandus 1500:f.135ra).

[20] … omnes illiterati sicut barberii, sortilegi, locatores, insidiatores, falsarii, alchemistae, meretrices, metatrices, obstetrices, vetulae, Judaei conversi, Sarraceni, et quasi omnes qui … fingunt se cyrurgicos … (Pagel 1892:65).

[21] hoc opus feci ob hoc quia uidi quod erat necessarium humane nature quia autores non plene tractauerunt de ista scientia sicut fecerunt de alijs scientijs … et nullum uidi tempore meo qui recto tramite sciret exercere secundum artem inter christianos (Naples MS, f.48 [51]r).

there were very few books on surgery available in Latin. If Scalinci's (1935) careful and plausible dating of Benvenutus is correct, we can only conclude that he was not widely acquainted with developments in the study of surgery that were taking place around him. If he had lectured at Montpellier, or at any medical school, such lack of awareness would surely have been unlikely.

The second section of the *De probatissima arte oculorum* is the curious discussion of the anatomy of the eye. I say 'curious' because it reflects in part the limited nature of Benvenutus' knowledge of medical authority and in part his own strange theories. In prefacing his descriptions of diseases and cures with a chapter on anatomy, the author is on solid ground, for surgeons increasingly stressed the need for such theoretical grounding as the only reliable basis for medical and surgical treatment. William of Saliceto early in his *Summa conseruationis* mentions the major division of surgery into *scientia* and *practica* and remarks that any particular surgical operation depends on *scientia*, just as any particular depends on the universal from which it derives. And he goes on to berate the ignorant who pretend to medical ability when they lack the scientific knowledge that makes proper treatment possible.[22] By the fourteenth century this attitude has become standard. Guy de Chauliac, writing in 1363, cites Rasis' *Continens* as his authority for the necessity of a knowledge of anatomy. In the first place, he says, a physician needs to be wise in his knowledge of the parts of the body; and if this knowledge is useful for a physician, it is even more necessary for a surgeon—and Guy notes that Rasis cites Galen as his authority. Surgeons without proper knowledge of anatomy, he continues, blunder in many ways and may mistakenly cut into nerves and ligaments.[23] Guy goes on to cite Henri de Mondeville, Galen, Haly Abbas, and Avicenna (McVaugh 1997, I:24) to the same effect—without a proper grounding in anatomy a surgeon

---

[22] Sed bene dependet operatio particularis ex cyrurgia que est scientia particulare ab universali. … Et propter hoc multi sunt operatores huius artis que irrationabiliter et sine causa in vno casualiter operantur tanquam homines ignorantes, et que non didicerunt eorum operationes a scientibus sed ab ignorantibus et causis infirmitatum nullo modo se exercuerunt (William of Saliceto 1502:f.134vb).

[23] … medicus debet esse sagax in notitia membrorum veniencium in quolibet loco. Et si hoc est utilis physicis, multo magis, ymo necessarium est cyrurgicis, iuxta doctrinam ipsiusmet [sc. Galieni] in 6° Terapentice … Cyrurgici ignorantes anathomiam peccant multotiens in incisionibus neruorum et colligacionum (McVaugh 1997, I:23).

is like a blind man cutting wood: both cut either more or less than they ought.

Benvenutus does not mention the place of anatomy in his ophthalmological scheme of things, but he does deal with the anatomy of the eye. He begins with a definition of the eye, mentions the hollow optic nerve[24] and the visual spirit, then cites Johannitius for the names of the seven tunics or membranes that cover the eye as well as for the four colours of the eye.[25] Johannitius' *Isagoge,* or introduction to Galenic medicine, formed part of the *Articella*, an introductory medical text that served as a basis for medical education at Salerno and elsewhere during the first half of the thirteenth century (Siraisi 1990:58; Conrad, et al. 1995:141-2), when it was almost everywhere replaced by Avicenna's *Canon.* Apart from general references to Hippocrates and Galen, which indicate more a perfunctory reverence than a careful reading, Johannitius is the only medical authority Benvenutus cites by name. And having cited him, he immediately disagrees. For according to Benvenutus the eye has only two tunics, the 'saluatrix,' so called because it preserves and retains the eye, and the 'discolorata,' so called because it has no colour.[26]

This disagreement with Johannitius leads to a further speculation on the nature of eye colour and its relation to both the acuity of vision and its duration or deterioration in old age. Here Benvenutus both expands upon and argues against Johannitius' theories about eye colour. Where Johannitius had claimed that variations in the crystalline humour produced different eye colours, Benvenutus theorises that eye colour is determined by the depth of the crystalline humour, generally the deeper the crystalline humour, the darker the eye.[27] This discussion takes more space in the manuscripts than I

---

[24] Modern ophthalmological anatomy recognises that the optic nerve is not hollow, though normally ophthalmologists do not feel it necessary to state this. An ordinary nerve structure is presupposed in, for example, Kanski 1999:587-644.

[25] ... per quam spiritus uisibilis ueniendo per neruum concauum habet exitum suum intra aquas et tunicas, de quibus tunicis dicit Johannitius quod sunt septem ... et dicit quod colores oculorum sunt iiij (Naples MS, f.48 (51)v, with corrections from Vat. Lat. 5373, f.166v).

[26] ... dico quod tunice oculorum due sunt ... et uoco primam saluatricem quia saluat totum oculum et retinet omnes humores oculorum. Secunda uero discoloratam quia non est color in ea (Naples MS, f.48 (51)v, with corrections from Vat. Lat. 5373, f.167r).

[27] illi qui habent humores in profundo ... apparent oculi eorum nigri ... et illi qui habent

have allotted to it here, but much of it is repetitive and in any event speculative rather than based on authority. Benvenutus finishes his anatomical section with an account of the three humours or fluids in the eye, where he again follows Johannitius though without acknowledgement, and a brief description of the complexions of the various parts of the eye together with an account of how each part is nourished.

And this completes Benvenutus' anatomy of the eye. It does not include everything that was known at the time. For example, there is no mention of theories of vision: whether vision takes place by intromission, or the reception by the eye of light from a source outside the eye, or by extromission, where the eye itself sends out a ray to encounter a lighted object. There is no description of the course of the optic nerve from the brain to the optical chiasmus to the eye. The crystalline humour is not identified as the actual organ of sight. All these theories formed part of the ophthalmological views current in Benvenutus' day, but he seems ignorant of them and depends wholly upon Johannitius' brief *Isagoge* and his own notions.

5. Conclusion

Without plunging further into the whole corpus of Benvenutus' medical and surgical techniques, his diagnostics and pharmacology, any judgement one can make must at best be tentative. With that caveat I would tentatively suggest the following conclusions. First, Benvenutus may well have been educated at a Salernitan school, perhaps at Salerno itself, but after leaving he made little further contact with any university setting, neither as student nor as lecturer. Second, while he knows the form that a medical/surgical treatise should take and has the wit to organise his work to conform with the pattern, the content of his prologue and anatomy often seems no more than a parody of the actual university discourse that has survived. Finally, Benvenutus' strength, and it is an undeniable strength, lies in his skill as a practising ophthalmologist, not as a university lecturer. His talent was enough to impress Guy de Chauliac, who cites him extensively (McVaugh 1997, I:323-

---

humores in medietate ... apparent oculi eorum mediocriter nigri ... et illi qui habent humores iuxta tunicas sunt uarii (Naples MS, f.49 [52]r, with corrections from Vat. Lat. 5373, f.167r).

46), and to endure well into the seventeenth century (Eldredge 1999). However narrowly I have restricted the extent of his expertise, he is still an impressive expert.

References

Albertotti, G. 1901. *I codici napoletano, vaticani, e boncompagni ora albertotti dell'opera oftalmojatrica di Benvenuto.* Modena: Memorie della Regia Accademia, ser.3, vol. 4.

Borgognoni, Theodorico. 1500. *Cyrurgia*. In *Cyrurgia Guidonis de Cauliaco.* Venice: Scotus.

Bullough, V. 1959. 'Training of the Non-University Educated Medical Practitioners in the Later Middle Ages'. *Journal of the History of Medicine* 14:446-58.

Catalogus codicum Latinorum Bibliothecae Regiae Monacensis. 1868-81. 2 vols in 7 pts. Munich: Bayerische Staatsbibliothek.

Conrad, L. I., Michael Neve, Vivian Nutton, Roy Porter, & Andrew Wear. 1995. *The Western Medical Tradition 800 B.C. to A.D. 1800.* Cambridge: Cambridge University Press.

DeRenzi, S. 1857-9. *Storia documentata della scuola medica di Salerno*. 5 vols. Naples: Nobile.

Eldredge, L. M. 1993. 'The Textual Tradition of Benvenutus Grassus' "De arte probatissima oculorum"'. *Studi medievali* 3rd ser. 34:95-138.

———. 1999. 'The English Vernacular Afterlife of Benvenutus Grassus, Ophthalmologist'. *Early Science and Medicine* 4:149-63.

Kanski, J. K. 1999. *Clinical Ophthalmology: A Systematic Approach.* 4th ed. Oxford: Butterworth/Heinemann.

Kristeller, P. O. 1986. *Studi sulla scuola medica salernitana.* Naples: Istituto Italiano per gli Studi Filosofici.

Laborde, C. 1901. *Un oculiste du xiie siècle: Bienvenu de Jérusalem et son oeuvre: le manuscrit de la Bibliothèque de Metz.* M.D. thesis. Montpellier: Hamelin.

Lanfranc of Milan. 1500. *Ars completa totius cyrurgie*. In *Cyrurgia Guidonis de Cauliaco*. Venice: Soctus.

———. 1500. *Parua cyrurgia.* In *Cyrurgia Guidonis de Cauliaco.* Venice: Scotus.

Lindberg, D. C. 1975. *A Catalogue of Medieval and Renaissance Optical Manuscripts.* Toronto: Pontifical Institute of Medieval Studies.

Mazza, A. 1723. *Urbis Salernitanae historia et antiquitates.* 2nd ed. in I. G. Graevius, *Thesaurus antiquitatum et historiarum Italiae*, IX, 4. Leiden.

McVaugh, M. R. 1997. *'Guigonis de Caulhiaco inventarium sive chirurgia magna.* 2 vols. Leiden: Brill.

Pagel, J. L. 1892. *Die Chirurgie des Heinrich von Mondeville (Hermondavilla) nach Berliner, Erfurter, und Pariser Codices.* Berlin: Hirschwald.

Pansier, P. 1904. 'Les maîtres de la Faculté de Médecine de Montpellier au moyen âge—xiie siècle'. *Janus* 9:443, 537.

Rolandus. 1500. *Libellus de cyrurgia.* In *Cyrurgia Guidonis de Cauliaco.* Venice: Scotus.

Scalinci, N. 1935. 'Questioni biografiche su Benvenuto Grasso jerosolimitano, Medico oculista del xiii secolo'. *Atti e memorie dell'Accademia di Storia dell'arte sanitaria* 2nd ser. 1: 190-205, 240-55, 299-313.

Siraisi, N. G. 1990. *Medieval and Early Renaissance Medicine: An Introduction to Knowledge and Practice.* Chicago: University of Chicago Press.

William of Saliceto. 1502. *Summa conservationis magistri Guglielmi Placentini.* Venice: Scotus. [Version revised by William in 1275.]

Some Observations on the Use of Manuscripts, Dates, and Preferred Editions in the *Middle English Dictionary*

Robert E. Lewis

1. Introduction

For as long as Matsuji Tajima and I have known each other, which now goes back nearly twenty years,[1] I have been involved in the editing of the *MED*, and he and I have kept in touch about our progress ever since, either through letters or in person. The *MED* was completed in the summer of 2001, with the publication of the X-Y-Z fascicle, and the celebrations of the completion took place in Ann Arbor a few months earlier, in May of 2001, at the biennial meeting of the Dictionary Society of North America. During those celebrations I gave a final lecture in which I spoke about the nature and achievement of the *MED*, changes in the editing plan over the years, innovations in the *MED* to the usual practice of historical dictionaries, and the people and the institutions involved in producing and supporting the project over the years. In that lecture I briefly described the *MED*'s treatment of manuscripts, manuscript vs. composition dates, and preferred editions and explained, as I conceived it, the underlying philosophy for that treatment.[2]

---

[1] To October of 1983, at the University of Ottawa, where he was defending his PhD dissertation. Though he thinks of me as one of his mentors, I consider myself rather a friend and a colleague in the same field, and I congratulate him on this Festschrift and on the milestone of his 60th birthday.

[2] The lecture, in revised form, will be published later this year, after the presentation date of this Festschrift, in the journal *Dictionaries: Journal of the Dictionary Society of*

In what follows here I want first to summarize (in Part 2) my remarks on these matters and then to make some general observations (in Parts 3 and 4) based on those remarks: Part 3 has to do with Christopher Cannon's comments in a recent article about one aspect of the *MED*'s treatment, the 'double-dating' system, and the *MED*'s sense of history; Part 4 has to do with an exception to the *MED*'s treatment of preferred manuscripts and preferred editions—a large one because it involves the best known ME author, Geoffrey Chaucer, and his works.

2. Treatment of Manuscripts

Since the purpose of the *MED* is to describe, or recover, the English language current between circa 1100 and circa 1500, we are interested in what the actual witnesses had to say, that is, what the medieval scribes put down on parchment and paper, and our bias towards these witnesses can be seen in our basic, overall approach to our material.

First of all, 'For every text and for every version of a text a *preferred MS* is selected, from which the quotations are normally taken.... The earliest complete, or fairly complete, MS that has been edited is chosen as the preferred MS'.[3] This usually turns out to coincide with what the editor believes is the most important manuscript or the one closest to the author's original, though 'If the most important MS...has not been edited, or poorly edited, a facsimile of that MS may be used as the preferred MS' (*Plan*:17).

The manuscript date is the first item in the short title for nearly every text and takes precedence over the composition date, which is usually conjectural. If the composition date is more than twenty-five years earlier than the manuscript date, then we put it in parentheses after the manuscript date, though only in the short title for the preferred manuscript; otherwise we omit it, leaving just the manuscript date. There are two main exceptions, or rather refinements, to this practice—'Quotations taken from documents (if they are assumed to be contemporary...), or from works for which the composition

---

North America, and I thank Luanne von Schneidemesser, the Executive Secretary of the Society, for permission to quote a few paragraphs, in revised form, from it in Part 2 below; see Lewis (2002).

[3] *Plan and Bibliography* (1954:17); subsequent references to this work are cited as *Plan* and incorporated in the text.

date is well established and less than 25 years earlier than the MS, bear only the composition date, *enclosed in parentheses*' (*Plan*:17)—but the principle still holds: the manuscript date is the one we consider the more important.

Then, 'For each MS of a text that has been edited by two or more different scholars, a *preferred edition* is selected, from which the quotations are normally taken.... In selecting the preferred edition, fidelity in the reproduction of the MS is the primary consideration' (*Plan*:17); in the case of competing critical editions, the ease with which we can recover and restore the manuscript readings is the crucial factor in our choice of preferred edition. That means that the easiest editions for us to use are the diplomatic or semi-diplomatic (that is, those that reproduce the manuscript exactly as it stands or that put variant texts in parallel facing columns), and the hardest to use are the eclectic (that is, those that select readings now from one manuscript, now from another, according to the editor's sense of what the author intended) or those that make use of conjectural emendation.[4]

In short, we treat each manuscript, whether preferred or non-preferred, as a witness (more coherent or less coherent, more reliable or less reliable, as witnesses are), and our short title stands for that witness—*not* for the edition in which it happens to appear. If we believe that a manuscript reproduces a garbled or an erroneous reading, we sometimes add a bracketed reconstructed reading after it to indicate what we think the reading was intended to be or was derived from, but we leave the manuscript reading intact. We thus preserve the integrity of the scribe, the actual witness, and of his manuscript, his testimony.

I do not want to imply by this that we think we are dealing with running passages of spontaneous writing, that is, the kind of data one might find used as evidence for an unabridged contemporary English dictionary. In dealing with a scribal copy of someone else's original, it is of course difficult, if not impossible, to sort out what part is the scribe's language and what part is the language of the original. This is a perennial problem in medieval studies,[5] but the principle still holds: the scribal copy is the closest thing we have to the running passage of spontaneous speech or writing of

---

4 See Lewis (2002:fn.13) for some examples; it is unnecessary for the purpose of this paper to repeat them here.

5 See, for example, *LALME*: especially Volume I, Chapter 3 of the Introduction and Appendices I and II.

the modern informant, and only by treating this copy as our primary evidence will we come close to being able to recover the language of the ME period.

3. The 'Double-Dating' System

The interpretation of the underlying philosophy for our dating system that I have set forth in the preceding section, with its reliance on manuscript dates as a reflection of the testimony of actual witnesses,[6] is nowhere to be found in the writings on the *MED* of my predecessors, Hans Kurath and Sherman Kuhn, so far as I am aware. The initial impetus for the system of privileging manuscript dates came from a very practical consideration, which Kurath explained in the annual report on the project for 1947:[7]

> The bibliographical apparatus of the MED, as it was in 1946, was found to be quite inadequate for our purposes. It had simply accumulated over a period of years and had never been systematically reviewed. Much of it had been taken over uncritically from the O[E]D or culled piece-meal from the introductions to edited texts. Some texts were assigned composition dates, others MS dates (which sometimes are a century apart). For some texts the MS date reflected the opinions of early paleographers who were inclined to push the MS dates rather far back; for others the more conservative dating of recent paleographers was accepted. In some cases different texts from one and the same MS, written by one and the same hand, had very different dates. Some texts were quoted under two or three different titles without anyone being aware of it.

The bibliographical system that was eventually adopted, after 'a thorough overhauling of the bibliographical apparatus' between 1946 and 1949,[8]

---

[6] Laing (2001:90) makes a similar point, but from the perspective of an historical dialectologist, about the scribe 'as an authentic user of language'.

[7] 'THE MIDDLE ENGLISH DICTIONARY Report for 1947', pp. 2-3; this unpublished report, along with most of the other *MED* records and materials, is now housed in the Bentley Historical Library at the University of Michigan.

[8] The quotation is from the *Plan and Bibliography* (1954:x). Revisions to the bibliographical apparatus were begun, apparently in late 1946 and certainly by early 1947, by editors Margaret S. Ogden and Charles E. Palmer, and it was they who presented to the *MED* staff on April 1, 1947, the idea of 'double-dating', which was subsequently incorporated into the bibliographical system and apparatus. Their unpublished presentation, along with most of the other *MED* records and materials, is now housed in the Bentley Historical Library at the University of Michigan.

contained the innovation of the 'double-dating' feature. As Kurath put it in the same report, 'We have decided to assign the MS date to all texts, and to add the composition date in parentheses if the text was composed a quarter of a century or more earlier than the date of the MS from which we quote. Paleographic evidence gives us a fairly reliable approximate date for all the MSS, whereas the composition date is often highly conjectural. Mixing MS dates and composition dates, as in the past, is very misleading' (p. 3).

This 'double-dating' feature constitutes the primary, and indeed most striking, innovation in the *MED*'s bibliographical system. Some years later Kuhn (1982:24) summarized its virtues in this way: 'The double date is desirable because a text composed in one year and preserved in a MS many years later has obviously lived through some changes in the language. Any specific word in it may have the shape originally given it, or it may have a shape given it at any time down to the period of the MS. Medieval scribes frequently modernized the texts they were copying, but never consistently'.

In a recent article Cannon discusses the *MED*'s general approach to lexical history and argues that the practice of 'double-dating' obscures the 'sequential history' of a word (2001:15),[9] concluding that, because of this and other practices, the *MED* 'is not a "historical" dictionary if history must be as sequential, progressive, and rectilinear as the editors of the *OED* are sure it is' but rather 'is "historical" as it reconstructs the endless motion [or recursiveness] inherent' in 'the unchangeableness of so many words' (2001:15).[10]

This is not the occasion for an extended analysis of Cannon's article, which makes a number of interesting and valuable points, but, before going on to his main one, I would like to make two general observations about his interpretations of the *MED*'s dating system and especially the 'double-dating' feature. First, he says that the composition dates 'are to be nowhere

---

[9] See also Cannon (2001:1-2, 9-10, *et passim*). Subsequent references to Cannon's article are incorporated in the text.

[10] Cannon's contrastive example of the *OED* gerund 'Misleading' versus the *MED* gerund 'misleding(e' on page 1 is an unfortunate one because of the *OED*'s practice of frequently defining the gerund as 'The action of the [corresponding] verb'. The *OED* could easily have made finer distinctions with 'Misleading', as it does with the verb 'Mislead', just as the *MED* does with its gerund. This example does not invalidate Cannon's point, however, but his example of the noun 'cloistrer' on page 2 is, as he says, 'more typical' of the practice of the *MED*.

heeded for the purposes of historical arrangement' (2001:3). Though this is true when both the manuscript date and the composition date are given for a single bibliographical entry, the *MED* does use the composition date in place of the manuscript date, as I pointed out above, when there is *less* than 25 years between them. Secondly, and more important, his interpretation that 'The doubled timeline...is, in fact, a direct result of the skepticism [regarding historical semantics that] the "Editors of the *MED*" direct at the very documentary record they survey' (2001:5) is historically incorrect. As I also pointed out above, the present dating system grew out of shortcomings and inconsistencies in the bibliographical apparatus as Kurath found it in 1946 and preceded his remarks on meaning and historical semantics as found in the *Plan and Bibliography* (1954).

But to respond to Cannon's main point, which is correct, that the 'sequential history' of a word is obscured by the *MED*'s 'double-dating' system, it is inevitable, given our decision to privilege the manuscript date over the composition date (if and when it exists), that the 'history' of a word, insofar as that means the historical development proceeding from first authorial use to second authorial use, etc.[11] would be somewhat obscured. But, in view of the fact that so few ME texts have reliable, or even ascertainable, composition dates, any dating system based on such dates would be impossible to sustain. Ultimately the only way to produce a consistent and relatively reliable dating system for the ME period is to use manuscript dates.[12] This results in the history of the usage of individual scribes rather than the history of authorial use, and, as I have pointed out in Part 2 above, such usage is the best evidence we have available for recovering the language of the ME period.

An interesting question raised by Cannon's article, however, is how one can trace the history of authorial use, if one wishes to do so, within a system that is based on scribal usage and manuscript dates. The data for carrying

[11] Cannon's formulation for this is 'a word's history according to the dates of a text's composition' (2001:5).

[12] The forthcoming third edition of the *OED*, unlike the first and second (which Cannon used for his examples), will normally follow the *MED* in its dating practice, using the 'double-dating' feature where appropriate; see the online 'Preface to the Third Edition', the section entitled 'Documentation', last paragraph (I am indebted to John Simpson, Chief Editor of *OED*3, for calling my attention to this paragraph).

out this exercise is available, of course, in both the print *MED* and the online *MED*,[13] but it would normally be easier to use the online *MED* to extract such data. Unfortunately, however, the parentheses enclosing composition dates, whether they come first in a bibliographical entry or follow the manuscript date, have not been tagged, and so the work cannot be done at this time on the Compendium screen. One would need to download the data and rearrange the quotations in chronological order offline, or perhaps write a program to sort and chronologize the downloaded data. For entries that have no composition dates, but only manuscript dates, one would then have to decide whether to ignore them or to fit them into the chronological scheme. I believe that it would be a little misleading to fit them in if one is interested in only authorial uses. But even without them the result would give only an approximation of the history of authorial use because one can never be absolutely certain that the word in question was actually in the author's original and not added during the course of transmission by the scribe.

4. Chaucer Editions

The one exception to the practice of the *MED* regarding preferred manuscripts, and preferred editions based on them, as I have described it in Part 2, is our treatment of Chaucer's works, for which we have used as our preferred editions—without restoration or recovery of the readings of the base manuscripts—the eclectic edition of Manly & Rickert (1940) for the *Canterbury Tales* and Robinson's edition of 1933, and more recently the Riverside edition (Benson 1987), for most of the other works.[14] Indeed, the

---

[13] The online *MED* is one part of the Middle English Compendium, available at the website listed under McSparran (2002) in the References at the end of this paper; see further the description of it in McSparran's paper.

[14] We have of course acknowledged our practice in the *Plan and Bibliography* (1954:17, 31), and for works other than the *Canterbury Tales* we have put 'Rob.', and more recently 'Riverside', into the short title when necessary in place of the usual preferred manuscript, as we also do with other eclectic editions, for example, G. Warner's edition of *The Libelle of Englyshe Polycye* or K. Brunner's edition of *Richard the Lionheart*, for which see Lewis (2002:fn.13). I have treated the exception of Chaucer's works in a paper entitled 'Chaucer Editions and the *Middle English Dictionary*', presented at the 6th International Congress of the New Chaucer Society in Vancouver in August 1988, of which Part 4 of this paper is an adaptation.

notion of a base manuscript did not even enter into Manly and Rickert's thinking. They were interested in reconstructing O[1] (= the exclusive common ancestor, or archetype, of all the extant manuscripts), which is one remove from O (= the author's original), and they did this by classifying the extant manuscripts and then using the classification to reconstruct O[1]. Though their final text looks most like the Hengwrt manuscript, it is not that manuscript used as a base but rather an eclectic text containing readings from various manuscripts.[15] Robinson (1933) adhered to the principle of a base manuscript in his texts, but he too emended from other manuscripts and in addition freely corrected grammatical errors by the scribes and restored final *-e*'s 'when necessary to the meter'.[16] Riverside follows the practice of Robinson (1933), though in its editions of the majority (though not all) of the texts is somewhat more conservative in retaining the readings of the base manuscripts.[17]

The reason we made the exception for Chaucer's works, I suspect, is that we began life as a Chaucer dictionary (going back to the days of Ewald Flügel at Stanford University),[18] and since we have tried throughout our long history to use one or more quotations from Chaucer, wherever possible, in every sense of every word used by him,[19] it must have seemed important to my predecessors to use editions that were accessible to most readers of the *MED*. But in view of our basic philosophy they were not good choices. For the *Canterbury Tales* it would have been better to have used the transcripts of the Hengwrt or Ellesmere manuscripts done for the Chaucer Society or the more recent transcript of Hengwrt on facing pages of the facsimile published by the New Chaucer Society (1979) (supplemented by Ellesmere) or perhaps N. F. Blake's edition (1980) based on Hengwrt (again

---

[15] For a convenient explication see Dempster (1946:390-2, 394-5, 413-14). On the method of editing see G. Kane's chapter on Manly and Rickert in Ruggiers (1984:208-12, 228).

[16] Robinson (1933:xxxix). See further the general section entitled 'The Text' in Robinson (1933:xxxii-xl) and G. F. Reinecke's chapter on Robinson in Ruggiers (1984:esp. 238-41). We did not change to Robinson's second edition when it appeared in 1957, for it is primarily an 'extension' of the first edition; on this second edition see Reinecke's chapter in Ruggiers (1984:249-51).

[17] See the general section entitled 'The Texts' in Benson (1987:xlv-xlvii).

[18] For a brief history of Flügel's Chaucer dictionary see Blake (2002:section I).

[19] See Cannon (1998:206-9, 227-33) for how the *MED*, as well as the *OED*, has

supplemented by Ellesmere). For the other works it would have been better, since it is impossible to restore the full texts of the base manuscripts from the limited textual apparatus in either Robinson (1933) or Riverside, to have used the transcripts of the preferred manuscripts prepared for the Chaucer Society or the various separate editions available (J. Koch, *Kleinere Dichtungen* (1928); R. K. Root (1926), then B. A. Windeatt (1984), for *Troilus and Criseyde*; M. H. Liddell (1898) for *Boece*; H. Phillips (1982) for *Book of the Duchess*; the Chaucer Variorum edition (1982) for some of the short poems; etc.).

We have made some adjustments during my time to bring our treatment of the *Canterbury Tales*, the *Romaunt of the Rose*, and *A Treatise on the Astrolabe* more in line with our basic philosophy, but in only one case (that of the *Romaunt*) did this amount to a change of policy. For the *Canterbury Tales* we have continued to use Manly and Rickert, but we have tried to be as full as possible in the variant readings we cite, both substantive and orthographic, from volumes five through eight of Manly and Rickert or from the Chaucer Society transcripts (if more context was needed). For the *Romaunt of the Rose* we changed from Robinson (1933) to Kaluza's edition of the Hunterian manuscript (1891) at the beginning of the *sc-* words (except for those portions that were lacking in the Hunterian manuscript, which we have taken from W. Thynne's edition (1532), using a different short title) and have continued in that manner through the end of the alphabet.

For the other works we changed from Robinson (1933) to Riverside soon after it was published. Because of the nature of its texts and the fuller textual notes,[20] the Riverside edition was for us a considerable improvement over Robinson (1933). Of the two prose texts in Riverside, *Boece* and *A Treatise on the Astrolabe*, the edition of the former is based on a full collation of the manuscripts, with comparisons from the Latin text, the French translation, and Nicholas Trevet's commentary; the textual notes themselves are selective, but they do include lists of readings in the base manuscript from which the editors have departed, and my understanding is that final *-e*'s and inflectional endings have not been 'corrected', as in Robinson (1933).[21] The

---

'privileged' Chaucer in its pages.

[20] See the introduction to the 'Textual Notes' section in Benson (1987:1117).

[21] See Benson (1987:xlv-xlvi) and the textual introductions to the various poems.

edition of the *Astrolabe* in Riverside is based on a collation of nearly all of the manuscripts, and though the text itself is eclectic, the textual notes are unusually full; the spelling has been modified in accordance with Chaucer's grammar, but we often corrected that in our quotations with reference to the transcripts of the base manuscripts, Oxford, Bodleian Library, MS. Bodley 619 and (for the supplementary propositions) Oxford, Bodleian Library, MS. Digby 72 and Cambridge, St. John's College, MS. E.2, made by the editor (John Reidy, who was also a member of the *MED* staff) and deposited in our project library.

Leaving aside the *Canterbury Tales* and the *Romaunt*, the poetic texts in the Riverside edition do not differ as much as the prose texts from those in Robinson (1933). Thanks to the Chaucer Society transcripts, which exist for most manuscripts of the poetic texts (except *Troilus and Criseyde*), Robinson had access to nearly as much of the relevant data as the Riverside edition, but the fuller textual notes in Riverside, especially when used along with the Chaucer Variorum editions, the Chaucer Society transcripts, and B. A. Windeatt's edition of *Troilus and Criseyde* (1984), allow the reader to make more informed decisions about the relationships of the manuscripts—and thus about their language—than those in Robinson (1933) do.

Chaucer's works, as I have shown, are an exception to our practice regarding preferred manuscripts and editions, but for works other than Chaucer's our basic policy remains, that is, to treat each scribe as a witness and his manuscript as the record of his testimony, for only in this way, we believe, will we be able to capture, or recover, the language current in the ME period.

References

Benson, L. D., gen. ed. 1987. *The Riverside Chaucer*. 3rd ed. Boston: Houghton Mifflin.

Blake, N. F. 2002 (forthcoming). 'The Early History of, and Its Impact upon, the *Middle English Dictionary*'. *Dictionaries: Journal of the Dictionary Society of North America* 23.

Cannon, C. 1998. *The Making of Chaucer's English: A Study of Words*. Cambridge: Cambridge University Press.

———. 2001. 'The Unchangeable Word: The Dating of Manuscripts and the

History of English'. *Middle English Poetry: Texts and Traditions*, ed. A. J. Minnis. Woodbridge: Boydell and Brewer. 1-15.

Dempster, G. 1946. 'Manly's Conception of the Early History of the *Canterbury Tales*'. *Publications of the Modern Language Association of America* 61:379-415.

Kuhn, S. M. 1982. 'On the Making of the Middle English Dictionary'. *Dictionaries: Journal of the Dictionary Society of North America* 4:14-41. A revised version of the article originally published in 1976 in *Poetica: An International Journal of Linguistic-Literary Studies* 4.

Kurath, H., S. M. Kuhn, R. E. Lewis, et al., eds. 1952-2001. *Middle English Dictionary*. 13 vols. Ann Arbor: University of Michigan Press.

Kurath, H., M. S. Ogden, C. E. Palmer, & R. L. McKelvey. 1954. *Middle English Dictionary Plan and Bibliography*. Ann Arbor: University of Michigan Press.

Laing, M. 2001. 'Words Reread. Middle English Writing Systems and the Dictionary'. *Linguistica e Filologia* 13:87-129.

Lewis, R. E. 2002 (forthcoming). 'The Middle English Dictionary at 71'. *Dictionaries: Journal of the Dictionary Society of North America* 23.

McIntosh, A., M. L. Samuels, M. Benskin, et al. 1986. *A Linguistic Atlas of Late Mediaeval English*. 4 vols. Aberdeen: Aberdeen University Press.

Manly, J. M., & E. Rickert, eds. 1940. *The Text of the Canterbury Tales*, 8 vols. Chicago: University of Chicago Press.

McSparran, F. 2002 (forthcoming). 'The Middle English Compendium: Past, Present, Future'. *Dictionaries: Journal of the Dictionary Society of North America* 23. The website for the Compendium is http://www.hti.umich.edu/m/mec/

Plan and Bibliography = *Middle English Dictionary Plan and Bibliography*. See Kurath (*Plan*) & Ogden, Palmer, & McKelvey (*Bibliography*) (1954).

The Riverside Chaucer. See Benson, gen. ed. (1987).

Robinson, F. N., ed. 1933. *The Complete Works of Geoffrey Chaucer*. Boston & New York: Houghton Mifflin.

Ruggiers, P. G., ed. 1984. *Editing Chaucer: The Great Tradition*. Norman, Oklahoma: Pilgrim Books.

Troilus and the Law of Kind[1]

Joseph Wittig

1. Introduction

Ideas from Boethius' *Consolation of Philosophy* permeate Chaucer's writing from the time he seriously encountered that work, and nowhere is this more true than in the *Troilus*. The most extended intrusion of *Boece* into that poem is the speech, one hundred and twenty-one lines long, of Troilus about 'predestination' in Book 4 (4.958-1078).[2] This material, drawn directly from the fifth book of the *Consolation* (the end of Prose 2 and the first part of Prose 3) has often struck modern readers as tedious, inappropriate, even bizarre (see for example Patch 1918:399 and Curry 1930:150-1). Such sentiments may have been shared by medieval readers: some scribes simply omitted the lines altogether.[3]

---

[1] An earlier version of this article was presented at the Southeastern Medieval Association's 26th Conference in September 2000.

[2] All references to and quotation from Chaucer's works use *The Riverside Chaucer* and are given parenthetically in the text. Boethius' Latin text is quoted from the edition by L. Bieler (1957). Translations of Chaucer or Boethius into modern English are my own.

[3] The textual situation is summarized in S. A. Barney's note to Book 4, lines 953-1085 in the Riverside edition. Earlier editors, particularly Root, had suggested the absence of the passage in some MSS indicated it was a later addition, by Chaucer or another reviser. Windeatt (1979) has argued that this and similar passages were integral to Chaucer's original plan and that his mode of composition (first translating those lines of the *Filostrato* he intended to use, then going back to add other material) may have resulted in a draft which led to scribal omission. Hanna finds Windeatt's case a 'compelling demonstration' (1984:186, n. 8).

2. Reasons for the Addition

Yet since the arguments by Patch and Curry no modern scholar has seriously doubted that Chaucer took some pains to introduce these lines into his story; his reasons for doing so have been variously explained. Patch had argued that the speech was dramatically appropriate, 'an outburst of human emotion' in which Troilus 'exonerated himself of all guilt for his disaster so that he might pity himself the more justly' (1918:405, 410).[4] Curry agreed that the speech created a dramatic effect, showing Troilus in an emotional revolt against a destiny whose earlier effects he had happily accepted, in which his instinctively philosophical mind momentarily reasserts itself in relentlessly logical pursuit of the question of freedom versus destiny (1930:152-4); the whole passage shows Chaucer 'an extremely intrepid artist who conceived that the action of a great tragedy should be under the direction of a stern necessity' (156). Readers have subsequently tended to agree that the passage is significant: it adds to the presence and pressure of Fortune and Fate in the tale; it contributes to the characterization of Troilus (for example as one who leaps to extremes, who is instinctively an idealist, perhaps even inclined to metaphysics,[5] adds to our sense of his passivity, and can even be read as humorous at Troilus' expense. More recently S. Knight has read it as a means through which Chaucer attempts, using the intellectual apparatus available to him, to dramatize the limitations on individual freedom in the face of collective values and social constraints (1986:56). But without dismissing any of these appreciations, I would here like to suggest that the passage also functions in a very specific way, one which so far as I know has not been fully articulated.

Barry Windeatt, comparing the *Troilus* passage with Chaucer's translation of the same matter in the *Boece*, recently pointed to a difference in tone between the prose translation and the poem; he finds 'a more resignedly predestinarian prejudice on Troilus' part, in which the *Consolation*'s arguments are absorbed but re-expressed by Troilus with a reverent sense of God's power' (1992:106).[6] He continued: 'The way in which Troilus'

---

[4] Patch restated this argument some dozen years later (1931:225-43).

[5] Pandarus has recently remarked this tendency: 'Devyne not in resoun ay so depe / Ne preciously …' (4.589-90).

[6] Windeatt's sense of a tonal difference may arise from the difference between prose and

soliloquy is both more explicitly resigned to a lack of free will, and would also be judged as incompletely argued by any reference to its celebrated source, makes it one of the Boethian borrowings in *Troilus* which most turns upon a comparative sense of how the borrowed passage relates to its original context in the *Consolation*' (107). My argument addresses the significance of this 'incompletely argued' aspect of the speech and of its context of the *Consolatio*: for both place Troilus in a context recognizable to those familiar with the *Consolation*, the context of the human soul at a specific stage in its quest for happiness.

3. Context: General Considerations

One must begin by recalling the general situation. As Book 4 of *Troilus* opens, the Trojan parliament has agreed to exchange Criseyde for Antenor; Troilus has left the parliament devastated by grief; Pandarus has gone off to arrange a meeting between Troilus and an equally devastated Criseyde. Pandarus now returns to Troilus. Boccaccio's version simply says:

> Rintrovó Pandar Troiolo pensoso,
> e sí forte nel viso sbigottito,
> che per pietá ne divenne doglioso,
> ver lui dicendo:—Or se' tu sí 'nvilito
> come tu mostri, giovin valoroso?
> Ancor non s'è da te 'l tuo ben partito;
> perché ancor cotanto ti sconforti
> che gli occhi in testa ti paion giá morti? (*Filostrato* 4.109)

> Pandarus found Troilus heavy-thoughted and so downcast in look that he was stricken with pity for him, and said unto him: 'Art thou now so low-spirited as thou appearest, valorous youth? Thy love has not yet left thee. Why then art thou so melancholy that thy eyes already look dead in thy head? (Gordon 1934:83)

Chaucer adapts this stanza as follows:

> Goth Pandarus, and Troilus he soughte

---

dramatic versification. Huber (1965:120-5) had argued to a similar end that Chaucer characterizes Troilus by making him more adamant in rejecting free will than the Boethian persona and by deliberately mistranslating a clause of the Latin (at *Tr* 4.1057). Though neither of Huber's claims affects the point argued here, both seem to me open to question.

> Til in a temple he fond hym al allone,
> As he that of his lif no lenger roughte; (946-8)
> ...
> 'O myghty God', quod Pandarus, 'in trone,
> I! Who say evere a wis man *faren so*? (1086-7, emphasis added)

The gaping space between lines 948 and 1086 contains the 'carrying on so' that Pandarus remarks in line 1087.

Lines 974-1078 are a very close paraphrase of Chaucer's own prose translation of the argument against free will advanced by the character Boethius in *Boece* V Prose 3; it constitutes lines 8-99 of the *Boece* (the passages are printed side by side in the Appendix). On one level, the speech is a *tour de force* by Chaucer; he says here, more clearly in rhyme royal, the same things he says there in prose, often using phrases identical with those in the *Boece*.[7] And sometimes Chaucer seems to be having fun, at the expense of both the character Troilus and philosophical discourse. Compare, for example

> 'and ayeinward also is it of the contrarie', (*Bo* 56-7:)
> *and on the other hand is it also [true] of the opposite*

with

> 'And further over now ayeynward yit / Lo, right so is it of the part contrarie', (Tr 1027-8:)
>
> That is,
> *and furthermore besides now on the other hand still, Lo, exactly so is it [true] regarding the opposite*

But such touches apart, even an audience not familiar with the *Consolation* must sense the scene's major effect in depicting Troilus. He, in the temple, is praying that the gods end his life. Why? Because he is lost (956-7). Why lost? Because, he says, it's his destiny, and everything that happens, happens necessarily (958-9). Yet at this point, though parliament has agreed to the exchange (and although the narrator has made sure *we* know what will eventually happen), Troilus does not. Pandarus has made some suggestions (e.g., 532 ff.) and though Troilus does not know the outcome of Pandarus'

---

[7] See, e.g., *Tr* 995 ff. and *Bo* 30 ff.; *Tr* 1003 ff. and *Bo* 37 ff.; *Tr* 1009 ff. and *Bo* 44 ff.

efforts yet, he knows that Pandarus has gone to arrange a meeting with Criseyde for that evening. As Pandarus will soon point out, Troilus does not yet know what Criseyde will do or suggest. Nevertheless here Troilus is, expecting the worst and crying out to die. Even without much knowledge of *Boece* one can see that the underlying learned debate is about *whether what will happen, must happen.* But in this speech, Troilus equates what he *fears* will happen with his destiny. He assumes that what *will* happen will be the worst thing that *can* happen. After all, to prove that what *will* happen *must* happen is not to prove that what *might* happen *must* happen. Thus even on the surface this speech characterizes Troilus as one who leaps to extremes and absolutes.[8]

But I think Chaucer, who knows his *Boece* so well, is inviting others who know it to recall the original context of the 'free will and predestination' passage and to reflect on its relevance for this uniquely conflicted lover; and it is to that context I now turn.

4. Specific Context in the *Consolatio*

At the end of book 4 (4.7.1 ff.) Philosophy, addressing the question of 'fortune', asserted that all fortune is good when viewed rationally. Its apparent adversity provides occasions and stimuli for the development of virtue, and the virtuous thus shape all fortune into good fortune by accepting its corrections and challenges. Meter vii, which closes Book 4, ends:

> Superata tellus / sidera donat (4.vii.34-5)
> For the erthe overcomen yeveth the sterres. (*This to seyn, that whan that erthly lust is overcomyn, a man is makid worthy to the hevene.*) (*Boece* 4M7, 69-72)

As Book 5 begins, the character Boethius accepts this and goes on to ask about 'chance'; Philosophy explains that *casus* is the confluence of independently acting causes, coordinated by Providence. Boethius is moved to ask (5 Pr. 2) if this leaves room for free will. It is Philosophy's response

[8] I do not suggest this is simply comical at Troilus' expense, or a caricature. Chaucer has made Troilus somewhat more mature-seeming in Bk 4 than Boccaccio's *Troiolo* of Part 4. Take for instance the faint of *Troilo* in *Fil* 4.17-21, which Chaucer eliminates here, and also the somewhat bigger play Chaucer gives to Troilus' debate between love and reason (compare *Fil* 4.16 with *Tr* 4.162-75).

to this question that triggers the long 'predestination' speech and is crucial to the line of thinking I wish to suggest.

Philosophy says that rational creatures have judgment which enables them to choose good and spurn evil; but such judgment, she continues, is easily clouded by immersion in the corporeal: in general, by soul's being enmeshed in body; more particularly by one giving oneself over to the pursuit of 'goods', of objects of desire in this mutable world:

> *Nam ubi oculos a summae luce ueritatis ad inferiora et tenebrosa deiecerint, mox inscitiae nube caligant, perniciosis turbantur affectibus, quibus acccedendo consentiendoque quam inuexere sibi adiuuant servitutem et sunt quodam modo propria libertate captiuae.* (V.2.19-23)
>
> [For when they have cast down their eyes from the light of highest truth to lower and shadowy things, at once they are befogged in a cloud of stupidity, troubled by destructive desires; by acceding and consenting to these they aggravate the servitude which they have brought on themselves and are, in a way, captives because of their own freedom.]

It is for this reason, Philosophy continues, that Providence arranges to strip away false goods so as to enable the captive spirit to have a new lease on freedom:

> *Quae tamen ille ab aeterno cuncta prospiciens prouidentiae cernit intuitus et suis quaeque meritis praedestinata disponit.* (V.2.23-5)
>
> [Nevertheless that attentive gaze of providence sees all these things from eternity and disposes to each as it is proper those things which have been determined beforehand.]

Boethius now fixes on the word *praedestinata* and launches his assault on free will and its consequent ethical responsibility.

Philosophy's point is that providence, foreseeing the human tendency to become tangled in the yarn of earthly desires, so shapes the flow of events, of Fortune and chance, as to strip people of their 'dark', beclouding distractions, thus potentially freeing them from the prison they have made for themselves by the misuse of their liberty.[9] This is, after all, what has

---

[9] Curry appreciated this idea, but found it not in Boethius but in Thomas Aquinas, whom he quoted about men who, governed by their passions, are governed by what the stars can influence. Curry added 'Therefore, the man who does not exercise his free will in

happened to Boethius, who began this psychic quest stripped of power, wealth, family, and civil liberty.

The character Boethius' conclusion to his predestination speech (5.3.77 ff.) is that, if there is no free will, then there is no virtue or vice, no just reward or punishment; even vices must come from the author of all good! There is no purpose in hoping or praying for or against anything, and there is no hope of any interaction between humans and the deity. Finally, there is no hope of returning to *ille summus princeps rerum* (5.3.99) which, all of Book 3 of the *Consolation* had argued, is the object of all informed desire and the conferrer of true happiness. Humans are left torn apart and disjointed, distant from their origin (*humanum genus ... dissaeptum atque disiunctum suo fonte fatiscere*, 5.3.100-1). In the *Consolation* Lady Philosophy reasons Boethius out of this conundrum and back onto the path towards happiness.

5. The Context and Troilus

Troilus, in the temple and in despair, prepares to die because he 'is but lost' (953-7).

> 'For al that comth, comth by necessitee:
> Thus to ben lorn, it is my destinee.
> 'For certeynly, this wot I wel', he seyde,
> 'That forsight of divine purveyaunce
> Hath seyn alwey me to forgon Criseyde,
> Syn God seeth every thyng, out of doutaunce,
> And hem disponyth, thorugh his ordinaunce,
> In hire merites sothly for to be,
> As they shul comen by predestyne'. (4.958-66)

As we have just seen, lines 963-66 in fact come from the end of *Philosophy's* speech in 5 Pr 2 and thus forcibly remind us of the context: Fortune and chance are meant to free humans from the enslaving entanglements of their passions (quoted just above); restated in modern English, 'that attentive gaze of providence sees all these things from eternity

---

the control and direction of his emotions, finds himself presently without free choice in the guidance of his actions when the power of the stars descends upon him or when he comes in contact with the destinal force inherent in other people's influence' (1930:161). This is exactly the point made here in the *Consolatio*.

and disposes to each as it is proper those things which have been determined beforehand'. After a stanza recounting how old and great clerks have held different opinions concerning the relationship between destiny and free will, Troilus restates Boethius' argument, as we have seen.

But Troilus does not carry it even to the character Boethius' immediate conclusion. Boethius, remember, ended by arguing that there is no purpose in hoping or praying for or against anything, and no hope of any interaction between humans and a deity. Troilus, by contrast, concludes with a prayer to Almighty Jove on his throne which expresses the hope that all may not be lost, after all:

> Thanne seyde he thus: 'Almyghty Jove in trone,
> That woost of al thys thyng the sothfastnesse,
> Rewe on my sorwe: or do me deyen sone,
> Or bryng Criseyde and me fro this destresse!'
> And whil he was in al this hevynesse,
> Disputyng with hymself in this matere,
> Com Pandare in, and seyde as ye may here: (4.1079-85)

Troilus, thus, does not have the intellectual staying power or the logical consistency of the character Boethius in whose situation he finds himself and whose language he extensively appropriates—up to a point. Nor does he have Boethius' guide: it is Pandarus, not Lady Philosophy, who comes to lead Troilus from his 'heaviness'.

And so I am suggesting that one major effect of Troilus' predestination speech is to identify him as a human being, beset by an ill fortune which, in a larger, philosophical perspective, he might accept as a challenge, as a stimulus to virtue and corrector of vice. Providence would, by depriving him of distracting and distraining mutable 'goods', free his spirit to pursue the lasting, unchanging, and ultimately satisfying object of desire. This is, for the author of the *Consolation of Philosophy*, the nature of human desire and the nature of human experience. It is, in its main lines, a view of human nature completely in harmony with that articulated by the philosophy and theology of Chaucer's culture.

6. Conclusions

If this argument is plausible, what are its implications for understanding the poem? I am emphatically *not* proposing a monochromatically 'moral' reading. On the other hand, I think appreciating these implications of the predestination speech adds complexity to the poem's meanings. It argues, for example, that the poem's closing lines are already implicit in Book 4.[10] The concluding prayer expresses, in Christian terms rather than Neoplatonic ones, the *summum bonum* for which the questing, incipient philosopher was groping. But the only transcendence Troilus achieves is a violent one, delivered, not by intellectual or moral discipline, but by death. Does Troilus find happiness?

> Swich fyn hath, lo, this Troilus for love!
> Swich fyn hath al his grete worthynesse!
> Swich fyn hath his estat real above!
> Swich fyn his lust, swich fyn hath his noblesse!
> Swych fyn hath false worldes brotelnesse!
> And thus bigan his lovyng of Criseyde,
> As I have told, and in this wise he deyde. (5.1828-34)

What end? We do not know, do we? We've just been told:

> And forth he wente, shortly for to telle,
> Ther as Mercurye sorted hym to dwelle. (5.1826-7)

In the *Parliament of Fowls*, the transcendent vision of Scipio, the temple of Venus, and Nature's garden cohabit the panels of a triptych, each panel of

---

[10] Disagreement about the significance of the poem's conclusion was prominent even among the early defenders of the 'predestination speech'. For Patch, the ending seemed part of Chaucer's larger perspective, in which 'pagan' fortune and destiny were incorporated within a larger Christian framework which subjects them to a rational God (1931:235). For Curry, it spoiled the sense of tragedy which he took to be the poem's most significant effect (1930:168). Much recent criticism has been unsympathetic to the conclusion. S. Knight caricatured 'a priestly caste of American professors [who have] baptized the text in a shower of footnotes and pronounced it a devout Christian allegory' (1986:32). D. Aers, in an essay which offers an illuminating discussion of Troilus, enthusiastically endorsed Knight's characterization and would read the poem's conclusion as merely 'diversionary' on Chaucer's part (148); his comments that the predestination speech, with its 'metaphysical questions', does not in itself provide any 'consolation' (1988:147) seem to miss the point.

which serves to enrich our appreciation of the others. In this poem, Troilus the 'fine lover' and Troilus the human soul both search for the ultimate love. On one level the 'law of kind' drives Troilus, along with proud Bayard, to sexual desire; on another, the conventional ideals of love talk and lovers' behaviour encounter Troilus' surprising expectations that they be taken for what they purport to be; on yet another the predestination speech reminds us of human nature seeking permanent happiness which, in the long perspective of philosophy (and religion), can only be obtained by accepting the buffets of Fortune as liberating the spirit and redirecting desire towards a transcendent good. In all of this we experience, and respond to, human aspiration, frustration, grief, and loss. All are real, and true. Chaucer, as poet, puts them all before us. My purpose has been to argue that the philosophical, and religious, note is one intended to make up a resonant part of the whole chord.

References

Aers, D. 1988. *Community, Gender, and Individual Identity: English Writing 1360-1430*. London: Routledge.

Benson, L. D., gen. ed. 1987. *The Riverside Chaucer*. 3rd ed. Boston: Houghton Mifflin.

Bieler, L., ed. 1957. *Anicii Manlii Severini Boethii Philosophiae Consolatio*. Turnholt: Brepols.

Boccaccio, Giovanni. *Il Filostrato e il ninfale fiesolano*. See Pernicone (1937).

Curry, W. C. 1930. 'Destiny in Chaucer's *Troilus*'. *PMLA* 45:129-68.

Gordon, R. K. 1934. *The Story of Troilus*. Rept. for Medieval Academy Toronto: University of Toronto Press, 1978.

Hanna, R., III. 1984. 'Robert K. Root'. *Editing Chaucer: The Great Tradition*, ed. P. G. Ruggiers. Norman: Pilgrim. 191-207, 285-9.

Huber, J. 1965. 'Troilus' Predestination Soliloquy'. *Neuphilologische Mitteilungen* 66:120-5.

Knight, S. 1986. *Geoffrey Chaucer*. Oxford: Blackwell.

Pernicone, V., ed. 1937. *Il Filostrato e il ninfale fiesolano*. Scrittori d'Italia. Bari: Laterza.

Patch, H. R. 1918. 'Troilus on Predestination'. *JEGP* 17:399-422.

———. 1931. 'Troilus on Determinism'. *Speculum* 6:225-43.

Windeatt, B. 1979. 'The Text of the *Troilus*'. *Essays on Troilus and Criseyde*, ed.

M. Salu. Cambridge: Brewer. 1-22.
———. 1992. *Oxford Guides to Chaucer: Troilus and Criseyde*. Oxford: Clarendon.

Appendix

Troilus IV

974 'For som men seyn, if God seth al biforn—
975 Ne God may nat deceyved ben, parde—
976 Than moot it fallen, theigh men hadde it sworn,
977 That purveiance hath seyn before to be.
978 Wherfore I sey, that from eterne if he
979 Hath wist byforn oure thought ek as oure dede,
980 We han no fre chois, as thise clerkes rede.
981 'For other thought, nor other dede also,
982 Myghte nevere ben, but swich as purveyaunce,
983 Which may nat ben deceyved nevere mo,
984 Hath feled byforn, withouten ignoraunce.
985 For yf ther myghte ben a variaunce
986 To writhen out fro Goddis purveyinge,
987 Ther nere no prescience of thyng comynge,

988 'But it were rather an opynyoun
989 Uncerteyn, and no stedfast forseynge;
990 And certes, that were an abusioun,
991 That God sholde han no parfit cler wytynge
992 More than we men that han doutous wenynge.
993 But swich an errour upon God to gesse
994 Were fals and foul, and wikked corsednesse.
995 'Ek this is an opynyoun of some
996 That han hire top ful heighe and smothe yshore:
997 They seyn right thus, that thyng is nat to come
998 For that the prescience hath seyn byfore
999 That it shal come;

999 but they seyn that therfore
1000 That it shal come, therfore the purveyaunce
1001 Woot it byforn, withouten ignoraunce;
1002 'And in this manere this necessite
1003 Retorneth in his part contrarie agayn.
1004 For nedfully byhoveth it nat to bee
1005 That thilke thynges fallen in certayn
1006 That ben purveyed; but nedly, as they sayn,
1007 Byhoveth it that thynges whiche that falle,
1008 That they in certayn ben purveyed alle.
1009 'I mene as though I laboured me in this
1010 To enqueren which thyng cause of which thyng be:
1011 As wheither that the prescience of God is
1012 The certeyn cause of the necessite
1013 Of thynges that to comen ben, parde,
1014 Or if necessite of thyng comynge

Boece V *Prosa* 3

8 For yif so be that God loketh alle thinges
9 byforn, ne God ne mai nat ben desceyved
10 in no manere, thanne moot it nedes ben that
11 alle thinges betyden the whiche that the
12 purveaunce of God hath seyn byforn to comen.
13 For whiche, yif that God knoweth byforn nat
14 oonly the werkes of men, but also hir conseilles
15 and hir willes, thanne ne schal ther be no liberte
16 of arbitrie; ne certes ther ne may be noon
17 othir dede, ne no wil, but thilke whiche that the
18 devyne purveaunce, that ne mai nat ben disseyved,

19 hath felid byforn. For yif that thei
20 myghten writhen awey in othere manere
21 than thei ben purveyed, thanne ne sholde
22 ther be no stedefast prescience of thing to
23 comen, but rather an uncerteyn opynioun; the
24 whiche thing to trowen of God, I deme it felonye
25 and unleveful.

26 'Ne I ne proeve nat thilke same resoun (as who
27 seith, I ne allowe nat, or I ne preyse nat, thilke
28 same resoun) by whiche that som men wenen
29 that thei mowe assoilen and unknytten the
30 knotte of this questioun. For certes thei
31 seyn that thing nis nat to comen for that the
32 purveaunce of God hath seyn byforn that it is to
33 comen, but rathir the contrarie; and that is this:
34 that, for that the thing is to comen, that therfore
35 ne mai it nat ben hidd fro the purveaunce of
36 God;
36 and in this manere this necessite slideth
37 ayein into the contrarie partie: ne it ne byhoveth
38 nat nedes that thinges betiden that ben
39 ipurveied, but it byhoveth nedes that thinges
40 that ben to comen ben ipurveied—

41 it were Y travailed (as who seith, that
42 thilke answere procedith ryght as though men
43 travaileden or weren besy) to enqueren the
44 whiche thing is cause of the whiche thing, as
45 whethir the prescience is cause of the necessite
46 of thinges to comen, or elles that the necessite of

1015 Be cause certeyn of the purveyinge.	47 thinges to comen is cause of the purveaunce.
1016 'But now n' enforce I me nat in shewynge	47 But
1017 How the ordre of causes stant; but wel woot I	48 I ne enforce me nat now to schewen it, that
1018 That it byhoveth that the byfallynge	49 the bytidynge of thingis iwyst byforn is
1019 Of thynges wist byfore certeynly	50 necessarie, how so or in what manere that
1020 Be necessarie, al seme it nat therby	51 the ordre of causes hath itself; although
1021 That prescience put fallynge necessaire	52 that it ne seme naught that the prescience bringe
1022 To thyng to come, al falle it foule or faire.	53 in necessite of bytydinge to thinges to comen.
1023 'For if ther sitte a man yond on a see,	54 'For certes yif that any wyght sitteth, it byhoveth
1024 Than by necessite bihoveth it	
1025 That, certes, thyn opynyoun sooth be	55 by necessite that the opynioun be soth of
1026 That wenest or conjectest that he sit.	56 hym that conjecteth that he sitteth.
1027 And further over now ayeynward yit,	
1028 Lo, right so is it of the part contrarie,	56 and
1029 As thus—now herkne, for I wol nat tarie:	57 ayeinward also is it of the contrarie:
1030 'I sey that if the opynyoun of the	57 yif the
1031 Be soth, for that he sitte, than sey I this:	58 opinioun be soth of any wyght for that he sitteth,
1032 That he mot sitten by necessite;	
1033 And thus necessite in eyther is.	59 it byhoveth by necessite that he sitte.
1034 For in hym, nede of sittynge is, ywys,	60 Thanne is here necessite in the toon and in
1035 And in the, nede of soth; and thus, forsothe,	61 the tothir; for in the toon is necessite of
1036 There mot necessite ben in yow bothe.	62 syttynge, and certes in the tothir is necessite of
	63 soth.
1037 'But thow mayst seyn, the man sit nat therfore	63 But therfore ne sitteth nat a wyght for that
1038 That thyn opynyoun of his sittynge soth is,	64 the opynioun of the sittynge is soth, but the
1039 But rather, for the man sit ther byfore,	65 opinioun is rather soth for that a wyght sitteth
1040 Therfore is thyn opynyoun soth, ywis.	66 byforn. And thus, althoughe that the cause of the
1041 And I seye, though the cause of soth of this	67 soth cometh of that other side (as who seith,
1042 Comth of his sittyng, yet necessite	68 that althoughe the cause of soth cometh of the
1043 Is entrechaunged, both in hym and the.	69 sittynge, and nat of the trewe opinioun),
	70 algatis yit is ther comune necessite in that
	71 oon and in that othir.
1044 'Thus in this same wise, out of doutaunce,	71 Thus scheweth it that
1045 I may wel maken, as it semeth me,	72 Y may make semblable skiles of the purveaunce
1046 My resonyng of Goddes purveyaunce	73 of God and of thingis to comen.
1047 And of the thynges that to comen be;	
1048 By which resoun men may wel yse	
1049 That thilke thynges that in erthe falle,	
1050 That by necessite they comen alle.	
1051 'For although that for thyng shal come, ywys,	73 For althoughe
1052 Therfore is it purveyed, certeynly—	74 that for that thingis ben to comen therfore ben
1053 Nat that it comth for it purveyed is—	75 thei purveied, and nat certes for thei be purveied
1054 Yet natheles, bihoveth it nedfully	76 therfore ne bytide thei nat; yit natheles byhoveth
1055 That thing to come be purveyd, trewely,	77 it by necessite that eyther the thinges to comen
1056 Or elles, thynges that purveyed be,	78 ben ipurveied of God, or elles that the thinges
1057 That they bitiden by necessite.	79 that ben ipurveyed of God betyden.
1058 'And this suffiseth right ynough, certeyn,	79 And
1059 For to destruye oure fre chois every del.	80 this thing oonly suffiseth inow to destroien
	81 the fredom of oure arbitre (that is to seyn,
	82 of our fre wil).
1060 But now is this abusioun, to seyn	83 'But certes now schewith it wel how fer fro
1061 That fallyng of the thynges temporel	84 the sothe and how up-so-doun is this thing that

1062 Is cause of Goddes prescience eternel.
1063 Now trewely, that is a fals sentence,
1064 That thyng to come sholde cause his prescience.
1065 'What myght I wene, and I hadde swich a thought,
1066 But that God purveyeth thyng that is to come
1067 For that it is to come, and ellis nought?
1068 So myghte I wene that thynges alle and some
1069 That whilom ben byfalle and overcome
1070 Ben cause of thilke sovereyne purveyaunce
1071 That forwoot al withouten ignoraunce.
1072 'And over al this, yet sey I more herto:
1073 That right as whan I wot ther is a thyng,
1074 Iwys, that thyng moot nedfully be so;
1075 Ek right so, whan I woot a thyng comyng,
1076 So mot it come; and thus the bifallyng
1077 Of thynges that ben wist bifore the tyde,
1078 They mowe nat ben eschued on no syde'.

85 we seyn, that the betydynge of temporel thingis
86 is cause of the eterne prescience.

86 But for to
87 wenen that God purveieth the thinges to comen
88 for thei ben to comen—what oothir thing is it
89 but for to wene that thilke thinges that
90 bytidden whilom ben cause of thilke
91 soverein purveaunce that is in God?

91 And
92 herto I adde yit this thing: that ryght as whanne
93 that I woot that a thing is, it byhoveth by
94 necessite that thilke selve thing be; and eek
95 whan I have knowen that any thing schal
96 betyden; so byhovith it by necessite that thilke
97 same thing betide; so folweth it thanne that the
98 betydynge of the thing iwyste byforn ne may nat
99 ben eschued.

The 'Eight Points of Charity' in John Rylands University Library MS English 85

Margaret Connolly

1. *Contemplations of the Dread and Love of God*

Typical of the devotional reading material which was produced in vast quantities towards the end of the fourteenth and throughout the fifteenth centuries, is *Contemplations of the Dread and Love of God.*[1] The writer of this devotional prose text addressed the work to a readership comprised of both lay and religious readers, men and women, but clearly intended to appeal mainly to the lower end of this mixed market. The work assumes little previous knowledge or learning on the part of its readers, and makes extensive use of techniques designed to facilitate the less educated. Frequent repetition ensures that a point cannot be missed or misunderstood, and the division of the text into manageable sections and subsections helps the reader to negotiate the material easily. In addition, a *kalendar* or list of contents precedes the text, thus allowing it to be read sequentially or selectively as the individual desired. Perhaps because of such user-friendly features the text achieved considerable popularity, to judge from the relatively large number of surviving manuscripts, and in addition to the circulation of the full text (usually in devotional anthologies), individual sections were themselves anthologized. This happened most frequently with the text's final chapter (AB), but other chapters were also selected and

---

[1] See Connolly (1994a); all quotations are from this edition. The text is divided into lettered rather than numbered chapters which run from A-Z, with the final chapter designated AB; this method of ordering is reflected in citations from the text, which are given first by chapter letter and line number, and then by page number.

reproduced, as for example in the case of chapters C (on dread) and M (on sin) which were included in a Carthusian commonplace book, Westminster Cathedral Diocesan Archives, MS H.38. Sometimes the process of extrapolation also involved alteration, as with the short text on temptation in Oxford, MS Bodley 423, ff. 167r-168v which was fashioned mostly from chapter X, with parts of chapters Y and Z pasted in.[2]

2. The 'Eight Points of Charity'

Another derivative of *Contemplations of the Dread and Love of God* which has not yet been properly assessed or edited is a text on charity which is untitled in its manuscript witnesses, and which, for convenience and following its contents, I have entitled 'Eight Points of Charity'. This text survives completely in four manuscripts: Manchester, John Rylands University Library MS English 85, ff. 25v-37r (J); Durham Cathedral Library A.iv.22, pp. 105-16 (D); Cambridge, Trinity College, R.3.21, ff. 12v-16v (R); and Cambridge, Trinity College, O.1.74, ff. 29r-50v (O). A fifth manuscript, Cambridge, Corpus Christi College, 385 (C), pp. 221-2, contains only the introductory section of the text. In the four manuscripts which contain the complete work the 'Eight Points of Charity' occurs in the company of two other devotional texts, 'The Twelve Lettyngis of Prayer' and 'A Short Declaration of Belief'.[3] That this association was intentional and not just accidental is demonstrated by J where the three texts are coherently linked together into a clear sequence introduced by a prologue.[4]

The existence of this text was noted by Jolliffe (1974:85) who identified it as an instance of chapter D of *Contemplations* and recorded four of its manuscripts. In fact the text is considerably more substantial than Jolliffe realized, as Gillespie (1988) correctly noted.[5] The 'Eight Points of Charity'

---

[2] See Horrall (1990) and Connolly (1992).

[3] For these texts see Raymo (1986:2377, B2582; & 2291, B2518-19). For editions of both see Lloyd (1943:98-9).

[4] This manuscript has been described fully by Ker (1983:409). For the prose contents see Lester (1985:14-24), but also the review by Gillespie (1988). Tyson (1929:168) gives a list of the names inscribed in the manuscript. For a discussion of the three-text sequence, see Connolly (2003).

[5] The text, described simply as 'Charity I' is also noted by Raymo (1986:2292 & B2518).

is based on nine chapters of *Contemplations of the Dread and Love of God*, taking its starting point from Chapter D, which is one of the four introductory chapters, and which deals with the topics of charity and the love of God. The treatise then follows the substance of Chapters E, F, G, H, and I, which are grouped together in *Contemplations* as the five elements which constitute the degree of ordained love, and Chapters K, L, and M, which represent the three elements of the degree of clean love. This five- plus three-part structure of the main text of *Contemplations* is abandoned, and a new format of eight points of love, with an introduction and conclusion, is adopted. A great deal of the substance of the original text is also abandoned in the process, so that the resulting treatise is much shorter than the corresponding sequence of nine chapters in *Contemplations*, and parts of it represent new writing, rather than borrowing. It is the extent of this re-writing, borrowing, and new writing, which I wish to examine in detail now.

3. Re-writing and new writing in the 'Eight Points of Charity'

The introduction to the treatise begins by following the introductory part of Chapter D, whilst at the same time contracting the material covered. In contrast, the first part of the introduction, the explanation of what it means to love God with all one's heart, soul and virtues (lines 6-12), is longer and more detailed than that given in *Contemplations*, and is also different in substance. For example, Chapter D (D/9-12, p. 10) says:

> Whan þou puttest away fro þe, or wiþstondist wiþ al þi power, alle þing þat ys plesing or liking to þi flesche for þe loue of þe blessed flesche of Crist, þan þou louest him wiþ al þin herte and al þi soule,

whereas the treatise takes each aspect—heart, soul, virtue—and explains it in turn, before adding more generally:

> Also to be not led awei þoruȝ flateryngis, to be not disseyued bi falsnesse, and to be not brokun bi wrongis, is for-to loue God wiþ al þin herte, in al þi soule, and in al þi vertu (10-12).

The treatise then follows Chapter D, apart from a few minor alterations, up until line 23, but the explanation of the second point which is made here ('hou þou shalt knowe whanne God puttiþ grace in þee to wille lerne to loue him', 22-3), is again different. Chapter D tells us that this will be clear: 'whan þe trauaille wiche þou hast for þe loue of God is liȝt and likinge to þe' (D/25-6), whereas no mention is made in the treatise of 'trauaille' at all. The next section (lines 31-7), follows Chapter D, but most of the rest of Chapter D is then discarded, and we have instead a discussion of the ordered nature of love. This leads naturally into the introduction of the eight points, which are described as 'an ordynat loue' (line 45). It is interesting that the treatise keeps the terminology of *Contemplations*, whilst altering its structure, assimilating the three points of the degree of clean love with the five points which properly belong to the degree of ordained love. The idea of the 'fundement' (line 47), the foundations on which these eight points should be set, is not mentioned in *Contemplations*.

The eight points of the treatise follow the sequence of eight chapters, E to M, in *Contemplations* with reasonable closeness, sometimes condensing the material of the original, sometimes expanding it. Often the same ideas are expressed, but that expression is more succinct, as for example in the first and third points which cut down the material they inherit from Chapters E and G. For instance, the first point locates the problem of sustaining the flesh very precisely, warning against 'two þingis': excess and delicacy (line 67). These dangers are also outlined in Chapter E, but at greater length, and supported by three quotations from Gregory's *Moralia* which are not reproduced in the treatise. Similarly, Chapter G of *Contemplations* explains the idea of loving one's neighbour in a lengthy manner, as follows:

> To þis þou art bounde bi þe hest of God wher he comaundeþ an seiþ: 'Þou schalt loue þi neiȝbour as þiself.' Yif þou schalt loue him as þiself, nedis þou most loue him; þou schalt loue him also for God. Of þis loue spekeþ Seint Austyn and seiþ: 'Þou schalt loue God for himself, wiþ al þin herte, and þi neiȝbour for God as þiself.' Þat is to sey, lok wharto and for what þing þou louest þiself, so þou schalt loue þi neiȝbour. Þou schalt loue þiself in al goodnes and for God, riȝt so þou schalt loue þi neiȝbour for God and in al goodnes but in noon euil (G/1-9, p. 14).

This is reduced in the third point to the much more compact:

> To þis þou art boundun bi Goddis heeste, and vndirstonde wel þat þou shalt loue þi neiȝbore for God, and þou shalt loue God for himsilf, and so þou shalt loue þisilf in al goodnesse and for God, and in þe same wise þou shalt loue þi neiȝbore for God and for goodnesse and vertu, and not in noon yuel (115-19).

Specific methods of reducing the length and content of the text include the cutting of quotations. For example, the third point cuts the quotation from Gregory, 'Bi þe loue of God þe loue of þi neiȝbour is purchased, and bi þe loue of þi neieȝbour þe loue of God ys nurschid' which is present in Chapter G, lines 19-21, although two other quotations, from Augustine, are retained. Similarly the sixth point dispenses with a quotation from Jerome, 'A gret cunning and a hie cunning it is to knowe vices and vertues, for albeit vices and vertues ben contrarious, yet þei be so liche þat unneþis þe vertu mai be knowe from þe vice, ne þe vice from þe vertu' (K/18-21, p. 16). And the fifth point cuts the biblical quotation of Christ's commandment to his disciples, 'Loueþ youre enemis, doþ good to hem þat yow hateþ, and preieþ for hem þat pursuythe yow to deseise and for hem þat yow despiseþ, þat ye mowe be þe children of yowre Fader þat is in heuene' (I/12-15, p.15). Note, however, that the opening line of the fifth point contrives to include the rejected material obliquely, by adding the clause: 'and þis is a comaundement of Cristis gospel generali to alle men' (lines 151-2), which is not present in the original Chapter I.

Another method of reducing the volume of material is to dispense with passages of the original text which are repetitive or which, within the framework of the new treatise, have become redundant. For example, the fifth point, which follows Chapter I, omits the second part of that chapter (I/18-31) because its contents—a recapitulation of the five aspects of the degree of ordained love, and a rehearsal of the three aspects of clean love which are to be discussed next, are obviously inappropriate for the new treatise with its eight point structure. Similarly, the eighth point declines to follow the second part of Chapter M, which restates the three aspects of the degree of clean love, and looks forward to the five aspects of steadfast love—material not covered by this treatise. Other material, which is simply repetitive rather than inappropriate, is excised, for example the following sentence at the end of Chapter L:

> Thus þou maist wiel see þat yif þou be used in eny sinne it wol be ful hard to wiþstonde it, and but þou leue al manere sinne to þi power þou hast no clene loue to þi God (L/17-19, p. 17).

which is not reproduced in the seventh point, though its substance is still conveyed.

At the same time, the content of *Contemplations* may actually be expanded and developed in the new work. This may be achieved by a more explanatory discussion of the original ideas, as, for instance, in the fourth point, which states that one should love one's friend 'for his good lyuyng' (line 135). The fourth point follows its source, Chapter H, to begin with, but then departs from this (lines 143-8), developing the idea of how 'fleshli frendship' (line 144) may mislead one into supporting vices, so that one may be 'eþer necligent in vndirnymmyng, or ellis in councelynge, or ellis appreuynge, or ellis to helpe him to defende his synne' (lines 145-7). Whilst this is an addition to the original text, the material is not really new, but an expansion, by several examples, of the old idea. But the writer of the treatise does make the addition of new ideas of his own, most notably in the introductory section, as shown above, but also in other places throughout the treatise, for example in the second point (lines 82-9), we have the exploration of the idea that one may appear to be less in the eyes of God than in the eyes of the world,

> But whanne þou reseyuest þis worship of þe peple, loue it not, and be not enhauncid in þin herte arettynge þat worship for þi greet staat þat þou art more bifore God, and supposist þat God wole deeme þee greet as þe peple deemeþ þee greet; but wite þou wel þat þi staat or þi richesse or þi greet kyn makiþ not þee greet bifore God,

and the suggestions of how one might improve one's standing with God:

> But to gouerne þi staat wel aftir Goddis lawe and in þin owne reputacioun holde þee more vnworþi bifore God þan þe leeste of hem that doen reuerence to þee. And so for þese causis þou art gretter bifore God …

none of which occurs in Chapter F. In the third point (on how to love one's neighbour), there is an interesting addition concerning merchants (126-31), and how especially bad they are at neighbourly love; and the eighth point supplies a new conclusion to the treatise (227-40), setting out its objectives, having first dispensed with the latter part of Chapter M, as outlined above. This final passage also serves as a conclusion to the text-sequence as a whole, and may have been intended primarily as such, but whatever its original purpose, its presence in all four manuscripts, even those such as R and O which lack the prologue to the sequence, proves that it had become firmly identified with the text of the 'Eight Points of Charity'.

4. MS New York, Pierpont Morgan 861

None of the sixteen extant manuscripts of *Contemplations of the Dread and Love of God* shows evidence of having been used as the quarry to create the 'Eight Points of Charity'. In one manuscript, British Library Arundel 197, the text of *Contemplations* has been extensively revised, seemingly by the original scribe, but the purpose of these changes seems to have been personal engagement in reading rather than the creation of a new work, and other material in this manuscript has also been subjected to alteration.[6] Moreover, since the text of the relevant chapters of *Contemplations* reappears in the 'Eight Points of Charity' in such a changed form, it is difficult to trace agreements in variant readings between the source and its derivative. However, it is worth noting that there are a limited number of textual agreements between the 'Eight Points of Charity' and the heavily abbreviated version of *Contemplations* contained in the mid fifteenth-century manuscript New York, Pierpont Morgan 861 (Mg).[7] It has been suggested that this shorter version of the text might represent an earlier form of *Contemplations* but, whilst this might be true (and there is no way of proving conclusively which came first), there is no evidence amongst the manuscript tradition to support the view that the original version of the text was the shorter one.[8] The earliest manuscripts of the complete text of *Contemplations* date from the first quarter of the fifteenth century, whereas most of the manuscripts which contain shorter forms of the text seem to be later. It might be noted that there are other similarities between Mg and J. Mg begins with a treatise on the ten commandments, and then has a number of short manual texts (on the sins, works of mercy, senses, virtues, etc), before concluding with *Contemplations*. The version of the 'Ten Commandments' in Mg is similar to that in J, and both are characterized as 'rhetorical' by Martin (1981-2:202). He uses the term to mean 'a kind of text that is compact (when compared to other and different extant texts), rigidly organized, and, with respect to the internal structure of each

---

[6] See Connolly (1994b).

[7] On this manuscript see Faye and Bond (1962:365) and Bühler (1954). The following agreements in variant readings may be noted between the text of the 'Eight Points of Charity' and the version of *Contemplations* in Mg: 14 principal; 14 louede us first; 35 slakiþ; 64 stiryng; 164 mennes; 199 doun aȝen; 211 not.

[8] See Bühler (1954:687).

commandment, repetitive', a description which might be applied to other texts in these manuscripts, or even, with some modification, to the anthologies themselves. The similarities in content between J and Mg, and the agreements between the text of the 'Eight Points of Charity' and the version of *Contemplations* contained in Mg, seem significant and might indicate a centre of manuscript production where the text of *Contemplations* was systematically quarried and reduced, perhaps more than once, for inclusion in ever more specifically tailored manual-type anthologies.[9]

5. Edition of the 'Eight Points of Charity'

The text of the 'Eight Points of Charity' is edited in the appendix below from J, with emendations and variants cited as appropriate from the other four witnesses (since C is merely a fragment, for the most part the treatise has four witnesses, rather than five). I have generally followed instances of agreement and assumed that the reading of the single manuscript in each case constitutes an isolative error; however, there are points where I have preferred the isolative reading of J to the readings of the other manuscripts. In general emendations have been kept to a minimum, and the substance of all five manuscripts can be reconstructed from the list of variant readings.

Editorial policy is as follows. Emendations that consist in the addition to, or alteration of, the readings of J, are denoted by square brackets, thus: [ ]. Emendations that result in the suppression of the readings of J are recorded in the variants. Modern punctuation and capitalization have been substituted for those in the manuscript, modern paragraph division and word division have been introduced. The beginning of a new folio in the manuscript is signalled in square brackets in the text. All abbreviations have been silently expanded, the expansions being carried out as far as possible according to J's spelling of similar unabbreviated forms elsewhere. All substantive variants to the readings of J are recorded, but linguistic variation, i.e. morphological, dialectal, and orthographical variations, are not recorded. The scribe of J repeated one large section of the text in error (the list of eight points, from lines 51-9 inclusive), but having noticed the mistake he

[9] An alternative point of view, voiced by Gillespie (1988:112), is that the 'Eight Points of Charity' and *Contemplations* may not be interdependent in the way that I am suggesting here, but that both may derive from a common ancestor treatise.

cancelled the duplicated portion of text; this is not recorded in the apparatus. The sigla are cited from the sequence JDROC in that order. The following abbreviations are used in the variants:

canc.	previous word(s) cancelled
ins.	previous word(s) inserted
om.	word(s) omitted
rev.	order of previous words reversed

References

Bühler, C. F. 1954. 'The Middle English Texts of Morgan MS 861'. *Publications of the Modern Language Association of America* 69:686-92.

Connolly, M. 1992. 'A New Tract on Temptation: Extracts from *Contemplations of the Dread and Love of God* in MS Bodley 423'. *Notes and Queries* n.s. 39:280-1.

———, ed. 1994a. *Contemplations of the Dread and Love of God*, EETS o.s. 303. Oxford: Oxford University Press.

———. 1994b. 'Public Revisions or Private Responses? The Oddities of BL Arundel MS 197, with Special Reference to *Contemplations of the Dread and Love of God*'. *British Library Journal* 20:55-64.

———. 2003. (forthcoming) 'Books for the "helpe of euery persoone þat þenkiþ to be saued": Six Devotional Anthologies from Fifteenth-Century London'. *Medieval and Early Modern Literary Miscellanies in Manuscript and Print,* ed. Phillipa Hardman, special issue of *Yearbook of English Studies* 33.

Faye, C. U., & W. H. Bond. 1962. *Supplement to the Census of Medieval and Renaissance Manuscripts in the United States and Canada*. New York: Bibliographical Society of America.

Gillespie, V. 1988. Review of *The Index of Middle English Prose, Handlist II: John Rylands and Chetham's Libraries, Manchester*. *Medium Ævum* 57:111-12.

Horrall, S. M. 1990. 'Middle English Texts in a Carthusian Commonplace Book: Westminster Cathedral Diocesan Archives, MS H.38'. *Medium Ævum* 59:214-27.

James, M. R. 1912. *A Descriptive Catalogue of the Manuscripts in the Library of Corpus Christi College Cambridge*, II. Cambridge: Cambridge University Press.

Jolliffe, P. S. 1974. *A Checklist of Middle English Prose Writings of Spiritual Guidance*. Toronto: Pontifical Institute of Mediaeval Studies.

Ker, N. R. 1983. *Medieval Manuscripts in British Libraries* III. Oxford: Oxford University Press.

Lester, G. A. 1985. *The Index of Middle English Prose, Handlist II: The John Rylands University Library of Manchester and Chetham's Library, Manchester*. Woodbridge: Brewer.

Lloyd, D. J. 1943. 'An Edition of the Prose and Verse in the Bodleian MS Laud Misc. 23'. Dissertation, Yale University.

Martin, C. A. 1981-2. 'The Middle English Versions of *The Ten Comandments*, with Special Reference to Rylands English MS 85'. *Bulletin of the John Rylands University Library* 64:191-217.

Raymo, R. R. 1986. 'Works of Religious and Philosophical Instruction'. *A Manual of the Writings in Middle English 1050-1500,* vol. 7, gen. ed. A. E. Hartung. New Haven, CT: Connecticut Academy of Arts and Sciences. 2255-378, 2467-582.

Tyson, M. 1929. 'Handlist of the Collection of English Manuscripts in the John Rylands Library, 1928'. *Bulletin of the John Rylands Library* 13:152-219.

Appendix: 'Eight Points of Charity' (John Rylands University Library MS English 85)

The þridde tyme it is to speke sumwhat of loue.[1] Charite is a loue þat [f. 26r] we shulden haue to God for as moche as he[2] is almyȝti. Also charite is a loue to oure neiȝbore for God, and þese ben two principal heestis of God, whiche includen alle þe comaundementis of God. Now hast þou [what is] charite[3]; se now how þou shalt loue God.

Þou mostist loue him wiþ al þin herte, and[4] wiþ al þi soule, and wiþ alle þi vertues. Of al þin herte, þat is, of al and ful desijr of herte to loue him; of al þe soule is in al[5] wakyng and bisi loking aboute resoun to loue him; wiþ al þi vertu, þat[6] þou drede not to die for his loue, forwhi loue is stronge as deeþ. Also to be not led awei þoruȝ flateryngis, to be not disseyued bi falsnesse, and to be not brokun bi wrongis, is for-to loue God wiþ al þin herte, in al þi soule, and in al þi vertu. Now hast þou sumwhat hou þou shalt [f. 26v] loue God. Now se ferþer whi we shulden loue him[7] best wiþout noumbre. Two skilis I fynde principal[8]. Oon is for he louede us first, wiþ al his herte and[9] al his soule, sweetli and strongli: sweetli for he took fleish and blood and bicam man for oure loue; strongli for he suffride deeþ for loue of man. Þe secunde skile [is][10] for þer is noþing þat mai be loued more riȝtfulli ne more profitabli: more riȝtfulli is þer noon þan to loue him þat made man and diede for man; noþing is more profitable þat mai be loued þan almyȝti God, for if we louen him as we ben boundun, he wole ȝyue us ioie and blis wiþout eende, where noþing lackiþ but al þing is plenteuous.

Se now hou þou shalt knowe whanne God puttiþ grace in þee to wille lerne to loue him[11]. Oo to- [f. 27r] -kene is whanne þou hast a greet will to

---

[1] The … loue] *om.* DC, Here sueth somwhat of charyte R
[2] he] it *canc.*, he *ins.* O
[3] charite] sumwhat of *canc.* charite J, what is charite DROC
[4] and] *om.* O
[5] al] al þi O
[6] þat] is þat O
[7] him] god R
[8] principal] principally OC
[9] and] and of J
[10] is] *om.* J
[11] him] *ins.* J

rule þi wittis, inward and outward, and al þi lyuyng, aftir þe heestis[12] of God. And whanne þou hast biholdun hou[13] God haþ putt in þee a good will, loke þanne bisili þat þou aske help of God to sende þee[14] grace to contynue þi good will, [and] to[15] fulfille it in dede aftir his bidding. And ferþermore mekeli to aske and lerne of wiser men þan þou, and speciali of hem þat dreden God, to lerne þe lawe of þi God and truli to vndirstonde it, and rule þi lijf þeraftir; and þanne þat[16] is a tokene þat God haþ sett in þee a bigynnyng of loue dreed. And whanne þou hast such a bigynnyng, wiþdrawe þee not for no[17] disese, ne[18] noon[19] sugestioun of þe fleish, of[20] þe world, and of[21] þe feend. For manye men and wymmen þe whilis þei ben in prosperite, and welþe, and reste, [f. 27v] gladli þei wolen shewe loue to God as þei kunnen; but if[22] God sende hem ony disese, anoon her loue slakiþ and leuen her first purpos, and þis is no sad[23] loue. And þerfore man[24] most haue a strong[25] and wise[26] purpos to loue God in aduersite as he doiþ in prosperite.

Here is shewid sumwhat to knowe whanne God stiriþ þee of his grace to wille loue him. Now for as moche as þer is ordre in loue, sum in oo degre and sum in anoþer, as is loue to þi God, and loue to þisilf,[27] and loue to þi neiȝbore, and loue to oþer creaturis; but loue to þi God most be moost in þin affeccioun, aboue alle þingis in heuene and in erþe; and þe loue of[28] þisilf and of[29] þi[30] neiȝbore askiþ anoþer ordre of loue, and lower[31] creaturis

[12] heestis] commaundmentes R
[13] hou] howe that RC
[14] a good will … sende þee] *repeated* O
[15] and to] to JDO
[16] þat] hit C
[17] no] *om.* C
[18] ne] ne ne C
[19] noon] no D
[20] of] *om.* RC
[21] of] *om.* RC
[22] if] and O
[23] no sad] non sadnes of C
[24] man] a man C
[25] strong] strong wyll RC
[26] wise] sad RC
[27] and loue to þisilf] *om.* C
[28] of] to C
[29] of] to C
[30] þi] *om.* D

anoþer ordre of loue[32]. Þerfore next folowing, wiþ Goddis grace, shal sue an ordynat loue, þat[33] is a loue þat shulde be kept of alle men[34] [f. 28r] and to[35] þis comoun loue is neeful[36] eiȝte poyntis. But first þou mostist haue a fundement to sette on þese eiȝte poyntis, þat is þou mostist haue a ful feiþ, as al hooli chirche bileeueþ, ourned wiþ werkis of Goddis comaundementis, and þou mostist hate and fle þe seuene deedli synnes, and þat þi will be sett þat þou noldist[37] wraþþe God for noon erþeli þing.

Þe first poynt is þis[38]: þou shalt loue þi fleish oonli þat it be susteyned.

Þe secunde: þat[39] þou loue þe world to no superfluite.

Þe þridde is[40] þou shalt loue þi neiȝbore for God.

Þe ferþe: þat[41] þou loue þi freendis for her good lyuyng.

Þe fifþe: þat[42] þou loue þin enmye for þe more meede of God.

Þe sixte: þat[43] þou loue no vice wiþ vertu.

Þe seuenþe is[44] þat þou dispise and leue al yuel custom.

Þe eiȝtþe: þat þou [f. 28v] sette not litil[45] bi synne,[46] wheþer it be litil or moche.[47]

As[48] to þe firste: þou shalt loue þi fleish oonli þat it be susteyned as þus. Þou shalt take mete and drynk, and cloþing, and al oþir þing þat is needful to þi bodi, in resonable manere, to kepe þi bodi in his[49] staat[50] in counfort of þi

---

[31] lower] loue of D
[32] and …loue] *om.* O
[33] þat] þer C
[34] þat is … men] *om.* D
[35] to] to to C
[36] neeful] nedeful DC
[37] noldist] woldest nat R
[38] þis] *om.* R
[39] þat] is þat O
[40] is] ys that R
[41] þat] is þat O
[42] þat] is þat O
[43] þat] is þat O
[44] is] *om.* D
[45] litil] liȝt D
[46] synne] synne þat is þat þou hate gretli euery synne DR
[47] moche] greet R
[48] as] now as R
[49] his] his in *canc.* his J
[50] staat] astaat D

soule; and not [f. 29r] for-to norisshe þi fleish in lust and likyngis wiþ delicat metis and drynkis, for þerof comeþ not[51] but stiryng of[52] synne and many bodili sijknessis. So in þis loue þou shalt not seke but needfulnesse to sustentacioun of þi bodi, be it of boistous þing or ellis of more deynte. And so here þou mostist be war of two þingis: oon is excesse or out of mesure of mete and drynk and cloeþ, and anoþir is delicacie or sweete taast of þe[53] bodi, for oonli þoruȝ sum of þese þou maist falle into þe synne of gloteny and drunknesse, þe which is a[54] dampnable synne, for but if þe wombe of glotonye be aswagid, and bridils be sett to[55] mouþ and þrote, alle þi vertues shulen be cast doun. Fle þerfore excesse and delicacie, and so loue þi fleish oonli þat it be susteyned.

Þe secunde is þou[56] shalt loue þe world [f. 29v] to no superfluite. And[57] þus, if þou desirist to be Goddis seruaunt þou shalt not desire to loue vanytees of þe world. In what degre þat euer þou be yn, if þou be ordeyned to be a souereyn, as lord or ladi, or[58] domesman, or oþer spirituel or te[m]porel[59], resoun wole þat reuerence be don to þee more þan to anoþer man or womman. For aftir tyme þe first man Adam was inobedient to Goddis heeste[60], it was ordeined bi almyȝti God þat man shulde be suget to man. Also nede dryueþ þat þe peple most haue gouernail, and þerfore it is resoun to do reuerence to hem þat han power and gouernail aboue oþir. But whanne þou reseyuest þis worship of þe peple, loue it not, and be not enhauncid in þin herte arettynge þat worship for þi greet staat[61] þat þou art more bifore God, and [f. 30r] supposist þat God wole deeme þee greet as þe peple deemeþ þee greet; but wite þou wel þat þi staat or þi richesse or þi greet kyn makiþ not þee[62] greet bifore God. But to gouerne þi staat wel aftir

---

[51] not] *om.* R
[52] of] to R
[53] þe] þi D
[54] a] *om.* RO
[55] to] to þe O
[56] þou] þus *canc.* þou O
[57] and] as DRO
[58] or] *om.* DR
[59] temporel] teporel J (*contraction mark omitted by scribe*)
[60] heeste] commaundment RO
[61] staat] *om.* D
[62] not þee] the nat R

Goddis lawe and in þin owne[63] reputacioun holde þee[64] more vnworþi bifore God þan þe leeste of hem that doen reuerence to þee. And so[65] for þese causis þou art gretter bifore God, and so mekeli ȝilde al þat worship to God, which myȝte haue maad þee a suget; and þis is confermed of Crist, to sette[66] in þe last place. Also to loue not þe world to[67] superfluite is to loue no worldli goodis but in mesure, as nede askiþ. Þerfore lord or suget, pore or riche, holde þee apaied wiþ þi[68] degre and desire to be no gretter, but as Goddis will is, and as he wole dispose for þee. If þou holdist þee not[69] a- [f. 30v] -paied wiþ þi degre, nameli where as God haþ sent to þee a resonable lijflood, but euere desirist to be gretter and gretter in þe world, þanne þou louest þe world to superfluite, for þou desirist of þe world more þan þee nediþ, and so bi þat foul desijr þou fallist into þat[70] foule synne of couetise, which is repreued bi al Goddis lawe for a foul deedli synne. Wherfore I rede þat where þe synne of couetise is in ony man, he is maad suget to alle maner yuels. Pride and couetise ben gladli yknyt togidir þat where couetise regneþ, þere is pride. Þis synne is so wickid and greuous, þat as long as it is wiþ ony man he shal haue no grace to drawe to God. And þerfore seiþ Seynt Gregor: 'Oþerwise we moun not drawe ne come to þe bigynner and maker of al goodnesse, but þat we caste from us þe synne[71] [f. 31r] of couetise'. Þre þingis I rede, þat a man desiriþ aboue alle worldli þingis: þe first is richesse; þe secunde is lustis; and þe þridde ben worships. Of richesse comen wickid dedis, of lustis comen foule dedis[72], of worships comen vanytees. Richesse gendriþ couetise, lustis norisshen glotony and lecherie, worship norisshiþ boost and pride. Þus[73] þou maist knowe what peril it[74] is to loue þe world. Þerfore if þou wolt stonde sikirli, make þe world to be þi seruaunt and not

---

[63] owne] *om.* O

[64] þee] *om.* O

[65] and so] also O

[66] sette] sitte D, sytte R

[67] to] to no DR

[68] þi] þe D

[69] þee not] *rev.* O

[70] þat] *om.* RO

[71] þe synne] þe synne *repeated and canc.* J

[72] of ... dedis] *ins.* J

[73] þus] and *canc.* þus J

[74] it] *om.* R

þou seruaunt to þe world, and þanne þou kepist þe secunde poynt of þis degre of loue.

Þe þridde poynt is þou shalt loue þi[75] neiȝbore for God. To þis þou art boundun bi Goddis heeste[76], and vndirstonde wel þat þou shalt loue þi neiȝbore for God, and þou shalt loue God for himsilf, and so þou shalt loue þisilf[77] [f. 31v] in al goodnesse and for God, and in þe same wise[78] þou shalt loue þi neiȝbore for God and for goodnesse and vertu, and not in noon yuel. Þerfor he verili loueþ men, þat is to seie, þe kynde of men, þat loueþ hem[79] forþi þat þei ben goode and riȝtful, or ellis þat þei moun be goode and riȝtful. In þe same wise þou schuldist loue þisilf. Also whanne þou forsakist a synguler profit for loue of þi neiȝbore, þanne þou louest þi neiȝbore as þisilf; and also doist þi neiȝbore noon harm, but desirisit þe same goodnesse and profit, goostli and profitabli to him þat þou desirist to þisilf. Loue þou þi neiȝbore or ellis þou louest not God. And þis loue of neiȝbore is brokun[80] of many[81] men, and speciali of marchauntis, for seldom or neuere þei comen to grete richessis wiþoute þre cursid falshedis, þat [f. 32r] is, to wite[82] bi fraude or gile, bi lesyng or[83] bi forsweryng[84], and þus usynge þese cursid menes þou louest neþer God ne þisilf ne þi neiȝbore, and þanne it wole sue þou[85] art no lyme of Crist ne of his chirche. But whanne þou wiþdrawist þee fro þese cursid menes and oþer, and bigynnest haue sauour in þe loue of þi neiȝbore, þanne þou bigynnest to entre into þe loue of þi God, and kepist þis þridde poynt of loue.

The ferþe point[86] is þou shalt loue þi freend for his good lyuyng. If þou haue a freend þat is a good lyuer þou shalt[87] loue him on double manere, oon

---

[75] þi] þe world *canc.* þi J
[76] heeste] commaundment RO
[77] and so … þisilf] *om.* R
[78] wise] *om.* O
[79] hem] *om.* R
[80] brokun] bro O (*scribal error at line break*)
[81] of many] in many maners of many O
[82] wite] seie O
[83] or] and R
[84] forsweryng] for *ins.* sweryng J
[85] þou] þat þou O
[86] point] poynt of loue O
[87] shalt] shuldest R

is for he is þi freend, and[88] for[89] þe goodnesse þat is in him. If þi freend be vicious ȝit þou mostist loue his kynde but not hise vicis. For parfit frendship is whanne [f. 32v] þou louest not in þi freend þat þat[90] shulde not be loued, and whanne þou louest in him, or desirist to him, goodnesse, whiche is to be loued. As þus, if þi freend lyue folili, þou shalt not loue him for his foly lyuyng, but for he mai bi Goddis grace amende him and be parfit in lyuyng and herto þou art i-boundun to helpe wiþ alle manere leeful menes. But here þou mostist be war þat for no fleshli frendship þat is bitwix þi freend and þee þat þou be fauorable to his vicis in consentinge, eþer necligent in[91] vndirnymmyng, or ellis in councelynge, or ellis appreuynge, or ellis to helpe him to defende his synne, and so to be necligent to not helpe him out of his synne; alle þese spicis of consence[92] ben euene peyne worþi wiþ þe doer. Þer- [f. 33r] -fore if ȝe louen ȝoure freendis, loueþ not þe vicis of ȝoure freendis, and þou shalt kepe þe ferþe poynt of þis degre of loue.

Þe fifþe is[93] þou shalt loue þin enmye for þe more meede and þis is a comaundement of Cristis gospel generali to alle men. A greet dede of charite and meedful it is to forȝyue hem wiþ al oure herte whiche[94] han trespasid aȝens us. It is but litil[95] goodnesse and ful lasse meede to be wel-louyng and willynge to hem þat doen þee noon harm, but it is a greet goodnesse and a greet meede þat þou be louynge vnto þin enmye, and þat þou[96] wille good and do good, wiþ al þi power, to him þat is in will or doiþ yuel to þee, wiþ al his power. And þerfore seiþ Gregor[97], 'It is holdun a greet vertu among word- [f. 33v] -li men to suffre pacientli her enmyes, but it is a[98] moche gretter vertu a man to loue his enmye, for þis vertu is for a[99] sacrifice present

---

[88] and] and anoþere is D
[89] for] *om.* R
[90] þat] *om.* O
[91] in] in þin D
[92] consence] consent DR
[93] is] poynt R
[94] whiche] *om.* D
[95] litil] a lytyll R
[96] þou] thow be louyng vnto thyne enemy and that thow R
[97] Gregor] Seynt Gregor DO
[98] a] *om.* O
[99] a] *om.* DR

bifore þe si3t of almy3ti God'. Loue þanne þin enmye for þe more meede, if þou wolt kepe þe fifþe[100] poynt of loue þus declarid to þee.

Þe sixte poynt is þou shalt loue no vice wiþ vertu, as þus. What euere þou be in mennes i3en be war þat þou be not vicious inward in þi soule, vndir colour of vertues whiche þou shewist opunli. Þe feend haþ many wilis to disceyue mankynde, but among alle it is greet disceit whanne he makiþ a vice lijk to[101] a vertu and a vertu lijk to[102] a vice, for þis is ypocrisie. And se per[103] ensaumple, for þou3 merci be a greet vertu in almesse doyng and in for3yuynge of trespassis, wher þat[104] it is[105] do[106] wiþ clene entent in þe wor- [f. 34r] -ship and in þe name of God, 3it þis vertu is turned to vice where it is[107] do for plesaunce of men and not for God. Also ri3twisnesse is a greet vertu, and 3it it is turned in[108] to vice, as whanne a man wolde chastice his seruaunt or his nei3bore for his amending þat he shulde þe beter knowe his synne and amende, 3it þis vertu is turned to vice whanne it[109] do for couetise or ellis for angir and vnpacience. Also þe vice of pride is hid sumtyme vndur mekenesse, as whanne a man lowiþ him[110] and mekiþ himsilf in speche and in berynge, for þis entent, þat he wolde be holdun meke and lowli. Also þe vertu of pacience semeþ in many men whanne þer is noon, as whanne a man wolde take veniaunce if he my3te for þe wrong þat is doon[111] to him, but for he mai not, or ellis þat[112] he haþ no tyme, or ellis shame of þe [f. 34v] world restreyneþ him, þat he ne[113] wolde be a wreke[114] on his enmye; for suche skilis he suffriþ, and not for þe loue[115] dreed of God, and þus þe vertu of

---

[100] fifþe] furst R
[101] to] *om.* D
[102] to] *om.* DR
[103] se per] so bi D, se by RO
[104] þat] *om.* D
[105] is] *ins.* J
[106] do] so O
[107] is] *ins.* J
[108] in] *ins.* J
[109] it] hit ys R
[110] him] himsylf D, *om.* R
[111] doon] do *ins.* O
[112] þat] for D, *om.* R
[113] ne] *om.* RO
[114] a wreke] avengid DR
[115] loue] loue and DR

pacience is turned to[116] vice. And þus for-to parte[117] vice fro vertu it is speedful in euery werk þat þou shalt[118] do[119] to biholde þin[120] entent and purpos þat it be not corrupt, but þat it haue roote in God or for God bi þe foorme of his lawe; but þis is ful hard for-to do but[121] þou[122] haue clennesse of lyuyng. Be war þerfore and loue so sadli vertues wiþoute ony feynyng, þat þou hate alle maner of vicis, and so þou maist bi grace kepe þe sixte poynt of loue.[123]

Þe seuenþe poynt is þou shalt dispise alle yuel customs. A greet peril it is to haue an yuel dede in custom, for þouȝ synnes be neuere so grete ne so orrible, whanne þei ben drawen[124] into custom þei semen but [f. 35r] litil synnes to him þat vsiþ hem in custom, in so moche þat it is to hem a greet liking, and þei shewen ofte tyme[125] her wrecchidnesse to alle men[126], wiþoute shame. And þerfore seiþ Seynt Gregor þat whanne synne comeþ so[127] in vse[128] þat þe herte haue a lust and a likyng þerinne, þat synne shal be feyntli wiþstondun, for it byndiþ so soore þe herte, and makiþ þe soule[129] bowe to him, þat it mai not rise aȝen[130] and come to þe riȝt weie of clene lijf, for whanne he is in will[131] to rise, anoon he slidiþ and falliþ doun aȝen. And þerfore þe same Gregor seiþ: 'Many þer ben þat desiren to come out of her synne, but for as moche as þei ben closid in þe prisoun of yuel custom, þei moun not come out of her yuel lyuyng'. To þis purpos I rede þat he þat wole not vse him to no vertu [f. 35v] in his ȝong age, it shal be ful hard to[132] wiþstonde vicis whanne he comeþ to oold age. And þerfore striue and aske

[116] to] into D
[117] for-to parte] to depart R
[118] shalt] schulde D
[119] do] do firste D
[120] þin] to thyne R
[121] but] but if D
[122] þou] *om.* R
[123] and so … loue] *om.* O
[124] drawen] dra O
[125] tyme] *om.* O
[126] alle men] other pepyll R
[127] so] *om* D
[128] vse] us D
[129] þe soule] *om.* D
[130] aȝen] *om.* D
[131] will] poynt R

bisili help and grace to leue al synne, and brynge noon in custom, and þanne þou shalt kepe þe seuenþe poynt of þis degre of loue[133].

Þe eiȝte poynt and þe laste is þou shalt not sette liȝt bi synne; be it greet[134], be it smale[135], charge it discreetli in[136] þi conscience, and sette not litil þerbi. For as I rede, what man passiþ mesure in etyng and drynkyng more þan him nediþ, þat man offendiþ God. And ȝit to many men it semeþ but[137] litil trespas, but Austyn seiþ it is not litil, for as moche as we[138] trespassen euery dai þerinne for þe more partie. In as moche as we synnen þerinne eueri dai we synnen þerinne ofte[139], and so we multiplien oure synnes, and þat is [f. 36r] ful perilouse; and so Seynt Austyn preueþ bi ensaumple of litil beestis: where[140] þei ben many togidir, be þei neuer so litil, þei doen moche harm. Also greynes of sond ben ful litil, but ȝit where a ship is ouerchargid wiþ sond, it most nedis synke and drenche. Riȝt so it fariþ bi synnes, be þei neuere so litil þei be ful perilous, and so necligence to not wiþstonde hem ne to drede hem discreetli, mai charge so moche þat at þe laste þei drenche þee to[141] helle. Þerfore be war of idil speche þat profitiþ not and also of foli speche wiþoute discrecioun. Also be war of oolde synfull þouȝtis[142] þat rennen vp[143] in[144] þi mynde, þat þou haue no likyng in hem, but trauele to putte hem awey bi preier and grace. For Crist seiþ þat[145] of euery idil word [f. 36v] man shal ȝilde rikenyng at domesdai and[146] þerfore stryue and fiȝte[147]

---

[132] to] to hym to R
[133] of … loue] þus declarid to þee DR
[134] greet] litil DO
[135] smale] myche DO, lytell R
[136] in] and in R
[137] but] *om.* R
[138] we] *om.* D
[139] þerinne ofte] *rev.* O
[140] where] þat þat where D
[141] to] downe to R
[142] synfull þouȝtis] *om.* D
[143] vp] *om.* R
[144] in] into D
[145] þat] *om.* R
[146] and] *om.* D
[147] stryue and fiȝte] *om.* D

strongli as a good knyȝt of Crist, duyk of oure batel, aȝen synne, more and lasse, and þanne þou shalt kepe þe eiȝtþe poynt of þis degre of loue.[148]

Now in þe eende of þis short tretijs þou shalt vndirstonde þat al Goddis lawe and al[149] declaracioun þerof as in þis short co[m]pilacioun[150] and alle oþir tretijs, is not ellis but to brynge mankynde to two þingis. Oon is to loue God and[151] drede God[152] and his lawe aboue alle oþir þingis, in heuene and in erþe; and þe secunde is to brynge man to loue his euene cristen in goodnesse as himsilf, and for-to come herto þou mostist loue vertues and hate vicis. Vertu stant herinne: þat þou obeie to þe lawe of þi God in gouernynge þi lijf þeraftir, and þat þou mesure euery dede þat þou do, þat it be not [f. 37r] to moche ne to litil, and þis most be do in God and for God. Vice stant herinne: to do þat[153] God haþ forfendid to do, or ellis to leue vndo þat good þat þou ouȝtist or myȝtist esili do. Þerfore enforce þee to loue vertu and to[154] hate vice, þat at þe laste þou myȝt come bi grace to dwelle wiþ him þat is lord of vertues, wiþ him to reste aftir trauel, in ioie and blis wiþoute eende. Amen.

---

[148] of þis … loue] that ys to set not lyte by synne whether that hit be moche or lytell R
[149] al] al the R
[150] compilacioun] copilacioun J (*contraction mark omitted by scribe*)
[151] and] and to R
[152] drede God] *om*. D
[153] þat] not *ins*. þat J
[154] to] *om*. O

Caxton, Malory, Arthurian Chronicles, and French Romances: Intertextual Complexities

Edward Donald Kennedy

1. Introduction

Caxton argues in the preface to his 1485 edition of Malory's *Morte Darthur* that Arthur was a real king and that contrary to what some were saying, books about him were not 'fayned and fables'; however, he also indicates that all the stories in the book might not be true, but readers could nevertheless derive moral instruction from them (Vinaver 1990:cxliii-cxlvii). The preface was written to help sell a book that, as N. F. Blake plausibly argues, might have been a financial gamble for Caxton: unlike Caxton's editions of works such as the *Canterbury Tales* and the *Confessio Amantis*, it probably had not circulated much and would have been relatively unknown (Blake 1976:274, 279; also E. D. Kennedy 2000:224). Caxton might also have been concerned about its author's reputation as a criminal (Blake 1976:280), particularly, one might add, since he had been a Lancastrian enemy imprisoned by the Yorkists for whom Caxton had published his earlier works. However, possibly the most important reason for *Morte Darthur's* being a financial risk for Caxton is that the French romances upon which Malory based most of his book would have presented an Arthur who was at times quite different from the king of the chronicle versions of the Arthurian story that would have been familiar to readers of English. The preface could suggest that Caxton himself had reservations about how the book that he was publishing would be accepted by English readers. In arguing for the historical truth of Arthur's existence while at the same time pointing out that the book's chief value lay in its moral *exempla* rather than its truth, Caxton may have been expressing concern about how the English readers who were expected to buy it might react to it.

Many modern readers who have been influenced by the King Arthur of Tennyson's *Idylls of the King* (an Arthur who, at least by Victorian standards, was idealized) could have reactions to Malory's book similar to those of Caxton's contemporaries and might be surprised to find that medieval writers often had a considerably less exalted conception of Arthur than Tennyson had. Although Arthur in medieval literature can be a mighty conqueror and a chivalrous king, he can also be weak cuckold or a relatively insignificant master of ceremonies at a court where the important figures are his knights. In fact, in some medieval works he is both strong and weak, and in such works his character seems to many modern readers to be an inconsistent mixture of conflicting traits. Thus an understanding of the background of medieval English and Continental Arthurian literature against which *Morte Darthur* was written can help one better understand some of the problems Malory faced in adapting Continental Arthurian romances for English readers and why Caxton's English readers might have been expected to have misgivings about Malory's Arthur.

2. The Character of King Arthur in Medieval Literature

Arthur's actions in *Morte Darthur* often do not correspond to the high regard that Malory appears to have for the king he describes as the 'moste man of worshyp crystynde' (Vinaver 1990:1147). It is indeed easy to find in *Morte Darthur* a number of Arthur's acts that either are or that seem to some critics to be far from praiseworthy: his incestuous relationship with his sister and his attempt to destroy his son/nephew Mordred by having all the children in his kingdom that were born at the time of Mordred's birth destroyed; his later refusal to permit Lancelot to defend Guenevere in trial by combat after the two have been captured together; and his acquiescing in the final book to Gawain's desire for vengeance against Lancelot are a few examples. While most scholars consider Malory's Arthur to be basically a good king,[1] some have argued that Malory was critical of Arthur and that Malory presented him negatively as a king who was to a great extent

---

[1] See, for example, McCarthy (1988), Lambert (1975), Brewer (1968:9-12), and Benson (1976).

responsible for the destruction of his realm.[2] P. Korrel (1984:255-67), while acknowledging Malory's positive attitude toward Arthur ('Malory wanted Arthur to be the best king of the world'), nevertheless devotes about twelve pages of his book to a discussion of Arthur's shortcomings and observes that when 'one looks at the king's real actions, one may wonder indeed how he ever got his splendid reputation'.

Although Korrel, in my opinion, at times overstates Arthur's flaws in *Morte Darthur*, the question he raises is a valid one, and it is one that would probably have been of concern to Caxton; but while Korrel's book raises some valid questions about Malory's portrayal of Arthur, the interpretations of those who feel that Malory wished to make Arthur largely responsible for the downfall of his realm are difficult to accept. Such views ignore the comments Malory adds from the beginning to the end of his book that indicate that he had great admiration for Arthur. He mentions the king's sense of justice, his generosity, his heroism, his concern for the ideals of chivalry, and his love for his men. When he becomes king, Arthur promises to rule with 'true justyce'; he establishes a Round Table in which his knights are charged 'never to do outerage nothir murthir and allwayes to fle treson, and to gyff mercy unto hym that askith mercy'; early in the book he is praised above all kings for his 'knyghthode' and 'noble counceyle'; during his campaign against the Romans he promises to do his 'trew parte' fighting with his men, and Malory tells us, 'Was never kyng nother knyghtes dud bettir syn God made the worlde' (Vinaver 1990, 1:16, 120, 188, 221). At the end of *Morte Darthur*, he is the 'floure of kyngis,' the 'noble kynge' whose 'grete goodnes' made the pope want to end the war between him and Lancelot; when in the final tale Mordred rebels against him, Malory expresses dismay at the English desertion of Arthur, and the reason he gives is not the negative one that Mordred was worse, but the positive one that Arthur was so good: 'Lo, ye all Englysshemen, se ye nat what a myschyff here was? For he that was the moste kynge and nobelyst knyght of the worlde, and moste loved the felyshyp of noble knyghtes, and by hym they all were upholdyn, and yet myght nat thes Englyshemen holde them contente with hym' (Vinaver 1990, 3:1252, 1237, 1194, 1229).

The only way to accept arguments that Malory did not have great

---

[2] Pochoda (1971), Dean (1987:91-106), Thornton (1991 & 1992).

admiration for Arthur is to believe that Malory created a narrator whose remarks are to be interpreted ironically, and a book with an ironic narrator is not the kind of work Malory was creating (see Brewer 1981:108-9). What seems most logical is to accept Malory's admiration for Arthur as part of his conception of the Arthurian story. Like the other major characters Lancelot, Guenevere, and Gawain, Arthur makes mistakes that contribute to the tragic destruction of his realm; and like the other major characters, he shows an awareness of those mistakes and an acceptance of responsibility that gives *Morte Darthur* an ending reminiscent of Aristotelian tragedy.[3] Arthur's mistakes, however, do not negate the words of praise that indicate that Malory had much greater admiration for Arthur than some modern critics do.

Malory's book, completed sometime between March 1469 and March 1470, draws upon earlier French and English romances for its major sources and also reflects the author's extensive reading of still other Arthurian works, particularly English ones (Vinaver 1990; E. D. Kennedy 1981). All of these, French and English, would probably have been easily obtainable in England in the fifteenth century (Meale 1984). Furthermore, Malory's handling of his sources suggests that while working within the limits allowed to a medieval adapter who lacked the freedom to create his own story, he objected to some of the material in both his French and English sources and attempted to find ways to change his account in order to improve the character of Arthur that he found in them (E. D. Kennedy 1975, 1981; Wroten 1950; Dichmann 1964). His efforts to enhance the picture of Arthur that he found in the sources by adding comments about Arthur's being 'the moste kynge and nobelyst knyght of the worlde,' even when his actions did not always appear to justify such praise, reflect the intertextual relationship of Malory's book to earlier often different medieval conceptions of King Arthur.

---

[3] After the final battle Arthur says: 'A, sir Launcelot! . . . alas, that ever I was ayenste the! For now have I my dethe, whereof sir Gawayne me warned in my dreame'. Cf. the statements of the other major characters: Gawain: 'for thorow my wylfulnes I was causer of myne owne dethe'; Guenevere: 'Thorow thys same man [Lancelot] and me hath all thys warre be wrought, and the deth of the moste nobelest knyghtes of the worlde; for thorow oure love that we have loved togydir ys my moste noble lorde slayne'; Lancelot: 'I remembre me how by my defaute and myn orgule and my pryde that they [Arthur and Guenevere] were bothe layed ful lowe' (Vinaver 1990, 3:1238, 1230, 1252, 1256).

One of the most important of these is the conception of Arthur found in the many chronicles that were produced in England in the Middle Ages (E. D. Kennedy 1996a:xiv-xxii). There Arthur was presented positively as a great king who conquered France and most of Europe before being killed in his final battle against Mordred. This King Arthur is ultimately derived from Geoffrey of Monmouth's *Historia Regum Britanniae* (ca1138). Although Geoffrey does not mention Fortune, the story is nevertheless a medieval tragedy in which a character at the height of his power falls, not because of sin or error, but because things of the earth are transient and one may lose them at any time. As E. Vinaver (1971:129) describes Arthur's fall in Geoffrey's *Historia*, it is 'a military disaster for which the chances of war were alone to blame'.

By the end of the twelfth century, however, a less positive conception had been introduced in the later romances of Chretien de Troyes. Although in one of Chretien's early romances *Cligès*, Arthur is the powerful king of the chronicles, his later works *Chevalier de la Charrete (Lancelot), Chevalier au Lion (Yvain)* and *Conte du Graal (Perceval)* did much to diminish Arthur's reputation (Noble 1984; E. D. Kennedy 1996a:xxii-xxiv). In these romances Arthur, although not evil, is at times weak and unable to defend his realm, create knights, or even stay awake at the table. And this conception influenced the Arthur portrayed in such early thirteenth-century prose romances as the non-cyclic *Lancelot en prose* and the Vulgate *Mort Artu*, works in which Arthur, although at times admirable, at times becomes too depressed to carry out his duties, neglects his people, and is dominated by others. In these prose romances he is often presented as a king whom E. Peters has aptly described as a *rex inutilis* or *roi fainéant* (Peters 1970:170-209; also E. Kennedy 1965 & 1984).

A medieval author familiar with English and French Arthurian literature could thus draw upon two disparate traditions concerning Arthur, and it was not unusual for a writer to use both traditions in a single work. In France, readers of Arthurian literature were familiar with the romance tradition through the works of Chrétien de Troyes and his successors; they knew the chronicle tradition through Geoffrey's *Historia* and Wace's French verse adaptation of this work. Elspeth Kennedy, in discussing both Chrétien de Troyes' romances and the non-cyclic French *Lancelot en prose*, observes that those listening to or reading these works were capable of placing each romance, in which Arthur was presented as an often minor and weak character, against the background of the Arthurian world of the chronicles in which Arthur had the more important role of warrior king (Elspeth Kennedy 1986:2; also Brewer 1981:95-6). The same would be true of a work such as the thirteenth-century French Vulgate *Mort Artu.* As J. Frappier (1972:328-9) remarks, in this romance Arthur's character, with its strengths and weaknesses, has many inconsistencies. Such a portrait is apt to trouble modern readers who expect consistent characterizations; a medieval audience, unaccustomed to the conventions of realism, would be less likely to have been disturbed by inconsistencies, and much of the delight that they probably took in such portraits would have been in recognizing their intertextual affinities with earlier Arthurian literature from both chronicle and romance traditions.

The thirteenth-century French prose romances, judging from the number of surviving manuscripts and the number of translations into other languages, were well known throughout Europe; and a number of them were in England in the Middle Ages and are frequently mentioned in book lists and wills (Meale 1984; E. D. Kennedy 1993b:79-80, n. 3; Riddy 1991:326-9). It is doubtful, however, that most of Malory's English readers would have been familiar with these French romances and would have been able to recognize intertextual affinities between them and Malory's work, and it is doubtful that inconsistency in the characterization of Arthur would have been as irrelevant to them as it was to French readers. To be sure, some of Malory's readers would have been like the probably fictitious 'noble and dyvers gentylmen' who supposedly asked Caxton to publish an account of Arthur (Vinaver 1990:cxliii) and who would have been familiar with the French romances and thus able to react in the same way as French readers. Caxton would probably have been in this category himself: he at least implies this when in the prologue he expresses regret that so many of the stories about Arthur have been unavailable to English readers: 'And also he is more spoken of beyonde the see, moo bookes made of his noble actes than there be in Englond…And many noble volumes be made of hym and of his noble knyghtes in Frensshe, which I have seen and redde beyonde the see, which been not had in our maternal tongue' (Vinaver 1990:cxlv). However, by the end of the fifteenth century, most readers of a romance written in English would not have been like Malory, Caxton, and the 'noble and dyvers gentylmen'. Most would have been unable to read French and would not have known the romances upon which *Morte Darthur* was based. Caxton acknowledges this in *Charles the Grete*, the life of Charlemagne he published in 1485, a few months after *Morte Darthur:* 'the moost quantyte of the people understonde not Latyn ne Frensshe here in this noble royame of Englond' (Blake 1973:67). Thus many of Caxton's potential customers would have been unable to place *Morte Darthur* against the background of these works.

Of the French romances that Malory used as major sources (*Merlin* of the Post-Vulgate *Roman du Graal*, the Vulgate *Lancelot*, the *Perlesvaus*, the Prose *Tristan*, the Vulgate *Queste del Saint Graal*, and the Vulgate *Mort Artu*) only the *Mort Artu* had previously been adapted into English as a metrical romance known to modern scholars as the stanzaic *Morte Arthur*, a work that like Malory's book presents Arthur more positively than its French source (E. D. Kennedy 1994). Malory was an innovator in adapting into English French Arthurian romances that other English writers had left untouched.[4]

The conception of a weak Arthur would have been known to some of Malory's English readers, however, since it appears in several Middle English romances. Dean (1987:89), in fact, suggests that the presentation of Arthur in these works in a way that is contrary to his conventional portrait in the chronicles indicates that 'he was not an established figure in the serious history of Britain; otherwise such liberties could not have been taken'. Admittedly, some of these authors may not have taken Arthur seriously as a historical figure; since, however, a number of the romances that present Arthur as a weak king were written in northern England or Scotland, they could reflect the unpopularity of the historical Arthur in that region as much as French tradition (Göller 1962; Alexander 1975). The chronicle accounts of Arthur's dominion over Scotland had been used to justify English attempts to conquer Scotland; and in presenting a portrait of Arthur whose

[4] The French prose Vulgate *Merlin* had been adapted into English three times before Malory wrote his book. Malory at some time had read this work, in French if not in its English versions (Wilson 1950:46-9). It was not, however, one of his major sources. It, like the *Mort Artu*, is different from the other romances of the Vulgate Cycle in that it was strongly influenced by the chronicle tradition. It presents a generally positive picture of Arthur.

stature has been diminished, these northern romances could testify to belief rather than disbelief in his historicity. Although most of these survive in only single manuscripts, and it is not certain how widely they circulated, Malory was familiar with some of them, for there is evidence in his text that he had read romances such as *Syre Gawene and the Carle of Carelyle, The Weddynge of Sir Gawen, The Avowynge of King Arthur, The Awntyrs off Arthure*, and the alliterative *Morte Arthure* (Wilson 1950; E. D. Kennedy 1981).

Although Malory derived only minor details from most of these, one of them, the alliterative *Morte Arthure,* was the major source for his second tale concerning Arthur's campaign against Rome. In adapting this work, however, Malory omitted the tragic ending and had it end in triumph with Arthur crowned Roman emperor, a detail that was probably derived from the metrical chronicle of John Hardyng (Matthews 1960:172; E. D. Kennedy 1969). He presented Arthur as a more humane king than he was in the alliterative *Morte*. Those of Malory's readers who knew this work would have been struck by the ways it contrasted with Malory's account (Wroten 1950; Dichmann 1964).

Malory's approach to the alliterative *Morte Arthure* is characteristic of his selective approach to those French romances that his readers probably would not have known. Thus although he appears to have read all of the Vulgate *Lancelot*, he avoided the parts of it that present the most negative picture of Arthur (E. D. Kennedy 1993a), and, as noted above, he similarly enhanced the character of Arthur that he found in other French romances that he used. Malory's attempt to put Arthur in a better light is probably due to the influence of the chronicles.

3. Arthur in the Chronicles

English and French readers would have responded differently to the portrait of Arthur found in the chronicles. Most French readers would not have taken the English chronicles seriously as history. France had its own chronicles, and most of these did not mention being conquered by Arthur. In fact, resentment of such tales of conquest could have led to a desire to negate Arthur as a heroic figure and may help account for the portrayal of Arthur in some French romances as a weak king (Morris 1991:121). To the English, however, the story of Arthur was an important part of the history of the island they now occupied. Although the historical Arthur would have been a Celtic enemy of the invading Angles and Saxons, by the late twelfth century he was considered a king deserving of the admiration of the English and Normans as well as the Welsh (Gransden 1976:354-6; Chambers 1927:123-4). While the Latin text of Geoffrey's *Historia*, surviving in at least 215 manuscripts, was one of the most influential works written in England in the Middle Ages (Crick 1989), the fact that it was written in Latin indicates that it was intended for the limited readership of scholars, and much of its importance consists of the influence it had on later chroniclers. As Felicity Riddy points out, when later chroniclers repeated the story of Arthur in Anglo-Norman and English, they made it available to a much larger audience than Geoffrey could ever have conceived (Riddy 1991; E. D. Kennedy 1996a:xvii).

Medieval chroniclers certainly did not have the concern for factual accuracy that modern historians have. Chronicles were valued for the moral truths they could teach, and Ranulf Higden, in citing in his *Polychronicon* St Paul's belief that all is written for our doctrine, raised doubts about the truth of much that even he wrote in his chronicle (Guenée 1980:27-9). Nevertheless chronicles were considered to be generally true accounts of past events even if some facts in them were questionable. Some books, medieval readers believed, were more likely to contain truth than others. The Bible, at one end of the spectrum, was seen as a completely true work that people were expected to believe; fables, at the other end, were obvious fictions written to teach moral lessons. Other works were somewhere in between. Information found in chronicles would have been considered basically reliable. Although some English chroniclers questioned the veracity of Geoffrey of Monmouth's account (Treharne 1967:75-81; Kendrick 1950:12-13; Chambers 1927:106-8), most seem to have considered Geoffrey's account to be a fairly reliable account of past events. They sometimes embellished their adaptations of it with minor details drawn from romances and other sources, and some, like Robert Mannyng, at times alluded to Arthur's adventures in the romances and even referred to times during his reign when the adventures in the verse and prose romances might have occurred (Johnson 1991; Putter 1994). Nevertheless, for the four hundred years following the appearance of Geoffrey's *Historia*, most of the chroniclers repeated without much change the basic events of Geoffrey's account. By incorporating Geoffrey's *Historia* into their own vernacular chronicles that told the whole history of England, the later chroniclers gave Geoffrey's work a credibility that it would never have achieved had it remained simply a history of the British. Because they were accepted as basically true accounts, chronicles were important politically; the Arthurian ones in particular offered support for imperialist and other political ambitions of English rulers from Henry II to James I (E. D. Kennedy 1996a: xvii-xx).

The chronicles were more widely read than most of the Middle English romances taught today, and in England much of the conception of King Arthur would have been derived from them. Most English Arthurian metrical romances, including ones well known today like *Sir Gawain and the Green Knight* and the alliterative *Morte Arthure*, survive in single manuscripts, although admittedly allusions to various romances in works like Chaucer's *Tale of Sir Thopas* and Malory's *Morte Darthur* indicate that some were more widely read than the single surviving manuscript of each work might suggest. Surviving manuscripts of the Arthurian chronicles are far more numerous: the English metrical chronicle attributed to Robert of Gloucester is found in fourteen manuscripts and two different fifteenth-century translations into prose; the Anglo-Norman chronicle of Pierre Langtoft, in 21 medieval manuscripts; the second version of the fifteenth-century chronicle of John Hardyng, in sixteen; Higden's Latin *Polychronicon*, in at least 127; and Trevisa's translation of it, in eighteen. The most widely read of the chronicles was the prose *Brut*, which in its French and English versions survives in at least 50 and 173 manuscripts respectively. The printing between 1480 and 1528 of thirteen editions of the English version (including two by Caxton) offers further evidence of its influence (E. D. Kennedy 1996a:xviii-xix; E. D. Kennedy 1989:2629-37, 2818-21; Matheson 1998).[5] L. Matheson (1990:254) describes the prose *Brut* as the 'standard vernacular history textbook of late medieval England' from which a great many people in England would have derived their

[5] One more *Brut* manuscript has been discovered since my list appeared in 1989: Brogyntyn 8 (Porkington), on deposit in the National Library of Wales. The difference in number between my list and Matheson's is primarily due to Matheson's classifying as 'peculiar versions' of the *Brut* works that I classified as different chronicles.

knowledge of the Arthurian story. And there were many other Latin, French and English chronicles that survive in fewer manuscripts that would have helped spread the story of King Arthur (E. D. Kennedy 1989; Keeler 1946).

But if chronicles were popular sources of information about King Arthur, with the exceptions of Geoffrey of Monmouth, Wace, and Layamon, they are not well known today. This is understandable: The chronicles are long, there are no good modern editions or translations of many of them, and to the modern mind they lack quality. The verse of the chronicle attributed to Robert of Gloucester was described by his nineteenth-century editor as being 'as worthless as 12,000 lines of verse without one spark of poetry can be,' and one of the few assessments of John Hardyng's verse, written about two hundred years ago by Thomas Warton, described it as being 'almost beneath criticism,' an assessment that most today would still find accurate (Wright 1887, 1:xl; Warton 1774-90, 3:124). These later chronicles are works that until relatively recently few medievalists have read. Scholars have often been out of touch with what people in England were reading and with the conception of King Arthur that many of Caxton's contemporaries would have had before they read *Morte Darthur.*

Malory's positive conception of Arthur was probably derived from the chronicles. Malory had read as one of his earliest accounts of Arthur the enthusiastic version in John Hardyng's chronicle (E. D. Kennedy 1981), and he might also have read Lydgate's equally positive version in *Fall of Princes* (Withrington 1987), which was based on earlier chronicles (Perzl 1911:191). Moreover, with so many manuscripts of the French and English *Brut* in circulation, it is difficult to believe that Malory had not at some time read it as well. The portrait of Arthur in Hardyng and other chronicles can account for Malory's praise for Arthur throughout his book as well as his attempt to present Arthur more positively than he found him in the French romances and in an English source like the alliterative *Morte Arthure*. But although Malory expresses his admiration for Arthur, weaknesses, such as the attempt to kill all of the children in the kingdom born at the time of Mordred's birth, nevertheless remain;[6] and many English readers would have cared little for some of his actions in *Morte Darthur.*

[6] P. J. C. Field describes the child-killing episode 'plainly incompatible with Arthur's character as presented elsewhere in Malory's book' (Field 1998:101).

4. Caxton, the Chronicles, and Malory

As mentioned above, Caxton, like Malory, knew earlier stories about Arthur, and that would include both the positive English portraits in the chronicles and the less positive French ones in the romances that Caxton says he had read 'beyonde the see'. Like Malory, he had great admiration for Arthur and apparently believed that there had been an historical Arthur. In his prologue to *Godeffroy of Boloyne* (1481) Caxton had described Arthur as the 'best and worthyest' of the Nine Worthies. Arthur's story is so 'gloryous and shynyng' that he is 'in the fyrst place of the mooste noble, beste and worthyest of the Cristen men' (Blake 1973:139). In his prologue to *Morte Darthur*, Caxton again describes Arthur as one of the Nine Worthies, the 'fyrst and chyef' of the three Christian worthies, and he 'coude not wel denye but that there was suche a noble kyng named Arthur'. As evidence for the existence of an historical Arthur, he mentions the chronicle tradition: in his argument, he says that there were accounts of Arthur in Geoffrey of Monmouth's *Historia*, Higden's *Polychronicon*, and in Boccaccio's *De Casibus Virorum Illustrium*, which Caxton probably knew through Lydgate's *Fall of Princes* (E. D. Kennedy 1996b:46-50). He also mentions the French romances several times. Malory's book was based on material that Malory 'dyd take oute of certeyn bookes of Frennshe and reduced...into Englysshe'. Caxton had also indicated his interest in these French works in his prologue to *Godeffroy of Boloyne*. There he mentions Arthur's 'knyghtes of the Round Table, of whos actes an historyes there be large volumes, and bookes grete plente and many...volumes of Seynt Graal, Ghalehot, and Launcelotte de Lake, Gawayn, Perceual, Lyonel and Tristram, and many other' (Blake 1973:139).

Although Caxton knew both traditions, he was particularly interested in the historical one. Oddly enough, in citing in his prologue historical evidence for the proof of Arthur's existence, he does not mention the English prose *Brut*. But he knew this work well. Before the publication of *Morte Darthur* in 1485, besides publishing an edition of Trevisa's translation of Higden's *Polychronicon* in 1482, he had published in 1480 and in 1482 two editions of the *Brut,* which he entitled *The Chronicles of England*, a work that presented Arthur unabashedly as a great king and champion of Cristendom (see Brie 1906:86-7). At the time Caxton was publishing his two editions of the *Chronicles of England* and the *Polychronicon*, he was either planning his edition of Malory or perhaps even trying to decide whether to publish it. Studies of the surviving Winchester manuscript of *Morte Darthur* have shown that it was in Caxton's print shop during this period: it has ink smudges on it that came from damp printed pages of books that Caxton printed between 1480 and 1483 and that had been placed on the manuscript (Hellinga 1981). Thus, the Winchester version of Malory's book could have been in Caxton's shop for five years or even longer before *Morte Darthur* was published, a period in which Caxton published three editions of chronicles that included the most widely read accounts of Arthur in England. These chronicles would not have been gambles; they would have been proven best sellers.

Malory's work, however, was a different matter. Unlike the chronicles, it was a work that had not circulated widely and that drew upon French romances not previously available in English. On the one hand, Caxton must have felt that the book would appeal to English readers who could not read French but who were interested in reading the kinds of romances that the aristocracy read. On the other, it was a work in which Arthur at times appeared in sharp contrast to the Arthur of the chronicles that these same readers would have known.

The one part of Malory's book that comes closest to the chronicle tradition is his second tale, the account of Arthur's war against the Romans. This is a part that has also been controversial because the version in the Caxton edition is considerably different from the version in the surviving Winchester manuscript. While the second tale in the Winchester manuscript is written in heavily alliterative prose, the corresponding section in Caxton's edition has had the alliteration removed, has been shortened and has other changes. Some have argued that Malory made the changes; others that it was Caxton.[7] The evidence, however, strongly indicates that Caxton was the reviser, particularly since scholars have shown that a number of the details that were added to the second tale appear to have been derived from Caxton's editions of the English prose *Brut* and his edition of the *Polichronicon* (Withrington 1992; Nakao 2000; Takagi & Takamiya 2000). The possibility that Caxton could have changed Malory's account to make it

[7] For both sides of this controversy, see Wheeler, Kindrick & Salda, eds. (2000).

conform, both in style and to some extent in substance, to the *Brut* suggests that he may have had readers in mind who knew the chronicle tradition.

Caxton's familiarity with the chronicles can help explain the reservations he seems to have had about recommending Malory's book to his readers: He says 'to passe the tyme thys book shal be plesaunte to rede in,' but 'to gyve fayth and byleve that al is trew that is conteyned herin, ye be at your lyberté.' He echoes St Paul (Romans 15:4) in a statement that, as mentioned above, Higden had also used in the *Polychronicon*: '[A]l is wryton for our doctryne.' Malory's book may not be entirely true but it has didactic value. It is, like many of Caxton's other publications, a work that offers moral *exempla*: 'I ...have doon sette it in enprynte to the entente that noble men may see and lerne the noble acts of chyvalrye, the jentyl and vertuous dedes that somme knyghtes used in tho dayes . . . and how they that were vycious were punysshed and ofte put to shame and rebuke.... Do after the good and leve the evyl'.

Some scholars have argued that Caxton, unlike such later writers as Sir Philip Sidney, did not distinguish between history and fiction (Levine 1987:45, 50; Kretzschmar 1992). Admittedly some medieval writers' attitudes toward what they wrote were ahistorical, and they valued history primarily for its moral *exempla*, some of which might not be true and which they at times felt free to create (Morse 1982). Many nevertheless had a sense of history (see Patterson 1987:198) and would have distinguished between chronicles, which were basically true, and romances, which were not. E. Kirk (1985) has argued that Caxton's prologue to his edition of the *Polychronicon* indicates that he was aware of some of the distinctions between history and fiction that became more evident among writers of the sixteenth century. Kirk's observation is plausible. In the prologue to his edition of the *Polychronicon* Caxton defined 'historye' as 'a perpetuel conservatryce of thoos thynges that have be doone before this presente tyme and also a cotydyan wytnesse of bienfayttes, of malefaytes, grete actes, and tryumphal vyctoryes of all maner peple' (Blake 1973:130). Moreover, Caxton's implicit questions about the truth of Malory's book contrast with his remarks in the prologue to *Godeffroy of Boloyne*, a book about another of the Nine Worthies, published four years before *Morte Darthur*, when Caxton had the Winchester manuscript of Malory in his shop and when he was probably contemplating an edition of Malory. *Godeffroy*, Caxton writes, is 'no fable ne fayned thynge, but alle that is therin trewe' (Blake 1973:140). Caxton's comments about Malory's book contrast sharply with this. In contrast to his remarks about Godeffroy, Caxton writes that 'dyvers men holde oppynyon that there was no suche Arthur and that all suche bookes as been maad of hym ben but fayned and fables' (Vinaver 1990:cxliv). Caxton, to be sure, attempts to destroy this argument by having one of the 'noble and dyvers gentylmen' who wanted him to publish a book about King Arthur give historical evidence for Arthur's existence. Even though the argument of Arthur's existence appears to be settled in the affirmative, Caxton does not assert as he had with his edition of *Godeffrey* that 'alle that is therin trewe'. In the case of Godeffrey of Boloyne there would not have been as many competing stories about him, and even if there had, few English would have been concerned about him. It was different with Arthur, who by this time was considered a national English (not just British) hero. On the basis of his familiarity with the chronicles, Caxton would have known that Malory's book had to be distinguished from them.

Although Caxton expressed in his prologues and epilogues interest in the didactic value of virtually everything he published, his emphasis upon the didactic value of Malory's book and his indicating that not everything in it is true suggests that he was aware that Malory's book was quite different from the chronicle accounts of Arthur that many of the readers could have known through Caxton's editions or through a rival edition of the *Brut* that had been printed at St. Albans at about 1483 or through the many manuscripts of the *Brut* and other chronicles that were in circulation. Caxton's readers had to be told that Malory's book was important for its moral lessons, rather than for its historical truth.

Caxton's successor Wynkyn de Worde, who published an edition of the *Polychronicon* (1495) and two editions of the *Brut* (1497, 1502) as well as two editions of *Morte Darthur* (1498, 1529) placed similar emphasis on the moral lessons to be learned from Malory's book. He added, for example, moral exhortations to his editions reminding readers that one could see that 'this mighty conqueror Arthur' and 'the noble queen Guenever… now lie full low in obscure foss or pit covered with clods of earth and clay' and how readers should fear 'the unstableness of this deceivable world' (Parins 1988:52; also Mukai 1993). Wynkyn de Worde, unlike Caxton, was not born in England and would probably have had continental scepticism about the existence of Arthur, and it is therefore not surprising that he would have emphasized the moral value of the stories. Of course, by the time of Caxton and de Worde many readers would have doubted that Arthur had ever lived. Nevertheless, those who believed that there had been an Arthur would have known his story through the chronicles; and they would have had some of the same reservations about Malory's Arthur that a modern reader would have after reading Tennyson and that Malory's changes in his sources and reassurances about Arthur's being a great and noble king have never been able to eradicate. Publishing such a work may indeed have been a gamble for Caxton.

References

Alexander, F. 1975. 'Late Medieval Scottish Attitudes to the Figure of King Arthur: A Reassessment'. *Anglia* 93:17-34.

Benson, L. D. 1976. *Malory's 'Morte Darthur'*. Cambridge, MA: Harvard University Press.

Blake, N. F., ed. 1973. *Caxton's Own Prose*. London: André Deutsch.

———. 1976. 'Caxton Prepares His Edition of the *Morte Darthur*'. *Journal of Librarianship* 8:272-85.

Brewer, D. S., ed. 1968. *The 'Morte Darthur': Parts Seven and Eight*. York Medieval Texts. London: Edward Arnold.

———. 1981. 'Malory: The Traditional Writer and the Archaic Mind'. *Arthurian Literature* 1:94-120.

Brie, F. W. D., ed. 1906. *The Brut or the Chronicles of England*. Part 1. EETS o.s. 131. Reprint, London: Oxford University Press, 1960.

Chambers, E. K. 1927. *Arthur of Britain*. London: Sidgwick & Jackson. Reprint, Cambridge: Speculum Historiale, 1964.

Crick, J. 1989. *The 'Historia Regum Britannie' of Geoffrey of Monmouth, III: A Summary Catalogue of the Manuscripts*. Cambridge: D. S. Brewer, 1989.

Dean, C. 1987. *Arthur of England: English Attitudes to King Arthur and the Knights of the Round Table in the Middle Ages and the Renaissance*. Toronto: University of Toronto Press.

Dichmann, M. E. 1964. '"The Tale of King Arthur and the Emperor Lucius": The Rise of Lancelot'. *Malory's Originality*, ed. R. M. Lumiansky. Baltimore: Johns Hopkins Press. 67-90.

Field, P. J. C. 1998. 'Malory's Mordred and the *Morte Arthure*'. *Malory: Texts and Sources.* Cambridge: D. S. Brewer. 89-102. Originally published in *Romance Reading on the Book: Essays on Medieval Narrative presented to Maldwyn Mills*, ed. J. Fellows, R. Field, G. Roers, & J. Weiss. Cardiff: University of Wales Press, 1996. 77-93.

Frappier, J. 1972. *Étude sur 'La Mort le Roi Artu'*. 3rd ed. Geneva: E. Droz.

Göller K. H. 1962. 'König Arthur in den schottischen Chroniken'. *Anglia* 80:390-404. Translated in E. D. Kennedy (1996a), pp. 173-84.

Gransden, A. 1976. 'The Growth of the Glastonbury Traditions and Legends in the Twelfth Century'. *Journal of Ecclesiastical History* 27:337-58.

Guenée, B. 1980. *Histoire et culture historique dans l'Occident médiéval.* Paris: Aubier Montaigne.

Hellinga, L. 1981. 'The Malory Manuscript and Caxton'. *Aspects of Malory*, ed T. Takamiya & D. Brewer. Cambridge: D. S. Brewer. 127-42.

Johnson, L. 1991. 'Robert Mannyng of Brunne and the History of Arthurian Literature'. *Church and Chronicle in the Middle Ages: Essays Presented to John Taylor*, ed. I. Wood & G. A. Loud. London: Hambledon Press. 129-47.

Keeler, L. 1946. *Geoffrey of Monmouth and the Late Latin Chroniclers 1300-1500.* University of California Publications in English 17. Berkeley: University of California Press.

Kendrick, T. D. 1950. *British Antiquity*. London: Methuen.

Kennedy, E. 1965. 'King Arthur in the First Part of the Prose *Lancelot*'. *Medieval Miscellany presented to Eugène Vinaver*, ed. F. Whitehead, A. H. Diverres, & F. E. Sutcliffe. Manchester: Manchester University Press. 186-95.

———. 1984. 'Études sur le *Lancelot en prose*: 2: Le Roi Arthur dans le *Lancelot en prose'*. *Romania* 105:46-62. Translated in E. D. Kennedy (1996a), pp. 71-89.

———. 1986. 'The Re-writing and Re-reading of a Text: the Evolution of the *Prose Lancelot*'. *The Changing Face of Arthurian Romance*, ed. A. Adams, A. H. Diverres, K. Stern, & K. Varty. Woodbridge: Boydell & Brewer. 1-9.

Kennedy, E. D. 1969. 'Malory's Use of Hardyng's Chronicle'. *Notes and Queries* 214:167-70.

———. 1975. 'Malory's King Mark and King Arthur'. *Mediaeval Studies* 37: 190-234. Revised in E. D. Kennedy (1996a), pp. 139-71.

———. 1981. 'Malory and His English Sources'. *Aspects of Malory*, ed. T. Takamiya & D. Brewer. Cambridge: D. S. Brewer. 27-55.

———. 1989. *A Manual of the Writings in Middle English, vol. 8: Chronicles and Other Historical Writing*, gen. ed. A. E. Hartung. New Haven, CT:

Connecticut Academy of Arts and Sciences.

———. 1993a. 'Malory's "Noble Tale of Sir Launcelot du Lake", the Vulgate *Lancelot*, and the Post-Vulgate *Roman du Graal*'. *Arthurian and Other Studies Presented to Shunichi Noguchi*, ed. T. Suzuki & T. Mukai. Cambridge: D. S. Brewer. 107-30.

———. 1993b. 'Gower, Chaucer, and French Prose Arthurian Romance'. *Mediaevalia* 16:55-90.

———. 1994. 'The Stanzaic *Morte Arthur*: The Adaptation of a French Romance for an English Audience.' *Culture and the King: The Social Implications of the Arthurian Legend: Essays in Honor of Valerie M. Lagorio*, ed. M. B. Shichtman & J. P. Carley. Albany: State University of New York Press. 91-112.

———. 1996a. 'Introduction'. *King Arthur: A Casebook.* New York: Garland. xiii-xlvii.

———. 1996b. 'Generic Intertextuality in the English *Alliterative Morte Arthure*; The Italian Connection'. *Text and Intertext in Medieval Arthurian Literature*, ed. N. J. Lacy. New York: Garland. 41-56.

———. 2000. "Caxton, Malory, and the 'Noble Tale of King Arthur and the Emperor Lucius'. In Wheeler, Kindrick, & Salda, eds. (2000), pp. 217-32.

Kirk, E. 1985. '"Clerkes, Poetes and Historiographs": The *Morte Darthur* and Caxton's "Poetics" of Fiction'. *Studies in Malory*, ed. J. W. Spisak. Kalamazoo, MI: Medieval Institute Publications. 275-95.

Korrel, P. 1984. *An Arthurian Triangle: A Study of the Origin, Development and Characterisation of Arthur, Guinevere, and Modred.* Leiden: E. J. Brill.

Kretzschmar, W. A., Jr. 1992. 'Caxton's Sense of History'. *Journal of English and Germanic Philology* 91:510-26.

Lambert, M. 1975. *Malory: Style and Vision in 'Le Morte Darthur'.* New Haven: Yale University Press.

Levine, J. M. 1987. *Humanism and History: Origins of Modern English Historiography.* Ithaca, NY: Cornell University Press.

Mattheson, L. M. 1990. 'King Arthur and the Medieval English Chronicles'. *King Arthur through the Ages*, vol. 1, ed. V. M. Lagorio & M. L. Day. New York: Garland.

———. 1998. *The Prose 'Brut': The Development of a Middle English Chronicle.* Tempe, AZ: Medieval & Renaissance Texts and Studies.

Matthews, W. 1960. *The Tragedy of Arthur: A Study of the Alliterative 'Morte Arthure'.* Berkeley & Los Angeles: University of California Press.

McCarthy, T. 1988: *Reading the 'Morte Darthur'.* Cambridge: D. S. Brewer.

Meale, C. 1984. 'Manuscripts, Readers and Patrons in Fifteenth-Century

England: Sir Thomas Malory and Arthurian Romance'. *Arthurian Literature* 4:93-126.

Morris, R. 1991. 'King Arthur and the Growth of French Nationalism'. *France and the British Isles in the Middle Ages and Renaissance: Essays in Memory of Ruth Morgan*, ed. G. Jondorf & D. N. Dumville. Woodbridge: Boydell & Brewer. 115-29.

Morse, R. 1982. '"This Vague Relation": Historical Fiction and Historical Veracity in the Later Middle Ages". *Leeds Studies in English* n.s. 13:85-103.

Mukai, T. 'De Worde's Displacement of Malory's Secularization'. *Arthurian and Other Studies Presented to Shunichi Noguchi*, ed. T. Suzuki & T. Mukai. Cambridge: D. S. Brewer. 179-87.

Nakao, Y. 2000. 'Musings on the Reviser of Book V in Caxton's Malory'. In Wheeler, Kindrick, & Salda., eds. (2000), pp. 191-216.

Noble, P. S. 1984. 'Chrétien's Arthur'. *Chrétien de Troyes and the Troubadours*, ed. P. S. Noble & L. M. Paterson. Cambridge: St Catherine's College. 220-37.

Parins, M. J., ed. 1988. *Malory: The Critical Heritage*. London: Routledge.

Patterson, L. 1987. *Negotiating the Past*. Madison: University of Wisconsin Press.

Perzl, W., ed. 1911. *Die Arthur-Legende in Lydgate's 'Fall of Princes': Kritische Neu-Ausgabe mit Quellenforschung*. Munich: Wolff.

Peters, E. 1970. *The Shadow King: 'Rex Inutilis' in Medieval Law and Literature 751-1327*. New Haven: Yale University Press.

Pochoda, E. T. 1971. *Arthurian Propaganda: 'Le Morte Darthur' as an Historical Ideal of Life*. Chapel Hill: University of North Carolina Press.

Putter, A. 1994. 'Finding Time for Romance: Mediaeval Arthurian Literary History'. *Medium Ævum* 63:1-16.

Riddy, F. 1991. 'Reading for England: Arthurian Literature and National Consciousness'. *Bibliographical Bulletin of the International Arthurian Society* 43:326-9.

Takagi, M. & T. Takamiya. 'Caxton Edits the Roman War Episode: The *Chronicles of England* and Caxton's Book V'. In Wheeler, Kindrick, & Salda, eds. (2000), pp. 169-90.

Thornton, G. 1991. 'The Weakening of the King: Arthur's Disintegration in *The Book of Sir Tristram de Lyones*'. *The Arthurian Yearbook*, ed. K. Busby, 1:135-48. Reprinted 1992 in *Sir Thomas Malory: Views and Re-views*, ed. D. T. Hanks, Jr. New York: AMS Press. 3-16.

Treharne, R. F. 1967. *The Glastonbury Legends*. London: Cresset.

Vinaver, E. 1971. *The Rise of Romance*. Oxford: Clarendon Press.

——, ed. 1990. *The Works of Sir Thomas Malory*. 3rd ed. Revised by P. J. C. Field. 3 vols. Oxford: Clarendon Press.

Warton, T. 1774-90. *History of English Poetry*. 4 vols, ed. W. C. Hazlitt. vol. 3. London: Reeves and Turner, 1871.

Wheeler, B., R. L. Kindrick, & M. N. Salda, eds. 2000. *The Malory Debate: Essays on the Texts of 'Le Morte Darthur'*. Cambridge: D. S. Brewer.

Wilson, R. H. 1950. 'Malory's Early Knowledge of Arthurian Romance'. *Texas Studies in English* 29:33-50.

Withrington, J. 1987. 'The Arthurian Epitaph in Malory's "Morte Darthur"'. *Arthurian Literature* 7:124-44.

——. 1992. 'Caxton, Malory and the Roman War in the *Morte Darthur*'. *Studies in Philology* 89:350-66.

Wright W. A., ed. 1887. *The Metrical Chronicle of Robert of Gloucester*. 2 vols. Rolls Series 86. London: Eyre and Spottiswoode.

Wroten, H. I. 1950. 'Malory's Tale of King Arthur and the Emperor Lucius Compared with Its Source, the Alliterative *Morte Arthure*'. Dissertation, University of Illinois. University Microfilms, no. 2231.

The Lineage and Variations of the Biblical Phrase *while the world standeth*[1]

Hideki Watanabe

1. William Tyndale

Reading *I Corinthians* in the *Authorized Version* (hereafter *AV*), we encounter a strange phrase 'while the world standeth' in 13.8: 'Wherefore if meate make my brother offend, I will eat no flesh while the world standeth, lest I make my brother to offend'. The meaning of the phrase is apparent as it is a rendering of the Greek phrase '*εἰς τὸν αἰῶνα*': 'for ever'. Dr Johnson notes and quotes this strange expression for the fourteenth sense definition of the verb *stand*.[2] The *OED* also refers to the biblical phrase for 23b of *stand*: 'Of the world: to exist; to remain stable, last. Chiefly in phrase'.[3] Here are rendered five examples of the phrase and its variation, of which the first one is from Layamon's *Brut* and the last is from the translation of Terence at the end of the sixteenth century. Before the bracketed reference to *AV* comes the counterpart from Tyndale's earlier version of the New Testa-

---

[1] Facsimiles of the early editions of the English Bible were used for reference after initial searches with *Bible in English on CD-Rom*.

[2] In his first edition of *A Dictionary of the English Language* Dr Johnson quotes from Dryden: That sots and knaves should be so vain / to wish their vile remembrance may remain; / And stand recorded, at their own request, / to future days a libel or a jest.

[3] *OED* stand 23. b: Of the world: To exist; to remain stable, last. Chiefly in phrase: cf. quot.1526. c1205 Lay. 18850 þe wile þe þis world stænt [c1275 steond] ilæsten scal is worðmunt. a1225 *Leg. Kath.* 1490 Of marbrestan a temple, þet schal aa stonden, hwil þet te world stont. 1340-70 *Alex. & Dind.* 587 ȝe were alle..bred of þat modur þat is stable to stonde. 1526 Tindale *1Cor.* viii. 13 Whill the worlde stondeth [So 1611; Gr. *εἰς τὸν αἰῶνα*]. 1598 R. Bernard tr. *Terence, Adelphos* i. ii, Neuer was there since the world stood, any thing more vnreasonable.

ment (1526), which suggests that it was Tyndale who first employs this phrase. Actually he renders 'whill the world(e) stondeth/ endureth' to 'εἰς τὸν αἰῶνα' six times in both of his two versions:[4]

'while the world standeth/endureth' in Tyndale in the order of appearance

Mark 11:14:	never man eate frute of the here after whill the world stondeth.
John 13: 8:	Thou shalt not wasshe my fete whill the worlde stondeth.
1Cor. 8:13:	Wherefore yf meate hurt my brother/ I will eate no flesshe whill the worlde stondeth because I will not hurte my brother.
1Pet. 4:11:	That god in all thinges maye be glorified thorowe Jesus Christ/ to whom be prayse and dominion for ever and whill the worlde stondeth Amen.
1Pet. 5:11:	To hym be glory and dominion for ever/ and whill the world endureth Amen.
Heb. 13:21:	To whom be prayse for ever whill the world endureth Amen.

We should note that Tyndale switches the verbs in the phrase from *stondeth* to *endureth* in the course of translating *I Peter.* The fourth and the fifth chapters thereof are divided into five and three parts, respectively, by the translator. In both chapters the phrase 'whill the world stondeth/endureth' with *amen* appears at the end of a part.

The purpose of this paper is to review the historical development and divergence of the Tyndalian phrase 'while the worlde standeth/endureth' with special reference to its OE counterparts, ME variants, and Modern English remnants. We will also consider, with the view point of discourse, the peculiar use of the phrase by Tyndale as it is employed to finish a unit of passage.

2. English Bible Translations

In the sixteenth century most important English Bibles after Tyndale followed him to some extent: while Thomas Matthew's Bible (1549) copied all of the six examples, Cranmer's Bible (Great Bible) (1539) adopts the phrase in the renderings of Mark 11:14 and Heb. 13:21, Geneva Bible (1560) also in Mark 11:14 and 1Cor. 8:13, and Bishops' Bible (1568) follows suit. As *AV* does not follow Bishops' Bible in Mark 11:14, the tradition in the renderings of the Gospels was discarded before the

[4] Tyndale printed I Peter and II Peter before Hebrews.

seventeenth century. Table 1 below shows the incidence of the phrase 'while the world standeth/ endureth' from Tyndale to Webster:

Table 1. 'while the world standeth/ endureth' from Tyndale to Webster

Tyndale (1526/ 1534)	Cranmer's (1539)	Matthew (1549)	Geneva (1560)	Bishops' (1568)	AV (1611)	Wesley (1755)	Webster (1833)
Mark 11:14	○	○	○	○			
John 13:8		○					
1Cor. 8:13		○	○	○	○	○	○
Heb. 13:21	○	○					
1Pet. 4:11		○					
1Pet. 5:11		○					

Allen and Jacobs (1995) show that the collators for *AV* made a revision in the text according to alternate readings in the margins of the Bishops' Bible. They found that 'alternate meanings for words and phrases are designed in the Bishops' Bible by parallel vertical lines, as they are in *AV*. Only where an alternate meaning in the margin of the Bishops' Bible has influenced a revision in *AV* does that meaning appear in this collation'.[5] They print specimen pages of collation from the four Gospels which include the chapter eleven of Mark, where the collator(s) wrote in *for ever* on the phrase 'while the world standeth'.[6] It was eventually deleted in *AV*, leaving 1Cor. 8:13 as the only inheritance from Tyndale.

The tradition in 1Cor. 8:13 thereafter was continued by John Wesley (1755) and Noah Webster (1833). Preserved in *AV*, the phrase 'while the world standeth' seems to have exerted influence on preachers in church or religious treatises, too. We have two instances of the phrase employed by religious people in the quotation columns for the two religious nouns as the headwords in the *OED*:

---

[5] See *The Coming of the King James Gospels: A Collation of the Translators' Work-in-Progress* (University of Arkansas Press, p. 44).

[6] p. 233. We might perhaps note that H. Wheeler Robinson mentions this phrase at John xiii. 8 in relation to Tyndale's interpolations and paraphrases (*The Bible in its Ancient and English Versions*, pp. 157-8). But he is silent about the occurrences of the phrase elsewhere in his New Testamant.

a1679 T. Goodwin *Knowledge of God* iii. Xiii, Whilst the world stands he [Christ] governs it, easeth God of that burden, and is his *prorex* for him. (*OED*, *prorex*)

1784 Cowper *Task* ii. 332, I say the pulpit .. Must stand acknowledg'd, while the world shall stand, The most important and effectual guard, Support, and ornament of virtue's cause. (*OED*, *pulpit*)

Thus in the modern Christian tradition this phrase was first employed by Tyndale, established, though lessened in number, by *AV*, and continued by later translators and preachers until the nineteenth century.

3. Old English

The first instance of the phrase in the *OED* is from Layamon but it was already used in OE poems with *þenden*:

Þu on ecnysse wunast awa, drihten;
wunað in gemynd, þenden worold standeð. (*The Paris Psalter,* 101:10)

Næfre him deaþ sceþeð
on þam willwonge, þenden worold stondeþ. (*Phoenix,* 88b-9)

ne mæg him bitres wiht
scyldum sceððan, ac gescylded a
wunað ungewyrded, þenden worold stondeþ. (*Phoenix*, 179b-81)

þæt ic monnum þas
wære gelæste, þenden worold standeþ. (*Genesis*, 1541b-2)

tuddor bið gemæne
incrum orlegnið a þenden standeð
woruld under wolcnum. (*Genesis*, 914b-6a)

These appear in b-verse when alliteration falls on <w>. The three works, *Phoenix*, *Genesis*, and *The Paris Psalter*, are religious pieces retold on the basis of Latin originals. The Latin counterpart in *The Paris Psalter* running as 'tu autem Domine in aeternum permanes memoriale tuum in saeculum saeculi' does not seem to prompt the OE translator to use a clause with the verb *standan* here, as he uses *wunian* for the notion 'to continue' elsewhere:

Him wuldur and wela wunað æt huse,
byð his soþfæstnys swylce mære,

þenden þysse worold wunað ænig dæl. (*The Paris Psalter*, 111:3)

OE writers, poets and preachers alike, have a variety of phrases for the notion in stock.[7] *The Paris Psalter* poet uses such variations for the notion as ‘awa to worulde’, ‘on ealra worulde’, or ‘þurh ealra worulde’, which perfectly fit the situation and the metre.

The two instances from *Phoenix* also deserve our close inspection. The poem is clearly divided into eight sections (or stanzas) in the manuscript (f. 55b-f. 65b, *The Exeter Book*).[8] At the beginning and the end of the second section (ll. 85-181) ‘þenden worold stondeþ’ appear. The poet is very likely to have intentionally repeated the phrase in order to impress immortality of the bird. From discoursal point of view we should take note of its use in the concluding remark of a section of the poem, a distinctively marked position of a text. Note that Tyndale employs the phrase at the end of a section in 1Pet. We will discuss this further in section 5.

Then, what is the implication or connotative meaning of the collocation of *woruld* and *standan*? The noun *woruld* etymologically represents ‘a life time, generation’ for it is a compound of *weras ‘man’ and *alð- ‘old, time’, as can be compared with Gothic *fairhwus* (cf. OE *feorh*) denoting ‘life, man’s lifetime, men, world’. Naturally it was used to render Latin *saeculum*, when its temporal sense was prevalent; for example, *þurh ealra worulde* does not mean ‘all over the world (spatial)’ but ‘through all the generations (temporal)’. Its spatial sense is a later development.[9]

We have some instances of *standan* denoting duration of time in OE:

sy eure elmnesse ykest. ȝerhwamliche. Oȝe land se þe oȝe þe wille þe Cristendom stondez. (*The Will of Wulfgyth* (Sawyer 1503), E 25-6)

And seo feorð eyld þissere worulde stod fram Daniele þam witegan; (*Ælfric’s Letters* 4 (Sigeweard Z), 471)

---

[7] Wulfstan has a variety of phrases for the notion ‘for ever’: a worulde (VIIIb. 87); aa butan ende (II. 72; IV. 96; VI. 217; VII. 174; VIIa. 48); æfre to worulde (III. 73; VIIa. 37; XV. 73), on worulde ær worulde ende (II. 48); in ealra worulda woruld a/æfre butan ende (III. 80; V. 119-20; Xc. 202; XII. 94; XIIIc. 179-80; XVIII. 148; XX(BH). 131-2); etc. (Section Numbers are according to Bethurum (1957).

[8] Blake (1964).

[9] Compare the contrastive notions represented by *mundus* and *saeculum* in a late ME religious piece: ‘Mundus is materual [read: material] worlde, but seculum is take for the induryng world’ (*Pilgr. Soul* 5. 2. 90b in 2. (a) of the headword *enduren* of *MED*).

se tima stod on þusend wintrum & on twa & hundsefontigum wintrum.
(*Byrhthferth's Manual* (Crawford), 236.28)[10]

With these we can compare the following instance where the subject *woruld* appears with a predicative verb *standan*:

Swa stent eall weoruld stille on tille, streams ymbutan,
(*The Metres of Boethius*, 20.171-2)

Here 'the world' is presented as a body, an ordered construction created by God, which 'stands' firm in its place. It is a physically tangible structure as it is encircled by 'streams'.

All things considered, the phrase 'þenden worold standeð' emerges as a native formulaic expression employed to render the notion 'for ever' irrespective of forms of its counterparts in the Latin originals. In this phrase the two distinct but closely interrelated notions of 'the world',—man's life time or a generation and an ordered structure by God—are amalgamated as the verb *standan* has twofold implications, too: 'to (continue to) be' and 'to remain standing/to stand firm'.

4. Middle English

We have examples of 'while the world standeth' from the thirteenth century onward as well. *MED* quotes the following three instances for the sense-division 22. (a) of the verb *stonden* (to last, endure; continue), though it does not clearly specify the collocation:

Longe beoð æuere; dæd ne bið he næuere,
Þe wile þe þis world stænt; ilæsten scal is worð-munt
(*Brut*, MS Caligula, 9406-7)[11]

And he was the wyseste in witt that euer wonnende in erthe,
And his techynges will bene trowede *whills þe werlde standes*
Bothe with kynges and knyghtis and kaysers therinn.
(*The Parlement of the Thre Ages*, 603-5)[12]

---

[10] When the manual is concerned about the history and periodisation of the world, it often employs the verb *standan* in the forms of *stod* or *wæs standande* to render Latin (*con-*) *stabat*.

[11] In the Otho Manuscript the corresponding line runs: 'þe wile þat þe worle steond, me wolw of him telle'.

[12] 'King Solomon's teaching in *the Books of Wisdom* and *Ecclesiasticus* will be believed

His body euer shal be dwelling In erþe *while þe world is stonding.*
(*Medical lore from Sidrak and Bokkus,* 11898)

But it gives two further examples under the headword *world* 1b. (a), designating here 'so longe so this world ilaste' and 'while that the world stondeth' as the typical constructions:

On ende þu schalt habben hehliche as an of ure heuenliche lafdis of marbre-stan a temple þat scal ai stonden *hwil þat te worlde stont* to witnesse of þi wurð mund. (*Seinte Katerine,* MS Titus D XVIII, 1001-7)

O oonly god...Save Calais...That euer it mot wel cheve Vnto the crovn of England, *As longe as the world shal stonde.* (*Siege Calais,* 167)

I have found two more examples:

Yf it worth sall to wy, *whil þe world standes,*
Oure burgh agayn to be beld, þat brytynd is to noght?
(*The Wars of Alexander,* 2382-3)[13]

I axe more god of you, for all the seruyse at I shall do yow *whyll the world standyth,* (*Paston Letters*, Letter 354, 'To John Paston II')

In *Brut* and *Seinte Katerine*, both early ME pieces, the compound noun *wurð-mund* 'honour, glory' following the phrase indicates its Christian colouring and formulaic character. In OE the phrase always appears in present indicative mood. But in the course of ME it is also used in the future tense or in the expanded form (for the rhyme scheme) as is seen in *Medical lore from Sidrak and Bokkus* and *Siege Calais*. The instance from *Paston Letters* testifies a non-religious use and suggests a proliferation of the phrase in secular literature, though its use in alliterative verse was still prevalent.

In ME alliterative verse there are many phrases for the notion 'for ever' observed. Let us see here an example with the verb *lasten* from *Wynnere and Wastoure*:

Dare neuer no western wy *while this werlde lasteth*
Send his sone southwarde to see ne to here

for ever'.

[13] In the Dublin Manuscript the two lines run: 'If euire it worthe sall to wee, *quen þe werd stand,* / Oure bu[r]ȝe agayne for to bigge, þæt bretted is to noȝt?'

That he ne schall holden byhynde when he hore eldes.
(*Wynnere and Wastoure,* 7-9)

It is notable here that the demonstrative *this* takes the place of the definite article *the*. As we have seen above, *MED* allocates the definition column 1b. of the noun *world* for phrases denoting a long time span or 'emphasizing the world's duration', citing two typical constructions: 'so long as this world ilaste' and 'while that the world stondeth'. The dictionary does not give or suggest any difference between the two phrases, but we have observed some distinction thereof. See the following three examples:

Jesu Crist Winndweþþ hiss corn… *Whil þatt tiss weorelld lassteþþ.*
(*Ormulum,* 10515)

Giif ðu liuedest *swa lange swa ðes woreld ilast*, and æure þoledest pine,
ne miht ðu of-earmin swa michel eadinesse swa ðe is behaten.
(*Vices and Virtues,* (1) 33.21)

Presented him þe presoneres in pray þat þay token,
Moni a worþly wyȝe *whil her worlde laste.* (*Cleanness,* 1297-8)

In this formulaic expression the noun *world* goes with the definite article when it is combined with the verb *standan*, whereas if it goes with the demonstrative *this* or a possessive pronoun, it appears more frequently with (*i-*)*last*. J. J. Anderson in his edition of *Cleanness* renders 'many a man of noble rank in his time, lit[erally] 'while their prosperity lasted' or line 1298.[14] He goes to the lengths to give 'prosperity' as a definition for the noun *world* here in the glossary, which should have been treated as a contextual meaning. Tauno Mustanoja in *A Middle English Syntax* cites an instance of 'while the world schal laste' from *the Fifty Earliest English Wills* 6 to show that '[*w*]*orld* normally takes the definite article'.[15] But we have observed that *this* is also frequently used in the construction. In this connection the latter type can be compared with another variant with a demonstrative adverb *thus*:

Few þer be outhe of owr alliance.
Wyll þe worlde ys thus, take we no thought! (*Wisdom*, 659-60)

---

[14] Anderson (1977:94).
[15] Mustanoja (1960:249).

In the second type ephemerality of the present world seems to be highlighted by the demonstrative *this*, 'this mortal world', 'this wretched world' as against 'the next world'.[16]

5. Chaucer

We have seen the use of 'while the world standeth' and the related constructions in ME in the preceeding chapter. Chaucer is conspicuous by his non-use of the phrases 'while the world standeth' or 'so long as this world lasts'; he resorts to 'whil that the world may dure' instead:

When that Arcite to Thebes comen was,
Ful ofte a day he swelte and seyde "Allas!"
For seen his lady shal he nevere mo.
And shortly to concluden al his wo,
So muche sorwe hadde nevere creature
That is, or shal, *whil that the world may dure.* (*The Knight's Tale*, 1355-60)

But certes, than is al my wonderinge,
Sithen she is the fayrest creature,
As to my doom, that ever was livinge,
The benignest and beste eek that Nature
Hath wrought or shal, *whyl that the world may dure*,
Why that she lefte Pite so behinde? (*Complaynt D'Amours*, 50-5)[17]

It is also notable that Chaucer employs the phrase with the verb *duren* to end a stanza:

But finally, whan that the sothe is wist
That Alla giltelees was of hir wo,
I trowe an hundred tymes been they kist,
And swich a blisse is ther bitwix hem two
That, save the joye that lasteth everemo,
Ther is noon lyk that any creature
Hath seyn or shal, *whil that the world may dure.*
(*The Man of Law's Tale*, 1772-8)

---

[16] *OED* registers the phrase 'this world' as a subordinate headword under *this*, giving nine examples from *Lindisfarne Gospels* to M. E. Braddon (1883). It also gives further examples for 1. a. of *world*.

[17] Skeat comments on 'whyl that the world may dure' here at his note 54 in his seven-volume edition, referring to *The Parliament of Fowls* 616. He is silent about the other instances.

Lyve thow soleyn, wormes corupcioun,
For no fors is of lak of thy nature!
Go, lewed be thow *whil the world may dure*!"
(*The Parliament of Fowls*, 614-6)

And Troilus wel woxen was in highte,
And complet formed by proporcioun
So wel that kynde it nought amenden myghte;
Yong, fressh, strong, and hardy as lyoun;
Trewe as stiel in ech condicioun;
Oon of the beste entecched creature
That is or shal *whil that the world may dure.*
(*Troilus and Criseyde*, V 827-33)

He uses a variant phrase in the concluding remarks of *The Romaunt of the Rose*, a long narrative poem of 7692 lines:

And, Abstinence, full wise ye seme.
Of o talent you bothe I deme.
What counceil wole ye to me yiven?"
"Ryght heere anoon thou shalt be shryven,
And sey thy synne withoute more;
Of this shalt thou repente sore.
For I am prest and have pouste
To shryve folk of most dignyte
That ben, *as wide as world may dure.* (*The Romaunt of the Rose*, 7671-9)

MED cites the instance from *The Man of Law's Tale* for 1. (a) to continue, go on, last' and the instance from *The Romaunt of the Rose* for 3. To extend in space, reach, stretch' of the verb *duren*, not relating the two constructions. It does not register 'whil that the world may dure' under the definition 1 b. of the noun *world*, either, where 'so long as this world ilaste' and 'while that the world stondeth' are presented as illustrative of the usages of *world* in this sense. It is incredible that *MED* should have committed this oversight.

Repeated use of the phrase, and non-use of the other two variants, by Chaucer attests that it is another variant formulaic construction with the noun *world* in ME. His use of the phrase at the concluding part of a unit of discourse, together with those instances from the OE *Phoenix* and the Early Modern Tyndale, conclusively demonstrates its formulaic character. These have been formulaic in that they end a unit of discourse. The *Phoenix* poet also employs one with *standan* at the beginning of a stanza as well as at its end. Tyndale uses two variants with *stand* and *endure* to end what can be called a paragraph of a chapter in his translation of the Bible. In this line we can re-consider Chaucer's use of a variant with the verb *duren* in *Troilus* and *Romaunt*.

Chaucer employs most variant constructions with the noun *world* for the notion 'for ever'. In *The Man of Law's Tale* 157 he says 'syn the world bigan', in *The Monk's Tale* 2638 'unto the worldes ende' or in *The Reeve's Tale* 3876 'whil that the world wol pype'. His notion of 'the world' may be typically seen in 'the edifice of this world is kept stable and withouten corrumpynge' (*Boece,* 78-9) or in 'Somtyme the world was so stedfast and stable / That mannes word was obligacioun, / And now it is so fals and deceivable/ That word and deed, as in conclusioun, / Ben nothing lyk, for turned up-so-doun / Is al this world for mede and wilfulnesse, / That al is lost for lak of stedfastnesse' (*Lak of Stedfastnesse*, 1-7). For him the world is an edifice, steadfast and stable. 'Thanne goth the world al to destruccioun' (*The Summoner's Tale*, 2110).

6. Grimm's Dictionary, Martin Luther, and Germanic Counterparts

It has been shown that the phrase 'while the world standeth' is of OE provenance and develops its variants in the course of ME. We must go still further back in history to discover the origins. It has the counterparts in Germanic cognates:

Icelandic:	svá lengi sem heimrinn stendr.
Swedish:	så länge världen står.
Danish:	så længe verden står.[18]
German:	so lange die Erden stehet.

These parallel expressions suggests its genesis back in Germanic.

Grimm's *Deutsches Wörterbuch* enumerates examples and variations of this phrase from Old and Middle German as well as other languages under

[18] In Danish there are variations concerning tense or aspect of the verb: 'Så længe verden står' and 'Så længe verden har stået'. These two variants are registered under the noun *verden* 'world' in a dictionary of modern Danish idioms. See *Dansk Sprogbrug* (1978, Gyldendal), p. 555. The difference in meanings is observable and might be rendered 'for ever, till the end of time' for the former and 'since the beginning of the world' for the latter.

the definition 15.b) häufig von erde und welt, bes. in formelhaften redeweisen. In a subsection α) 'von der erde, mit deutlicherer sinnlicher vorstellung .. geht von der bibelsprache aus' it mentions, but does not render the passage of, 1 Mos. 8:22, which should be Luther's *Genesis*, explaining the Hebrew origin of the phraseology. It goes on to show its variants in Old and Middle German with their counterparts in Italian in β) 'häufiger und abgeblaszter von der welt, was wohl auf α zurückgeht. so in bezug auf die vergangenheit': fin che … il mondo è (sarà) mondo, fin che dura (durarà) il mondo'.[19] Let us recall here Chaucer's preference of the verb *duren* to *stonden* discussed in the preceeding chapter.

Because of its relation with Tyndale it is interesting to see Luther's *Genesis* here: 'So lange die Erden stehet/ sol nicht auffhoren/ Samen vnd Ernd/ Frost vnd Hitz/ Sommer vnt Winter/ Tag vnd Nacht' (Luther (1922) *Genesis* 8:22). Grimm also cites a passage from Luther's religious treatise: 'die Trucken werden auch yhren stosser finden, sol die welt lenger stehen'.[20] He uses his favorite phrase to render the passage in 8:22 of *Genesis*, or the other way round, borrowing a biblical expression for religious discussions.

Compare its counterpart in Tyndale:

> Neither shall sowing time and harvest, cold, and heat, summer and winter, day and night cease, as long as the earth endureth. (Tyndale (1530) *Genesis*, 8:22)

Tyndale uses a variant with the verb *endure*, not following Luther's *stehen* here. *AV* also employs a clausal expression, not an adverbial phrase, for the rendering of the verse: 'while the earth remaineth'. It gives an original sense in Hebrew here as 'Heb. as yet all the days of the earth' in the marginal note. It might be interesting to see how the translators after Tyndale and before *AV* treat the passage:

Genesis* 8:22 from Tyndale to *AV

Tyndale (1525):	as long as the earth endureth
Coverdale (1535):	so longe as the earth endureth
Cranmer's (1539):	all the daies of the earth
Geneva (1560):	so long as the earth remaineth
Bishops' (1568):	all the days of the earth

---

[19] Stehen (II, D, 15), pp. 1701-2.

[20] Luther, 19, 360, 17 Weim (p. 1702).

Doway (1609):	Al the days of the earth
AV (1611):	while the earth remaineth

AV here seems to have directly followed *Geneva Bible* with a slight change of the conjunctions. But this brief glance at the two types of renditions which alternated over one century shows that *AV* in fact adopted a Tyndalian phraseology followed by the two puritan Bibles in variations, making terms with Catholic and other disciplines to mention their alternate reading in the marginal note. Now it is obvious that the clausal rendering of the notion 'for ever' in 8:13 of *Genesis* in *AV* is a legacy of Tyndale, who was influenced by the German translator and assimilated his phraseology.

In the tradition of translating the Old Testament there are several editions which employ one or two of the variations of 'while the world standeth.' *Geneva Bible* (1560) renders 'One generation passeth, and another generation succeedeth: but the earth remaineth for euer' at *Ecclesiastes* 1:4 with a marginal note 'One man dieth after another, and the earth remaineth longest, euen to the last day, which yet is subiect to corruption'. *Bishops' Bible* (1568) renders 'He hath compassed the waters with certayne boundes vntill the day and night come to an ende', to which it gives a side note 'That is, so long as the worlde endureth' at *Job* 26:10. *AV* has at *Ecclesiasticus* 39:9 'Many shall commend his vnderstanding, and so long as the world endureth, it shall not be blotted out, his memoriall shall not depart away, and his name shall liue from generation to generation'. Webster (1833) follows *AV* to adopt 'While the earth remaineth' at *Genesis* 8:33. In the twentieth century *Goodnews Bible* (1976) has at *Genesis* 8:22: 'As long as the world exists, there will be a time for planting and a time for harvest. There will always be cold and heat, summer and winter, day and night'.

Then what is the case with the six passages in question in the New Testament? Luther does not use the formulaic clause but employs such adverbial expressions as 'ewiglich' or 'von ewickeyt zu ewickeyt' for the notion 'for ever':

Lutheran Counterparts to the Six Instances in Tyndale's New Testament

Mark 11:14:	Nu esse von dyr niemant keyne frucht ewiglich.
John 13: 8:	Nymmer mehr solltu myr die fussz wasschen.
1Cor. 8:13:	Darumb, szo die speyse meynen bruder ergerti, wolte ich nicht fleysch essen fleysch essen ewiglich, auff das ich meyne bruder nicht ergere.

1Pet 4:11:	durch Ihesum Christ, Wilchem sey preysz vnd gewalt von ewickeit, Amen.
1Pet. 5:11:	Dem selbigen sey preysz vnd macht von evickeyt zu ewickeyt, Amen.
Heb. 13:21:	wilchem sey preys von ewickeyt zu ewickeyt Amen.

Luther's Bible was also enormously influential in formulating Danish Protestant translations of the New Testament in the sixteenth century. See for examples the six passages in question:

The six counterparts in Danish New Testament (1524)

Mark 11:14:	her efftir / skal ingen ede fruct aff tig / indtil euig thijdt /
John 13: 8:	thu skalt aldri thwo myn føddir /
1Cor. 8:13:	nw ethers kerlighed & thegen oc worber ømelses / om ether til thennom / oc obenbarlige for menhedene.
1Pet. 4:11:	wed Jesum Christum / huilken skee ere / oc macht fran euighed til euighed /Amen.
1Pet. 5:11:	thend same skee ere oc magt/ fran euighed til euighed / Amen.
Heb. 13:21:	huilken skee ere fran evighed oc til evighed / Amen.[21]

Tyndale does not follow Luther in rendering these passages.[22]

---

[21] See the six counterparts in Danish New Testament (1529):

Mark 11:14:	Der skall aldrig nogen ade fruct aff dig her effter till euig tid /
John 13: 8:	Dw skalt aldrig to mine føder
1Cor. 8:13:	Da ville ieg helder aldrig ade kød til ewig tid / en ath ath ieg ville fortørne hannem der meth.
1Pet. 4:11:	ved Jhesum Christum / huilken ske are och macth fra ewig tid och till ewig tid Amen.
1Pet. 5:11:	hannem ske are oc magt fra ewig tid och till ewig tid amen.
Heb. 13:21:	huilken ske are fra ewig tid och til ewig tid amen.

[22] H. W. Robinson observes that 'Luther's German translation appeared in 1522, Tindale's early version in 1525, and it was inevitable that contemporaries should regard the latter as an English rendering of the former…Tindale, in the Cologne fragment, adopts Luther's order of the books, takes over a substantial part of his prefaces and prologues, uses nearly all his marginal references, errors included, adopts his paragraph division, and incorporates a large number of his marginal comments (pp. 156-7)'. He furthers notes that '[h]e works close to Erasmus's Greek text, using the second edition of 1519 and the third of 1522, he is much indebted to Erasmus's Latin rendering, takes full advantage of Luther's example in three different editions, and is not unmindful of the Vulgate text. (p.157)' and that '[h]e interpolates and paraphrases and fills in ellipsis, as Acts x. "a captayne of soudiers of Italy", John xiii. 8, "[t]hou shalt not wesshe my fete while the worlde stondeth" (p. 158)'. This is the only reference to the phrase that I have ever met in many histories of English Bible. But note that both in earlier and later versions Tyndale prints the conjunction *while* as *whill*.

7. 'world without end'

As seen above, *MED* lists varied constructions 'emphasizing the world's duration' with the noun under 1b. (a) of the headword *world*: 'from the ginninge of the...', 'from the worldes frume', 'sin that this...first bigan', 'sitthen this...was astald', 'sitthen that god this...wrought', 'in-to the endinge of this...', '(un-)to the worldes ende', 'oth þissere worldes ende', 'so longe so this...ilaste', 'while that the...stondeth'. Among the many variations, however, we could perhaps note the most popular and longlasting one: *world without end. MED* does not register this phrase under the headword *world,* but under *end,* giving just one example from *Cleanness* 712: 'Þat wyȝeȝ schal be by hem war worlde withouten ende'. *OED* contrastively gives nine examples of (*world*) *without end* under the headword *end* 18. from *the Metres of Boethius* to Milton's *Paradise Lost.* It also has as many as twelve examples under *world* 6.b. from *Ancrene Riwle* to Francis Brett Young.[23] To these can be added one from *Wynnere and*

---

[23] *OED world* 6. b. *world without* (*ME. abuten* or *buten*) *end*; later used hyperbolically: Endlessly, eternally. Hence as adj. phr. = perpetually, everlasting, eternal; and as subst. phr. eternal existence, endlessness, eternity.

a1225 *Ancr. R.* 182 þeo þet hebden ofearned þe pinen of helle world a buten ende. c1305 *St. Swithin* 109 in E. E. P. (1863) 46 þat vuel..ne schal no leng ileste, Ac þu worst þer of hol and sound, wordle wiþouten ende. c1460 *Townelet Myst.* Ii. 465, I must nedis weynd, And to the dwill be thrall warld withoutten end. 1483 Caxton *Gold. Leg.* 94/1 Many benefetes ben gyuen to thonour of our lord Jhū crist whiche is blessed world wythouten ende. Amen. 1548-9 *Bk. Com. Prayer, Matins*, As it was in the beginning, is now, and euer shalbe, world without ende.

1588 Shakes. *L.L.L.* v.ii. 799 A time me thinkes too short, To make a world-without-end bargaine in. 1649 Milton *Eikon.* xxi. Wks. 1851 III. 484 This man..thinks by talking world without end, to make good his integrity. 1753 in *Life Ld. Hardwicke* (1847) II. 499 Ld Chesterfield writes Worlds without End. 1881 Morris *Mackail's W.M.* (1899) II. 34 This world-without-end-for-everlasting hole of a London. 1888 *Advance* (Chicago) 20 Dec. 831 A city pastor, with a world-without-end of things to be done. 1896 A. E. Housman *Shropsh. Lad* xiv, My heart and soul and senses, World without end, are drowned. 1905 F. Young *Sands of Pleasure* i. v, Small wonder if the embodiment of the world-without-end should prove no encourage of man's happiness!

Further examples of the phrase are found under such headwords as *a, abide, abuten, rixle, smod, wandreth,* or *weary*:

c1175 Lamb. Hom. 25 From þan helle..us bureȝe þe lauerd þe is..wuniende and rixlende on worlde a butan ende. (*rixle*)

1225 Juliana 22 For ne werȝeð he neauer to wurchen ow al þat wandreðe world a buten ende. (*weary*)

Wastoure 261-2: 'For siche a synn haste þou solde thi soule into helle,/ And there es euer wellande woo, worlde withowtten ende'.

In OE there were a variety of phrases for the notion 'for ever': *a worulde, aa butan ende, æfre to worulde, in ealra worulda woruld a/æfre butan ende*, etc. There was, however, no variant in the form of the noun followed by *butan ende* without any preposition or adverb. The noun *worold* in inflected forms can be used adverbially but it always appears with *in/on* or *to* or with *a/awa*. So the phrase *world without end* is a hybrid, made in the course of ME, of those variants with prepositions before the noun *woruld* and something like *aa/æfre butan ende*. Its longevity is all the more remarkable when compared with 'while the world standeth', since in the body of the text of the Bible the two variants are equally very rare from the seventeenth century downward. *The Authorized Version* has only two instances of 'world without end' at Isaiah 45:17 and Eph. 3:21 with a single instance of 'while the world standeth' at 1Cor. 8:13. Tyndale did not use the phrase 'world without end' in his translation of the New Testament and parts of the Old Testament. It is Coverdale's Bible which started to disseminate the phrase. See Table 2 below. In the body of the Bible the phrase is peculiar to the Old Testament and the Apocrypha. Coverdale's phrase had been taken over in several books of the Old Testament, with some additions or rephrasings and deletions, by later translators for thirty years up to Bishops' Bible. At the end of the sixteenth century the phrase 'world without end' suddenly slid into obsolescence, leaving sporadically just one or two marks in the later editions. The table clearly shows that the middle of the sixteenth century was the high point in the use of the phrase.

1225 *Ancr. R.* 156 Godes þreatunge is wondreðe & weane ine licome & ine soule, world a buten ende! (*wandreth*)

1230 *Ancren Riwle* 36 World a buten ende. (*a, abuten*)

13.. *E. E. Allit. P.*B. 711 Hem to smyte for þat smod smartly I þenk þat wyȝes schal be by hem war, worlde with-outen ende. (*smod*)

1535 Coverdale Ps. xci. 7 But thou Lorde o most hyest, abydest worlde without ende. (*abide*)

Table 2. 'world without end' from Coverdale to Webster

Coverdale (1535)	Cranmer's (1539)	Matthew (1549)	Geneva (1560)	Bishops' (1568)	Rheims-Douai (1582-1610)	AV (1611)	Wesley (1755)	Webster (1833)
			Psalm 41	○				
Psalm 44			○(45)	○				
	Psalm 90	○						
Psalm 91		○ (92)						
Psalm 105	○(106)	○ (106)						
Isaiah 33				○				
Isaiah 45	○	○	○	○		○		○
				Isaiah 59:21				
	Lamentations 5			○				
Daniel 12	○	○						
Esdras 4	○	○		○				
Tobit 9	○	○						
Tobit 13		○			○			
Song of Three		○	○	○				
				Manasseh				
					Ecclesiasticus 42:21			
	Eph. 3:21			○		○	○	○

Coverdale also uses the phrase three times in the front matter of his edition. Almost all the instances appear at the end, or the closing part, of a prayer, a hymn, a dedication, or a chapter. The phrase is typically followed by *amen*, which definitely ends a form of discourse. His dedication, too, ends with a prayer featuring the final adverbial phrase:

> To whom for ye defendynge of his blessed worde (by your graces most rightfull administracyon) be honoure and thankes, glory and dominyon, *worlde without ende*, Amen. Youre graces humble subiecte and daylye oratour, Myles Couerdale.

In relation to the period (1535-68) it is to be noted that the *OED* makes two citations of the phrase from *the Book of Common Prayer*:

> 1549 *Bk. Com. Prayer, Gloria Patri*, As it was in the beginning, is now and ever shall be: world without end. (*OED, end*)

> 1548-9 *Bk. Com. Prayer, Matins*, As it was in the beginning, is now, and euer shalbe, world without ende. (*OED, world*)

David Lyle Jeffrey explains the genesis of the phrase and attributes it especially to the *Gloria Patri* in the *Book of Common Prayer*.[24] However, Jeffrey's explanation is rather impetuous, since in that influential book the phrase is repeatedly employed together with 'for ever and ever' to end a prayer, a hymn, or a collect, as in Holy Communion, Litany, Morning Prayer, or Evening Prayer. A wide progagation and the popularity of the phrase as the final remark in a prayer should then be attributed to the book itself, not to a single hymn therein. The form 'worlde withouten ende' first appeared, taking the place of 'worolde (a) butan ende' in the fourteenth century. Before it was adopted by Coverdale first into the text of the Old Testamant, it was repeatedly used and had been a common phrase in ME religious works. Its later broad diffusion was promoted, and its survival was secured, by the masses sung by a preacher and a congregation, who read *the Book of Common Prayer*. While the clausal expression 'while the world standeth' has long become obsolete, the phrase 'world without end' survived beyond the period of its full use in the text of the Bible in the sixteenth century. James Joyce's allusion to the biblical expression attests its survival well into the twentieth century: 'In the beginning was the word, in the end the world without end. Blessed be eight beatitudes' (1922 J. Joyce *Ulysses*, Episode 15).[25]

8. Conclusion

This survey of each period of English literature has shown the lineage of the clausal expression 'while the world standeth'. The phraseology had its genesis back in Germanic and since its earliest examples it had a Christian colouring. In OE the typical construction was 'þenden worold standeð', which occupied b-verse. In the course of ME a small group of variants appeared with such verbs as *duren*, *enduren*, and *lasten* to substitute for *stonden*. It was William Tyndale who introduced and revived the time-honoured expression in a Christian context: he used it six times in his translation of the New Testament in 1526. But during the sixteenth century most of these were rephrased and discarded by later translators, leaving a single mark in *AV*, which kept just one in 1Cor. 8:13. As the most important edition of the English Bible, *AV* long exerted its influence over a series of

---

[24] Jeffrey (1992:851).
[25] *Ulysses: Annotated Student's Edition*. Penguin Books, p.626.

modern editions of the Bible and it is still possible to see its trace in 1Cor. 8:13 as late as in Webster (1833). But by the eighteenth century this was already a very strange expression, as is testified by Dr Johnson, who registered in his dictionary the old temporal meaning of the noun *world*, equivalent to Latin *saeculum* or Greek *αἰών*. In the twentieth century the phrase has become antiquated or obsolete as the temporal meaning of *world* has been utterly lost. So the *OED* puts the phrase under a subsection of definition 23 of *stand*: Of an edifice: To remain erect and entire; to resist destruction and decay.[26]

References

Allen, W. S. & E. C. Jacobs. 1995. *The Coming of the King James Gospels*. Fayettville: University of Arkansas Press.

Anderson, J. J., ed. 1977. *Cleanness*. Manchester: Manchester University Press.

Bethurum, D., ed. 1957. *The Homilies of Wulfstan*. Oxford: Clarendon Press.

Blake, N., ed. 1964. *The Phoenix*. Manchester: Manchester University Press.

Bodelsen, C. A. & H. Vinterburg. 1986. *Dansk-Engelsk Ordbog*. København: Gyldendal.

Bruun, E. 1978. *Dansk Sprogbrug: En stil- og konstruktionsordbog*. København: Gyldendal.

Cleasby, R., G. Vigfusson, & W. Craigie. 1957. *An Icelandic-English Dictionary*. Oxford: Oxford University Press.

Det Ny Testamente: Oversat af Christiern Pedersen Antwerpen 1529. 1950. København: Roskilde og Baggers Forlag.

Duggan, H. N. & T. Turville-Petre, eds. 1989. *The Wars of Alexander*. EETS s.s. 10. Oxford: Oxford University Press.

Hardy, W., ed. 1938. *The New Testament translated by William Tyndale 1534: A reprint of the Edition of 1534 with the Translator's Preface & Notes and the Variants of the Edition of 1525*. Cambridge: Cambridge University Press.

Harlock, W. 1964. *Svensk-Engelsk Ordbok*. Stockholm: Nordstedt.

Jeffrey, D. L., ed. 1992. *A Dictionary of Biblical Tradition in Early English*

[26] I searched *Great Literature Plus* for the phrase and found one example used in a work with imitative archaism: 'Now so it is, that whoso heareth these tidings sayeth, that no such an one as was Sigurd was left behind him on the world, nor ever was such a man brought forth because of all the worth of him, nor may his name ever minish by eld in the Dutch Tongue nor in all the Northern Lands, while the world standeth fast' (Chapter XXXIII, *The Story of the Volsungs and Nibelungs*).

Literature. Michigan: William B. Erdmans Publishing Company.

Johnson, S., ed., 1755. *A Dictionary of the English Language*. London.

Kiberd, Declan, ed., 2000. *Ulysses: Annotated Student's Edition*. London: Penguin Books.

Lowe, K. A. 1989. 'A New Edition of the Will of Wulfgar'. *Notes and Queries* n.s. 36 (3):295-8.

Luther, Martin, *Die gantze Heilige Schrifft Deudsch* (Wittenberg 1545). Munchen: Rogner & Bernhard GmbH & Co.

Mustanoja, T. 1960. *A Middle English Syntax*, Part I. Helsinki: Société Néo-philologique.

Robinson, H. W. 1940. *The Bible in its Ancient and English Versions*. Westport: Greenwood Press.

The English Hexapla: A Reprint of the 1841 Edition Published by S. Bagster, London. 1975. New York: AMS Press.

The Cambridge Geneva Bible of 1591: A Facsimile Reprint Marking 400 Years of Bible Production by the World's Oldest Bible Printer and Publisher. 1991. Cambridge: Cambridge University Press.

The Geneva Bible: A Facsimile of the 1560 Edition. 1969. Madison: University of Wisconsin Press.

The Rhemes-Douay Bible (1600-11)*: A Facsimile*. 1990. Kyoto: Rinsen Book Co.

Thet Nøye Testamenth: Christiern II's Nye Testamment, Wittenberg 1524. 1950. København: Roskilde og Baggers Forlag.

William Tyndale's New Testament: A Facsimile of 1526. 1976. London: David Paradine Developments.

Electronic Texts

Bible in English on CD-ROM. Cambridge: Chadwyck-Healey Ltd.

Great Literature Plus. 1993. Bureau of Electronic Publishing, Inc.

Chaucer: Life and Time. CD-ROM. Reading: Primary Source Media.

The Oxford English Dictionary, 2nd ed. on CD-ROM. Oxford: Oxford University Press.

A List of the Published Writings of Professor Matsuji Tajima

BOOKS

1985 *The Syntactic Development of the Gerund in Middle English*. Tokyo: Nan'un-do; Exclusive Distributors outside Japan, Amsterdam & Philadelphia: John Benjamins. xi + 154 pp.

1986 (with E. F. K. Koerner) *Noam Chomsky: A Personal Bibliography 1951–1986*. Library and Information Sources in Linguistics, 11. Amsterdam & Philadelphia: John Benjamins. xi + 217 pp.

1988 *Old and Middle English Language Studies: A Classified Bibliography 1923–1985*. Library and Information Sources in Linguistics, 13. Amsterdam & Philadelphia: John Benjamins. xxxiii + 391 pp.

1994 (with David Burnley) *The Language of Middle English Literature*. Annotated Bibliographies of Old and Middle English Literature, 1. Cambridge: D. S. Brewer. viii + 280 pp.

1995 (with Keiji Konomi, et al.) *Present-day British and American English Usage: A Corpus-Based Study*. Tokyo: Kaibunsha. xii + 233 pp. [in Japanese]

1998 (Editor-in-Chief, with Yoko Iyeiri, et al.) *A Bibliography of English Language Studies in Japan 1900–1996*. Tokyo: Nan'un-do. xvii + 1,196 pp. [in Japanese]

2001 *One Hundred Years of English Language Studies in Japan: Retrospects and Prospects*. Tokyo: Nan'un-do. 225 pp. [in Japanese]

ARTICLES

1965 'Participial Constructions in Shakespeare'. *Cairn* (Kyushu University) 6:72–90. [in Japanese]

1966 'Verbals in Langland (I): Participle'. *Cairn* 8:76–90. [in Japanese]

1968 'Verbals in *Piers the Plowman* (II): Gerund'. *Essays in Literature and Thought* (Fukuoka Women's University) 31:29–53.

1968 'Verbals in *Piers the Plowman* (III): Infinitive'. *Essays in Literature and Thought* 32:1–55.

1968 'The Gerund in Fourteenth-Century English'. *Festschrift for Prof. Shun-ichi Mayekawa*. Tokyo: Eihosha. 339–52. [in Japanese]

1970 'On the Use of the Participle in the Works of the *Gawain*-poet'. *Essays in Literature and Thought* 34:49–70.

1971 'English Loan-words in Japanese: A Sketch'. *Bulletin of the Training Institute for Government Officials* (Fukuoka) 31:17–28. [in Japanese]

1971 'On the Use of the Gerund in the Works of the *Gawain*-poet'. *Essays in Literature and Thought* 35:1–24.

1972 'On the Use of the Infinitive in the Works of the *Gawain*-poet'. *Essays in Literature and Thought* 36:1–56.

1975 'Some Notes on the Correlative Conjunction "NOT ONLY…BUT (ALSO)" and its Similar Expressions'. *Hokkaido University Essays in Foreign Languages and Literatures* 21:341–57. [in Japanese]

1975 'The *Gawain*-poet's Use of *Con* as a Periphrastic Auxiliary'. *Neuphilologische Mitteilungen* (Helsinki) 76:429–38.

1976 'The Neuter Personal Pronoun *Hit* in the Works of the *Gawain*-poet'. *Linguistic Science* (Kyushu University) 11/12:23–36. [in Japanese]

1977 'The Gerund in Fourteenth-Century English, with Special Reference to the Development of its Verbal Character'. *Studies in English Literature* (Tokyo) 54:113–33. [in Japanese]

1978 'Additional Syntactical Evidence against the Common Authorship of MS. Cotton Nero A.x.'. *English Studies* (Amsterdam) 59:193–8.

1978 (with E. F. K. Koerner) 'Saussure in Japan: A Survey of Research 1928–78'. *Historiographia Linguistica* (Amsterdam) 5:121–48. [Repr. in E. F. K. Koerner, *Saussurean Studies/Études saussuriennes* (Geneva: Éditions Slatkine, 1988), 175-202.]

1980 'Gnomic Statements in *Beowulf*'. *Studies in English Language and Literature* (Kyushu University) 30:83-94.

1980 'The Gerund in the *Katherine* Group'. *Linguistic Science* 15:30-5.

1982 'The Gerund in Medieval English Drama'. *Studies in English Language and Literature* 32:81-96.

1984 'Images of a Medical Doctor in *Piers Plowman*'. *Studies in English Philology and Linguistics in Honour of Dr. Tamotsu Matsunami*. Tokyo: Shubun International. 259–64.

1985 'Some Notes on the Syntactic Development of the Gerund in Middle English'. *Studies in English Language and Literature* 35:117–36. [in Japanese]

1985 'The Common-/Objective-Case Subject of the Gerund in Middle English'. *Linguistic Science* 20:13–20.

1985 'The Gerund in Chaucer, with Special Reference to the Development of its Verbal Character'. *Poetica: An International Journal of Linguistic-Literary Studies* (Tokyo) 21/22:106–20.

1989 (with Yumiko Iwamoto) 'Noun-Name Collocations in the American Weekly *Time*'. *Linguistic Science* 24:53–70. [in Japanese]

1989 'Authorship and Syntax: The Case of the *Gawain*-Poems'. *Essays on Middle English Alliterative Poetry*, ed. E. Suzuki. Tokyo: Gaku-shobo. 98–135. [in Japanese]

1990 'The Development of the Modal Auxiliary *Ought* in Late Middle English'. *Studies in English Philology in Honour of Shigeru Ono*. Tokyo: Nan'un-do. 227–48. [in Japanese]

1992 (with Yumiko Iwamoto) 'Subject-Verb Concord in Shakespeare'. *Linguistic Science* 27:1–19. [in Japanese]

1993 (with Keiji Konomi) 'A Corpus-based Study of Present-day British and American English Usage (1): "prevent me (from) going" and "prevent my going"'. *Studies in English Language and Literature* 43:145–60. [in Japanese]

1993 (with Keiji Konomi) 'A Corpus-based Study of Present-day British and American English Usage (2): "in (the) light of"'. *Studies in Languages and Cultures* (Kyushu University) 4:31–6. [in Japanese]

1993 (with Keiji Konomi) 'A Corpus-based Study of Present-day British and American English Usage (3): "not so much A as/but B"'. *Bulletin of the Faculty of Computer Science and Systems Engineering* (Kyushu Institute of Technology) 6:39–48. [in Japanese]

1993 (with Keiji Konomi and Sukeaki Matsuda) 'A Corpus-based Study of Present-day British and American English Usage (4): "have difficulty (in) doing something"'. *Reports of the Faculty of Engineering, Oita University* 28:129–34. [in Japanese]

1993 (with Sukeaki Matsuda and Keiji Konomi) 'A Corpus-based Study of Present-day British and American English Usage (5): "aim at doing" and "aim to do"'. *Reports of the Faculty of Engineering, Oita University* 28:135–41. [in Japanese]

1994 'A Corpus-based Study of Present-day British and American English Usage (6): "despite" and "in spite of"'. *Studies in English Language and Literature* 44:125–36. [in Japanese]

1994 'A Corpus-based Study of Present-day British and American English Usage (7): "*many a(n)* + noun" and "*many another* + noun"'. *Studies in Languages and Cultures* 5:81–6. [in Japanese]

1994 (with Keiji Konomi) 'A Corpus-based Study of Present-day British and American English Usage (9): "apart from" and "aside from"'. *Bulletin of the Faculty of Computer Science and Systems Engineering* (Kyushu Institute of Technology) 9:89–97. [in Japanese]

1994 'A Corpus-based Study of Present-day British and American English Usage (11): "*rather a* / *a rather* + adjective + noun"'. *Linguistic Science* 29:21–8. [in Japanese]

1994 (with Yumiko Iwamoto) 'Flat Adverbs in Shakespeare'. *Linguistic Science* 29:28–41. [in Japanese]

1994 (with Sukeaki Matsuda) 'A Corpus-based Study of Present-day British and American English Usage (12): "busy (in/with) doing"'. *Reports of the Faculty of Engineering, Oita University* 29:75–8. [in Japanese]

1994 (with Sukeaki Matsuda) 'A Corpus-based Study of Present-day British and American English Usage (13): "cannot but do, cannot help doing, cannot help but do"'. *Reports of the Faculty of Engineering, Oita University* 30:63–70. [in Japanese]

1996 'How to Study Middle English Syntax: Some Notes on Olga Fischer, "Syntax" (*The Cambridge History of the English Language*, Vol. II)'. *Studies in English Language and Literature* 46:1–15. [in Japanese]

1996 'The Common-/Objective-Case Subject of the Gerund in Middle

English'. In: *A Frisian and Germanic Miscellany: Published in Honour of Nils Århammar on his Sixty-Fifth Birthday, 7 August 1996* [=*NOWELE* 28/29]. Odense: Odense University Press. 569–78. [Rev. version of 'The Common-/Objective-Case Subject of the Gerund in Middle English' (1985)]

1996 'When did the Phrase "cannot help but do" Appear First in Writing?' *The Kyushu Review* (Fukuoka) 1:47–53. [in Japanese]

1998 'The Gerund in Chaucer, with Special Reference to its Verbal Character'. *English Historical Linguistics and Philology in Japan*, ed. J. Fisiak & A. Oizumi. Berlin & New York: Mouton de Gruyter. 323–39. [Rev. version of 'The Gerund in Chaucer, with Special Reference to the Development of its Verbal Character' (1985)]

1998 'The Earliest Instance of the Expression "American Dream"'. *The Kyushu Review* 3:33–9. [in Japanese]

1999 (with Nobuko Suematsu) ''Busy (in/with) doing' in Nineteenth-Century English'. *Linguistic Science* 34:15–20. [in Japanese]

1999 'The Compound Gerund in Early Modern English'. *The Emergence of the Modern Language Sciences: Studies on the Transition from Historical-comparative to Structural Linguistics in Honour of E. F. K. Koerner, vol. II: Methodological Perspectives and Applications*, ed. S. Embleton, J. E. Joseph & H.-J. Niederehe. Amsterdam & Philadelphia: John Benjamins. 265-77.

2000 '*Piers Plowman* B. V. 379: A Syntactic Note'. *Notes and Queries* (Oxford) 245:18–20.

2000 'Chaucer and the Development of the Modal Auxiliary *Ought* in Late Middle English'. *Manuscript, Narrative, Lexicon: Essays on Literary and Cultural Transmission in Honor of W. F. Bolton*, ed. R. Boenig & K. Davis. Lewisburg, PA: Bucknell University Press; London: Associated University Presses. 195–217.

2000 'English Lexicography in Japan: An Overview'. *The Kyushu Review* 5:73–7. [in Japanese]

REVIEWS

1986 'Y. Terasawa and A. Oizumi (eds.), *Eigoshi Kenkyu no Hoho* [The Methods of English Historical Linguistics] (Tokyo: Nan'un-do, 1985)'. *Eigo Seinen* (Tokyo) 132(1): 38. [in Japanese]

1997 'S. Ono, *On Early English Syntax and Vocabulary* (Tokyo: Nan'un-do, 1989)'. *The Kyushu Review* 2:89–91. [in Japanese]

1999 'E. F. K. Koerner (ed.), *First Person Singular III: Autobiographies by North American Scholars in the Language Sciences* (Amsterdam & Philadelphia: John Benjamins, 1998)'. *The Kyushu Review* 4:111–14. [in Japanese]

2000 'T. Saito, *Eigoshi Kenkyu no Kiseki* [Studies in the History of the English Language] (Tokyo: Eihosha, 1998)'. *Studies in English Literature* (Tokyo) 77(1):89–93. [in Japanese]

OTHERS

1980 'Medieval English Studies in Canada: A Report'. *Medieval English Studies Newsletter* (Centre for Medieval English Studies, University of Tokyo) 3:1–2. [in Japanese]

1987 'Bibliographies of the History of English, Old English, and Middle English'. *Eigo Seinen* (Tokyo) 133(3):137. [in Japanese]

1987 'Recent Studies in Chaucerian English'. *Eigo Seinen* 133(6): 295. [in Japanese]

1987 'Syntactic Variation Studies in Scandinavia'. *Eigo Seinen* 133(9):449. [in Japanese]

1988 'Young Philologists in the UK'. *Eigo Seinen* 133(12):603. [in Japanese]

1989 'Twenty Years of Friendship with EFKK'. *E. F. Konrad Koerner Bibliography*, ed. W. Cowan & M. Foster. Bloomington, IN: Eurolingua. 79–80.

1991 '*Middle English Dictionary* Soon to Be Completed'. *Eigo Seinen* 136(1):34–6. [in Japanese]

2000 'Professor W. F. Bolton'. *The Kyushu Review* 5:101-2. [in Japanese]

2001 'English Language Studies in Japan: A Bibliographer's Musings'. *Eigo Seinen* 147(8):498–500. [in Japanese]

2001 'In Memoriam Professor David Burnley'. *The Kyushu Review* 6:105-6. [in Japanese]

2001 'Bibliography of Writings by (John) David Burnley'. *The Kyushu Review* 6:107–11.

Index

And gladly wolde he lerne and gladly teche
Essays on Medieval English
Presented to Professor Matsuji Tajima on his Sixtieth Birthday （検印廃止）

2002年11月1日 初版発行

編著者	家入葉子
	Margaret Connolly
発行者	安居洋一
印刷所	平河工業社
製本所	株式会社難波製本

〒160-0002 東京都新宿区坂町 26
発行所 開文社出版株式会社
電話 03(3358)6288・振替 00160-0-52864

ISBN4-87571-577-3 C3082